GLIMMERFIN

THE SECOND BOOK IN THE DOMINANT SPECIES SAGA

by

Kingsley Pilgrim

Grosvenor House
Publishing Limited

This book is published by
Grosvenor House Publishing Ltd
28-30 High Street, Guildford, Surrey, GU1 3EL.
www.grosvenorhousepublishing.co.uk

A CIP record for this book
is available from the British Library

ISBN 978-1-78148-674-0

"She's not my girlfriend, she's my date,
a date who I wouldn't mind seeing before
she gets eaten."

DEDICATION

To Frisky and Friday, goodbye you silly old cats, thanks for the company.

ACKNOWLEDGEMENTS

As always, thanks to my family for their continued support and thanks to the following people for a variety of reasons;

Dexter 'Rudy' Roberts, my editor Natasha Fletcher, Darren Baker, Paul 'Shifty' Lay, Olivia Pollard, the Maguire family, Brendan, Shelagh and Marie, Natasha Roye, Steven and Joanne Higham, Kay Jones, Ross Carmichael, Michael Feasey, Anthony Lewis, Karl Rose,

Lee and Mandy Ship, Mike O'Sullivan, Rod Murrell, Ashly Rae, Krysten Mallet,

Lori Macfadden, Katy Heffernan Smith, Tia Magno, Samantha Soar, Cristina Barratt, Tara Billinge, Jason Louis, Stephen Cole, David Pugh, Albert Locke and Beehive Illustrators.

If I've missed anybody out, I wasn't being rude, just probably couldn't remember how to spell your name.

Cheers to all the people who paid good money to read my books. As long as you guys keep buying them, I'll keep writing them!

ABOUT THE AUTHOR

Kingsley Pilgrim lives in Milton Keynes and still considers himself an actor…even though he can't get any work for love nor money these days. When he isn't writing he occasionally does stand up comedy and eats peanut butter sandwiches (smooth).

CONTACT

Kingsleypilgrim.co.uk

Twitter:@Kingsleyland

Guess. Try. Hope.

ALSO BY THE AUTHOR

In the Dominant Species saga

Paintshark

PROLOGUE

Olympia City – twelve years before the events in *Paintshark*

"MUMMY! I CAN'T SLEEP!"

Hannah Wylde heard the shout from her daughter and gripped her phone tightly, took a deep breath and spoke quietly into the mobile phone receiver. "Look…I can't talk right now, give me a second."

The voice on the other line sounded disappointed. "*So when can I see you?*"

The young child, restless in her bed, called out again. "MUMMY! WHERE ARE YOU?"

Hannah placed her hand over the receiver and leaned her head back. "COMING HONEY!" She spoke again into the phone, more stressed this time. "Look, I said I can't talk, let me deal with her and I'll ring you back."

"*But—*"

"I'll deal with it!"

A tear dropped from Hannah's eye as she ended the call and whispered, "Mummy's coming."

The woman walked along the long corridor of her upstairs landing until she came to a door covered in a child's paintings and food collages. Knocking gently she entered. Her pretty little daughter sat upright in her cabin bed, her bulging blue eyes looked like they were about to dart out from her head as her mother walked in.

"Who were you on the phone to, Mummy?"

Hannah casually dismissed it. "Nobody honey, so why aren't you asleep my little peanut?" The little girl huffed and folded her arms petulantly. "There's a dragon in my wardrobe, Mummy."

Hannah's own eyes bulged in mock astonishment too. "A dragon? In my house? How did it get here?" A giggle from the youngster made her mum continue. "So this dragon is in your wardrobe, is he?"

"It's a she."

"Oh it's a 'she' is it? Well I'm the only woman in this household."

"Except from Daisy the nanny?" the little girl said dubiously.

"Ok."

"Rita the cook?"

"I forgot about her."

"Ollie the maid?"

Hannah made a face. "Do you want me to get this dragon out of here or not, peanut?"

The girl slumped back into her bed. "I'm sorry, Mummy." She pointed with confidence to the wardrobe. "It's in there."

"Does this dragon have a name?"

The little girl wriggled her nose in thought. "It's the Glimmer...thing."

"Glimmerfin?"

"No...thing, as in thingy me bob."

"Oh I see...Glimmer thing?"

"Yeah, she glows quite a bit, well her head does, it's got a bright glittering thing on her head, so I call her Glimmer thing."

Hannah nodded her head in acceptance. "Ok, let's call her 'Glimmer thing' then."

Hannah crept slowly towards the wardrobe, over-enthusiastically looking around at each step, she reached the handle and gave a knowing glance to her daughter. "Are you sure it's in here?" The girl nodded her head with purpose as her mother gripped the handle tightly. "Ok...ready...1...2...3..." Hannah flung the wardrobe doors wide open. "READY OR NOT?...HERE I—"

Looking inside the wardrobe warily Hannah turned her head round to her daughter. "Nope, nothing here, honey."

The little girl rose from her sheets. "Are you sure?"

The confident mother stepped aside and showed the little girl the wardrobe, filled only with a child's clothes and an absent dragon. "No dragon here, honey."

The girl slumped back into her bed as her mother walked over. "Well it was there earlier."

The mother smiled as she tucked her in. "Now what's this really about, peanut?"

Stifling a yawn the little girl's blue eyes met her mother's.

"What do you mean, Mummy?"

"I mean you're a big girl now and I know you don't really believe in dragons, so why the long face?"

"I'm hungry."

"You're hungry? After all those double chocolate ice-creams for dessert?"

"How did you know?"

"Rita the cook told me... I remember her now."

"Ridiculous."

Hannah sat in the middle of the bed and began to tuck her daughter in. "Why won't you sleep, peanut?"

A slight frown appeared on the girl's face. "I don't want to go into school tomorrow."

Hannah fluffed up the pillows, slightly concerned. "Ok, go on and tell me why?"

"The other kids are picking on me," she murmured to her mother.

Hannah's eyes grew wide. "What kids?"

"The kids in my class."

The mother mulled over her daughter's response before continuing calmly. "So what are these kids saying to you?" A shrug of the shoulders was the only response. "Tell me, what are they saying to you? Are they hitting you?"

The girl shook her head defiantly. "No, just calling me names really."

"What names?"

"They call me 'Stinky' and 'Skank'...and..."

"And what?"

"They say you only married Daddy for his money and that you're a whore."

Hannah shrank back in shock. "Why would you say something like that?...That's an awful thing to say."

"But I didn't say it, those other kids did."

"Stop lying."

The girl flung her arms up in protest and then began to beat down on the bed covers. "IT WASN'T ME! I DIDN'T SAY ANYTHING!"

Hannah's eyes looked squarely to her daughter's. "Are you sure?"

The scared little girl's voice quavered. "That's what everyone is saying, Mummy, I'm telling the truth."

Observing the girl's distress, Hannah changed her frown and held her daughter's hand. "I'm sorry I didn't believe you, peanut." A hard knot formed in her stomach. "Do they hit you?"

"No, they just tease me, that's all."

"Well that's enough, I think." Her husky voice deepened. "Look's like I'm going to pay your headmaster a visit."

The little girl's resolve was stronger than her mother's. "You don't have to, Mummy, it won't make a difference."

Hannah's phone began to purr from her pocket, she took it out and turned it off with scant acknowledgement to the caller.

"Who was that?"

"No one, peanut."

"Why are there bullies, Mummy?"

A grim-faced Hannah looked back down to her daughter. "Some people bully because they have low-self esteem."

"What does that mean?"

Hannah's eyes wandered around the child's room trying to pinpoint any pop stars' eyes for support on the girl's many posters. "It means someone who doesn't have a very high opinion of themselves, they may have a fear of being left out or sometimes they're being bullied as well." The girl gestured towards the covers and Hannah pulled them up tighter for her. "Let me speak to your father and I'll see what he says, ok?" The little girl nodded slowly. "You were very brave for telling me about this, peanut."

Clearly trying hard to contain her anger, Hannah stood up and a tear formed, making her vision blurry. "Remember what I always said, baby, tough times don't last…"

"…tough people do." The little girl finished it off for her mother. "Yes I know, Mummy, tough times don't last…tough people do, you say it all the time."

"Because I mean it."

Hannah found herself welling up and moved quickly towards the door, her phone buzzed again from her pocket and she let it continue until there was silence apart from her tears.

"Don't cry, Mummy, I'll be fine and…"

She paused.

"What?"

"I will go to school tomorrow…and I love you." Hannah paused for a while, long enough for her daughter to show concern. "Mummy?"

Composing herself, Hannah turned back and kissed her daughter on the temple.

"I will always love you, my little peanut…remember that."

"Where are you going?"

"Mummy has to do something, but…" She paused, frustrated. "Daddy has gone out."

The mother opened the door and was very grateful that there were no more questions from the little girl lying face up from her bed, she wiped away another tear and left the room in a hurry. She ran as fast as she could down the corridor and swung the doors open into her bedroom, she tried hard not to appear devastated but the tale of her daughter being bullied was too much. Tears erupted from her eyes, she reached into her pocket and pulled out her phone frantically pressing down on the buttons to reach a number. As soon as the voice on the other line spoke, Hannah blurted, "I CAN'T DO THIS! I'M NOT STRONG ENOUGH!…DON'T SAY 'EVERYTHING WILL BE ALRIGHT' BECAUSE IT WON'T!…DO YOU HAVE ANY IDEA WHAT I'M ABOUT TO DO?…YOU'RE NOT SACRIFICING

ANYTHING...but I am still coming though...I'm still leaving...love you too."

Hannah cancelled the call and stared at the two suitcases packed and standing by her huge double bed. There was half a glass of wine sitting on her bedside table, she had been stressing about this day yesterday and the wine had helped her get some sleep. She picked up the glass and finished it, wiping the trickling remnants from her mouth.

The remaining bottle of wine caught her eye, she grabbed it and continued the routine she'd started with the glass. Tossing the rest of it down her mouth she looked at her reflection from the full-length mirror at the end of the bottle. She glared at contempt at herself with the now empty bottle swinging from her right hand. "What are you looking at?"

A flare of rage hit her and she threw the bottle to the other side of the room, smashing it into tiny pieces against the wall.

The tears came back as Hannah grabbed the cases and ran out of her bedroom, sobbing more as she ran down each step, the cases weighing her down. Her dark eyes flashed to the bottom step and she collapsed into a heap as she finished her descent.

Looking back knowingly at the upstairs bedrooms, Hannah wiped her wet face, picked up her cases and struggled out of the front door, bawling her eyes out into the night.

As the door was slammed shut, the whole house was silent, but only for a while, a little voice, a young boy's voice called out from one of the bedrooms. "Mummy? Where are you?...I'm scared." The house stayed silent. "Mummy, please?"

The eerie silence was finally broken when somebody slowly entered the boy's room.

"Whoopsy daisy!" another voice exclaimed brightly. "Time to get you back in the land of the sleep, young man."

The boy's eyes examined the new person's face, his eyes squinted as the glare from the landing light hit him, he grew calmer as the voice entered.

"What are you doing here?" the young boy asked with a voice filled with inquisitiveness more than fear.

The new person answered with another question. "Why aren't you asleep?"

"My mummy won't come to me, Mr babysitter, do you know where she is?"

Taking a few steps closer, the man bent over to the youngster and brushed his hair gently. "Your mummy called me earlier, asked me to come over and watch you and your sister while she had to pop out."

"When is she coming back?"

The man arched his back and removed his glasses carefully. "She had to sort some stuff out, little man, but I'm sure she'll be back soon."

"Is my daddy here?"

"No, he's not here."

A strange expression crossed the young boy's face. "Is he coming back?"

The man craned his neck under the youthful interrogation. "Yeah, he'll be back, he's just got things to do, you know?"

"I know, the usual stuff right?"

The babysitter smiled. "You are your father's son alright, you know the crack! But you don't have to call me Mr babysitter you know, you can call me by my real name."

Giggling, the boy pulled his sheets above his head and then dropped them down again to reveal his cheeky smile. "I like calling you Mr babysitter! I think it's cool."

Slowly, with easy care, the man smiled. "Ok, I like being cool, Would you like me to read you a story?"

Nodding enthusiastically the little lad stuck his thumb in his mouth and rolled around excitedly in his bed. "Yes please!"

Putting his hand back on the boy's forehead, the man bent forward and cooed his voice. "Let's see."

He left the boy's side and rummaged through some books sat at the foot of the bed. "Ah ha! Here we go, what about this one?"

The man stretched for the book and walked around to the boy's side of the bed with it clutched firmly in his hands. "Here we go, what about this one then?...*The Green Man Rides a Bike*."

Rolling around excitedly in his bed, the youngster spoke from beneath the covers.

"Yes please, Mr babysitter. I love that book!"

Thumbing through the pages of the book, the brown-haired man held his breath slightly until a grin was ready to emerge. "Oh ok...The Green Man? I like the sound of that." He closed the book and looked at the cover. "I like his green hat too."

Some years later, two years after
the events in Paintshark.

Apology Day at Olympia, outside
Big Man's Messiah's Complex

"Look at that guy down there, I bet he shaves his toes."
Big Man tapped the microphone attached to the podium
he stood behind. "Is this thing working?"

He pointed to an old woman walking past, with a
grey cardigan wrapped over her shoulders. "Wow! Look
at that, mutton dressed as mutton."

Still dressed in a crisp clean black suit and perfectly
smooth skin, the hair had greyed and was started to thin
a little but not too much to warrant him whipping out
the box of hair dye.

The static feedback made him jump and most of the
people gathered around the foot of the podium. He
wanted the audience to be made up of what he classed as
'His sort of people'. Fashionable movers and shakers
and the best society people the city of Olympia had to
offer. He wanted the most elegant and the prettiest
people at this gathering and they did come, along with
some others he wasn't too keen on at first.

Under the words of his advisors, if he wanted to make
this day special, he had to invite everybody from all
walks of life to this party, plumbers, dustmen, even
primary school teachers got the nod for the invite.

That was the hardest of bitter pills to swallow, but life goes on, as countless people constantly told him after the break-up of his marriage, and if he was honest, the break-up of his empire was more pressing than his wife's infidelity.

So it seemed most of the city had gathered outside of the Messiah's Complex – the grand tower, the massive office and residential complex were still the most glorious buildings in the city and definitely the tallest, housing a lot of staff and a few family who he still managed to keep out of the limelight.

The theme for the day, again from the advisors' mouths, was to have a mini funfair in his giant backyard and fancy dress costumes.

Big Man sent the invites out and people turned up in their droves, eating candyfloss and hotdogs, riding on bumper cars and generally taking part in all the funfair activities.

A woman sauntered through the crowds and walked past the podium, she wore a very tight red evening dress with red shoes to match, her appearance even made Big Man double take, she had her face completely covered with a child's cheap 'Monster' mask, but her hair was what had caught everybody's attention.

Her hair was a mass frenzy of what seemed to be live snakes, they pulled her head from left to right swarming and launching themselves at passers by only held back by the woman's skull. Much of the crowd seemed nonplussed by her appearance, whilst others just simply gave her the thumbs up sign, which she replied back in kind and carried on walking without a word.

"That outfit was pretty shit hot," Big Man idly mentioned out loud, which the whole crowd heard as the microphone was working perfectly. "Shit! Sorry! Shit! Swore again, shit! So sorry!"

He composed himself and started again. "Right, can I have everybody's attention please?" The loud sounds of the funfair carried on regardless as he tried again. "A little quiet here please, people!"

Big Man was no match for free rides and food and he finally gave up and leaned down to whisper to an aide standing beside him, the man also in shades nodded and pressed a button on his earpiece and muttered something before relaxing again with his arms behind his back. Suddenly all the rides came to a halt, the bumper cars stopped bumping and the ferris wheel stopped turning, much to the annoyance to the people stuck at the top.

Big Man laughed and wriggled his nose before turning back to his aide. "Ok, we are good to go. Thanks man, by the way, do you shave your toes?"

Instead of answering he simply shrugged his massive shoulders. "I bet you do," Big Man pressed him.

The aide stood as still as a rock and crossed his huge arms across his chest, his mouth moved a little. "Sometimes."

The microphone picked up the moans of disappointment from the crowd as all the rides came to a halt. Big Man turned to his audience.

"Thank you for showing an interest in me and my free funfair, I appreciate it, this is the second annual 'Apology Day' and I know it's not the oldest of public holidays and I had to pull a lot of strings with the government to get this new holiday after they stitched me up after blaming the television ban on me…"

Big Man's aide tugged at his shirt and whispered in his ear, which Big Man nodded in reply.

"I meant to say I liaised with government officials and we came to an agreement which would benefit all citizens of Olympia due to the disappointment of the television ban, I can only apologise profusely about what happened two years ago and the distress of seeing my TV empire crumble before your eyes must have been terrible for you. I know you probably blame me for wrecking your lives and entertainment values as apparently my violent game show was to blame for our current financial climate.

I know thousands of you lost their jobs thanks to me which is a bit of a bummer but I just wanted to say it wasn't my fault, it was due to the little shit kids in that school I tried to close down years ago that done me in..."

The aide poked at Big Man again. "I meant...due to an unforeseen chain of events involving some quite remarkable bright children from a local school who turned out to be quite adept at escaping from high security prisons and destroying them in the process..."

He stared at the aide like a child looking for reassurance from his parents. The aide nodded his approval.

"I would like to thank myself for hosting the event and I suppose I should thank you for turning up for this free shindig, I have made one or two mistakes in the past and believe me I am paying the price for it as my money is dwindling, however..."

Before Big Man could continue his inept apology, the sound of a huge engine rumbling through the funfair crowd cut him off. An armoured military car roared through the grounds to Big Man's plaza. Big Man studied the car sceptically. *What's happening now?* he thought.

The hatch to the car opened and a figure wearing a long green raincoat emerged. He wore a battered old fedora hat, which was green also.

Silver eyes beamed above a strange device fixed to its mouth – it was an odd-looking black breathing apparatus which covered his nose as well, each breath the masked man took made a strange squelching sound, like a boot stuck in mud. Two tubes ran from where his nostril should have been and coiled around his head and ran down his back, connected to some misshapen battery pack attached by straps just under his coat.

Big black steel toe-capped boots clunked hard against the ground as he made his way forward.

The astonished crowds parted to allow him through, he tipped his hat in gratitude and Big Man could quickly see the sun reflecting off the metal which seemed to be his head.

Big Man had seen a lot of strange things since he started his violent game show series many years ago, genetically engineered animals and teenagers with superpowers, but something about the masked man in green was intriguing.

"Can I help you?" Big Man raised an eyebrow as he spoke.

"I believe you've already helped yourself, Big Man."

The voice of the figure was confident but strained each time it spoke sounding like it took tremendous effort, the sound of gas escaping accompanying each word that left his mouth. Big Man listened intently to the metallic grate of his voice.

"Who are you again?"

"Who I am doesn't matter, but what I do next will give you grave concern."

Big Man thrust his chest forward like a young buck, itching for fight. "I don't take well to empty threats, mister—"

"It's as well I don't make them," the deep voice interjected. "Let's just say I'm Olympia's saviour."

Big Man responded immediately. "Well I'm savouring the moment you leave my premises."

He went to touch fists with his aide who remained motionless. "The words have different meanings, sir."

"You're quite the comedian, Big Man, but I wonder if your gags will still rain down after the events which will transpire."

"Dude, stop talking in riddles, look I'll spell it out to you..." He spoke slowly and mockingly. "W-H-A-T D-O Y-O-U W-A-N-T?"

The man in green had expected this behaviour from Big Man and carried on regardless.

"You have bought pain and discomfort to so many people."

"And 'Here's the church and here is the steeple'," Big Man said, using his hands making the movements for the children's nursery rhyme.

"Fair enough."

The former TV executive yawned. "Mate, I've got the rest of Apology Day to enjoy without some nutbag outside my front door spouting gibberish, you sound like you can do with a tune up, why don't you take yourself to McLean's garage down the road, tell them Big Man sent you."

The stranger hesitated and walked back to his vehicle, he paused again before banging his fist on the side. The hatch opened and a man dressed in a poncho handed the masked man a megaphone and a small radio receiver.

"Thank you."

He spoke into the radio. "Gentlemen, it is time."

Suddenly more men working for the man in the green coat appeared out of nowhere and swarmed around all of the rides of the funfair."

"WHAT THE HELL IS THIS?" Big Man yelled.

The man in the green coat eyed him steadily. "This is your penance." He shouted into the megaphone.

"GOOD AFTERNOON, LADIES AND GENTLE-MEN, THOSE OF YOU STRANDED ATOP THE AMUSEMENT RIDES, STAY STILL, MY MEN WILL GET YOU DOWN MOMENTARILY."

With a nod from their boss's head, the men all wearing ponchos climbed up the various rides attached with harnesses and with military precision started moving down the people stuck on the tops of the funfair rides.

Big Man was gradually losing patience with the gate crasher, it had been a long morning and he was getting too tired for this.

"Is there any point to this? You disrupting my party?"

"THERE IS ALWAYS A POINT TO PROVE TO THE MASSES, BIG MAN, BUT I WILL NOT TRICK THEM."

"Excuse me?"

The huge figure turned to the people gathered now by the sides of the rides, all rescued by his henchmen.

"PEOPLE OF OLYMPIA, I'M SURE YOU ARE WELL AWARE OF THE EVENTS THAT HAVE TRANSPIRED OVER THE LAST FEW YEARS, WITH WHAT YOU HAVE LOST, ALL DUE TO THE THEATRICS AND DECEPTION OF THE MAN WHO STANDS BEFORE YOU.

A MAN OF TAINTED BUSINESS, A RICHER THAN GOD TYPE.

"THERE IS A BAN ON MOVING PICTURES, TELEVISION AND FILM INCLUDED, A NOTION PUSHED THROUGH BY THIS LIBERAL NEW GOVERNMENT AND THANKS TO THE GAME SHOW, KNOWN SIMPLY AS 'GAME SHOW' THE BAN WILL NOT BE MOVING ANYTIME SOON.

"A WARRANT FOR HIS ARREST CAME AND WENT THANKS TO HIS MANY CORRUPT CONTACTS WITHIN THE POLICE FORCE. HOW MANY OF YOU LONG FOR THE PULL OF THE SMALL SCREEN? AFTER A DAY OF SWEEPING UP VOMIT FROM THE GROUND AT TRAIN STATIONS, CHASING WINOS AND JUNKIES OFF THE PREMISES? A CAR SALESMAN OR WOMAN FOR THAT MATTER WHO HASN'T MADE THEIR TARGETS...HOW MANY OF THEM MISS THE DAILY CATCH UP FROM THEIR BELOVED SOAP CHARACTERS WHEN THEY RETURN HOME FROM WORK?

"WITHOUT YOU EVEN KNOWING, OUR CITY IS MORE DANGEROUS WITH BIG MAN STILL HERE, THE THREATS WILL BECOME MORE FREQUENT WHEN HE TIRES OF THE CHARADE OF FORGIVENESS, OUR ENEMIES WILL BE SEEMINGLY ENDLESS WITH BIG MAN STILL RESIDING IN OLYMPIA.

"I KNOW WHAT HE'S DONE TO YOU, PEOPLE OF OLYMPIA, I KNOW WHAT HE'S TAKEN FROM YOU, AND THE ANIMAL HE'S CREATED. BUT I CAN HELP YOU GRIEVE FROM YOUR LOSS, MY BROTHERS AND SISTERS, AND IF YOU LET ME IN

I BELIEVE I CAN HELP YOU, JUST LISTEN TO ME, I THINK WITH A LITTLE TIME AND SOME EFFORT, YOU MIGHT SURPRISE YOURSELF WITH WHAT YOU CAN DO TO TAKE BACK THIS LOYAL CITY.

"WE WERE HEADING FOR A WORLD WHERE PEOPLE LOOKED PAST THEIR INNER TRIBAL INSTINCT WHERE PEACEFUL COHABITATION COULD HAVE HAPPENED, BUT THAT WAS UNTIL BIG MAN STARTED HIS MANIACAL HOLD ON THE ARTS, REVENGE AND HATRED ARE ALL THAT BOILS IN HIS ENGINE.

"SOME TRIED TO STOP THIS HEINOUS MADMAN...AND DIED FOR THEIR EFFORTS SO IT'S TIME TO AVENGE THESE BRAVE SOULS. BIG MAN IS A MURDERING COWARD AND IT'S TIME HE PAYS FOR HIS CRIMES."

Straining his eyes and flaring his very delicate nostrils as he breathed harder after listening to the man's intensive speech, Big Man yawned and spoke.

"Is that it? That's quite an impressive spill of rubbish, did you write that yourself sitting alone in the loony bin? Were you allowed crayons or did your nurse do it for you? That's classic dude, you're a riot."

"I WILL AVENGE OUR FALLEN, BIG MAN, THIS WILL BE THE FINAL TIME YOU MOCK ME."

"Wearing that outfit? I doubt it matey."

This time Big Man and his security aide punched fists successfully.

"YOUR MEDDLING HAS BURST THE DAM, THE FLOW WILL BE RELEASED NOW."

"The dam has burst? Dude, you're killing me! But I'm still waiting." Big Man folded his arms impatiently mimicking his aide.

The man in the very dark green coat fiddled with the controls on the megaphone, increasing the volume.

"VERY WELL, MY BROTHERS AND SISTERS OF OLYMPIA, BIG MAN HAS YET TO TRULY PAY FOR HIS CRIME AGAINST OUR BELOVED CITY, YOU HAVE BEEN ROBBED OF THE LUXURY OF TELEVISION AND FILM, YET BIG MAN STILL LIVES THE LIFE OF LUXURY IN HIS GLORIOUS TOWER, UNAFFECTED BY THE PAST."

A teenage boy stepped forward and raised his hand, the man in the green coat motioned him to speak.

"But we have books to learn sir, I like reading again."

The green coat shook as the man laughed. "OH THE AGONY OF YOUTH, YOU WILL LEARN MY YOUNG FRIEND, WE HAVE DODGED A BULLET WITH THE COLLAPSE OF BIG MAN'S NETWORK AND THIS IS WHERE I COME IN, I OFFER THE REWARD OF 500 MILLION CREDITS FOR THE CAPTURE OF ZEUS A.K.A THE BIG MAN, ALIVE NOT DEAD, BATTERED IF NEEDS BE BUT ONCE HE IS IN MY GRASP, THE RISE OF OLYMPIA WILL RETURN."

A feeling like a punch to the gut hit Big Man and he swayed like he was on the ropes in a one-sided boxing match.

The man in the green coat's eyes closed in scrutiny at Big Man, his face mask shifted to the right slightly as if the mouth underneath was smiling. "WHAT? NO WORDS OF AMUSEMENT? NO JOKES AT MY EXPENSE? YOU'VE GONE ALL QUIET BIG MAN, NO WITTY RETORT?...COME ON, SAY SOMETHING FUNNY."

The crowd were already very quiet as they heard the speech, but then suddenly a tidal wave of applause and cheers equalled the sound of the funfair earlier. "So it begins," the man said quietly as he took the megaphone from his mouth.

"WHAT THE HELL IS THIS?" It was Big Man's turn to yell.

The crowd were getting more rowdy by the second, the man in the green coat was the perfect ringmaster.

"It's been interesting observing you, Big Man, your sacrifice to the great city of Olympia will not go unnoticed, you are a powerful force of nature and I respect that in some way, any last words before we take you in?"

Big Man ran a hand through the top of his thinning grey hair.

"Yeah, I've got two words…and the second one is 'you'."

"Charming to the last."

The man in the green coat laughed and clutched his stomach, he waved to the crowd when he had composed himself. "Are we ready for the reckoning, Olympia?" The crowd roared their approval as the man in the green coat continued waving. "Then here we…go!"

The crowds of people surged forward as if it was the first day of sales for a high street department store. Women and children battled with each other to reach the front of the surge, old men with walking sticks swung wildly in any direction connecting with anyone who stood in their path.

It was a stampede, people slipped and fell in their frantic chase but were trodden underfoot by other more cash hungry party goers who wanted a piece of Big Man.

"WHOA! WHOA! WHOA! WHAT'S HAPPENING HERE?" Big Man shouted.

Big Man's aide considered before answering. "Well I think they're after you, sir."

"WELL DO SOMETHING! PROTECT ME!"

The aide paid no attention to his boss's frantic questions and began to take off his radio mic and sunglasses. "I think it's too late for that sir, 500 million credits is a lot of money."

"What are you doing?"

"I'm taking you in sir, resistance is futile." He reached over for his boss.

Surprising himself as well as his aide, Big Man head-butted his bodyguard, knocking him to the ground. "Test tube baby," Big Man hissed.

He turned and bolted towards the plaza, his home.

His guests, the people he invited to his funfair, a fair he had built especially for them had now turned against him. The man in the green coat didn't move as hundreds of people moved past him for their reward.

"Shouldn't we go after him?" asked one of his men, wearing a bright yellow poncho.

"Not yet my friend, the turning point hasn't started yet, but the war has begun."

The guard shot him back a puzzled look. "I don't get it, sir."

A rough metal hand gave him a rub on the shoulder. "All in good time my friend."

Big Man sprinted to the front of his massive complex, it had a load of doors on the bottom level, but at the moment he only needed one of them to open but he began to panic.

"OH SHIT..OH SHIT...OH SHIT...OH SHIT!"

An old woman on a motorised buggy was blocking his path.

"Let me through please," Big Man huffed.

"Screw you dick head, I'm taking you in."

The woman put her foot down on the accelerator and went for a ramming speed albeit a very low one. Big Man easily side-stepped the cart and gave her a dig to the head for good measure.

Another party goer appeared from nowhere and grabbed him from behind, an elbow from Big Man put the man to the ground with ease. The man shook like he was having a seizure, but that didn't bother Big Man.

He saw how the chasing people had spread out and were coming from both sides opposite the plaza, he had to keep his eyes on targets coming from two directions. Big Man banged his little fists hard on the main front door. "LET ME IN! PLEASE SOMEBODY, YOU GOTTA LET ME IN!"

A panel revealing a screen flipped open and a computerised vocal track with a woman's voice switched on.

"AUTHORISATION CODE REQUIRED: ACCESS LEVEL ONE."

He frantically banged on the screen. "IT'S ME! IT'S ME! BIG MAN! BIG MAN! IT'S MY HOUSE LET ME IN GOD DAMMIT!"

The computer wasn't programmed to notice panic in somebody's voice and remained firm.

"AUTHORISATION CODE REQUIRED: ACCESS LEVEL ONE."

Big Man shook his head resolutely. "ANYBODY INSIDE OPEN THE DOOR! ROGER! ROGER! WILCO! WILCO!" He touched the screen and then swiped his finger across it to no avail. "OH COME ON!"

The fast-moving city folk were almost upon him, including his bodyguard who was back on his feet and moving in fast, forcing his way through the others to get at his boss. Big Man saw his guard knock three people down in order to get to him and his stomach twisted with shock and disappointment, his heart was hammering hard inside his chest.

A gunshot sound made him freeze briefly before turning around at the baying crowd. One shot was followed by another and then another, until someone started firing a machine gun wildly at his direction.

"GUNS NOW? DIDN'T ANYBODY FRISK THESE PEOPLE?"

His mind flicked back to his bodyguard and thought about how useless he really was.

The young feminine computer voice coming from the speakers continued;

"AUTHORISATION CODE REQUIRED: ACCESS LEVEL ONE."

"I KNOW! I KNOW! CAN'T FIND MY—"

Then the realisation hit him and Big Man punched the air with delight and suddenly he didn't feel so terrified as he reached into a secret pocket inside his suit.

"SWIPE CARD!" he shouted.

Using the card in a slot below he typed in some numbers, the screen and then the computer voice changed.

"AUTHORISATION CODE ACCEPTED: RETINA SCAN REQUIRED."

Placing his head right up front to the screen a red beam of light scanned his face, the red line moved horizontally and stopped on his eyes, when the computer voice came on again.

"RETINA SCAN ACCEPTED, PERIMETER DEACTVATED."

The lights on the screen flashed briefly and then the red locked sign changed to green.

Huge clunking and whirring sounds came from the door as the locks were finally open and the door slowly began to rise. Big Man dived though the entrance and with moments to spare slammed his hand against the door lock mechanism. The door closed and he glanced around nervously before getting up and shouting into another computer screen behind him.

"ACTIVATE EMERGENCY LOCK OUT PROCE-DURE AT ALL ENTRY LEVELS CODE 112224 FILE NAME ZEUS WYLDE… OVERRIDE ALL RETINA ID SCANS!"

The familiar sound of the female computer voice followed.

"OVERRIDE ACCEPTED: EMERGENCY LOCK OUT PROCEDURE INITATED."

The voice made Big Man relax slightly, knowing that nobody could enter his tower now without his knowl-edge. Thanks to his override not even his bodyguard had the right codes to get in.

Big Man slumped against the door and listened to the fist pounding and machine gun fire from the outside that gradually died down. He thought about the mysterious man in the green coat and the huge bounty he had placed upon his head as well as the city folk he had invited to his grounds for Apology Day and who had now tried to turn him in, and his trusted bodyguard who in a split second forgot about years of service for Big Man and had his head swayed by The Green Man's money.

As the screams and shouts continued from the outside Big Man hunched his shoulders and dropped his head in thought about his bodyguard.

"I knew he shaved his toes."

1. THE TURNING POINT

Olympia City: Early Morning
Four Years Later

"GET BIG MAN OUT! GET BIG MAN OUT! GET BIG MAN OUT!"

The crowds swarmed around the giant tower like ants around a fallen ice lolly in the sun. The protesters held aloft giant banners and waved placards above their heads. Their anger was fervently directed at the former TV executive who watched them from a high room from within his fortress. His actions years ago had cost the city of Olympia dearly, he had underestimated the teenage collective of Cassandra, Kimberley and Sabrina, as well as their headmaster Elias Glaucas, and then there was a little nerd called Felcey and some teachers too, but he didn't care about them. They had successfully taken down his television empire as well as escaping from the most notorious prison on the planet. He was aware of Kimberley's sacrifice in helping the others escape due to the cameras on the prison ship, but since the ship went down, everybody on board was presumed dead.

But the damage had already been done, he had no money, his assets frozen and most importantly, the new government had banned television and only given the city a limited internet access. There was a warrant out for his arrest, it had been for many years now. The police knew exactly where he was, locked away in one of Olympia's biggest towers. His fortress was impenetrable, police battering rams and tanks had tried to bash and blast their way through with no avail; they couldn't find a way through to bring him in for questioning. So they were happy just to now sit back and wait for the Big Man to finally leave his safe haven.

But it was the tremendous bounty from The Green Man of 500 million credits that was the real reason why Big Man stayed in his tower; his eyes were now bloodshot and his vision wasn't at its best now. Citizens who couldn't break into the tower or simply grew tired of trying to were leaving the city in their droves, to other states where the TV ban wasn't in place.

As for the people who remained in the city, they took to venting their anger with a daily protest outside his tower, stones, paint and countless bunches of out of date fruit were flung against the doors of the reception area.

Big Man trusted no one, the remainder of his staff had to be vetted by him and him alone. He could barely afford to keep some of his staff. It was a matter of paying them way over their normal salary but it was either that or watch them one by one betray him and bring him in for the 500 million credit reward, although he could relax slightly knowing that to get into the tower was much harder than to get out.

He had been holed up in his office block home for some years now and was tired, he wondered what it would be like to breathe fresh air again, to see and feel the sun on his shades, plus how long the protesters would keep this up for, he took out his mobile phone and put it to the 'binocular' feature. Holding it close to his eyes he gave a further look to the people gathering outside.

The first was a fantastically dressed couple in their thirties clutching a bottle of wine and swaying apologetically with their inebriation, they moved in for a kiss before stumbling back and launching the bottle at the building. The crowd roared with delight as the bottle shattered against the window. Big Man scanned the crowd again. A father was crouching down with his young son to reach the boy's little height. The dad was wearing a Greymen Utd football top, which barely covered his protruding stomach. Snot dripped from his bulbous nose, as he obviously had a summer cold. The boy wore glasses with big lenses and he looked up nervously to his dad who handed him something small and round.

Big Man increased the zoom on his phone and sighed when he saw it was a rock. The dad rubbed his son's shoulders to give him support and began to egg him on with vile encouragement, buoyed up by the crowd who were now whipped up into a hysterical frenzy. Shutting his eyes the boy released the rock feebly and it bounced harmlessly off a window with no great effect.

Nevertheless, the crowd cheered the little boy's efforts and his football-mad father kept his hands around his shoulders, shaking him until the boy's glasses slipped from his face.

A thunderous sound from the skies made everyone look up, including Big Man. Four Olympian fighter jets skimmed through the air and joined in with the crowd in shattering the beautiful morning; the planes flew in low and began to circle the building. They weren't official Olympian protectors, they must have been from somebody's private collection of planes, obviously the lure of bagging 500 million credits to bring in Big Man was too much for the owner who gave the word for the planes to try. The crowd roared their approval as one of the planes turned to dip and unleash it's machine gun fire towards Big Man's observation tower – the sound tore through the morning sky as the protesters whooped and cheered below. More gunfire slammed harmlessly against the building as the tower's shields did their job. Big Man stepped aside from the window and walked over to a small fridge in the corner of the room. He took out a bottle of water and slowly unscrewed the top to take a drink as the sound of the planes zipping through the air continued. Clutching the bottle he sat down on a huge chair and put some earpieces in from his phone. He turned up the volume to full to drown out the sound of the machine gun attack on his building. As the sound of hip-hop music entered his ears, Big Man's shoulders swayed in tune as the fighter jets continued their onslaught.

Aphrodite

Two armed guards stood outside the huge black complex, their breaths were fast and heavy as they saw what was rushing towards them, the fighter planes didn't bother them, they had long since departed. It was the sight of the heavy mob on the ground which was their concern. The older man stood with a heavy sigh. "Here we go again."

His younger colleague looked at his watch. "Hope this doesn't take long, I've got things to do tonight."

The old friend nodded. "I know, that's all you've spoken about for the last few days."

The young guard shot an amused glance to his friend. "I'm always on the move."

"As are they!" the old man blurted.

The huge doors from the tremendous black tower slowly opened, it was the doors leading to the kitchen quarters of Big Man's fantastic complex.

The protesters lined the street and swarmed around them like a starving house cat hassling its owner for fresh food to go in its bowl.

"You ready for this?" the older man asked, looking understandably anxious.

"To be fair I'm a little bored of it, same old same old."

The police used to try and enforce the protesters with a line around them, but that was years ago, when the police used to work for Big Man, but now they joined the protesters, some were doing their job in trying to bring in Big Man for questioning, but others with cash lust in their eyes wanted the bounty sitting on the head of Big Man.

The guards kept their backs to the doors as some people hurriedly began to leave the building. They were dressed as waitresses and kitchen staff and ran quickly to their cars placed awkwardly in the complex's car park, the cars were left in all different angles as if they had been parked in a hurry and under duress.

The crowd of protesters targeted the workers like a pride of lions hunting zebra, they had their targets and picked out each worker one by one.

The dad who was with his son earlier pinned a frightened young worker to the wall of the building. "WHO ARE YOU?" he roared in her ears.

"I'M STAFF!" she shouted back, more through annoyance than fright, he released her and she scurried off to her car. Another protester, a woman this time, mirrored the attack of the father previously and had her hands around the neck of another employee. "WHERE ARE THEY?"

The younger girl struggled free and ran to her car, mouthing back a fierce reply. "SCREW YOU! I DON'T KNOW WHERE THEY ARE!"

The protesters vented their frustrations on Big Man's employees without rational thought, bullying the kitchen and waitress staff. To their credit the girls fought back admirably, kicking male protesters in the groin and scratching and punching their way free to the waiting transport.

A young woman ran zig-zagging a path to the front of the main protest group, she wore huge sunglasses and a long shawl covering her mouth, she caught a glimpse at Big Man's guards and began waving her arms frantically.

"GET BACK!" the younger guard shouted. The woman was fast and shoved her way through the dispersing crowd. "MADAM! PLEASE STAND DOWN!"

She began to unravel her shawl, struggling with the knot at the back. "I WON'T WARN YOU AGAIN." She glanced once or twice from side to side were as the now untied shawl fell to the ground. The guard stood with his restraining baton by his side as the woman approached him, her mouth finally visible, she smiled and the eyes behind the shades beamed, then her mouth moved. "Hi. I just wanted to—"

The guard swung the baton hard against the side of the woman's head, just above her ear. Dazed by the blow, the woman struggled on her feet to hang on to consciousness, she staggered to the left before some protesters came in and held her steady before leading her away.

"A little harsh wasn't it?" said the mature guard.

"Yeah maybe, but she asked for it."

"Did she really?"

The guard lowed his baton and checked his watch again. "I just want this day to end."

Two maids held hands and made a dart for the car park at the side of the building, both had their brown hair tied back, one carried a little backpack whilst the slightly taller one carried a glittering handbag; the taller one was more used to running in high heels then her partner. A sudden explosion hit the car park lifting the protesters and workers alike off the ground. An armoured troop transport vehicle rolled up through the remains of the staff's burnt out car wrecks. Its mounted cannons still smoking, ready for another blast. The cover slid open and a huge masked figure emerged followed by three more guards in combat gear, the last man to appear held a megaphone and handed it to the massive first figure dressed in a long green coat.

"Shit it's him," whispered the younger of Big Man's guards.

"Get the water cannons ready," replied the older man.

The man in the green coat clicked his massive head and rolled his shoulders before speaking into the megaphone.

"EMPLOYERS OF BIG MAN ALSO KNOWN AS ZEUS, WE HAVE DANCED THIS DANCE MANY A TIME NOW AND YET YOU STILL ARE UNAWARE OF THE CORRECT MOVES TO SATISFY ME. FOR THIS TO END ALL I REQUIRE ARE THE DAUGHTERS OF ZEUS AND THEN YOU CAN GO ABOUT YOUR BUSINESS. AS I'VE REQUESTED ON A WEEKLY BASIS, YOU ARE BUTTERFLIES OF YOUR BOSS,

TRAPPED IN AN UGLY GLASS CAGE OF A TOWER...
GIVE ME WHAT I WANT AND YOU HAVE MY
WORD OF A RELEASE FROM THE TOMFOOLERY
OF BIG MAN."

Both of Big Man's guards reached for their
communication tags on their collars.

"CODE BLUE! WE NEED WATER DOWN HERE
ASAP!"

A streak of powerful water fired out of cannons
from secret compartments from within the Messiah's
complex. The force of the cannons scattered the protesters like ants in slight shower. More cannons locked onto
the man in the green coat's vehicle, knocking over his
own guards, the water failed to move the man in the
green coat, he held his hand out deflecting the water in
all directions. "THAT TICKLES!" he wheezed.

The two maids had reached their car, which had
been unaffected by the explosion, the taller one rifled
through her bag for something. "Oh for goodness sake!
I can't find the bloody keys!"

The other girl quickly reached into her rucksack and
threw her a set. "Why are you always losing keys?"

"So sue me, get in."

Another protester put his big sweaty hands on the
taller girl and spun her around. "Nice maids outfit, now
where are daughters of Big Man?"

"Do you like it, darling? Why thank you so much,
I altered it a bit made it my own creation, a cut here,
a trim there, gives the men something to look at." The
other girl cleared her throat loudly for attention. "Oh
as for your question..." She raised her high heel and
bought it hard down on the man's cheap trainers,

piercing them with ease. He howled like a wild animal and fell backwards.

"What a complete waste of good air," she said.

"Are you trying to give me heart failure?" the smaller girl asked.

"If only it was that easy."

With both girls in the car, tower high heels slammed hard on the accelerator and the battered old car sped out of the burning car park. The rest of the protesters ran away and the water cannons died down. One of the guards of The Green Man wiped down his soaking wet outfit and gave his boss a concerned look. "That vehicle doesn't check out on our records, that car was probably them, shall we go after them?"

"Their ruse was expected my friend, but they will not suspect ours until it is too late," rasped the man in the green coat.

"So you never wanted the girls then, boss?"

"They have fled the building again as we have undertaken this charade for many a time now."

"So why is today any different?"

The man in the green coat placed his hand on the man's shoulder and gave a comforting squeeze, the pain was unbearable for the little man, but he didn't want to show any weakness.

"The difference is that they will not be returning today, they have left the building and that's all that matters because the turning point is about to begin and the fall of Big Man from grace will be complete."

Speeding along the high street and breaking every speed limit in the book, the older girl turned to her passenger. "Be a dear and take the wheel please."

"But—"

"Now! My wig is stuck and brown is so not my colour."

Taking the wheel gingerly, the other girl watched as the driver pulled hard at her fake brown hair. With a shake of her head the wig came free and the driver's true golden hair was allowed to flow.

Aphrodite ran her perfectly manicured nails through her golden mane, some years had passed since she had betrayed some of her classmates including her best friend Sabrina to her father's game show called 'Game Show' – she thought it was a stupid name but whatever her father said or did, she'd blindly followed.

She was still savagely beautiful and her ocean blue eyes closed with concentration as she shuffled in her black maid's outfit, fiddling with her white cuffs.

"I can't keep this up you know." A low annoyed growl came from the lips of Gemma Glaucas. She was a teenager now, still living with Big Man but the adoption fell through – he was her foster-father though and had fought hard to keep her.

She enjoyed living at the huge complex, she loved her new family even now after things had changed since the arrival of this strange man wearing a green coat and the bounty on her fosters-father's head and how she had to employ such drastic tactics in order to leave her house.

Gemma loved this, she was as dangerously arrogant as Big Man when it came to getting into trouble, a trait she had easily picked up from him.

"Why can't I have a green wig?" Gemma asked, putting the ginger wig on the back seat. "I would love green hair and I'm always getting red hair. Can't I change for once?"

"What I would love you to do is to be quiet whilst I ditch this car and find another one, they would have noticed us leave and listed it." Aphrodite took back the wheel. "So annoying we have to do this every time we leave the complex."

It was a lovely day, with only a few clouds in the sky as the glorious sun peeked through the gaps in the sky. Zooming through the various streets, she suddenly came up against a huge traffic jam.

Aphrodite smacked her hand onto the horn of her car, her brow was creased with pure annoyance. "COULD YOU POSSIBLY DRIVE ANY SLOWER?"

"We could have gone by bus you know?" Gemma lazily rubbed her eyes.

"Public transport is filled with morons and people who don't shower, we're not taking the bus."

Even the slightest bit of heat bought out the citizens in droves, even more so now thanks to the ban on television, the big summer holiday getaway was busier than usual with people escaping the city by plane, trains and on a long stretch of a non-moving traffic jam, by car – but most of them had gathered back at her father's complex, trying to break through and get their hands on him for the most delicious amount of money.

She took her frustration out on the steering wheel and the driver in front, shaking her head. "FOR GOODNESS SAKE, WHY AREN'T YOU MOVING?"

Aphrodite gave the horn another blast and turned towards the passenger seat, giving its occupant an icy stare. "This is all your fault."

The younger girl simply gave a blank stare and popped her bubble gum and chewed vigorously before answering, "Why is it my fault exactly?"

"I'll tell why it's your fault, darling," Aphrodite snapped back. "It was your stupid father's fault, if he hadn't have stopped Daddy from taking over his school, Daddy wouldn't have those ghastly kids come after him, destroying his stadium and TV studios. We took you in and they've banned television, so when he tried to make things better with the Apology Days, some madman puts a bounty on his head so big we have to go through a tedious assault course just to leave the house and play dress up with these maid outfits, risk getting blown up, buying a car every day, all to take my so called 'sister' swimming on the hottest day of the year…AND GETTING STUCK BEHIND THE SLOWEST DRIVER EVER!" A succession of small blasts from the horn failed to make the car in front move. Gemma Glaucus popped her gum once more and cleared her throat only to whisper, "Loser." Aphrodite honked the horn again and hissed at her foster sister, "Tramp." The two bickering sisters couldn't see the driver's face in the car in front, only the back of his head bore the brunt of Aphrodite's road rage, if they had been able to see his face they would have noticed how both his hands clutched the steering wheel as his body shook uncontrollably, his nose began to bleed and drip of blood fell into the foot well, followed by the tip of his tongue as his teeth sliced through it.

Taylor

Taylor Tristan *really* hated working on Apology Day. It was only a new holiday and he really couldn't understand why people wanted to buy carpet on it, it seemed to be the hottest day of the year and still punters came in their masses, dragging their screaming kids in tow, looking for the best deals for decent floor coverings.

He just had to get through the day and then he knew he could sink a 'few cold ones' with his mates Earl and Malik in the pub later after football training – sports were extremely popular now since the shutdown of television and the enforced restrictions on the Internet.

Earl was going to bring along his cousin Cameo. Taylor hadn't seen her in years and Earl was hoping to set the two of them up. Taylor was looking forward to it, it had been a year since his girlfriend had walked out on him and he thought now that he was ready to get back on the dating scene, he hadn't had a good track record with the ladies and hoped this could be the start of a beautiful but probable brief relationship.

Cameo was about to go on a college trip on Olympia's first zoo space cruiser, Taylor didn't have long to impress her.

The automatic doors slid open as a new customer entered the shop and broke Taylor's concentration and thoughts of his next ex-girlfriend; Taylor approached the customer with confidence.

"Good morning sir! Is there anything in particular I can help you with?"

"Just looking thanks," was the reply, which was friendly enough to warrant a smile from Taylor.

To be fair he was glad, even though he knew he needed the job to save up and go travelling later on in the year, he really wasn't in the mood for customers today and he thought he'd had just enough cash to quit before next Apology Day holiday. *This will be my last working holiday.*

The shop was getting busier now and Taylor was one of seven sales staff on the shop floor and also the youngest. He was twenty-one, fit and handsome with incredibly blond hair, bad with the ladies but good with money, young and in his so-called 'prime'.

The phone rang on the front desk. Jess, the second youngest member of the staff and sometime drinking partner of Taylor was on her lunch break; every other one of his colleagues was pitching or wrapping up a sale.

Taylor sighed and put his head down as he shuffled toward the desk and answered the phone.

"Good afternoon and thank you for calling Quick Lay Carpets, my name is Taylor, how can I help you?" He rolled his eyes as he hated saying such a cheesy line. The phone line was silent. "Hello? Anybody there?"

The voice on the other side finally answered – male, youngish and slightly agitated, "Hi, is Jess there please?"

"No, she went on her lunch break, can I take a message?"

The voice went quiet. "Umm...Umm...Umm...Err..."

Taylor pressed the voice. "Hello? Is that you again, Achilles? Look, Jess has made her feelings clear mate, she doesn't want to know."

"Umm...could you tell her that...I...er...it really doesn't matter." He hung up.

Taylor drew back the phone from his ear and stared at the mouthpiece with a quizzical look on his face. He simply put down the phone and rolled his tongue around his mouth. Then he realised that Jess was actually finished for the day, she had left to join her college friends on the same Olympia zoo space cruiser as Cameo, Taylor's would-be date. Taylor sighed. *God I don't need this today.* The odd phone call didn't linger in his mind for too long and Taylor wandered through the aisles of carpets deliberately avoiding customers now, he didn't care about selling now and losing his commission. Each time the automatic doors opened and a new customer entered Taylor thought, *When will this day end?*

A male customer bought Taylor out from his trance. "Excuse me, can I get some help please?"

Taylor wiped his nose with the back of his hand and smiled. "Certainly sir, what can I do for you?"

The middle-aged gentleman pointed to a selection of brown carpets rolled up and standing on their end in the shop corner. "I was thinking of getting that colour for my son's room."

Taylor took out a pen and notebook from his pocket. "Ok, well old is he?"

"He's ten, he was supposed to be here and help choose it but he's got football training."

Taylor raised an eyebrow. "Oh, really? Who does he play for?"

The dad smiled gently. "He plays for Greymen Utd Academy."

"Does he? That's nice, shame about the first time missing out on the play-offs."

Taylor feigned pity as he supported Greys FC, their biter rivals, and was in pleased they'd missed out.

The two men spoke about sizes and costs as Taylor scribbled hard on the pad with his pen and put his pen back in his pocket when he'd finished.

"Also," said the football dad, "I was looking to get some carpet protection for spills and..."

He went quiet and stared intently at Taylor. "Are you ok?"

Taylor didn't say anything, he simply swayed from side to side, his eyes blank, and his head pounding. He took out the pen from his top pocket and swung it neatly in a short arc, slicing the customer's throat.

Football dad clutched his throat as his blood splattered onto Taylor who showed no emotion. Blood gurgled in his mouth and he fell head first on to the carpeted floor. A woman who was about to buy a rug for her bathroom put her hands to her head and screamed the place down. Taylor tumbled back, his brand new shirt was torn as he was bundled to the ground by shocked customers. As he lay on the floor another customer smashed Taylor's front teeth through his gums with his foot. Making no resistance, more and customers swarmed around Taylor and put their boots in as well. The blood from the mess that used to be his face stained his shirt and quickly spread.

Taylor Tristan finally got his wish…he had worked his last Apology Day holiday. This was the beginning of the turning point.

The traffic jam had hardly moved, nobody was attempting to edge their cars out and this frustrated Aphrodite even more. "Why am I taking you swimming again? If my day doesn't going to plan I hold you responsible, just you, you're responsible for the crap I'm probably going to go through today."

"We're going swimming because I'm not allowed to go on the trip to the space cruiser zoo. Everyone else is going, why can't I?"

"Because I think you're too young? Colleges can go, schools can't, is there another reason why we're outside today?"

Aphrodite was in a very bad mood, she had lost her job at the city's top beauty salon for her disastrous attendance, which used to be down to laziness, but recently it was more the point that now just even wanting to leave the complex to grab a morning newspaper took weeks to plan thanks to the unwanted company parked outside her house. So her father had put her on babysitting duties, she didn't bother with further education, there wasn't much point after her father's arrest warrant and the huge bounty on his head; she needed to be with her father.

The new government had banned television and it was supposed to have a positive effect on the city. The government thought people would be leaving their homes and television sets and going out to exercise and play, going to the theatre, taking part in sporting activities, but it had had the reverse effect. There were riots and protests and everybody blamed Big Man, the Apology Day holiday did come close to making amends, but that was well and truly forgotten thanks to The Green Man.

He hadn't left his tower in years, staying in the tallest tower in his Messiah's Complex of buildings. The girls knew that despite his bravado, the loss of outside contact was getting worse. Aphrodite *did* care about that, but she still thought she was the prettiest girl in the world and had the most 'to die for blonde hair' plus having the longest tanned legs was a bonus – only wearing the shortest of shorts would do them justice, only her arms she still kept covered. So what if Olympia was getting fit and having fun? Aphrodite *still* thought she was the most beautiful girl in the city.

The little girl beside her pointed towards the sun, not saying a word, just replying to Aphrodite's earlier question. "Oh you think you're so clever don't you? Ok, can you tell me what bankrupt means?... as my dad is almost it."

Gemma peeled at the stickers on her sports bag, thinking hard. "No, what does it mean?"

Aphrodite's delicate features wrinkled into a smirk as she put on her eyelash tint as the car remained motionless. "Bankrupt means when a family takes in a silly little girl and loses all their money, because of what their stupid father did to mine."

"What did he do?"

"Doesn't matter."

"You don't like me, do you?"

"Not really, no."

The young girl sighed and gripped her bag tightly. "Even though I'm your sister?...Oh no!"

Gemma suddenly remembered something before Aphrodite could answer, unzipping her bag and allowing a small hairy creature to emerge. "Come baby." Buckby, Gemma's pet spider scuttled out the bag and onto her hand. "Poor baby, was it hot in my bag?"

The spider had found her again after disappearing after the fire at her father's house some years back. Gemma had gone back to the old house many times to find her spider with no avail but it wasn't until sometime later her spider had found her at her school, crawling up the window outside her classroom – a fright for her classmates but a huge relief for Gemma, reunited with her pet and the only connection with her father Elias, and Auntie Kay.

"Why did you have to bring that infernal creature?" moaned Aphrodite.

"He get's lonely in that cage alone and it's a nice day, so I'll bring him out for some company and fresh air."

Aphrodite honked the horn again and shifted to her side. "We should have got a taxi to bring you here today and I would have too, except the last cab I got was rubbish! The driver was waving his arms about, sweating, babbling and shaking. He didn't have a clue where he was going so I ended up driving myself to the beauty salon."

"What happened to him?"

"He was having a heart attack apparently."

"And you didn't take him to a hospital?"

Aphrodite took one of her hands off the wheel and flashed her new nails at Gemma. "That's the reason why, besides, I gave him a tip."

Through the slender gap between either side of the cars rode a large man on a push bike wearing a bright all-in-one bodysuit; he struggled to get by and wobbled as he passed Aphrodite's car, scratching the side.

"MY CAR!…Oh for God's sake!"

Aphrodite watched as the bike rider huffed further up the road failing to look back at the damage he'd caused. "Moron" she muttered. "Why do bike riders wear such ridiculous tight outfits? I mean if everybody can see the weight that they need to lose then chances are that skin tight Lycra isn't a good idea."

She turned her attention back to Gemma. "I'm stunned I'm related to you, but hang on…?" Her eyes glistened in the sun. "You're NOT my sister, everything was fine until YOU came along and for some reason Daddy took pity on you and brought you in. You're nothing to me but a skank who can't keep hold of their own family and has to pinch somebody else's…you're a magpie, a thief and WHY ISN'T THAT STUPID CAR MOVING?"

The horn was used and Aphrodite held her hand firmly in place as the car in front's door opened and the driver stepped out.

"Oh this is just perfect." Aphrodite shook her head and closed up her window by flicking a switch. "He's coming over, just sit tight and let me do the talking."

Gemma put her spider back in her bag and looked at her watch and then her eyes followed the well-dressed gentleman as he approached Aphrodite's window. Aphrodite looked dead ahead, refusing to acknowledge him as he leered forward.

It was Gemma whose eyes flicked over to look him up and down, a lovely suit with his nose bleeding and strange foam stuff coming from his mouth. Aphrodite had just enough time to see his fist break through the window, both girls screamed as fragments of glass showered them.

"GET OFF ME!" Aphrodite yelled.

No words came from the man, his hand, still in the window went for Aphrodite's throat.

A passer-by tried to come to her aid, pulling valiantly at the attacker, but the man in the suit casually turned and back-handed the helper, sending him spinning to the pavement. This was the chance Aphrodite needed, rubbing her aching throat she stuck the car in reverse, Gemma tugged impatiently at Aphrodite's sleeve.

"I KNOW!" Aphrodite shouted. "HOLD TO SOMETHING, WE'RE GETTING OUT OF HERE."

Clutching the door handle tightly, Gemma looked behind her as their car shot backwards and hit the car behind, she could see the driver throw his hands up in the air angrily as bumper crunched against bumper.

"Shit," Aphrodite said through gritted teeth.

The suited man was up and looked into the car, his head cocked to one side, Aphrodite went forward and then back again, shunting the car behind and in front. The angry driver from behind got out and whilst swearing repeatedly walked towards the damaged bumper but before he could confront Aphrodite, the suited man had picked him up and hurled him through a shop window.

"No way," Gemma mouthed silently.

The gap Aphrodite made was big enough now to ease her car past, and mounting the kerb, she drove up onto the pavement. In a flash the man in the suit instinctively started chasing the moving vehicle and leapt onto the driver's door, his mouth foaming whilst still grabbed at the wheel. Aphrodite tore through the parade of high street shops, pedestrians throwing themselves out of the way of the oncoming vehicle.

"GET OUT OF THE WAY!" screamed Aphrodite.

The gentleman still clung on to the steering wheel, his legs trailed on the ground, his expensive shoes scraping the pavement, turning the wheel towards him he threw his head back and snapped it forward, aiming directly at Aphrodite's throat. Dodging the attack, she gave him more of the wheel and the car veered right, crashing into the front of a garden centre shop, not even a well put together garden shed could shift the gentleman.

"HE WON'T STOP!" Gemma shrieked.

"I GATHERED," replied her sister.

The car moved on down the parade with Aphrodite struggling to maintain control of the wheel; the gentleman was strong and would not let go of his side of the steering wheel.

Drinkers enjoying a mid-morning coffee outside on the boulevard saw their drinks and tables fly off between their legs as the car forced a path through the middle of them.

Gemma blinked in disbelief at the strength of the madman clinging to the side of her sister's car door.

With frightening speed the man flung his right arm again into the car, making a grab for Aphrodite again, the car swerved yet again as she avoided the incoming blow. The car was coming to the end of the retail promenade and yet the man clung on to the side, reaching at every opportunity to reach Aphrodite. Roadworks blocked the end of the pavement, workmen were digging up some power cables from underground and the whole street was cordoned off, the cars in the traffic jam had to take a diversion but Aphrodite had other ideas.

"Sorry little girl, I don't like you very much but I dislike this ghastly gentleman even more, time to see if you have the guts to really be my sister."

Gemma frowned, still holding tight on to her door handle. "What are you going to do?"

Aphrodite smiled between grimacing. "Watch and learn."

With an almighty effort Aphrodite heaved the wheel to her left, the car bounced through the road barriers and hit a pothole hard, the car flipped up on its passenger side wheels.

The enraged man in a suit still clung on to the driver's side door his foaming mouth and bloodshot eyes were close to Aphrodite's as gravity brought him nearer to her.

She drove the car on two wheels down the high street and looked into the eyes of her unwanted passenger.

"Hang on to this, you bastard!"

Aphrodite pulled with one supreme effort and turned the wheel left, aiming for the nearest shop window and the car went straight through the front of a florist. The car spun around and pinned the gentleman up against the cash register desk, the young girl usually behind the till had fled as soon as the car had come through the window.

Aphrodite picked the glass from her dress and looked at her arms, which she went to great lengths to keep covered, she looked at her sister and saw her chest was still moving. "Gemma?"

The younger girl paused briefly and held her side. "Yes."

Aphrodite spoke calmly. "You do know we're not going swimming now." Then she passed out. The turning point continued.

Norton

Norton looked at his clothes laid out on his bed. These were what he was going to wear later for his special meeting, a meeting he'd been looking forward to for ages. He leaned forward onto his bed and gently rubbed out some left over creases on his recently ironed shirt. His date wasn't until later in the afternoon, but he liked to be prepared.

He glanced at his watch. *Anytime now,* he thought.

"NORTON! BRING ME MY CIGARETTES!"

Norton felt his chest tighten. "Just a minute," he called.

"I NEED THEM NOW, DUMMY!"

With a heavy sigh Norton left his bedroom and strode across the hallway to his spare room, where his mother had been staying with him ever since her bungalow had been destroyed. It was one of many houses in the vicinity of Big Man's stadium which was destroyed by the powered up girl Kimberley six years ago – it was only meant to be a temporary agreement, but his mother had no intention of moving out, even though accommodation had been sorted out for her.

Norton picked up her cigarettes and headed downstairs to the lounge where his mother sat. The room stank of cigarette smoke as she puffed away without a care in the world. He noticed a pack of cigarettes on her armchair where she sat.

"Mother, you just asked me for a pack of cigarettes?"

"Yeah, what's your point?"

"My point is you already have some next to you."

"I don't want to run out! Better safe than sorry. Is it too much to ask that you do a favour for your own mother once in a while?"

Norton sighed. "No mother."

"Now come here and let me look at you."

Her son hesitated. "Come boy." She patted the side of the armchair as if she was calling a pet dog, as her hand thumped the chair, it slid down the side and pulled out a bottle of wine within the ragged lining of the chair and secretly took a swig. "Chop chop." Norton reluctantly stood in front of his over-bearing mother and shrugged his shoulders. "Turn around and let me see."

Norton turned slowly like a dissatisfied catwalk model. "So this is what you're going to wear to your hussy meeting later?"

"No, I—"

"She's not going to give you a second look wearing those rags, dumb arse!"

"Mother, I'm not wearing—"

Norton's mother would not let him get a word in. "Why would any girl go out with you anyway? A grown man still living with his mother?"

"This is my house. Mum, you're living with me, remember?"

"Nobody knows that, everyone thinks that your just a thirty-year old joke still hanging on to his mother's apron, you're a sad sack bastard."

"Oh Mum," he whispered. "You've been drinking again, haven't you?"

With her scant disguise blown, Norton's mother drank from the bottle freely, as the wine trickled from her lips. "Oh please? Where are you going to take this girl? Can't bring her home because I live here and I will embarrass you, I'll tell you that for nothing, as if living at home at your age wasn't bad enough, and we can't risk her having a heart attack from laughing so hard can we?"

"Why are you being so mean?"

"*Why are you being so mean?*" she mimicked her son and blew out some more cigarette smoke. "Because you're a waste of space, no woman will give a second look at you, stop wasting your time and except the fact that you will NEVER meet a girl and you will never be a man, you useless sack of shit!"

The anger was festering inside Norton. "One more bad word from you, Mother, I swear to God I'll walk out that front door and never come back."

"Really, dip shit?"

"Yes, I mean it."

"You don't have the balls."

His lips seemed to tighten slightly, his mum raised her eyebrows and carried on smoking with a contented smile. "Thought as much, dickhead." Trembling, Norton took a deep breath and headed for the front door. "DO IT!" his mum urged him. As he opened the door slowly, Norton was suddenly pinned against the wall as somebody from the outside burst through, smashing the door against him. Mr Cameron, his next door neighbour charged through and ran straight for Norton's mother.

"WHAT THE HELL ARE YOU DOING?" she screamed.

Mr Cameron ignored her completely and pushed her over in her armchair with incredible force. He was a small quiet man, single and kept himself to himself, usually he would talk to Norton over the garden fence or chat for a short while outside the front door as Norton was leaving for work. But this was unlike him, especially the speed. Before Norton could shout out, Mr Cameron was upon his mum, she groaned in agony as Mr Cameron's fists pounded on her frail chest.

"Help me," she gasped to her son.

Wide-eyed and panic-stricken, Norton watched as Mr Cameron's fists continued to lay into his mother. Her ribs her cracked under the pressure, he could see from his viewpoint blood trickling from the corners of her mouth.

"Please?" she rasped.

Norton held his head in his hands and listened to his mother screaming in agony, he stayed rooted to the spot, and noticed that her glasses stayed on her head despite the massive beatings her body was taking. *That's odd,* he thought.

"Norton, help me?" her voice was nothing more than a croaked cry as her body struggled to function after its assault. He ran up to her and interrupted the attack from Mr Cameron; his next door neighbour turned around to see. Mr Cameron's face had completely changed from when the last time Norton had seen it, the eyes had turned black and his face had turned a ghostly white, his mouth was foaming uncontrollably and his head twitched as if there was an annoying fly buzzing inside his head.

Norton hesitated as did Mr Cameron, Norton caught the look from his mother as she lay on her back, beaten and dying, she could see in the look from her son's eyes that she knew what he was about to do.

"Bastard," she whispered as more blood dribbled from her mouth.

"Sorry Mother."

Before Mr Cameron could react to Norton, he'd already run through the door and headed towards town and his date. If he'd stayed a little longer he would have been able to hear his mother curse his name before Mr Cameron bit into her cheek and tore it off easily.

The turning point had picked up.

Kingston

Kingston White didn't like his job, he didn't *hate* it but it wasn't the job he had wished for. He was an actor, trained at the prestigious Susan White Drama Academy and had a fantastic graduation. Through his tremendous interpretation of the wronged son 'Oliver' in the classic fable *Slaughter of the Messiah* he had gained a tremendous agent with the 'Lucy Hudson Agency' and had acted in great television dramas and even had some film work lined up. Then came the nationwide ban on television, due to the events with the 'Big Man' corporation, the acting work dried up, his contacts didn't want to know him anymore and he couldn't get an audition for the theatre for love nor money. The phone calls stopped and questions were raised on Kingston's acting ability.

Money was an issue and he had to take a job in a warehouse – his mum's best friend's son worked at this warehouse and after a few phone calls and hesitant head nods, Kingston got the job at the washing machine distribution centre.

The company distributed washing machines and fridge freezers to shops around the country even though the economy was in a state, people still needed white goods and the warehouse known as 'Mules and Wertham' were the ones to deliver.

Kingston sat on his industrial clamp truck in the middle of the loading bay, the truck was like a large forklift but the attachment on the front was a giant clamp capable of holding fourteen washing machines stacked on top of one another in a single lift. Manoeuvring his vehicle round to load the trailer, Kingston slowly bought the clamps down on the trailer's flatbed and pressed the release button on the control stick and the washing machines came down to rest with ease, he had spent quite a while loading up the trailer and was near the end of his loading. Kingston held the bridge of his nose and squinted, his head hurt and he was tired. *Why am I still here?…why am I still working in this dump?*

An angry voice snapped him out of his trance. "HEY KINGSTON, HOW MANY TIMES DO I HAVE TO TELL YOU? THE 'POWERLAND' LOAD GOES ON TRAILER PW101, NOT EL 101, YOU'VE MESSED

UP AGAIN, IT'S ALL GOING TO HAVE TO COME OFF NOW, YOU'RE GOING TO HAVE WORK THROUGH YOUR BREAK."

The voice was Kingston's boss, Macon Phelps, an ox of a man – in size and manner – who only got the team leader's job due to his dad owning the warehouse, despised by many, if not all of the other warehouse workers.

Macon could not be trusted at any costs, he used to pay off the security guards and sneak back into the warehouse late at night and steal washing machines to sell on the black market. He bellowed again, wiping his lunch remains down his top.

"YOU ARE SUCH A WASTE OF SPACE WHITE, YOU'RE GOING TO BE WORKING HERE FOR THE REST OF YOUR LIFE, YOU'RE NEVER GOING TO MAKE IT AS AN ACTOR, YOU'RE JUST A JOKE."

Kingston ignored his taunts and continued to reluctantly remove the washing machines from the trailer as Macon reached into his overalls pocket and pulled out a half-eaten sandwich, took a bite and stuffed the remains back.

"ACTOR? YOUR DAYS ON THE SCREEN ARE DONE, YOU USELESS IDIOT, TV BAN AND LIMTED FILM? ...HAVE A NICE LIFE."

Kingston had a load of washing machines in his clamps and he lifted the telescopic mast to its limit as his colleagues pointed and shouted at his actions, he slowly reversed the clamp truck away from the trailer and into the centre of the yard; his nose was bleeding more profusely and his headache had grown worse. He had an anger inside of him and the hunger for violence grew in his shell. The rising actor's eyes had gone blank as he rotated his clamps around and pressed the release button. Macon Phelps hadn't even finished his sandwich when the fourteen washing machines came crashing down on him, killing him instantly.

Kingston's colleagues pulled him from the clamp truck and tried to restrain him but he just stared blankly into the confused eyes of the workers who had come to trust him and like him, and managed to free one hand and take a swipe, knocking one friend to the ground next to him, his mouth filled with blood from the rain of blows.

Kingston would never act again or go to another audition but he loved the violence, causing it and receiving, and that he knew…and that would have to do for now.

One more had turned.

Tayla

Tayla Doherty knew her boyfriend was having an affair; she didn't want to believe it but now she had the proof.

She had seen the messages on his mobile phone – the same phone he had warned her not to look at but she did anyway and it was like she was on the ropes in the final round of a boxing match, taking emotional blows to the stomach but just managing to stay on her legs when she had found the texts from his lover.

Sitting on the top deck of the double decker bus she clutched her handbag close to her chest as some teenagers ambled past her on the top deck. She watched as they took their seats and then turned back, bowing her head at her handbag. It wasn't the look of the youths that made her hold her bag so tightly, it was what was in her bag. A pistol lay nestled between her mobile phone and travel-sized tissues. She put her hand in the bag to check it was still there, her thumb and forefinger rubbed the cold metal barrel and she yanked her hand out immediately.

She looked around at the passengers on the bus, just fleetingly checking over their features but only one really stood out to her – the pretty blonde model sat at the front of the bus – she was the one having the affair with her boyfriend and it was her the gun was intended for.

She had followed her boyfriend to this girl's flat four weeks ago and had watched the model's routine for the last two, she didn't know how they met but she knew she was having an affair.

Tayla watched on as the beautiful young woman stood up and offered an elderly gentleman her seat, multi-tasking as she waffled away on her phone whilst holding firmly on to the handrail with her other hand as the bus swung around a corner. Tayla was in her mid-thirties, average sized with heavy set glasses. She tried to keep fit when she could but her office job was very demanding, but however she looked, she didn't deserve this, she thought.

Tayla and her boyfriend had been dating for a few years now, she had been on a work's night out and he was in the audience at the comedy club that both sets of friends had opted to attend. The comedian on stage was having a terrible time with his choice of material and the hecklers in the audience.

The struggling comic had invited the chief heckler to come on stage and see if he could do a better job. Much to the comedian's surprise the heckler took him up on his offer and shocked the crowd with a nicely constructed and well-timed routine. Tayla clapped hard after the guest had left the stage, which was noted by the heckler.

"Great set, have you done this before?" asked Tayla.

The new comedian smiled. "Nope, first time I've ever done this." He dodged an icy glare from the original stand up comedian as he walked past. "Do you fancy a drink?" Tayla nodded and after an exchange of numbers and fun dates later, they were dating.

Things were fantastic at first, moving in together almost instantly and doing everything together. Meeting each other's parents, music concerts, holidays away all followed.

It wasn't until he had lost his job recently and struggled to find another that the arguments started, he stayed out for longer, wasn't very responsive when he spoke to her and became very cold. It was only when she looked at the text messages on his phone that her suspicions were confirmed. Tayla looked on at the girl's slim figure, tottering on high heels, still keeping her balance on the bumpy bus journey. Tayla's mind switched back on. *All it takes is one little pull on the trigger and that lovely figure is gone.*

That figure that stole my man from me won't be able to steal anything again after I'm done with it. She breathed in as the model turned around and Tayla caught her eyes and felt the rage bubbling inside her. *Go on, look past me like you don't know who I am, well I know who you are and those pretty blues won't be fluttering later, is that how you trapped him? With those gorgeous eyes of yours? Are you going to meet my man now? Going to your little secret hideaway? Well you're not going to make it, you little bitch.*

Tayla reached into handbag and gripped the gun with authority, her rage was getting harder to bottle up. *I can smell you, that scent is wondrous, did he buy you that perfume? Did he buy you those clothes that drive men crazy? Did he promise you his love like he promised me at one time? Well it doesn't matter, I'm going to shoot you on this packed bus and turn the gun on myself, so he would have lost both the women he claims to have loved on the same day...bastard. You are too beautiful to live, you have stolen my man and now I'm going to steal your life, you little slut.*

Tayla rose from her seat with one hand holding her bag and the other gripped firmly on the weapon. She walked past a couple of teenage girls giggling and pointing at a magazine one of them was reading and then looked the model square in the eyes, and noticed that her nose was bleeding. The model noticed it too and wiped away the blood with an upward stroke of her palm and then the stunning model started banging the side of her head with the same palm.

Most of the top deck saw what she was doing, some looked on in shock whilst others were embarrassed, hiding their heads. The old man who now had her seat stood up and offered his hand to make the girl stop. Her once lovely blue eyes were now soulless and buoyed on by an unquenchable rage. The model grabbed the old man's hand from her shoulder and snapped his fingers back in a sickening crunch, making him sink to the floor on his knees.

Some passengers scrambled from their seats and headed for the stairs, a few yelled at the girl to "Leave the old man alone", which she did, he was useless to her.

One of the teenage girls stared directly into the model's eyes as she walked past and got a punch to the face for her effort, her friend screamed and leapt to her defence and took a backhanded slap from the model. Tayla backed away fearfully as her boyfriend's lover ambled towards her, the blue eyes were bleary and red. In a few quick steps the girl was on Tayla, kneeing her in the stomach and then wrapping her arms around her neck as Tayla wheezed, holding her gut. Tayla couldn't break free from the model's grasp and sank further to the ground, her slender tanned arms and perfectly manicured nails held tight and squeezed with all her rage, struggling and whimpering at the same time. Tayla's tame kicks began to stop as she began to lose consciousness and lay flat on her back as the model finally released her grip. She had one final thought as she saw the model raise her foot and angle her stiletto heel towards her eye. *Damn. I didn't get to use my gun.*

On the street below the bus's top deck, more had reached their turning point and the violence had company.

Odysseus

The scruffy-looking small man with the unkempt brown hair moaned when the same message kept flicking across the screen. No matter how many times he swiped his hand across it, the message read the same.

Insufficient funds in your account.

There was no reason to go to the bank to try and reason with the fresh-faced school leaver at the credit desk, he had no money and had to find other ways to get his hands on some cash. He then remembered it was an 'Apology Day' holiday and they were shut anyway.

Spitting his chewing gum to the hot pavement the man walked back to the bus stop with his phone back in his backpack which brushed against something soft and another item which was smooth and cold to the touch. He felt them both again and fought the urge to pull any of them out, he thought about his wife's words that danced in his mind earlier that morning. *Please! You've got a problem! What's wrong with you? You must stop doing this, or I'm leaving you, I'm giving you one last chance, don't let me down.*

A car sped by. Blaring rap music bought him fully out of his daze. The two other people at the bus stop took shade inside from the heat. An old woman with a long brown coat and a little white dog shuffled uncomfortably further down the bus stop, there were some cracker crumbs on the ground which the dog began to lick up greedily as the owner struggled with her coat under the sun's unforgiving rays.

The other person was a young woman in her mid-twenties, dressed in extremely smart office attire. She was attractive and the man noticed her good-looking body and golden hair. She held her jacket over her arms and she was in the process of taking off her high heeled shoes for trainers to make it a much easier journey home for her feet. She put her heels in a small brief case and smiled at the man as he watched her fiddle with the lock. "I couldn't spend all day in those shoes," she warmly remarked.

The man wriggled in his tight-fitting coat and attempted a half-hearted smile. "It is really hot today, isn't it?" Again the man lamely smiled so as not to appear too rude. "I really wasn't going to go into work today as it was so hot!"

The attractive young woman was very talkative and the man surprisingly felt this to be a welcome distraction as his hands began to tremble more, his head rocked from side to side as the urge to reach into his bag came back. He had smiled too many times and it was time to make himself and the girl feel at ease, he really didn't care about what she was waffling on about, but for what he was about to do on the bus, he really should be calm.

"You're going to work on an Apology Day holiday? What do you do?"

Damn! he thought. *Really didn't mean to say that... she's going to talk back to me now.* His voice was old and tired, it matched the years on his face.

The blonde girl snapped back the case successfully and answered with a relieved smile. "Well I'm studying law at the moment."

"Law? Your studying law?" *God, I'm doing it again.* She nodded politely. *I'm going to have to talk to her now.* "So why are you working today then?"

"Just catching up with some paperwork for a case I'm on, now seems the right time as the offices will be empty."

"Well it's the middle of the afternoon on Apology Day, can't get any emptier than that."

"My dream job is to be an actress though, would love to make it onto the big screen or even television."

The man raised his bushy eyebrows. "You do know that television has been banned and all film making put on hold indefinitely?"

She nodded slowly. "Yeah, all thanks to that idiot Big Man and his 'Game Show' rubbish years ago, this new government haven't overturned that ruling yet and it's ridiculous!"

The man surprisingly was showing some interest. "So you *have* done some acting then?"

The girl nervously began to fidget. "Oddly enough, I've done some 'underground acting'."

"Underground?"

"Illegal acting, short films made by the G.M.E."

"I may be showing my age here darling, but who are the G.M.E?"

"They're a bunch...sorry, *we're* a bunch of actors and filmmakers who have, I guess, taken drastic steps to keep the preservation of film alive, we meet up every now and then and make feature films, documentaries, children's shows, etc."

His eyebrows still raised, he continued. "So let me get this straight, you're studying law...you're studying *law* and you're making illegal films? Isn't that a little bit strange, why are you telling me this? I mean you don't even know me?"

The woman took a swig from her water bottle as the man watch it dribble down her lips. She giggled softly.

"Just like a little danger I guess."

Wiping the water from her lips, she gave him a deceptively harmless grin. "So what's your story?"

"Me?" the man asked pointing a questioning finger to his own chest.

"Yes you."

He sighed, her really didn't feel like talking, but she had shared something about her, so it was only fair, if only to keep her quiet.

"I'm in the dog house with my wife."

They exchanged a sheepish glance.

"What did you do?"

"I love to stare at women in bikinis."

"Ah yes, I can see that being a little bit of a problem," the woman said.

"Agreed, so I left her at home to blow off some steam, thought I'd go uptown for a bit."

"Good idea."

A large hulk of a man went past walking his dog, the man wore a black suit which probably didn't help him in the bright hot sun, he was wearing shades and had many rings on his stubby fingers. It was Mr Tidy, the muscle for hire who usually worked for Big Man along with Big Man's friend, Apollo.

Apollo hadn't been seen for years, not since Big Man shipped him across to run the prison faculty in Gommerstall. After the prison breakout it was assumed that Apollo became one of the many casualties on the day the prisoners made their great escape, Big Man didn't even send out a 'search and rescue' squad for any of his staff at the prison – Apollo included.

It was Apollo who was the 'brains' of their operation and since his disappearance, business was suffering greatly, Mr Tidy had no money and the only comfort in his life since the loss of his friend was his little dog which had made a beeline for the old woman's dog and surged forward, barking furiously. The lady's dog stood its ground and yapped back as both dog owners struggled to restrain their pets.

The man in conversation to the law student left her and went in aid of the old woman and her dog, helping her separate the two dogs as Mr Tidy did nothing. The man shouted, "WHY CAN'T YOU CONTROL THAT USELESS PIECE OF CRAP?"

"Watch your tongue!" Mr Tidy said, finally keeping his dog under control.

"I was talking to the dog actually," the man said with an easy to see grin.

Despite the vast difference in size, Mr Tidy was tired and slightly intimidated by the other man's presence and bravado judging his small, but stocky build. Mr Tidy vented his anger out on his dog, pulling at the lead and walked to the other end of the bus stop.

The old woman ventured out from the shade, nervously looking to see if the dog antagonist had gone.

"Thank you young man, I thought that beast was going to kill my poor dog."

The man laughed as sweat beaded his eyebrows. "Young man? Haven't been called that for a long time!"

It was the old woman's turn to laugh now. "Everybody's young compared to me, young man, but thank you again…"

The woman hung on her last word, waiting for a name.

"Odysseus."

"Well thank you again, Odysseus."

The old woman shuffled back into the sanctuary of shade in the bus stop, avoiding the man and his dog, leaving the girl and Odysseus out in the sun. Struggling with his bag,

Odysseus called out to Mr Tidy, "Hey pal, I think we got off on the wrong foot there, let me make it up to you."

Mr Tidy was just as inquisitive as his dog and walked forward. "What do you mean?

Odysseus never even hesitated, like he knew exactly what to say. "Ok wait there, right, have you ever played the game of 'statues'?"

"Is that like the game 'video recorder catch'?" Mr Tidy enquired.

Odysseus studied the sincerity of Mr Tidy's face, his own was quite perplexed. "No, but I have seen that game played and to my knowledge, someone usually shouts one of two things, either.... *'This game is crap let's play something else'* or *'OUCH!...You've just hit me in the head with a video recorder'*."

Mr Tidy wriggled his nose in thought. "So what is this game then?"

"You've got to stand perfectly still like a statue, without moving and I bet you one hundred notes that you can't stand still long enough for me to walk around you three times."

The girl fanned herself with a magazine and looked on puzzled, as did Mr Tidy. "So let me get this straight, if I really stand still whilst you walk around me three times you'll give me one hundred notes?"

"Pretty much."

"So If I move, I pay you one hundred notes?"

"Pretty much."

Mr Tidy wriggled his small nose one last time. "Ok... done."

Mr Tidy spat in his hand and shook Odysseus's hand. Odysseus grimaced slightly and wiped the remaining drool on his trousers, before attempting to move the man mountain into a suitable position. "Just a little to the left and...ok...stay there," he instructed Mr Tidy. "Right let's go."

Odysseus slowly began to walk around the huge frame of Mr Tidy as the old woman and the younger one looked on.

"That's once," Odysseus said cheerfully.

"Yep," smiled Mr Tidy.

"And that's twice…"

Odysseus walked away still beaming.

"HEY! WHERE ARE YOU GOING? YOU'VE ONLY WALKED AROUND ME TWICE, YOU SAID THREE TIMES!"

Odysseus casually looked behind at the man rooted to the spot. "Yeah I can't be bothered to walk around you a third time, I'll do it later."

"Oiii! COME BACK!" Mr Tidy yelled. "THAT'S NOT FAIR!"

The young woman folded her arms against her chest and grinned. "Looks like you've been stitched up good and proper there!"

Mr Tidy spun his neck round undefeated. "Oh no I ain't…I ain't moved yet."

"But you will soon, so you'd better pay up," taunted Odysseus.

"No! I'm not moving."

As the two men carried on with their grievances, a bus sidled up to the bus stop, it wasn't until the door opened and passengers got off that Mr Tidy suddenly paid attention. The door stayed open as the driver looked at the man and his dog.

"Are you going to Winstead Park?" asked Mr Tidy.

The driver glanced at his watch and then answered. "Yes sir, hop on if you're coming?" Mr Tidy didn't move. "Sir, get on the bus if you want to go."

"I can't."

"Why?"

"I can't move until he walks round me three times." Mr Tidy pointed to Odysseus who gave an apologetic shrug of his shoulders. The driver took off his cap to scratch his head in bewilderment.

"So you want to go to Winstead Park, but won't board this bus until the gentleman to your left walks around you three times?"

Mr Tidy looked to Odysseus, and in turn the two looked back to the driver.

"Yeah that sounds about right," Mr Tidy nodded.

"Ridiculous," the driver snorted.

The doors slid shut and the bus pulled off. Odysseus watched as Mr Tidy's huge chest heaved slowly. "You're really not going to move are you?"

Mr Tidy shook his head and Odysseus felt slightly guilty about his trick as he underestimated how stupid this man was, he had a feeling this man was probably going to stay in this spot for the rest of his life. The girl stepped forward and cocked her head curiously. "You really not going to walk around him?"

"Not sure, he really is the dumbest man I've ever met."

The girl smiled. "That was quite funny…Odysseus is it? That's the reason why I told you about my double dealings."

She resumed her earlier position up close to and right in Odysseus's personal space. "I just like trying new things out really, I can read things with some people, I can read you want something more in your life too."

Odysseus sensed the girl was about to talk more and took a step backward. "You don't want to read me darling, I'm nothing but bad news."

"You've got a sense of humour though, that must count for something?"

Odysseus's discomfort showed and the girl backed away as well.

"Sorry! Said a little too much there, I do tend to waffle on a bit, just a bit of a silly goose really."

His eyes narrowed slightly. "I'm just waiting for my bus to turn up, let the missus cool off and come back home in a few hours, nothing more and nothing less, darling."

He felt into his bag again, fingers feeling around something metal. "Anyway let's just wait for this bus shall we? And say no more."

The girl blinked rapidly and rubbed her hands slowly. "Yes, why not?"

The older man's eyes lifted as he finally saw another bus approaching, the girl acknowledged the bus too and held out her hand. "My name is—"

Odysseus instantly cut her off. "Sorry missy, don't want to know what your name is and don't have the time to be honest, I told you about my wife and that should be it."

Odysseus's face reddened as the bus approached, he pulled at his collar nervously and then went into his bag, keeping his hand in there, ready to pull something out. The girl saw his face twitch as the bus pulled into the bus stop down the road, their stop would be next, her eyes darted back and forth between the now temporarily stopped bus and Odysseus, whose fingers were tapping away inside his bag, her cheeks damp with sweat. The girl wiped them and commented on Odysseus's equally damp face.

"Are you sure you're ok? You're sweating like a pig, do pigs sweat? Not sure, but whatever they do, your doing it too."

Odysseus flashed a look back to her and then to the bus and suddenly grew desperate with a hint of anger. "Ok, you want to know what's really happening? You were pretty easy with the truth when it came down to your moonlighting with the acting so I'll let you into a little secret, it's not only about my wife...there's something else."

Odysseus gently pulled her towards him. "I'm going to catch this bus and do something...then you'll hear all about it."

"Why? What are you going to do?"

"I'm going to—"

"You're going to do what?"

The girl held her stare as Odysseus for the first time felt nervous. *I can't tell her,* her thought.

"What's happening with you and this bus? *Leave it,* his mind told him. Without even looking at the oncoming bus, the girl put her hand out to make it stop, her eyes still digging into Odysseus, she was still wondering curiously. "Still not going to tell me?"

Odysseus relaxed his hand and took it out of his bag, his silence told the girl that he wasn't going to tell her. "Doesn't matter, darling, let's just say I'm keeping this secret for the moment."

"Ok," she said tiredly.

The bus finally pulled up and the sign on the front grabbed everyone's attention, even the old woman peered out from her shelter and huffed her annoyance.

Available seats 0
Standing room 2

Three people stood at the bus stop looking at each other in bemusement, Mr Tidy didn't bother looking as his bus had already gone. Their eyes began to shift suspiciously around each other, everyone untrusting, until Odysseus was the first to relent, looking at the older woman.

"Listen lady, I may be a miserable curmudgeon from time to time, but I know how to treat a woman, so I insist you get on that bus." The young girl agreed with a reluctant head nod.

The old woman with her dog in tow beamed a smile towards Odysseus, her teeth all her own, white and warm, slightly lifted Odysseus's mood. A couple of irritated shouts came from the back of the bus as the passengers grew impatient as they realised none of the two remaining people at the stop had followed the old lady on.

The girl turned to Odysseus and held out her hands in an imploring motion. "Do you mind if I take that last spot?"

Odysseus shouted to the bus driver whose uniform was adorned with sweat patches. "Hey Bub! What time is the next bus?"

He watched as the rather large bus driver's face oozed sweat, wiping it away breathing heavy as he replied, "Next bus going into town won't be for a while, we just heard reports from our depot that a woman went crazy and killed another woman on one our buses earlier, the police have cordoned off most of the street and cancelled the rest of the remaining buses on that route." I mean there is a replacement train service put on for customers, but you have to go back the way you came to get it, walk back to Blissmead train station and then you can get a train out of town."

"So let me get this straight, in order to get out of town, I have to walk back *into* town to get a train heading in the opposite direction?"

The driver shifted uncomfortably in his tiny seat, the sweat from his back making it almost unbearable. "Yeah, that's pretty much it, so which of you two are getting on? I haven't got all day."

The girl still had her puppy dog eyes fixed on Odysseus as she whispered, "Please, I really have to take that last spot."

Odysseus blocked the door to the bus with his arm. "Why's that spot so important to you, Miss?"

Odysseus's voice was maddeningly calm as the girl crossed her arms. "I just have to be somewhere this evening, it's a business meeting...if I miss this bus I'll never make it in time."

"So why should I miss out on that last place, darling? You're no more important than me...what if I got things to do tonight?"

"Have you?"

"No, but that ain't the point, just because you're a skirt doesn't mean I have to bend over backwards to do what you want."

The girl raised her neatly plucked eyebrows.

"A skirt?"

"What? Did I stutter?...yeah I called you a 'skirt'."

"But you helped out the old lady?"

"Again, not the point, she's an old woman and gets priority, you're just probably going on a hen night or a date or something."

The bus driver blasted on his horn angrily and Odysseus took a step onto the bus, giving a signal to him just to *wait*...the girl looked at her watch, took a deep breath and leaned forward towards Odysseus.

"Please...I know you don't know me and I know I have no right to that final spot...but I really do have a very important business meeting later and I have to take this last bus."

Odysseus looked to the ground and then back to the girl and gazed into her eyes, his hand was still in his pocket, the cold metal item in there was turning hot in the sun as he stroked it for the umpteenth time.

"Please let me on the bus, sir."

"So it's 'sir' now is it? You know what darling, do you gamble? Are you a betting person?"

The girl pointed to Mr Tidy, who was oblivious to their conversation. "I've seen how your betting games go, I'm not getting involved in them."

"Ok, well what shall we do?"

The girl reached into her purse and pulled out a silver coin. "Let's flip this coin, heads I win, tails you lose."

Odysseus thought for a moment. "Fifty-fifty? Sounds good."

The girl confidently flipped the coin and caught it with ease. "Heads, I win!"

Odysseus gave a moan of disappointment and stood aside from the bus door. "It's all yours darling."

The girl slowly chose her next words carefully. "Are you really sure, babes?"

"Go before I change my mind."

The girl clapped her hands excitedly and screamed with delight, she hugged and reached back into her purse taking out a packet of bubble gum, she unwrapped it and took out a single stick and popped it into her mouth, she offered a stick to Odysseus.

"Want some?"

"No, but thanks kid."

She smiled sweetly and gave a gentle hug to Odysseus as she moved past him and entered the bus. A cheer erupted from some of the other passengers as the girl paid the driver and made her way through to the last remaining spot. Odysseus stepped onto the bus and called out to her.

"Good luck with your *acting,* hope it goes well."

The girl's eyes narrowed and she smiled with her answer. "Looks like you're going to have to tell me that secret on another day then, good luck with your wife."

"Maybe, but ma'am, we all have secrets, the ones we keep...and the ones that are kept from us."

"So it's 'ma'am' now is it?" the smile stayed on her face as she copied his earlier statement.

The bus driver's eyes searched the figure of Odysseus and was running out of patience.

"Sorry sir, but we're leaving now."

An angry passenger yelled out. "GET OFF THE BUS, DICKHEAD!"

Odysseus held his temper and mouthed 'Sorry', stepping backwards off the bus. The doors slid shut and the same passengers cheered again.

Walking through the bus the woman glanced at the array of people sitting and standing but all sweltering in the heat. She saw that someone had kindly given up their seat to the old lady and she squeezed past to stand at her side, the young girl waved at Odysseus as the bus pulled away.

Gripping the cold steel handle of the gun in his backpack, Odysseus pulled it out and put the safety catch back on. *Looks like I won't be robbing that bus after all, just have to show the Missus I'm a man in another way,* he thought. Mr Tidy grinned to him.

"You don't get it do you?"

"Get what, chuckles?"

Mr Tidy couldn't contain his glee. "Think about it...'*Heads I win...tails you lose?*' And I thought *I* was dumb!"

"Yeah, what do you mean?"

Then suddenly Odysseus's lower jaw hit the floor as he realised what had just happened, Mr Tidy was laughing uncontrollably now. "LOOKS LIKE YOU'VE BEEN STITCHED UP MY OLD SON!"

A small smile snuck onto Odysseus's face. "Good one."

The girl took out her stick of gum one handed as her other hand held on to the support railing above her head, she offered one to the old lady who sat with her dog on her lap.

"No thanks my lovely."

The old woman stroked her dog as did the person in the seat next to her, its tail wagged lazily pleased for the attention, she looked up at the young girl whose beautiful features took on a stillness which she found strange and unsettling. She tried to make conversation to bring the friendly girl at the bus stop back.

"It is very hot though isn't it my dear?"

The girl gripped on the overhead rail tightly as the bus took a bump in the road shaking everyone standing up, this threw her from her daze.

"I'm sorry?"

"The weather dear, it's quite hot today."

The girl lifted her gaze from the front of the bus and forced a smile.

"It's going to get hotter."

"Do you think so?" the old woman asked.

The girl leaned over and stroked the dog as well. "I'll put money on it."

Mitchy

"Is this all the food you've got in here?"

A thin man behind the counter put down his paper and peered over his glasses. "Pardon me?" he asked.

The full-figured lady with the loud voice and louder clothes repeated her question. "I said is this all the food you got in this place? No sausages, bacon, egg, steak?"

"Steak? This is a newsagents, not a fast food joint."

The woman scanned the fridge again, keeping it open just to let the cold air work its way around her nut brown face. The shopkeeper sucked in his breath and carried on staring at the lady who was giving his fridge an extreme inspection. He looked over the counter and around at his empty shop.

"Can I help you, lady?"

Closing the fridge with a sigh the woman walked over to the counter and started rummaging through her handbag. "No worries sugar, I think I have a chocolate bar in here or something."

"Can't allow you to eat your own food in here, lady," he waggled his fore finger in her face.

"I'm not eating it."

"That's what I said."

The woman had large cheeks which could have easily stored food in like a squirrel if she'd wanted. Her big brown eyes blinked behind huge rimmed glasses. The shopkeeper again looked up and down the empty narrow isles in his shop. "Listen, it's kind of quiet in here, let me rustle you up a sandwich."

Taken aback, the woman stood back from the counter. "Are you sure?"

He turned and walked behind the storeroom behind the counter, the woman could hear him moving things and shuffling around back there. "It's fine miss, I don't mind, besides we haven't had any of your sort in here for ages now."

She shook her head at hearing the man's statement, an uneasy chill went down her neck.

"Excuse me?"

Oblivious to the dip in the tone of the woman's voice, he carried on. "Yeah we don't get people like you around these parts, it's odd to see one of you."

The woman's head appeared abruptly around the corner of the counter. "WHAT THE HELL DO YOU MEAN?"

Walking back through with a sandwich on a plate the man didn't even react to her outburst, just had a smile on his face for the first time since they met, happy for the company, he placed the plate on the bar and looked pleased with himself.

"People like you? Your accent? You're not from around here are you?"

She relaxed a little when she realised the man wasn't a backyard bigot.

"Oh right! Yes, I mean no, I'm not from around here."

"I know, I could tell by your accent, your from Strallen, right? Strallen City?

"That's right sugar, I'm Strallish. Was my accent the only give away?"

A slow smile warmed over the man's face as he eyed up the woman's garish clothes. "Would you like a cup of tea?"

The woman warmly nodded as the man pulled out a cup and filled it with water from his kettle from under the counter and handed it back to her, he then poured himself a cup and raised it to her.

"A toast to the lady from Strallen City. The name is Hutson Ma'am, this is my shop." The woman clinked her dirty cup with his and returned the smile. She noticed a sign on the wall to her left.

Shoplifters will be punched in the mouth and kicked in the stomach. Have a nice day.

"That's an interesting shop policy you have, Hutson."

His smile remained. "Had no complaints so far Ma'am."

She took a sip. "My name is Mitchy."

"So what you doing around these parts then? Visiting friends?" Hutson said, taking a sip from his mug. Mitchy shook her head, her large earrings swinging against her head. "Nope, I'm here on holiday, never been to Olympia before, always wanted to go but my ex-husband wasn't too keen what with 'Big Man' and his game show thing.

"Ex-husband?"

"Yes, we're divorced now, he was having an affair."

"I'm sorry about that."

Mitchy leaned into the bar eager to carry on. "Don't be, I'm better off without him if I'm honest, I'm not the one who had problems keeping 'it' in my pants, he's been calling me recently on the phone, but I don't want to talk to him, we're history as far as I'm concerned…I never want to see him again." He noticed an inquisitive look appear on Mitchy's face. "What are those things glowing beneath the counter?" she asked.

Hutson raised his eyebrows. "Oh these things?" He put his hand down beneath the counter and slid back the display glass, reaching in and pulling out two cylindrical sticks, they were slightly smaller than a drumstick and their natural colour seemed to be luminous green, but the sticks caught Mitchy's eye for another reason, they were glowing softly, beating with a faint red hue.

"These are 'heart sticks'," said Hutson.

"Heart sticks? I've never heard of them."

"Really? That does surprise me."

Mitchy felt a little insulted, but put it down to it being a 'local thing'. "Heart sticks are what the kids dance with when they go clubbing, or used to use, not to sure myself on that one, basically, and I don't know how it works as I'm no scientist, but these sticks work however when heartbeats are in the vicinity, so if it's just me, then you won't get much light, but…" He waved it closer to Mitchy and the dull light pulsed slightly more. "So if you can imagine at a disco or rave, or whatever the kids call them these days, you'll have hundreds of kids dancing with these sticks and it'll light up most of the club."

Hutson threw one stick in the air and attempted to catch it, missing it cleanly.

"Damn, thought I still had the moves!"

Mitchy thought for a moment. "So why do you have them here then if the 'moves' have long since gone begging?"

Hutson threw them back behind the counter. "I use them on the front door sometimes if the bell isn't working? If I'm down the other end of the shop I can see the sticks glowing when there's punters coming into my shop." He looked around, as if noticing his tired shabby newsagent for the first time. "Obviously they haven't glowed in a long while."

Hutson sucked in a tired breath. "So you came to Olympia for the start of your holiday?"

Biting hard into her sandwich Mitchy pulled a face. "Yeah, what's wrong with that?"

"Not many folks come visiting Olympia now, most cities refuse to trade with us now after the 'Game Show' debacle."

Mitchy picked up a chocolate bar on display next to the counter and took a quizzical look when seeing it was three years out of date.

"It's a bit old," he said.

"I can well imagine."

Hutson remained motionless for a few seconds and then wiped his mouth. "So how you finding Olympia anyhow?"

The Strallish woman looked to the ceiling and laughed. "To be fair sugar, your heart stick and your crusty sandwiches have been the most welcoming sight I've seen since I hit Olympia. Nobody wants to talk to this 'big old lady' from Strallen City, I'm actually looking for Olympia's Natural History Museum but haven't a clue where it is."

"It's only just been re-opened after Big Man had all the museums in the city shut, he claimed 'why should people be looking at old stuff, when they should be at home watching my TV shows' but nobody can watch anything now as there's a television ban in Olympia."

"Is that all down to the game show?"

He nodded. "Amongst other things, Big Man has a lot to answer for."

Hutson relaxed on his stool.

"Anyway let's find this museum of yours, doesn't your phone have navigation tech on it?"

"My phone's so old it can vote."

Hutson's smile broadened. "I've got some maps down that aisle if you like?"

"Thanks."

"Happy to oblige ma'am," Hutson said.

Mitchy took another bite into her sandwich wincing again. "What is in this sandwich? It has a strange taste if I'm honest, is it a local delicacy?"

Hutson stared into Mitchy's eyes and then threw back his head and laughed.

"It's peanut butter, maybe a year or two old but still the lovely gum clinging taste!"

"Peanut butter? Never heard of it."

Hutson stopped to smile a gob-smacked grin and carried on laughing. He laughed hard until a loud bang on the shop front door stopped him shaking from his mirth, he leaned over the counter and called out, "Hello there, can I help you?" There was no reply. "Is there anybody there?"

Hutson gave an exaggerated roll of his eyes.

"It's probably just kids," Mitchy said.

She put down the half-eaten sandwich and opened her handbag, dipped her hand in and pulled out an old chocolate bar and lifted it to her mouth, giving Hutson an embarrassed smile as she flouted his shop rules.

The shopkeeper was more concerned about what was happening outside his store and walked towards the door.

"See anything?" Mitchy called out.

Hutson shrugged and smiled wearily. A woman's scream of pure terror from outside made the pair of them jump. Mitchy looked anxiously at the shop door as a bolt of ice shot down her back.

"What the hell was that?"

"I don't know," said Hutson. "But I'm going outside to take a look."

"Don't...it could be dangerous," Mitchy said in an urgent whisper.

Hutson looked back at Mitchy's tense face. "Thanks, but I'll be fine, just want to see if that girl is ok."

Cautiously opening his shop front door, Hutson poked his head out looked around before heading out to his left. Mitchy went up to the door and pressed her face against the glass; she could see nothing but her own reflection. There was no sign of Hutson and she couldn't think of what to do next. She couldn't hear the woman screaming anymore, just the many sounds of cars blasting their horns and revving their engines.

Mitchy sat back down and waited nervously for Hutson to return, her stomach began to rumble and she was not sure whether it was due to nerves or hunger.

She unwrapped a small doughnut from the cake counter and left some change on the side for Hutson.

Taking a huge bite, Mitchy felt guilty about enjoying the glorious texture and allowing the warm jam to ooze out the centre and trickle down her fingers. Almost forgetting about Hutson outside she closed her eyes and took another bite, it was only the sound of Hutson's voice outside screaming, which made Mitchy drop her doughnut heaven. The turning point was spreading.

Aphrodite opened her eyes, it was the noise that had awoken her, the screaming and shouting and the smell.

She could smell burning, it was close to her, the acrid smell of burning plastic kept her awake. Grimacing as she held her side, which felt stiff and painful, Aphrodite unclipped her seat belt and pushed her door open with no sign of the man in the suit. Falling to the floor she unsteadily rose on her heels, and her knees clicked as she stood full height.

Surveying the mess in the florist, it wasn't until she had sauntered a few steps around the car she saw the dead body of the man who had started all of this flower carnage.

"Charming," she sighed.

Walking to the hole in the window she stood in silence at what she saw. Car alarms blared as the sea of cars in the traffic jam stood empty with both sets of car doors open. Police sirens wailed over the car alarms but it was the sudden cracks of gunfire that shook her from her trance and then the distant sound of screaming from a block away. Aphrodite was having difficulty seeing what was actually happening so she stepped over the broken glass, turned left and walked a few steps away from the florist's.

"Shit," she grumbled as a soft alarm went off in her head. Turning around, she went back into the shop to collect her foster-sister. "Almost forgot about you."

Big Man and Melissa

Big Man relaxed in his master bathroom. There were twenty-nine bathrooms in the Messiah's complex, the gigantic set of buildings that Big Man had built in the inner city of Olympia. This bath tub was the only one he could stretch out fully in, the water was ice cold as the heat outside was becoming more unbearable by the minute, his shirt had been sticking to his back with sweat which was the reason for the unprecedented ice cube bath. Closing his eyes he sank back further into the tub but he could feel the strong sunlight through his eyelids.

He had been partying hard after his business was collapsing around him, every night was party time. Feeling worse for wear he reached for the glass of white wine perched precariously on the bath edge and sipped the cold liquid, smacking his lips loudly.

Suddenly the bathroom door was flung open and a woman dressed from head to toe in black stood there. Her hair was tied back with an extremely tight headscarf and her eyes were covered in wraparound shades. Big Man splashed up, irritated by the interruption.

"Don't you believe in knocking?"

"Don't you believe in locks?" came her reply.

This was Melissa Atkins, long suffering underpaid personal aide to Big Man. She had stayed with him through thick and thin and especially since he lost most of his money over the furore with his reality television show, the same show that made this mysterious person known only as 'The Green Man' put a tremendous bounty on his head.

The pay was awful but she was like a part of this dysfunctional family now. She knew how to deal with him and his stuck up daughter Aphrodite, Big Man wriggled his big toe into the tap, he was relaxed with Melissa's company and stretched back out again.

"Have the fighter planes gone yet?"

Melissa looked at her watch. "Yeah they gave up a few hours ago."

"Did they? Really didn't notice, what about the protesters?"

Melissa's laugh was a raspy one. "What's that phrase Aphrodite has? Oh yeah, you're quite an amusement."

"So they haven't gone then?"

"Sir, they've been gathered at the foot of the building for years now, don't think they'll leave now because it's your bath night."

"Shame," Big Man murmured tightly. "Every time I go to the window, snipers start firing from the adjacent buildings, I know they can't break the glass, but it is a little unnerving to say the least, also I just remembered you should have got me out of here earlier, I'm going to be late for my shareholders' meeting this morning, get my bags packed for the flight."

"Sir it's the middle of the afternoon and the flight was four weeks ago."

"Was it? How'd it go?"

She wrinkled her nose and sniffed. "Not good Sir, and good joke about leaving the building."

"That would be nice, just to be able to leave this place for a few hours."

Melissa nodded. "I can imagine."

"But even though you live here, the protesters don't bother you when you come and go?"

"Nope, they pretty much leave me alone."

"And nobody tries to barge past you when you leave and try to get in the building?"

"They tried, but now they just leave me alone."

"How's that?"

"I have my ways, sir."

Big Man found himself chuckling as Melissa continued. "They're just people sir, people who felt that you've let them down and that it's your fault that there's no television anymore."

"These are not people, just those protesters outside, they are freaking me out man, I just want them to go away so that I can finally leave this god forsaken building, it's killing me now, I'm bored shitless cooped up in here, wish I could just click my fingers and make them all just fall asleep."

"A bit ambitious isn't it, sir?"

"Well look at it, the power company are constantly trying to turn my energy supply off, just lucky I have my own generator, and there's constant drilling underground from the gas people trying to switch me off just to get their hands on that bounty, Look at me! I'm shaking like a nerd on a first date."

Melissa moved in to refill Big Man's glass. "What do you mean?"

"Well nerds don't date that often so they'll probably be a tad nervous and—"

Melissa cut in. "I meant…why are *you* so nervous?"

"Who do I trust? Anybody who walks through that door could be a protester or some sleaze after the 500 million credits on my head."

"By the way, it's now 550 million."

"FOR GOD'S SAKE!"

"But you've done the security checks on all your staff haven't you? Everybody checks out."

"That's on the new staff…not sure about the old ones, although we did have a new girl start today? She's the new housemaid boss, Enya or Enza I think."

Melissa flashed acknowledgment to her boss, ignoring his housemaid tale. "I'm an old member of staff sir, do you trust me?"

"550 million notes is a lot of money Melissa, imagine what you could do with that?"

"I also have a job here sir, a job you gave me ever since I left school."

"But you wouldn't have to work again if you turned me in?"

"The bounty on your head is only 550 million credits, when it gets to 800 million, we'll discuss my probable betrayal later."

Big Man looked at her flushed from the wine and laughed. "You are a silly goose aren't you!"

"Like I said...I have my ways."

Big Man offered some wine to Melissa, she shook her head politely. "I'm working, sir."

"It's a holiday today, Apology Day, which was my idea."

"Doesn't matter."

"Now that's why I hired you, you're not expecting to get paid for today are you?"

She shook her head again.

"Admin stuff sir."

"Good girl, where's that lab rat Ares?"

"Not sure, but don't you think you're working him a little too hard?"

Big Man took another sip from his wine. "Nope, besides any guy who lists peanut butter and bacon sandwiches as his favourite food can work a little harder until I say so, he's just a little weird that's all, so what about the meeting with the tech guys about my 'Dinosaur' project?"

"Done," she said yawning.

"They're already downstairs setting up, your 'Abolish and Dominate' project is underway."

There was a slight gasp from Big Man as he shifted some ice cubes; Melissa looked on resignedly.

"Sweet! Oh I was just wondering, have we sacked that chef Loydy yet? I don't want him wandering through here again."

Melissa squinted with distrust. "Was that a good idea? Getting rid of him like that, I think it was a little extreme."

"Why?"

She rolled her eyes at him. "Because he gave you his kidney when you were ill, that's why."

Big Man cackled. "Oh yeah, forgot about that, still he knows I don't like vinegar on my chips and he looks like a protester, with all that long hair, he was trying to burn the complex the other day, he bought in some flaming device with sparklers trying to kill me, singing some ritual cult folklore hippy song to sacrifice me."

"That was your birthday cake sir, he was singing 'Happy birthday', we really have to get you out of this building soon."

Melissa gazed at Big Man's glass and huffed, thinking the drink may have been an excuse for his colourful mood.

"The girls would love this, where are they?"

"They're not back yet from the swimming baths yet."

Big Man was silent for a time and then spoke a hint of uncertainty in his voice. "That's not right, they should be back by now and I gave Aphrodite strict instructions to come back here when Gemma had finished."

"Maybe she jumped on a man," said Melissa.

A vicious glint was in his eyes. "That's not funny."

"I wasn't joking."

"Have you tried ringing her friends?"

Behind her shades Melissa rolled her eyes. "She doesn't have any friends, remember?"

Big Man glanced along the broken bath tiles and rubbed his cold wet chin. This was a sly reference to her only friend Sabrina who Big Man had Aphrodite betray and sent to Gommerstall prison.

"Are you sure there isn't anybody else she could be with?"

Melissa causally examined the back of her hand looking at her bright red nails. "Yep, since you got rid of Sabrina I'm Aphrodite's only friend and you pay me to do that."

Big Man raised an eyebrow.

"Oh yeah, forgot about that and...you know about Sabrina?"

"I'm your personal aide sir, it's my business to go around and clear up your mistakes."

"Mysteries," he corrected her and carried on. "Ok maybe Aphrodite took her sister out for a milkshake or something?"

"Doubtful sir, she's lactose intolerant."

"Is she? You would have thought the adoption agency would have pointed that out to me."

A thin smile crept onto her face. "Not Gemma, Aphrodite."

"Really? Wow, who knew?"

Melissa turned to leave and remembered something else, swinging back round. "The dishwasher in kitchen three sector four still isn't working. Did you take a look at it?"

Big Man nodded his head slowly. "Yes I did take a look at it."

Melissa folded her arms impatiently. "Well?"

"Well it looked broke."

"Are you going to sort the problem out?"

"I already have," smiled Big Man. "I've bought paper plates."

Melissa's face contorted as she left.

As Aphrodite and Gemma wandered out of the florist, Gemma instinctively reached for Aphrodite's hand, who reluctantly took it. She tightened her grip when the smell hit her, some of the cars were on fire and now the car alarms were joined by the sound of shop alarms ringing unashamedly. Aphrodite could taste the smell of smoke at the back of her throat and she rubbed it smoothly, checking her nails as she did so.

The shop windows had been broken and were blood stained, Aphrodite cupped her hands to one window and peered inside, it seemed nothing had been looted but glass lay everywhere.

She looked up at the shop sign, 'Hutson's news and booze store.' From further inside the shop a dull shape emerged from a backroom. Gemma cheerfully waved her hand in a greeting manner but was ignored.

"Charming," huffed Aphrodite, who casually pushed her sister behind her. Let me try. "Excuse me? My sister and I were—"

Gemma beamed. "You called me your sister!"

"Slip of the tongue, anyway I'm ringing Daddy to send someone to pick me up from this dump, and what did I say earlier? If I was to have a bad day today then who would be responsible?"

"Me."

"Pardon?"

"It's me, if you have a bad day today then I'm responsible."

"Exactly, now I want a car to pick me up."

"Pick *us* up you mean? If not let's run back home anyway?" asked Gemma.

"You can do whatever you like darling but I'm leaving, with or without you, by car or by personal jet if need be but I'm leaving now, I'm wearing my glorious seven-inch expensive heels and even if it means us going through that whole ridiculous charade of wearing maids' outfits to sneak back into the complex, then so be it, besides which I really need to pee so running isn't an option."

She took her phone from her bag and began to dial, turning her attention back to the oncoming shape.

"This isn't my phone by the way, I borrowed it from Father's little goth aide Melissa, I lost mine again and she lent me one of hers this morning. For a leather-clad woman with no life? I must admit she always has a mountain of mobile phones on the ready, oh and wait a minute, there's someone on the line."

"Hello sir we were involved in a little car accident back there and…"

Her voice trailed away, she looked at the shape in the shop and then to her sister and put the phone away. "Ok…let's run."

"Sorry?"

"Run!"

"What?"

"NOW!"

The man stepped out of the shadow of the evening sun and into full view; his face was white and gaunt and he didn't even attempt to wipe the blood from his nose as it trickled down and stopped at his lip.

His jaw opened wider than Aphrodite thought was humanely possible as he focused his eyes on the girls and screamed and then ran forward arms outstretched. Aphrodite's heels clip-clopped on the pavement as she and her sister fled from the strange man. His movements were unorthodox and animated, his head and eyes swayed from left to right as if he was drunk but trying to stay conscious to chat up someone on a guys' night out, but he stayed on his feet and stumbled after the girls.

"I CAN'T RUN IN THESE BLASTED HEELS," Aphrodite yelled and leaned on Gemma's shoulder as she eased the seven-inch heels off her feet. "Knew I should have worn flats."

Gemma tugged at her sister's arm as the crazed man came closer. Aphrodite ran quicker in bare feet as she continued down the street with Gemma in tow. Her borrowed mobile phone slipped from her hand and fell to the ground and bounced behind her in its rubber protective case. Turning back to pick it up, Aphrodite saw the man had begun to give chase. "Sod it, cheap phone anyway," she said and sped up again, leaving Melissa's phone on the pavement.

The man's steps had quickened as he pursued the girls down the street. Gemma ran close behind her sister, wriggling her shoulders to make her backpack more comfortable and wondering what the shaking was doing to her poor spider. The man was running in full stride now, he made no sound as he ran, just that his breathing had become more frantic and his arms were outstretched in anticipation of grabbing his fleeing prey.

Aphrodite gave an awkward shriek to Gemma. "DO I HAVE TO DO EVERYTHING?" She slowed her pace to grab Gemma's arm and pull her towards safety, running side by side.

"WHAT DOES HE WANT?" yelled Gemma.

"I WOULD HAZZARD A GUESS NOT MY AUTOGRAPH, KEEP RUNNING."

They fled past the burnt out cars and deserted shops as Aphrodite held her side with a stitch settling in. She took a deep breath and swung down an alleyway to her left but

even as fast as they were running, Aphrodite was aware that the man was becoming faster with every step and they had to either stop and make a stand or let him catch up with them and make his intentions clear.

Gemma fretted, broke her sister's grasp to slow down and un-shoulder her bag and allow it to hang from her back. Swinging it around to her front she unzipped it and rummaged inside, her spider emerged from beneath her swimming outfit and crawled up the back of her neck. Gemma turned her head to speak to it. "Spray baby."

On hearing those words a fine spray of webbing drifted from Buckby's behind and sailed straight into the eyes of their pursuer. The man dropped to his knees trying to tear the webbing from his eyes, thrashing wildly as he now rolled along the ground, the scraping away of the webbing from his face became more frenzied and then he threw back his head and roared a guttural cry of anger, it was a feral cry which made both girls cover their ears, its scream grew louder and whatever it was calling...responded.

He called for help...how'd he do that? thought Aphrodite.

She spun around to see about thirty people creeping up behind her; they were people dressed in various clothing. Nurses, firemen, policemen, but they all were lost in their eyes, they were foaming at the mouths and even though Aphrodite could not see from where she stood, their noses were bleeding profusely and they were angry as they began to swarm around them. Their clothes were bloody and torn as if they'd been in battle. Seeing their fallen comrade a few of them wailed in anger whilst the others were stealth-like in their approach, appearing from behind damaged shop windows and easing themselves out of burnt out cars responding to the call of the first creature.

They then all roared a terrible shriek and sprinted towards the girls.

Aphrodite stood rooted to the spot with literarily nowhere to run, she bent down to Gemma, keeping her eyes on the oncoming horde of enraged creatures and with a voice soft and calm cupped her against Gemma's ear and whispered sarcastically, "Good one."

Suddenly the ground she was standing on moved and Aphrodite hopped off of the manhole cover she had inadvertently found herself standing on. A man who looked a good few years older than her with jet black hair moved the cover aside and emerged, shielding his eyes from the light. "You'd best come down here if you want live," he said surprisingly calmly.

The stench of the sewer made Aphrodite's stomach plunge as she looked into hole. "You have got to kidding, have you seen my nails?"

"Fine, stay here and die, see if I care, but if you are coming lock back the cover behind you." The man dropped back into the hole as fast as he appeared. Aphrodite looked at the descending 'strange loser people' which she had now nicknamed them and turned to her sister and mumbled, "You do know who's responsible for this don't you?"

2. THE CLEANSING

The afternoon was slowly beginning to fade and Big Man had noted this as he prolonged a long stare at his watch. The girls still weren't back from their trip to the swimming pool, he had tried Aphrodite's phone and the line was dead which concerned him as the city of Olympia had changed greatly since the television ban was enforced on the city.

Some had taken the ban well and gotten their lives back on track, especially with some the schools re-opening, but others didn't take to the ban as well as others. They were the ones still protesting outside of his glorious complex, they were the ones that wanted revenge.

Big Man was in the mood for more wine so his meeting with his tech support team would have to be brief. The elevator took him further down into his Messiah's complex until he had reached the basement. He brushed aside a secret panel in the lift, took out his swipe card and put it in the according slot, then pressed some buttons in a combination. There was a slight shudder as the floor beneath the elevator opened up and the lift moved further deep underground.

Finally reaching the bottom the doors slowly opened and standing there to meet Big Man was a man in a long white lab coat, with smears of oil all down the front, his shaggy long brown hair covering most of his cheeks, only his thick-rimmed glasses that covered the sunken tired pouches under his eyes could be seen, an air of smugness sat behind them. Ares knew Big Man needed him more than he let on.

The two men shook hands and Big Man cleared his throat and looked around at the vast underground complex, there were technicians also in lab coats with clip boards and hard hats walking around some large inanimate objects, covered from top to bottom in tarpaulin, the largest object almost reached the ceiling as the technicians pointed with pens to certain points. Big Man copied them, looking up in their inspection with birdlike accuracy and turned to his attention to his side.

"Hello Ares, how are the preparations going for the dinosaur droids?"

Ares wiped his hands though his huge mane of greasy hair and sighed, speaking in a voice which lacked sleep. "Production is running at forty per cent sir, most of the machines are complete and ready to roll, but their weapon capabilities aren't ready yet, we have to sort out the 3D software and the infrared targeting devices need some work, but other than that we're good to go with Project 'Abolish and Dominate.'"

Big Man turned away from Ares knowing what he wanted to say next. "Well 'Abolish and Dominate' was going to be the name of my next game show.

There was an urgency in Big Man's voice, which Ares recognised. "But now I just want these weapons to use on those protesters outside and anybody who thinks that they can come and take me. If all the scum in my beloved city of Olympia thinks that they can take me for five hundred or six hundred million, or however many notes, then I'm not going down without a fight." Big Man bought a hand up to slowly pinch the end of his nose.

Ares paused. "You have your serious voice on sir, anything wrong?"

Big Man shook his head, clearing it from his daughters and then looked to the ceiling of the lab.

"Yes I'm fine."

They continued down the long gloomy corridor through the busy laboratories and further down to the tech labs. "So can't I see the things that are going to take care of my protester problem then? I mean what little money I have is bankrolling this auspicious project, I'm meant to be officially bankrupt but here I am financing your robot toys."

Ares took off his glasses and wiped them on his lab coat, speaking only after they were back on his face.

"It was your idea, sir."

Avoiding Ares's hard gaze, Big Man carried on.

"Still no word from Jago or Apollo from Gommerstall?"

"No sir."

"You guys really messed up with Jago, didn't you? I mean we told him to befriend Elias and to keep him in Gommerstall until the Dinosaur droids were ready to take part in the final game, the final game that would have given me the ratings I would have needed to make me end the season on a high and be the ultimate network king, but now I can't bring Elias back because I'm trying to adopt his daughter, as you know...so he'll have to wait for a while, assuming he's alive of course."

Ares's green eyes, which were hard to see behind his thick glasses, were filling with doubt.

"I know it's been years sir, but what *is* the point of all this again?"

Big Man gave a reassuring smile and snaked his arm around Ares' shoulder.

"Do you ever listen to me, Ares?"

"Nobody listens to you since you went into hiding in this Messiah's complex, I was just trying to fit in with everybody else."

Big Man chuckled and squeezed Ares's shoulder in reassurance. "Well tell me what you do know, but make it quick, I'm going to nip out and get some pizza for me and the girls...when they eventually get back, do you want a slice?"

Ares stuck his hands in his pockets and rocked back and forth on his heels. "You *can't* go out sir."

"Oh yeah, I forgot."

Big Man sighed hard, remembering sadly what it was like to go outside. "I'll find a menu and a phone, you sure you don't want some?"

"No thanks I'll pass, here we go, this company, *your* company were losing ratings for the 'fight night' segment in the game show, so you took some creatures from various forests, made some modifications to them to make them more violent and put them in your show, then you wanted kids to vote for your show with their remote controls at home which is why you started shutting down schools so kids would stay inside and do it, and then you sprayed some other kids at a rave with this serum that my colleagues developed to enhance their DNA to give them superpowers and put them in the game show too to fight the monsters, however the kids won all their segments and you sent them to Gommerstall Prison along with their teacher, Elias Glaucas. Right?"

Big Man nodded as Ares continued.

"So the kids and their teacher were in Gommerstall as you waited for a bigger and better idea for your end game and to rebuild your sets after Kimberley destroyed them...hence why the dinosaurs were developed, however they escaped sooner than you thought they would from prison and you had to delay them, right?...Jago took care of that prematurely, but however, there is now a price on your head for god knows how many million notes and you can't leave this building thanks to those protesters outside and the warrant for your arrest."

"Pretty much," Big Man said. Big Man stepped to the side, his small smile trembled. "I've lost so much money since that 'game show' debacle, plus thanks to Kimberley destroying my stadium which had a domino effect on the houses on the east side wiping them all out so now my principle investors from overseas have pulled out, my physical assets like this complex and your laboratories are going to be sold for squat, your technology and your research will be gone unless I can pull this out of the bag and get out of this building.

"Speaking of money sir, we're kind of running low on funds at the moment for equipment for the droids? I was hoping you'd be able to give my team or at least me a raise, if possible?"

Big Man smiled. "You know what, Ares? I'm going to give you something better than a raise."

"Really sir?"

"Yes, I'm going to give you a raise, with a P at the front."

Ares thought for a moment. "Praise sir?"

"Yes, you and your nerds are working great at the moment, you really don't need more cash to get by, do you?

"I'm afraid so, sir."

"Well I'm sorry my little man, but the cash well has dried up. I don't have a thing anymore so unless you can find somebody else to sponsor you and your dino robots, then this conversation is pretty much it."

"Couldn't you squeeze some cash from another source, sir?"

Big Man threw his head back and laughed manically. "Ha! Are you kidding? What you see is what you get, Ares. I'm broke. All I want is to be left alone, to have these protesters off my back so I can go outside from time to time, once in six years would be nice, so now have you finished yet? Pizza shop will be closed soon."

Ares shook his head, his eyes looked as if he was ashamed at his own words.

"Sir, your last venture would have eventually failed anyway, even if Kimberley hadn't destroyed the Chimera, your tinkering to the behaviour and DNA of these complex creatures could have had large repercussions, it may have meant that they would stop adapting and if this same rule applies to human test subjects then the clone effects could become permanent."

Big Man tapped at his watch and pointed to his stomach, Ares cleared his throat and got the message. "Clone effects?" Big Man looked positively shocked. "Who said anything about making clones? I don't want clones, I want robot dinosaurs, ok? What's the point of wanting to take back the city when they're all clones? Where's the fun in that? Messing around with humans and animals made me skint in the first place as they cost me everything and now I have to deal with snipers, the fighter planes and the protesters? I just want a rest."

"Clones can help sir, they can deal with your protester situation."

"No, clones, Ares. Robots yes. Clones no."

Another tired nod came from Ares and he pointed to the largest object under the covers. "That is Tyrannanut."

Big Man grinned. "Tyrannanut? What kind of a stupid name is that?"

"Oh I'm sorry 'Big Man' don't know what I was thinking having a stupid name like that," Ares snorted derisively.

Big Man kept the grin and clicked his fingers at a technician, a tall black man with no name badge. "What's your name, mate?"

"Makin," said the man far too quickly and nervously.

"Ok Makin, is Ares a funny guy or what?"

Makin let out a sigh of relief and smiled sarcastically. "Oh he's a riot, he's as much use as a concrete parachute."

Big Man grinned as Ares snapped his arms in a cross against his chest and nodded towards the biggest structure still under wraps.

"Ok well it weighs in at 300 tonnes and its height is 30m, its weapon capabilities are 90mm double barrelled machine guns, triple barrelled 50mm beam cannon, surface to air beam gun, missile launcher, pulse laser gun, energy shields, catapult cannon, flick cannon, mixed nut cannon and plasma cannon, plus 80% dagger metal casing, solid and unlike my grandma…leak proof."

Big Man smiled. "Good one."

"Then we have 'Tarantulnut' who has—"

Big Man stopped him, squinted his eyes and then flashed them open in realisation.

"Nuts! I get it now, Tyrannanut, Tarantulnut? Nuts as in 'nuts and bolts', right?"

Ares remained expressionless.

"That's right sir, anyway the droid under that sheet has a flame thrower, beam cannon, power pincers, laser machine guns, battle enhanced silk webbing and—"

"Webbing? So it's a giant mechanical spider, right?" Big Man asked like an excited child.

"Something like that," huffed Ares.

"Can we not change their names to droids? Like Tyranadroid? That sounds better, but man, I can't wait to try all this stuff out on those protesters, they won't know what hit them! Anyway soft lad, I'm getting bored now and my pizza won't wait forever so is that it?"

"Well we still have the 'Steganut' to go or 'Stegadroid' now sorry, and—"

Throwing his hands in the air in mock surrender Big Man had had enough. "Stop it! You're boring me but I've got two questions for you."

Ares sniffed the air around him. "It was Makin who farted."

"Ok then, I've only got one question, why can't you just relax and stop being a nerd. You're an ok guy Ares, but you are the dullest person I know, I'd appreciate it if you stop taking things so serious and just chill out for a few seconds. Everyone thinks you have the personality of a fruit fly so take a chill pill and let it slide, stop being an embarrassment and just flow baby."

Ares looked around at his colleagues, who stood in silence watching both him and Big Man cautiously, he shrugged his shoulders and took a deep breath. "Sorry, if you feel like that sir, if you're still going to get some pizza then I'll take a slice."

He lowered his eyes to Ares.

"You don't have to keep on saying 'sir' you know, Ares."

Big Man rubbed his hand though the oily head of Ares, who nervously responded. "Sorry, get me a slice of pepperoni please...Father."

The Big Man grinned. "That's what I wanted to hear."

Even though she was involved in a car crash, the damage to Aphrodite's dress had been minimal, a few glass cuts and a splattering of blood, but it thankfully for her it didn't smell, unfortunately the damp sewer walls had now put paid to that, her expensive shoes sloshed along in the rank water, it was almost knee high and the waste that knocked around her legs began to make her retch. She and her little foster sister followed the man who had saved them from the horde of feral attackers from the surface through endless tunnels of putrid filth. Steeling herself for the worst, Aphrodite broke the silence. "Where are you taking us?"

Sweat dripped from her rescuer's forehead, he wiped his brow and whispered, "Almost there now, please be patient."

"NO," Aphrodite said abruptly. "Listen young man…"

The man glanced behind him and shook his head. "I'm older than you."

"Oh really? And how would you know that?"

A small smile shot across the man's face, but he did not face Aphrodite. "Saying that, you might be right, must be that botox."

Aphrodite's shoulder's tensed. "I SAID, WHERE ARE YOU TAKING US? AND WHAT WERE THOSE THINGS?" The man paused for a moment as Aphrodite screeched again. "DID YOU HEAR ME?"

There was no response from him as they reached the end of the passage way and came to a T-junction. To the left of them was another set of stairs, nodding his head in that direction they climbed up them taking them to another level, which was away from the water, giving Aphrodite the chance to shake the water from her shoes. He sniffed the air and turned around to the girls. He had curly black hair and his build was athletic – even in the dark Aphrodite could tell he took care of himself, but he did have yellow teeth which as she could see was his only physical flaw. *Imagine waking up next to those teeth,* Aphrodite thought.

The man began moving his lips as if he was singing a song or talking to himself.

"EXCUSE ME, I'M TALKING TO YOU."

He stopped and chose his words carefully. "Oh yes, I'm sorry, I *did* hear you and chances are so did our 'friends' above us and probably now in here with us, you did lock the manhole cover, didn't you?"

She gave an annoyed shrug as the man shook his head. "Then we haven't got much time."

"Time for what?" He could tell that she wasn't taking this too seriously.

His face hardened. "I'm sorry if this is a bit of an inconvenience for you, me saving your life and all, but this thing is more important than this season's new shoe range. I don't know what those things were, but I'll tell what I know or what I think I know when we get back to the others, just bear with me."

"BEAR WITH YOU? I'M IN A SEWER, STUCK WITH MY SISTER, SMELL LIKE SHIT AND..."

She swayed ever so slightly and then her stomach erupted, Gemma and the stranger stared in gross unison at the water.

"That's just great. I've just thrown up on myself, happy now?"

"Happier," was his reply. Annoyance stained across his face as Aphrodite picked at her mouth, finally adding her new nails to the death toll. He was guessing how frustrated Aphrodite would get, so he spoke up quickly. "Ok, my name is Jason."

"Should I be impressed?" Aphrodite said through clenched teeth.

"It's up to you," Jason said.

Aphrodite stood silently and crossed her hands.

"I'm not."

Jason glanced at Gemma who stood close to her sister, they locked eyes and Jason smiled with his.

"Let me guess your name young lady, I have special powers you know."

"Really?" Gemma said excitedly.

"Yep, now empty your mind and close your eyes." She nodded. "Is it Julia?"

"Nope."

"Is it Gillian?"

"Close."

"Jessica?"

Gemma huffed and folded her arms. "Your rubbish, mister!"

Jason smiled. "Ok, your name is Gemma Glaucas."

Gemma's mouth dropped and her brown eyes rose with bewilderment. "WOW! How did you do that?" She turned excitedly to Aphrodite. "See what he did? He's got special powers!"

"No he hasn't," Aphrodite sighed.

"He has! He knows my name, how did he know that?"

Aphrodite walked over and pulled at Gemma's backpack. "He read your name tag on your bag."

Jason winked at Gemma and carried on. "We're almost there now anyway. Let's hope we'll be safe for a while, most of us got caught out early when the fighting broke out and the violence got worse. I managed to round up a few people, who had enough sense to hide and run away and we hid down here, until the fighting stops."

"Why are people fighting then?" Gemma asked, still impressed by Jason's non-trick.

Jason tried to keep her sprits up and spoke with warmth in his voice so as not to scare the poor girl. "I don't know honey, all I know is earlier this afternoon, some people suddenly became very violent and started killing people. I'm not going to freak you out anymore than is necessary, so try and forget about it until we meet the others."

A ripple of frustration went through Aphrodite and she huffed loudly. "Oh please! I had a madman jump on my car today and try to get in whilst I was driving, then we crash and another nut job starts chasing me and *her* down the street and now I'm following some high school drop out ruffian through some crap covered sewers to god knows what? And have you seen the state of me? I look like a cheap slut thanks to you, so that kind of leaves an impression on someone, don't you think?"

The corners of Jason's mouth twitched as if a smile was brewing. "*Look* like a cheap slut?"

He led the girls further through the tunnel until they came to a small opening to their left. Squeezing through the gap Gemma's heart sped up as she entered this new space, it was a giant hexagonal room, with the only light beaming through a huge metal grate at the top. There were huge doors on each wall, at the centre of the room was a generator under a table-like metal grille, sitting on top were some more faces, waiting patiently.

Aphrodite sniffed the air. "The smell in here is worse, is it due to these delightful reprobates?"

Jason ignored her and showed his hand to a older man in his fifties wearing a loud chequered shirt and a cap. "That is Tero, over there we have Sampson, next to him are sisters Echo and Enya."

The teenage girls, who were dressed in black leather trousers and jacket and had hair to suit, waved in unison. Gemma grinned and waved. "Echo's my friend. We used to have sleepovers together!"

Echo waved back. "Hey you! Long time no see."

"Then we have Odysseus in the corner, next to him is Judy, that's Mitchy sat over there…ummm…" Jason closed his eyes and clicked his fingers at a young man repeatedly trying to remember his name.

"Quinn." The young man finished it for him.

"Quinn, that's right."

Odysseus sat quietly observing the newcomers, he had shifty pin-prick eyes and a face older than his years, it was as if someone had crumpled up a piece of paper and thrown in a waste paper basket, then realised they needed it, uncrumpled it and lay across someone's head.

Jason carried on rattling off names like he was calling out a school register and that he'd known them for years, but in truth they had been thrown together in the space of a barely an hour. Aphrodite shifted her stance and shook her head in disbelief.

"This place *really* needs some scented candles you know, Jason darling." She turned to Gemma. "We haven't eaten lunch yet have we, darling? You hungry?"

Gemma nodded in a slow, confused manner. "Good! I could eat a horse and chase the jockey."

Gemma cleared her throat, clearly embarrassed by her would-be sister. "Why are you being so sarcastic? Be serious for once."

Aphrodite tilted her head and threw her perfect blonde hair over her shoulder.

"So, you know what 'sarcastic' means but not 'bankrupt'? That's progressive of you."

Jason walked back round after checking on the others. "You sure you're ok? Look I know things seem bad but—"

Aphrodite slapped her forehead. "Seem bad? Seem bad? I don't know about you but I think the shit's already hit the fan, now as I actually do appreciate your help from saving me and 'Little Miss Useless' here, just point us to the nearest exit and I'll – we'll – be leaving you and your merry bunch of losers."

"That's not a good idea," Jason answered. "I think we should just wait here and stay together until we know what's happening up top, it's mayhem up there, it's safer down here…maybe."

This time Aphrodite kept her cool and merely shook her now dirt-tainted blonde mane.

Mitchy, a big black woman in her late thirties sat on the table grill wheezing gently. Her hair was long and braided and she wore bright blue shorts that were too small for a woman her size, she spoke with tender authority whilst pushing up her glasses.

"What you going to do then, sugar? Go back to the top with those creatures roaming around out there?"

Aphrodite winked at her. "Gold star for you, chunky, go to the front of the class, if you can squeeze past the chairs that is."

Mitchy was up immediately, an annoyed anger etched on her face. "Is this how it's going to be with us, sugar?"

Aphrodite adopted a too innocent expression on her own face. "I'm sorry, I didn't mean that, I get nervous sometimes and say silly things." Mitchy wasn't buying it as Aphrodite continued. "I wouldn't stand still for too long darling, the children might think you're a bouncy castle and jump on you."

That was it for Mitchy. "THAT'S IT, MISSY! YOU AND ME, LET'S GO!"

"ENOUGH!" Jason shouted. "ISN'T IT ENOUGH THAT THE WHOLE CITY HAS GONE MAD, WE HAVE TO START FIGHTING AMONGST OURSELVES TOO?"

Mitchy spoke through a clenched jaw, annoyed at herself for so easily losing her temper. "She started it."

"No I didn't, chubby," grinned Aphrodite.

"I SAID ENOUGH!"

Aphrodite erupted with laughter and clapped her hands sardonically. "Well, well, well look at this, little Jason is taking charge! You remind me of my brother, at school he was a jittery little freak, he had hay fever, asthma, nut allergies, milk allergies, dirt allergies, everybody beat the tar out of him on a daily basis, you and him are so alike, both useless and no good to anybody and now I'm supposed to listen to you because your horoscope today read that a nerd was going to lead a gaggle full of annoying idiots to safety? I don't need your help and I don't need them." She looked straight at Gemma. "You can keep her if you want."

"HEY!" her sister yelped.

"Worth a try I suppose, you coming then?"

"I really think we should listen to Jason, he saved our lives and there's more people here, we could be safe if we stick together, they seem a nice bunch of people."

Aphrodite grinned, baring her expensive white teeth. "You make me laugh Gemma, I think I'm going to actually burst a blood vessel only you can use the words 'Nice bunch of people' to describe a wretched bunch of vagabonds and brigands…and as for Jason? You can marry him and move in with him as far as I'm concerned but I'm leaving this dump."

Jason shook his head slowly.

"We really don't have time for this Aphrodite, like I said we have to stick together to figure out what's going on."

She brushed aside Jason's protests and stood firm holding her hand out to Gemma. "Come along you."

Gemma hesitated. "But what about the others?"

"What others? These people you met just five minutes ago, I don't care about them, I don't know them, they could be on fire and I wouldn't care." She raised an apologetic hand to Jason. "No offence."

"None taken."

Aphrodite paused for a moment, clicked her knuckles, shut her eyes and answered through gritted teeth. "Fine, who wants to stay here with Captain Courageous here or man up and leave with me?" Aphrodite started to point indiscriminately at the others standing around the make-shift table, starting with Mitchy. "You, behemoth, you coming?"

The hate in Mitchy's voice rolled slowly from the back of her throat. "Not with you, sugar."

Unfazed, Aphrodite carried on, looking at Tero. "What about you old man? Do you need saving from that bumbling douche bag? Thing is though you are a trifle old, hanging around me it would be like beauty and the deceased."

Tero was tired, scared and in no mood for confrontation. "I'm fine thank you, young lady."

Mitchy huffed. "She ain't no lady."

Aphrodite rubbed her temple. "Now I know I can't tempt you away can I, chuckles?

"Mmmm, you got that right."

"Shame, we could have used you as a human shield, would have taken those things weeks to walk round you."

Mitchy kept her anger cool and let Aphrodite continue.

"You, the Goth guy, what's your name?"

A tall teenage boy dressed in black stood from the table onto his steel toe-capped boots. "Connor."

"Well Connor, I love your nails by the way, and your hair, very 'Death chic'. What do you think?"

Connor threw an unperturbed shrug of the shoulders. "Death is all around us and we won't escape it, may as well face it head on I suppose."

"Delightful creature, bet you're great to have at a wedding. Who's next? What about you?" She just pointed randomly now and the responses were as she expected.

"You?"

"No thanks."

"What about you in the blue top?"

"I'm staying thanks."

"You with those ghastly eyelashes, you staying?"

"I'm staying with Jason."

"Fair enough, what about you sir? Sir? Oh I'm sorry madam, the moustache fooled me."

"Drop dead!"

"Ok, anybody else? You, the sisters, Enya and, what's her face?"

"It's Echo," who answered for herself, she looked over to Enya for support. "What do you think? Could be fun!"

Enya shook her head. "This is hardly the time, Sis, not the situation for fun I'd say, don't you think?"

"Oh please? Let's get out of here, I just want to go home, we can't do anything down here."

Enya's eyes filled with suspicion as she looked over to Aphrodite. "We don't know her."

"We didn't know Jason but we still followed him."

Enya's patience was being sorely tested. "Look, all I want to do is to get out and see if I still have a job. I only got it today. Please?"

"Fine."

Enya nodded to Aphrodite. "We'll go then, just for you though."

Aphrodite clapped gently. "Cools, what about you, sir?"

There was no answer from anybody. "Gone all shy have we?"

Enya's eyebrows dipped with uncertainty. "Who are you talking to?"

Aphrodite pointed in Enya's direction. "Him, behind you."

Enya turned in time to see a man swaying like a drunk by her shoulder, his eyes were blood red and the left side of his face was torn and shredded and flapped like curtains in the tunnel breeze.

That's odd, Enya thought as the man leaned forward and tore a chunk of flesh from her neck. She was dead before her sister screamed, a scream which echoed all around the sewer. "NOOOO!!!!"

Jason roared immediately, "THEY'RE HERE! THEY'RE INSIDE!"

From the shadows lumbered out the changed humans, they had found their way into the makeshift meeting room and began to tear through the small crowd. They were eating at the survivors now, the violence which started it all had been replaced with a new sense of terror…cannibalism.

The screams of the humans in hiding were simultaneous with their pursuers.

Aphrodite grabbed Gemma and squatted behind a waist high row of bricks. "Stay here squirt, I don't want to explain to Daddy that you were eaten on the way to swimming lessons."

With calmness beyond her tender years Gemma whispered to her sister, "Could you get us out of here please?"

Aphrodite gave her a cheap look. "Stay here. I mean it." Aphrodite stayed crouching and edged her way around the hexagon. She watched wide-eyed as some humans charged through one of the doors just in front of her, she turned around to grab her sister when she heard the huge metal door slam shut. "HEY WAIT," she yelled. The eighteen-year old girl Judy, was straggling behind them and got to the door just as it shut. She screamed to the departing others. "PLEASE OPEN THE DOOR, LET ME IN PLEASE." She reached her hand through the vertical grills in the door. "COME BACK PLEASE! DON'T LEAVE ME."

Aphrodite crawled closer to the girl and through a half-open mouth called to the girl. "Hey you, come here, come with me."

Judy swung her head round in a blind panic and noticed Aphrodite beckoning to her, Aphrodite registered the fresh sweat and tears on the girl's face and also the pure fear in her eyes, she called again. "I said come with me, take my hand for goodness sake."

Ignoring her, Judy pounded on the door for the others to come back, she grabbed the metal bars and rocked them with all her might to open. "COME BACK! WHY WON'T YOU COME BACK TO ME?"

Aphrodite shouted out to the girl now in anger. "FOR GOD'S SAKE, WOMAN! COME WITH ME, RUN WOMAN, RUN!"

Judy was too scared and didn't comprehend. "YOU HAVE TO LET ME IN PLEASE!"

Aphrodite moved closer with her arm outstretched. "FORGET THEM COME WITH ME!"

She still ignored Aphrodite and tugged harder at the door. "PLEASE. PLEASE." Judy begged, over and over again until she gave up and just slid to the ground. Anger came over Aphrodite as the girl failed to move. "GET UP YOU SILLY COW AND MOVE!"

Judy just sat and waited as some of the changed humans crowded around her. Aphrodite crouched low, powerless to help her, the girl nodded to her and smiled briefly to her, holding her gaze before she was torn apart, her screams joined countless others around the room.

Aphrodite didn't blink and just sighed heavily. "You had your chance."

Mitchy fell back against a wall as her legs wobbled, a girl with a torn blood stained dress ambled towards her, her left leg was bent at an angle that should have been impossible to walk on normally but she struggled on and dragged herself closer to Mitchy, her teeth were red with blood and her neck was broken and bent but it didn't seem to trouble the woman, she grabbed Mitchy by the throat.

"Oh no you don't." One swift head butt from Mitchy sent the girl reeling; she followed it up with a clean punch to the girl's face, blood from her now split lip sprayed back onto her already bloodied face as she hit the ground with force. Mitchy said, "Broke into the wrong tunnel didn't you, bitch?"

Echo sat in the corner rocking back and forth like a scared child, the realisation of her sister's death had shocked her into a catatonic state, she had been spotted by another of the 'changed', a man in a loose-fitting plaid shirt was fast approaching her, his shirt was blood stained and torn and it revealed his exposed rib-cage underneath.

Jason was trying to evacuate people for the second time that day, they were running through any available exit as these ravenous people tore into them. He noticed Echo sat not far from him with her head in her hands. He screamed at her, "ECHO. WE HAVE TO LEAVE NOW!"

She opened her mouth to speak but could only muster a whisper. "I can't." Jason made hard contact with a punch, flooring an elderly man wearing a cooking apron with a comedic slogan on the front, some lettering was obscured with dried blood.

"DON'T JUST SIT THERE PLEASE, WE'VE GOT TO GO."

Echo choked back a sob. "I don't want to leave her."

"ECHO PLEASE?"

"I SAID NO!" she snapped through the tears that had finally arrived. "I'm not leaving my sister."

Jason ran over, stooped down and held her quivering hand firm in his own and stroked it gently. He brought her tear-stained face towards his, looking her straight in the eye. "Echo, I'm really sorry about your sister, truly I am, but if we stay here we're going to die, we can't let these things get us they—"

"I KNOW WHAT THEY CAN DO JASON, LOOK AT HER!" Anger began to replace the fear and she pulled her hand from his grasp. She remained adamant, keeping Jason locked tight in her gaze. "You go, I'm staying with Enya."

Jason stayed low as he turned around to see two of the blood stained horde fighting over the body of a fallen nurse, she was still in her uniform, just going for her first day at work to start the first of many shifts for the week, she never made it to the hospital. He held his hand to his mouth as his eyes showed disgust easing into pity for the young girl being pulled apart without hesitation by these new savages; he kept low and focused back to Echo, whispering almost.

"Do you think this is what your sister would have wanted? I hardly knew her but from what I saw of her she loved you and cared for you, she protected you, it was her who dragged you from that smashed up car wreck, it was her who flagged me down for help, it was her who wouldn't let *anybody* touch you, do you think she really wanted you to stay here and watch those bastard things rip the flesh from your bones? Watch them pick their way through your entrails? Watch them!"

"OK I GET IT!" Echo nodded her head solemnly. "I understand, just promise me Jason that when all this is done and things get back to normal, we come back for her, right?" She was breathing deeply and quickly and Jason offered his hand again to her to try and calm her down.

"I promise we'll come back and bring your sister home, on my life."

He was interrupted by another horrific scream of another life being ended by another of these seemly endless creatures. Making him swing his head around nervously and lowing his voice, keeping hold of Echo's hand, he glanced up and noticed Aphrodite and Gemma crouching behind a small wall; he turned back round to Echo. "Come on, we're leaving."

Jason and Echo skittered over to Aphrodite's hiding place, his reactions were fast as he looked over to where the changed humans were still picking off the humans in the dark.

Aphrodite sighed as she saw him approaching her.

"Thought I'd got rid of you."

Jason smiled behind a whisper. "Can't get rid of me that easily."

Aphrodite's voice rose slightly. "Now let's get one thing clear, you do know I hate you, right?"

"I got that impression, yes."

"Good, well now that's settled let's do what I said we should have done from the start and get the hell out of here."

Jason sidled closer to Gemma. "You ok, squirt?"

Her brown eyes were barely visible in the dark but he could make out that there was hardly any fear behind them, the young girl was extremely calm given the circumstances. She flashed him a quick smile from her small elf-like face. "Yeah, I'm ok."

He gave her a thumbs up. "Good, there's a chamber over there which may lead to a ladder to the streets, I think...not sure but be have to see where it takes us."

Mitchy, Odysseus and Quinn hid across the other side of the hexagonal room, the creatures had just taken down Sampson and at least three of them were feeding off his insides. Jason watched as the body still twitched and he ducked down even lower as the blood smeared faces of the horde looked up from their fresh kill eager for more human meat, Jason almost vomited and shut his eyes. Taking a deep breath he opened them again and tried to catch Mitchy's own eye and made a patting motion with his left hand and a sweeping motion with the other. Mitchy eyed him warily and then nodded, she paused briefly and then rounded up the rest of her bunch, whispering to them to stay low and edge slowly around the back to reach Jason's makeshift crew, other humans were still scattered around trying to dodge the horde of these voracious killers, an uneasy quiet fell over Jason's group, he knew that only Mitchy and her people were in touching distance of joining him and leaving together, the others were on their own; he rolled his eyes at everyone until they got the idea.

"Time to go," he told his group. He pointed to the chamber and crawled out first and the others crowded out after him. Mitchy eased out of her hiding place and followed suit.

The hairs on the back of Jason's neck prickled as he slowly rose off his hands and knees and tried the door handle and with an uneasy heave opened the latch and pushed it open. Unseen by the changed humans, he led the way out of the hexagonal horror room and through the now twisting tunnels of the sewer.

Aphrodite was right behind him and looked around to Mitchy at the back and then at the door frame. "Is she going to be able to fit through here?" She could barely make out the scolding look Jason gave her in the dark, but it was enough to make her shut up. "I only asked."

The whole group made it through the narrow doorway with the eldest member Tero at the back. He began to push the door shut when he realised there was nobody behind him, with another man, Norton helping, Mitchy stopped them and called to Jason. "What about the others?"

Jason glanced down the corridor and then back to Mitchy. "This is all of us now, if no one's behind you then that's it, we have to leave now, so close the door, everybody inside."

More screams from humans being attacked came from behind. The group quietly left the hexagonal room, Tero turned his face to Mitchy and she nodded in agreement now with Jason. The door was slammed shut with force and locked. Norton lowered his chin and stared at the door. "I can still hear them screaming."

Tero nodded and spoke quietly, "Screaming and dying."

3. Whatever Happened to Blaze Morrisey?

Melissa sat at her desk staring blankly at the computer screen – it wasn't working and was really trying her patience. Nimble fingers tapped on to the keyboard, trying to work around the virus which the computer had obviously caught, the self-repair systems were apparently up and running but nothing was happening. Melissa ran her ringed fingers across the keyboard and still nothing. She looked up at the observation camera on the ceiling above her, baring her teeth and waving her fists. "ARRRRGGGGHHHH!"

In her anger Melissa failed to notice a figure ghost up beside her. "Everything alright there?"

"Hey Ares, I swear to God I'm going to throw this thing against the wall."

Ares chuckled and ran his fingers over the computer console. "Computers are like children, if you spoil them they take advantage of you."

Ares's hands danced across the keyboard, which to him seemed like a fairly easy procedure. "All you have to do is to let them throw their toys out the pram." He continued tapping away. "Lure them into a false sense of satisfaction." His eyes focused hard onto the screen. "Then strike."

Ares hit the 'enter' button and the screen glowed to life as Melissa clapped her hands and cheered. "Yaahhyy! My hero!"

"I have moments, sometimes apparently."

Melissa smiled sweetly as Ares made her saying his own. "Why do you always put yourself down? You're a clever nice guy, Ares."

He shrugged and pulled up a chair next to Melissa. "Nice guys finish last, Melissa, don't you know that?"

"That's not true, why you say that?"

"I was nice to my mum, and what good did that do me?"

"You don't see her anymore do you?"

Ares sighed. "No, Aphrodite apparently used to see her a few years ago, she never gave us her address just met her at a neutral venue on her own, not with her boyfriend, but even now that's stopped, she's just disappeared now, even my own mother didn't want to see me."

"You never saw your mother?"

"Nope,. Aphrodite yes, me...no."

She put her hand on his arm. "Ever since I've known you've always put yourself down, you may be a nerd, but at least you've got some brains in that scruffy little bonce of yours."

Ares looked embarrassed and flustered. "Tell that to the Big Man, sometimes when I think we're doing ok, he still gives me that *look*...like I'm something he's found on the bottom of his shoe."

Melissa scratched her scarf wrapped tightly on her head. "He's your dad, he does love you, in his own special way."

Ares gave her a fragile smile. "I remember when I was a kid and really believed Dad was a superhero with special powers, he'd put me on his shoulders and jump down the staircase."

"What changed?"

"I grew up and realised he was just a drunk in a cape."

Melissa stifled a laugh as Ares continued. "I'm way down the pecking list when it comes to love. Dad obviously still loves Mum, despite her leaving him but then you have the girls, Gemma is really nice and I'm glad we adopted her, but then there was Dad and that thing he did to Athena."

"Who?"

"Who what?"

"You said Athena, who's she?"

"Who's who?"

"I said who is Athena? You mentioned her name."

"Did I? Sorry, I meant Aphrodite, don't know where that came from."

"Are you sure?"

Ares stared at the screen, eyes unmoving. "I'm quite sure, I don't know anybody called Athena, are you sure you're not hearing things or that you may be coming down with something?" Ares pressed his hand on Melissa's forehead. "You haven't got a fever."

Melissa slumped back in her chair, the uncertainness in Ares's voice made her think about pressing him again for a decent answer. "What are you doing?" she asked.

"Just checking to see if you had a summer cold, because you're talking gibberish, anyway what where you saying before?"

"I was asking about Athena?

"Look, I don't know anybody by that name, ok?

Melissa relented. "Fair enough."

"Can we talk about something else please? Anything. Aphrodite maybe?"

Melissa suddenly snapped her fingers. "Do you mean about Aphrodite being a bitch? I know, I went to school with her."

"Thought she was one of your best friends?"

Melissa glared at him impassively. "You *really* going to go there, Ares? Are you? I'm not her best friend, I talk to her because she has nobody else. I talk to her because your dad asks me to, you know damn well what happened to Sabrina. You know what Big Man paid his own daughter to do, he paid her to betray her best friend and send her to Gommerstall prison because she had powers, powers that *he* gave her for entertainment."

There was a moment of brief silence broken by Ares.

"Are you sure he knew about it? A frosty silence was all he got as a reply. "I'm sorry Melissa, didn't know you felt this way."

"About the 'powers'? It doesn't matter if you have powers or not, it doesn't matter if you're different through having a super power, or being a different sex, colour or creed, you shouldn't have to be bullied into doing something you don't want to do."

Ares could feel any dignity he had working for his father drain from his body.

"You're right, I didn't think like that, I thought I was helping him for entertainment, I guess you miss a lot about humanity living cooped up in this dark tower all the time hiding from the protesters and police, snipers constantly shooting at us, well Dad mostly, I just want to do the things people just take for granted I can never do. I'm stuck in that laboratory for so long even things like dating I can't seem to do right."

Melissa looked up from the computer and grinned, entertained by his frankness. "Really?"

"Yes! Because it's *true*, I'm just everyone's friend, a confidante, nobody important, just a shoulder to cry on when things go wrong in other people's relationships. I'm best friend material not boyfriend material. It's fine, you get used to it after a while."

Melissa wasn't listening, she had turned her attention back to the computer, craning her neck forward with her shades almost touching the screen.

"Those sunglasses aren't doing you any favours, let me—"

He went to remove Melissa's shades. "DON'T TOUCH THEM!" she snapped.

Ares snatched his hand away. "Sorry, I didn't mean to upset you."

"It's ok, I shouldn't have shouted at you."

Melissa fiddled with her headscarf, pulling it tighter and keeping her hair covered. "It's just this condition I have with my eyes, just have to wear shades all the time."

Ares sighed. "I understand, but I remember you having this condition for ages I know he's kind of low on funds but why not let my dad's people look at them?"

Melissa laughed softly. "I think your father has done enough."

"What do you mean by that?"

She changed the subject. "Before my computer went dead there were some reports about rioting downtown, shops being looted, people fighting. It looks quite bad, there's a visual block but managed to get some audio, listen to this."

Melissa raised the volume on the control.

A woman's hideous scream burst from the speakers making them both shudder. "Shit! Let me turn this down."

The volume decreased but the looks of shock on both faces remained. There was the sound of police sirens wailing in the background and heading closer to the shouts of "KEEP BACK" from the officers on the ground.

Ares puffed in annoyance as he tried to make out what was happening with no picture on the screen.

"GET DOWN ON THE GROUND NOW," an officer could be heard shouting with authority.

"What's happening out there?" Melissa nervously asked.

Ares shook his head slowly. "No idea, but it sounds—"

Before he could finish an explosion ripped through the air, making them both jump and more screams and now loud moans were picked upon the microphone. The policeman's voice could be heard again. "I SAID GET BACK, I'M WARNING YOU TO STAY BACK."

The piercing crack of gunfire made Ares's eyes widen even more. Behind her shades Melissa's did the same, more and more shots were fired as the same policeman struggled to contain the frontline. His screams filled the room as whatever the policemen were shooting at had burst through their containment line and had taken them down. Ares leapt to his feet. "I'm going to try something, it's just an idea but I think it could work."

"What are you doing?"

Ares went to move Melissa from her seat. "Sorry, but I'm going to try and hack into that street camera, we're getting audio but no visual."

Melissa was quiet and sullen. "You can't do that Ares, visuals are banned for a reason, no television and restricted internet remember?"

Ares still drilled his fingers into the keyboard. "Can't you hear all that? Don't you want to see what's happening downtown? Well my father is right, I *am* a nerd and only a nerd would be able to do this, just give me a second as I'm almost—"

He didn't finish the statement as the as the computer screen flicked and an image sprang to life.

The barricade put up by the police had been overrun by strange looking people who screamed like banshees and others had a grating moan. Some moved awkwardly as if they were dancing at a wedding whilst others were quicker and moved with lightning reflexes. Melissa put her hand over her mouth, unable to comprehend what was happening in the square of downtown Olympia City. They were howling like mad dogs these things, so loud that Melissa covered her ears even from the safety of the complex miles away, policemen fighting frantically for their lives and were losing the battle.

Ares tapped again on the keyboard and the street level camera zoomed in. One of the policemen who had one of these things clawing away at him, lay on the street. His body had been protected by his body armour but his face was a mess. There was a big hole in his cheek, like an abscess had just burst.

Ares looked harder and saw the gaping hole in its head where its brains used to be when the creature turned around. Fresh and dried blood stained his neck and his eyes were black; this man should have been dead but he stumbled forward like a toddler taking its first steps.

"I need more light," Ares said and dabbled with more typing. A light from on top of the street camera flicked on and the detail on the policeman's injuries became more aware, he didn't register the camera at first but as soon as the light came on he reached out his hands and went for the camera. The others behind him turned to the light and ambled slowly like some clumsy drunken street dance.

The cop with the empty head grabbed the camera and howled as the others did the same, then the screen went dead for the final time.

Ares's breathless voice spoke first, his eyes still transfixed to the dead screen. "Where are Aphrodite and Gemma?"

Melissa still had her hand over her mouth. "I think I'm gonna be sick."

"WHERE ARE THEY?" yelled Ares.

Melissa paused and then the realisation kicked in. "Oh my God, they're downtown at the swimming baths."

A wave of fear washed itself around Ares's stomach. "Get Dad, get my dad now!"

A Lab with The Green Man: 1

The Green Man had taken the call from his assistant and returned to his rented laboratory. It wasn't as grand as the labs in the Messiah's Complex and the equipment was very basic and barely adequate.

No one could enter the buildings of Big Man, his towers were impenetrable, so The Green Man had to make do with borrowing some tech. His money credits weren't that great, with loads of foot soldiers on his payroll and jeeps and tanks to maintain, he was straining his cash flow, plus with the bounty money he offered for Big Man was going to be a stretch, so this new project had to work.

He moved quickly down the drably painted corridor walls towards his main lab and his technician.

The technician had said it was urgent on the phone and this made The Green Man hasten his steps. He anticipated trouble from the start and now the technician's voice made his fears more apparent. With his green coat flapping more with each stride, The Green Man pushed open the lab doors. The technician tied her long blonde hair up and pointed to a computer monitor. "You have to take a look at this sir, she's growing at an incredible rate."

The Green Man's body went tense with added anticipation. "Can I see her now?" His blonde assistant nodded and tapped and swiped the screen on her hand held computer.

Suddenly the ground began to shift and a cryogenic chamber rose from the centre the revealed floor. The chamber device was filled with countless lights flashing and beeping sounds from another monitor moving slowly from the centre of the floor attached to the chamber. The tube was filled with water and something else that made The Green Man stir, he smiled through his face mask as the whole chamber rumbled to a halt.

"She is growing isn't she? he asked his assistant.

She barely acknowledged him as she was engrossed in her own computer screen. "I know, I called to show you," she mumbled.

"Can she hear me?" The Green Man asked.

The bored lab tech closed her screen and walked over to the glass chamber and tapped it with her pen.

In the chamber was a young girl, a young human girl with hints of blonde hair showing through. Her eyes blinked as she observed the newcomers who had awakened her from her chamber sleep. The Green Man's expression was like a parent seeing their newborn child for the first time. He walked over to the tube and joined the reluctant assistant as she tapped the tube again; they both observed the many tubes and breathing apparatus attached to the child.

"Isn't she beautiful?" The Green Man asked.

"You get what you pay for," replied his assistant.

"Can she hear us?"

"Probably."

"Will she be abnormal?"

The assistant was growing tired of the questioning, and laughed a laugh with little humour in it. "She is supposed to be that way, she is very different, but isn't that how you wanted her?"

The Green Man nodded. "Indeed."

She prodded him with her pen, knowing that he wouldn't harm her. "Talk to her, go on."

"Can I?"

"She is a remarkable specimen and she is responding well, I think it's only fair you try and speak to her."

The Green Man studied the little floating girl in the test tube, the light blinded her and she closed her eyes as The Green Man peered into the chamber.

"Hello? Can you hear me?" he slowly asked. There was no reply from the girl. "I said can you hear me?"

Still no answer. The Green Man looked to his assistant. "It's not working."

Before she could reply, the young girl in the tube replied, her voice smooth and soft like velvet. "*Yes I can hear you.*"

Taking a deep breath, the assistant suddenly showed some interest and tried to steady her nerves as The Green Man continued.

"How are you feeling? he asked slowly.

The young girl with the blond hair in the cryogenic test tube focused intently on The Green Man, she tried to ease herself away from the tubes attached to her body to make herself more comfortable, her eyes opened again and she looked The Green Man square in the face. "*I'm afraid.*"

"I really have to pee you know."

Jason glanced up and down the long tunnel and back to Aphrodite. "What did you say, sorry?"

"I said I *really* have to pee...now!"

Jason scratched his head looking up and down at the large industrial pipes on the sewer wall. "These pipes must lead up to the surface, I think they're called laterals, we can follow them to the top."

Aphrodite threw her arms up and slumped them down at her side in frustration. "God, I'm not surprised you're a expert in crap, so where's the toilet around here?"

"We're in sewer, Aphrodite," Jason said nonchalantly. "The whole place is a toilet, so take your pick."

Aphrodite's body filled with rage and urine. "YOU'RE INCORRIGIBLE!"

"But I'm alive, which is something you won't be if we don't get out of this tunnel."

"You're very melodramatic aren't you darling? It's becoming slowly endearing actually."

"Don't mention it."

Jason turned to the group. "Ok people listen up, I don't know how much time we have until those things find their way into this tunnel, so we're going to follow *this* pipe here which should hopefully lead us out of here."

Odysseus, another man older than Jason with a short beard and tired shifty eyes, finally spoke up. "Are you really sure this is the way out? We can barely see anything in here."

"I'm not certain…" Jason paused, his mind recollecting. "…Odysseus, yeah I'm hoping this pipe leads us away from here, how's everyone bearing up anyway?"

Aphrodite flinched at the audacity of such a question. "Are you for real? Have you seen those people? They're disgusting creatures and I bet half of them could peel an orange through a letter box with their teeth."

Burdened with responsibility which he wasn't sure he could handle, Jason reluctantly shrugged his shoulders. "Yeah, I don't know where those things from the surface came from but if we just stay together we might just make it out of here alive."

Aphrodite grinned. "I wasn't talking about them, darling."

An uneasy quiet fell over the group as Gemma pushed forward closer to her foster sister. "Don't you ever change?"

"Nope, why should I?"

"Because you *can* be a nice person sometimes."

"I don't recall that."

"A beautiful face doesn't mean a beautiful heart you know."

"Nope, but it gets me into nightclubs for free so works for me."

Jason smiled weakly, hearing Aphrodite's remark and attempted some levity himself as they continued through the tunnel.

"So how is everybody bearing up? Everybody ok?"

A tepid response shifted among the group as their hands felt along the slime-riddled walls until Gemma suddenly remembered something and swung her bag from off her back.

"Oh shoot! I forgot all about you."

Norton frowned in confusion. "What are you talking about?"

Gemma loosened the straps and clicked her tongue, something sprung from the bag and ran up her arm willingly. Norton screamed and fell back against the tunnel wall waving his hands wildly. The whole group spun around in unison.

"What's going on now?" a tired Jason moaned.

"THERE'S SOMETHING ON HER ARM!"

"IT'S CRAWLING ALL OVER HER, HOLY SHIT! GET IT OFF HER!"

Gemma's eyebrow's dipped as she threw a mock frown at his outburst. "No, don't be silly he's my friend."

Buckby crawled all over Gemma's arms and back as the others squinted hard to see in the dark. Mitchy leaned forward and peered hard at Gemma.

"Baby, is that a spider crawling up all over your arms?"

Gemma nodded vigorously. "Yep, his name is Buckby, I think he needed some air."

Mitchy offered her hand out. "Can I hold him?"

"Yeah sure."

Gemma wriggled the great spider from off her back and allowed him to crawl down her arm and on to Mitchy's.

A stiff breeze blew through the tunnel blowing Aphrodite's hair up. She tied it up, looking at Mitchy as she played with her sister's pet.

"Be careful, it might eat you."

Mitchy smiled.

"No, he's fine and no trouble at all."

"I was talking to the spider actually."

Mitchy sighed heavily and gave Buckby back to Gemma, fronting up to Aphrodite when she was done. "Do you have a problem with me, sugar?"

"Nope no problem."

"Then why do you have the nerve to say these things to my face?"

"Well I would say it behind your back but this tunnel is too tight."

Mitchy stood firm, staring hard at Aphrodite.

"Anytime missy."

Jason stepped in. "LADIES PLEASE! WE DON'T HAVE TIME FOR THIS, WE DON'T KNOW WHAT WE'RE DEALING WITH OUTSIDE BUT WE MUST

STICK TOGETHER AND NOT FIGHT AMONGST OURSELVES."

The group looked at Jason open-mouthed at his outburst. Slowly he regained control of himself. "Ok, well Tero what...um? What do you do for a living?"

The old man was pleasantly surprised by Jason's question and after the massacre in the last chamber it was nice to feel somewhat normal again albeit briefly, whether Jason was being credulous about the situation or just polite, Tero rubbed his aching back before answering.

"I don't work anymore Jason, I'm retired thankfully. I'm now a writer, a crime writer, have you heard of the 'McLean McArther' series of books about the cop solving cases from the back of a second hand ice-cream van? Well I'm the author, that's the reason why I was in town this morning, there was a book signing and people were queuing around the building."

Aphrodite smirked. "Queuing for what? Refunds?"

Tero smiled in the dark.

"That was a good joke young lady, but I can honestly say being retired is the best thing that ever happened to me, I spent thirty years in my last job working for those ghastly chocolate people."

"WHAT DID YOU SAY?" exclaimed Connor, the young Goth.

Aphrodite gave an ugly smile. "Oh you're a racist too? I should have known with *that* shirt."

Tero put his hands up in mock surrender as the tension grew worse. "No, I'm not racist, I meant chocolate people as in a chocolate factory, I worked for McMorrow Chocolate in the Vishelly District? And after I retired I took up writing."

Tero reached into his shirt pocket and pulled out a handkerchief to wipe his brow. "As I say, I was doing a book signing in the town centre and I had a good queue forming, The head of my fan club follows me wherever I go to do a signing be it rain or shine, Blaze Morrissey was in the queue, she's a wonderful woman, a little older than me."

"So she's two hundred?" Aphrodite said.

Jason hushed her up. "Carry on, Tero."

The old man became anxious and wiped his brow feverishly again. "Well, yes ok, Blaze got to the front of the queue and we exchanged pleasantries as we normally do and—"

"Is this story going anywhere?" chipped in Aphrodite. "Because I've a couple of things I'd like to do before this decade ends."

"Would you shut up and let him finish?" asked Mitchy.

Aphrodite's smirk returned and she walked up to Mitchy only breaking eye contact with her to rummage through her bag and take out some lip gloss, as she skilfully applied it in the dark a mischievous glint came to her eyes as she returned the look to Mitchy.

"How much do you actually weigh?"

Mitchy waved her finger at Aphrodite. "Oh no, you didn't just say that."

Aphrodite mimicked her. "Oh yes I did!"

Mitchy fought hard to keep her anger at bay and finally just scowled at Aphrodite, who returned the look with her very best puppy dog face. Aphrodite cocked her head to one side and spoke in her most patronising voice.

"You're not going to cry are you?"

"From you? You wound me up once girl, not again besides I've come up against bigger and badder bullies than you."

Aphrodite's eyes narrowed. "Really? I'm no bully, I'm just having fun."

Jason again stepped in. "Ladies, I just want to get out of this tunnel and if I'm honest I would like to know what happened to Tero if that's ok with you?"

Mitchy put her hand to her mouth in embarrassment. "Oh yes, I'm sorry Tero, so what happened to the lady in the queue?"

Tero's eyes blinked to the direction of Jason's voice. "I'm sorry?"

"Blaze is it? The woman at the front of the queue?"

"Well yes, she was always a fun and chatty lady, she was full of life and charm, a smile on her face every time we met and I did enjoy our chats."

Tero paused again and wiped his brow, smiling apologetically, and then his eyes closed and the smile disappeared.

"When she got to the front of the queue her lovely eyes had changed – they had turned black, they burned with this rage, she looked so angry, this foam, this disgusting foam began to mouth and that's when she—"

Norton interrupted. "Hey, a door!" He stepped in front of the group and kept his eyes locked to left of the tunnel. "Yeah I was right! There's a door here."

Everybody turned their attention from Tero's tale and looked to where the animated Norton was pointing. The group crowded around the hidden door. Aphrodite picked at an eyelash, seemingly disinterested. "Well, it's not going to open itself darling,"

The bereaved Echo shivered fearfully. "What if those 'things' are in there? They're in there and they're going to get us?"

Mitchy stepped in and held Echo's hand tight, rubbing her back for comfort with her free hand as Jason carefully pushed past them to check the door.

"I'm not sure if we should go through, maybe we should just stick to the tunnel and make our way to the surface."

Norton shot Jason an intense look and thumped his fist into his palm.

"You're talking crap now, it was your idea to come through this tunnel and your idea to make it to the top, this door could be a chance to escape and I'm taking it."

Jason eyed Norton up and looked to the door once more.

"Yeah, you're right, any chance we could get out of here the better, open the door then."

Norton eagerly pulled at the door handle, paused and then pushed hard, instead forcing the door open. "We're in, let's go."

The door opened slowly and the rest of the group tentatively followed. It led to a large room with tables and upturned chairs scattered around just about visible in the dark. Gemma looked around cautiously and noticed something. "What's that big thing in the corner?"

Jason strained his eyes to her direction. "I think it's a serving hatch, hold on..."

Walking back through the group, Jason pressed his hands against the wall fumbling around until he found a switch. "Got it."

A wash of relief hit the others as they turned their heads away from the blinding light as Jason flicked the light switch on."

"God that's bright," Norton squinted shielding his eyes from the light. He blinked hard a few times as Mitchy walked past him.

"What is this place?"

Jason glanced around. "It's the serving quarters, the canteen for the sewage workers."

Aphrodite smiled wickedly. "Surprised you didn't know that Mitchy darling, should we leave you here while we escape?"

Mitchy smiled back. "Not going to work on me, sugar."

Gemma wriggled her nose and put her hand to her mouth as she coughed. "So they put the canteen next to the sewers? How gross is that?"

The usually silent Goth Connor spoke. "Crap and then curries? Back to front but I like it!"

Gemma cringed followed by a grin. "That's disgusting."

"I like it."

"Connor!"

"I mean it!"

"That's dirty."

"It's cool."

"You sure?"

"Definitely."

Aphrodite rolled her eyes.

"Wouldn't it be easier if you two got a room."

Norton chuckled and Jason allowed himself to relax. "You see those nozzles in the ceiling? They're decontamination taps, they release a spray to clean the workers as they come into eat."

Tero surveyed the chairs on the floor. "Looks like whoever was here left in quite a rush, I think under duress too."

The others gathered round him and also surveyed the damage to the room as Tero took a deep breath. "It's obvious the sewage workers weren't alone down here, those creatures must have got in here before."

Echo suddenly began to shudder uncontrollably and became hysterical. "THEN WHY ARE WE STILL HERE? THEY'RE COMING TO GET US! THEY'RE GOING TO GET US!"

"Could someone shut her up please?" Aphrodite said disgustedly.

"We're all scared and we're all nervous but there's no reason to be rude, Aphrodite."

"Then tell her to shut up, we've got enough problems without her going nutcake on us."

Jason quickly grabbed Aphrodite's hand and pulled her to the corner of the room. "Look, we're all tired, lost and hungry and everyone, despite Norton's bravado, is scared and we're dealing with some sort of breakdown outside that nobody understands what is going on, but that young girl over there has just lost her sister so it would be kind of you if for once in your privileged spoon-fed life that you could give someone else some slack and not to think about yourself."

Aphrodite shook herself free from his grasp and adjusted her hair, seething at Jason. "You're an idiot."

Jason looked bemused. "You going to apologise?"

Aphrodite pushed him gently aside as she again played with her hair, blonde locks sailed through her fingers as she turned to Jason.

"Nope."

Looking stunned Jason grabbed her arm again. "Apologise to Echo now, Aphrodite."

Aphrodite wriggled free again and turned to the frightened Echo, her words were calm and direct. "Not yet."

Jason let out another long breath. "For God's sake, Aphrodite!"

"STOP IT!"

The stunned group turned to the quivering Echo. "STOP IT! STOP IT! STOP IT!"

"Echo wait—"

"NO JASON! I DON'T CARE ABOUT HER, I DON'T CARE ABOUT AN APOLOGY, I JUST WANT TO GET OUT OF THIS PLACE ALIVE, PLEASE I JUST WANT TO GO HOME, I JUST WANT TO BE SAFE!"

Jason tried to calm down the frightened young girl as the others looked on in silence. "We're going to be fine Echo, we just have to stay calm and stick together, ok?"

Echo bit her lip. "I'll try."

Jason continued. "Ok people we're leaving. Let's try and find another exit and get out of here, if anybody can find some food for the journey then look around the kitchen and take what you need, but don't take too much we don't want to be weighed down with too much food."

Mitchy flashed a stare at Aphrodite. "Don't say a word, sugar."

"You beat me to it, darling," Aphrodite smirked.

Connor, quiet and sullen moved forward. "They're going to get back in here, aren't they?"

Jason paused and looked up and down at the young Goth. "There's always that possibility."

"So where can we be safe?"

Jason shook his head firmly at Connor.

"Not here, as soon as we stock up we'll head through that door to your left and try and head back to the surface."

Connor shrugged and brushed his black hair back. "It doesn't matter, there's nowhere else, there's nowhere else safe, death is all around this group, I've seen it, you've seen it, there's nowhere else to be safe, there's nowhere else."

A silence came between them as the idea that the end of Olympia might be coming to pass. Jason was not amused with the talk of death. "You're scaring everybody, Connor."

"I'm telling the truth, I can see death, I saw it with my dad and he died, I saw it over my aunt and she died too, I see it everywhere, in this room…over you."

"ENOUGH!" shouted Jason.

"WE SIMPLY DON'T HAVE ENOUGH TIME FOR THIS 'DEATH TALK', DO YOU UNDERSTAND, CONNOR? WE'RE SCARED ENOUGH AS IT IS."

"But—"

"I said enough! Now let's go through that door and get out of here."

Connor nodded numbly as the others took food from the canteen and watched as Tero and Norton cautiously tried the big grey door at the other side of the room and walked through. Mitchy held the hands of Echo and Gemma and followed with Odysseus. Aphrodite hung back and grabbed Connor's arm as he walked past and whispered, "Listen you freak, I don't care about those other clowns, but if you see can death as you say you can what do see for me?"

"Forget it," Connor said distractedly. "It doesn't work like that, I can't just turn it on and off like a tap, when I concentrate hard and focus on someone then I can see the death spirit."

"Spare me the melodramatics you repugnant insect, just spill the beans and tell me if I'm next."

"I don't know if I can."

Aphrodite snapped forward like a hawk and held Connor closer. "I know you like me, I can feel it, your hormones chatter like monkeys on a hotplate whenever I'm close, so just tell me whose next, and maybe I'll let your grubby little hands—"

"Drop dead, Aphrodite."

"When? That's all I'm asking!"

"I DON'T KNOW!"

Aphrodite stood there glaring at Connor until Jason's faint voice from down the new corridor stirred them. "Is everything ok back there? What's the hold up?"

Connor shook himself free and looked back at Aphrodite, still drawn to her powerful blue eyes. They answered simultaneously. "WE'RE FINE."

"One last thing," Aphrodite hissed.

"What about Jason? What's in store for him? You said you saw death 'over him', is he going to die?"

Connor stayed silent. Hovering menacingly around him, Aphrodite waited for a response. "Well?"

She clicked her fingers snapping Connor from his daze and he answered, "A little bit."

4. Shapes and Ladders

Melissa and Ares rushed through the corridors of Dillon's tooth, a long passage way in the Messiah's Complex – named Dillon's tooth as it curved near the end, resembling a tooth which the family cat lost years ago – the two dodging the remaining staff still on Big Man's books. Stopping at an office junction, Melissa shook her head in exasperation. "Where could he be?"

Ares looked awkwardly up and down the office blocks. "Well he's not here, we've tried everywhere."

Melissa adjusted her shades. "We didn't try his meeting room, he could be in there. In fact I know that's where he'll be."

"How do you know he'll be there?"

Melissa answered him impatiently. "Think about it, your Dad is broke and hasn't had a decent meeting with any clients in years."

"So?"

"So chances are he'll be still sitting in his chair reminiscing about the good old days and waiting for the phone to ring."

Ares nodded assertively, "Ok let's go."

As the two backtracked and turned around, Melissa turned to Ares. "Those things out there, they're not down to you are they?"

Ares shook his head, pressing his lips tightly as he ran. "I don't know what you mean?"

"You know *exactly* what I mean," she snapped back. "You spend ages in your lab day in and day out, I've seen what you can do down there, are you sure your father didn't ask you to do this? A new game maybe?"

Ares pointed to the left, his head still down. "Up here."

"I know. I *do* live here you know."

The tone in her voice made him look up. "There is some stuff you know should stay hidden."

Melissa swung her arm in front of Ares to stop him.

"HEY WHAT ARE YOU DOING? WE HAVE TO FIND DAD."

"NOT UNTIL YOU TELL ME ABOUT WHAT'S REALLY GOING ON. WHAT DID YOU DO TO THOSE PEOPLE OUT THERE? AND WHO IS ATHENA?"

She steadied her head tie as Ares slowly lowered her hand from his chest. "You still won't drop that Athena conversation?"

"No."

Ares cleared his throat. "I still think you're coming down with something." He paused to flick his hair back from his face. "Please listen carefully, I really need you to listen to me, I don't know who Athena is." Again he placed his hand on her forehead. "You really sure you're not coming down with a cold?"

Melissa pulled back and rubbed her face remembering to keep her shades in place, shaking her head at the bizarreness of it all.

Ares's mouth twisted slightly. "Do you really think if I had anything to do with this, I'd endanger my own sisters? Father too?"

"I guess not."

"Good."

Ares dropped his voice even more and spoke so quietly that only Melissa could hear away from the passing office staff, his voice as fragile as a baby bird. "Look, I know this isn't probably the right time to ask you this and stop me if you think it's a little inappropriate, but once all this dies down, do you think maybe you and me can go out for a drink or something?"

Melissa's voice dropped. "Excuse me?"

"I said would you like to—"

"Sorry, I heard what you said, I just can't believe it. Did you seriously just ask me out? After what we've just seen on that screen, after what's happening outside now as we speak?" Ares shrugged. "I think your timing is somewhat out," Melissa said.

They both carried on down the corridor again, walking not running, Ares didn't respond. "I said I think your timing—"

"I heard what you said! I just..." He made a strangled noise. "It's just that I like you, I like you a lot, ever since you came to work for my dad I've fancied you like crazy. You're funny, clever and I like the way how you never take off your shades, even indoors, you smell nice."

"Little creepy..."

"I mean you just have this thing about you which I like."

Melissa grunted her reply, her expression tense behind the same shades Ares liked. "I don't think it would be a good idea, especially as I work for your dad."

"WHOA, WHOA, WHOA." He grabbed her arm and blocked her path, staring at her for a moment. "Don't you start getting a conscience now, so you work for my dad, so what? You know what he has done and what he can do, you were with him throughout the whole 'Game Show' business years ago, you saw what he did with those kids, giving them superpowers and throwing them into the games for entertainment? And you won't go out with me because it may make your job awkward?" Ares's voice rose as he became more agitated. "You think you know everything, right? You won't go out with me for what I guess is respect for my dad right? Well tell me this did you know what my dad made me do for my work experience? I wasn't working at a garage or hairdressers, no he made me work on a serum, he didn't tell me what it was for, in all honesty I don't think even *he* knew exactly what would happen. But it was the main nightclub serum, some went into other school showers but this was the daddy, the one that gave all those kids special powers? Well I helped on that."

Melissa had no problem in conveying her anger. "So you were responsible for giving kids superpowers and those people who died in Gommerstall? I don't know how you sleep at night."

"In a bed on my own, as usual."

"A sense of humour, eh? Well looking at those creatures out there I think you're going to need it."

"You think I like doing what I do? Taking orders for my dad?"

"Well move out then, it's not difficult, besides how old are you anyway? It's quite sad you still living at home at your age." Ares blinked and looked down embarrassed as Melissa sighed. "Sorry, didn't mean anything by that, it's been a while since I spent any time around anybody who wasn't intimated by..." She paused before finishing off her confession. "My appearance."

"What do you mean?"

"My shades, my hair constantly under wraps, the dark clothes, it can put people off."

Ares relaxed a little. "Didn't you just hear what I said about why I liked you? Your shades are very cool."

"What did you say?"

Ares adjusted his glasses nervously. "I meant your shades and head scarf, why not take them off?"

"I can't, not yet."

"Why are they covered?"

"Long story."

For the second time today Ares tried to remove Melissa's glasses, he went to grab them but Melissa stood firm and then faked it like she was playing 'Dodge ball', trying to dive around him to the right, then running to left darting past him.

"HEY YOU!" He grabbed her waist and spun her around. "WHAT ARE YOU DOING?" she yelled.

"I don't know…I'm sorry, I'm just…" He smiled faintly. "I'm just having fun I guess, I haven't done that before, so are we cool now?"

Ares released her gently as Melissa twitched her sensitive nostrils and eyed him up suspiciously.

"Yeah we're cool, so is that important to you? Having fun?"

"Living with Big Man should be fun and it was before Mum walked out on us, but after that and the collapse of the Game Show series he became a little too much to live with, he's constantly looking for the next big break to get himself back into the public eye, but I guess that's not going to happen now thanks to the bounty on his head."

Melissa nodded slowly. "I mean you've moved in now so you must have noticed the change in him now surely?"

"Yeah, he's quite forgetful isn't he? I have noticed that definitely...oh shoot."

"What?"

"Your dad had an appointment with the opticians today, I was just wondering if he went, I stuck a note in his pocket to remind him."

Ares laughed and ran his fingers through his thick hair and mimicked Melissa's earlier statement. "Why are you worrying? After everything we've seen on the screen?"

Melissa snorted and shrugged. "I'm his PA, it's my job to worry."

"You like my dad don't you?

She smiled meekly. "Of course I do, I wouldn't be his PA if I didn't like him would I?" Ares stared into the distance sadly, which Melissa quickly noticed. "Not like that silly! No he's extremely arrogant and pig-headed but he can be cool sometimes."

"Do you like that in a man?"

"Sometimes, I guess all girls do in a way, they like a 'bad boy'."

Ares looked at her with a broken face, trying hard to be pleasant.

"But don't you go changing Ares, you're my friend, I can always rely on you."

"Yeah, good old dependable Ares, everybody's friend, couldn't hurt a fly."

Melissa smiled, not knowing how much her words had hurt him. He shook his head without looking at her and spoke looking to the ceiling.

"How were you going to get him out of the building?"

"The optician was coming here, don't worry, we had him checked out."

They suddenly came to a halt the corridor terminating into what appeared to be a pair of massive iron doors, there was loud sound coming from inside and the strains of someone rapping to Hip Hop music.

"Yeah he's here, maybe we should have checked here first."

Melissa nodded wildly. "I guess it would have made sense really."

She placed her ear to the door as the sounds of music blared through. "It's quite loud isn't it?"

Ares turned to his companion as he turned the door handle. "Big Man never does anything by halves, he's madder than a snake who married a hosepipe." He winced as the deafening music hit hard as the door opened.

Big Man had gone back to his main office and opted to listen to his rap music without the earphones this time, the speaker was belting Hip Hop tunes down the large corridors.

Melissa's eyes squinted uncomfortably beneath her shades and she put her hands over her ears. Huge speakers hung from the ceiling pumping out sounds and lyrics that Ares neither liked nor understood. Upon the huge board table danced Big Man; his eyes were shut and his hips wriggled out of time with the music, he pushed his arms up in the air in a 'raise the roof' motion. He then began to walk in a stumbling jerking motion mirroring the creatures outside, shouting the words to the song. Ares cupped his hands to his mouth.

"DAD! TURN IT DOWN! IT'S TOO LOUD!"

Big Man danced on oblivious to the visitors in his room.

"DAD! THE GIRLS ARE STILL MISSING! TURN IT DOWN."

Big Man finally acknowledged another presence in the room and flicked open an eye.

"YEEHH BOOYYYEEE! ARES, THE LITTLE CHICKEN SHIT IS IN THE HIZZLE!"

Ares turned confused to Melissa. "It means house," she said, removing her hands from her ears as keeping them there wasn't doing any benefit from keeping out the noise.

"BIG UP BIG UP!! THIS IS HOW I ROLL LIKE A GANGSTA G!"

Ares leaned forward shouting, "DAD, WHAT ARE YOU TALKING ABOUT? TURN THE MUSIC DOWN PLEASE?"

Big Man ignored his son's pleas and continued to gyrate on the table. "COME ON BOYS AND LET YA LIL PUNK ASS, ROLL WITH DA CRAZY RHYMES!"

Melissa's eyes narrowed. "WHAT ON EARTH IS HE TALKING ABOUT?"

An utterly flabbergasted Ares threw his hands up in the air before commenting in disbelief. "I HAVEN'T A CLUE WHAT'S GOING ON."

The former game show boss jumped down from the table and slumped into the master chair, then suddenly he paused and stared at Melissa in disbelief, he held the image of her for just a split second before leaping to his feet and pointing wildly. "PROTESTER! PROTESTER! ARES, GET AWAY FROM HIM! A PROTESTER HAS BROKEN IN!"

Big Man flung his back against his chair, flipping back a secret panel on the chair's arm, revealing some buttons as the Hip Hop blared away. He pressed one of them and suddenly the floor beneath Melissa disappeared and she fell through a trapdoor.

"BOOYAH! THAT'S WHAT I'M TALKING ABOUT!"

Ares screamed at his dad. "WHAT HAVE YOU DONE? WHAT HAVE YOU DONE?" He leapt on to the table and flew into his dad. "TURN OFF THE MUSIC! TURN OFF THE MUSIC."

Big Man jumped startled and strained his eyes hard to make out his son stooped on the edge of the table.

"ARES? WHAT THE F—"

"TURN THE MUSIC OFF!"

Taking umbrage, Big Man hit another switch in the same secret chair compartment and the music finally ended.

"WHAT ARE YOU DOING?" Ares's eyes were wild and pointed to the flapping trapdoor hinge.

A huge grin emerged on his father's face and he started to rock and sway, the sounds of the music still playing in his head. "Got rid of that punk arse protester, thought he could sneak up on me and take me in? No way man! So I dropped him."

"THAT WASN'T A PROTESTER! THE PROTEST-ERS ARE OUTSIDE!"

Ares swung his father's chair round and hauled him from the seat, dragging him to the main window pointing towards the streets below.

"LOOK OUTSIDE, THE PROTESTERS ARE DOWN THERE! NOBODY IS INSIDE!"

The two men barely flinched as a sniper from the building opposite took a shot and the bullet bounced off the toughened glass."

"Ok, well if it wasn't a protester, who did I drop through the trapdoor?"

"YOU DROPPED MELISSA THROUGH THERE!" Ares spluttered.

"I DID WHAT? NO WAY MAN!"

Incensed with rage Ares grabbed his father by his shirt and began to shake him. "WHERE DID YOU DROP HER? TELL ME!"

Confusion and uncertainty had entered Big Man's voice. "She's in my shark tank, I've got a giant panther shark down there, I thought if anybody breaks in to try and take me away for arrest or that bounty on my head, they'll make a meal for my pet shark."

"WHY WOULD YOU KEEP A SHARK IN YOUR TOWER? ARE YOU INSANE?"

Big Man sighed heavily. "My gun licence ran out."

"I'M SERIOUS, DAD!"

"I haven't left this building in years, I'm bored shitless so it was that or start knitting."

Looking away from his father in disgust he found himself drawn to the hole in the floor.

"DIDN'T YOU SEE IT WAS MELISSA?"

Big Man sat back down and shuffled uncomfortably, he couldn't look Ares in the eye and looked to the floor like a naughty child under interrogation from their head teacher. "I really thought it was a protester you know."

Ares growled hoarsely. "HOW COULD YOU THINK THAT? COULD YOU NOT SEE HER?" Then it suddenly dawned on Ares. "Shit, your glasses."

"Excuse me?"

Ares's voice rose again. "YOUR GLASSES! DID YOU NOT SEE THE OPTICIANS TODAY? YOU

WERE MEANT TO GET SOME NEW GLASSES! MELISSA LEFT YOU A NOTE IN YOUR JACKET!"

Big Man stood up and put both hands in his jacket pocket the left hand pulled out a crumpled piece of paper and he struggled to read it. "I can't read a thing without my glasses."

Ares angrily snatched it from him and proceded to read it aloud, what he saw was not encouraging.

"Yeah, it's Melissa's handwriting, it says; *Big Man, don't forget your appointment later with the opticians, please don't forget as you could end up hurting somebody with your bad eyesight lol!*"

Big Man took the note from Ares and put it back in his pocket; he stared at his son who was breathing heavily and panicking and then he looked hard at the trapdoor.

"Irony eh?...gotta love it."

"WHAT?" Aphrodite's face turned passive. "What did you mean by that?"

Before Connor could reply, an ear-splitting howl came from the direction of the others. Leaving the well-lit canteen, Aphrodite and Connor ran through the door and followed the voices of the group into the dark, the pair turned through three corridors until they finally reached them. They stood peering into a large open doorway.

"What have you done now?" a bored Aphrodite asked.

Gemma replied with grave concern, "Tero took a step through this door and fell down." Aphrodite allowed herself a chuckle. Norton strained his neck towards the hole. "I think we found the service lift, it must take the sewage workers to and from the top."

Echo piped up excitedly, "So we can get out of there then?"

Norton nodded slowly but seemed preoccupied. "Yeah hopefully." He cupped his hands to the side of his cheeks to amplify his shout below. "HELLO? TERO CAN YOU HEAR ME?"

A slight groan was heard from the darkness below. "Yes I'm ok, I fell on my ankle."

Jason shouted down too. "Well sit tight and we'll have you out soon." Another groan was heard from the pit. "What did you say, Tero?"

"That wasn't me, I didn't say anything." A moment of fear hit Tero in an instant. "I don't think I'm alone down here."

Jason reacted the quickest. "Quick! Has someone got a mobile still working?"

Aphrodite shook her head. "Lost mine."

Echo offered her phone. "There's no signal though."

"No I just need the camera."

Jason fiddled with the phone, it was similar to his own and he was familiar with the device. He called down again. "TERO, HOLD ON!"

He pressed the camera flash and the lift shaft was illuminated with a brilliant light, it was brief but enough for a horrified Jason feel his guts shift. As the light faded Tero noticed what Jason had seen – shapes approaching his side. It was the changed, zombie-like humans and the smell of death hit him. "Oh good lord."

Jason screamed. "TERO!!!"

Tero slipped onto the floor in a panic, crawling on his hands and knees trying to stand up. "FOR GOD'S SAKE GET ME OUT OF HERE!"

Jason tried to reach down in vain. "GRAB MY HAND! REACH MAN! REACH!"

But it was too late, the creatures were upon him and began to tear him apart. Tero died quietly, never making a sound as he was eaten alive, taking the dignity he kept throughout his life to his premature grave.

Echo threw up into lift shaft, what was left in her stomach came out and landed on the remains of Tero, making her retch even more, she fell backwards and rolled around into a ball screaming in terror.

Norton shook Jason who stood transfixed at the mouth of the lift shaft. The creatures in the pit had finished sifting through the remains of Tero's body and could smell the new blood presence of the group looking down on them, they ambled towards the lift shaft wall and tried to make their way up.

The first wave fell to the floor after scraping off their fingernails on the cold metal of the elevator shaft but as they fell, more climbed on top of them making an unhuman, ant-like ladder.

"THEY'RE CLIMBING OUT!" Norton yelled.

He picked Echo from off the floor and fled further down the corridor. Jason's head spun around at the departing others, his eyes still wide with shock, he called to the remaining girls, his voice choked with emotion. "COME ON, WE'RE LEAVING!"

Mitchy held Gemma's hand and led her away from the shaft followed by Aphrodite. "Do you have any idea where we're going?"

"Just follow Norton, Aphrodite," Jason said. "We're running up, not down, so we're heading in the right direction."

They swung left and right running unspeaking up the winding corridors until Norton pulled up out of breath, the air had thickened and there was a stench of decay behind them.

"I don't know where we're going, don't follow me, I'm lost, I don't know how to get out of here."

Jason caught up with him as Norton was bent over, wheezing.

"Any ideas mate? coughed Norton.

"Over there," Jason said breathlessly. "That ladder to the left. It must lead to a manhole."

"Must?"

"*Might* lead to a manhole," Jason corrected himself. "We're running out of options here and..." Jason paused for a moment to wipe his brow before shouting back, "MITCHY, WHAT'S IT LIKE BACK THERE?"

Peering from behind a wall Mitchy snuck a peek. "Shush! Shush! Shush! I hear something."

The slight wind in the tunnel shifted and Mitchy caught a smell of their scent a moment of nausea followed, her eyes had adjusted to the darkness and she could see the shapes lumbering towards her. "Oh God! They're coming! THEY'RE COMING!"

Jason saw what Mitchy was looking at and stared fascinated down the corridor at the approaching horror – these creatures were moving faster than before, adapting somehow and it intrigued Jason how their speed had improved from the lumbering beasts in the morning that the group had come across. "JASON!" Mitchy yelled, suddenly angry. "WE HAVE TO GET OUT OF HERE NOW!"

Jason arched his shoulders and suddenly became business-like and relaxed.

"Up the manhole now, everybody, quickly!"

Standing aside he let the women run past him and watched as Gemma reached for the first available rung on the ladder, she checked to see if her backpack was secure and whispered to her spider. "Hold tight baby, we're leaving." Gemma clambered up the ladder swiftly followed by Echo and Mitchy. Aphrodite stared at her and flicked her head back to Jason.

"Is she going to fit through there?"

"Now isn't the right time, now get up the ladder!"

Aphrodite blinked softly and saw nothing but the desperation in his eyes, saying nothing more she made her way up the ladder.

Connor and Odysseus were next, followed by the very quiet Quinn. Jason frantically beckoned to the last person with him. "NORTON, GO!"

Norton nervously nodded and hauled himself up the ladder as Jason watched him move up and then looked down the corridor to see the creatures heading towards him.

Zombies? Are they zombies? What the hell are they? Zombies are in films he thought. Still they were approaching fast and Jason finally headed up the ladder.

The air re-circulators built into the walls around the ladders, dotted around the sewage works had motion sensors. Whenever a figure passed them they would emit a blast of cold air.

Everybody moving up the ladder felt a shot of re-circulated air in their faces. Jason was the last to have a hit of air blast him in his face and it felt so good, for a moment almost making him forget about his pursuers and craving the true fresh air at the top of the ladder even more. "KEEP MOVING! KEEP CLIMBING!" Jason yelled, remembering the situation.

Each member of the collective had different styles to work their way up the ladder, some were frantic whilst others had a cool, calm method to climb the ladder. Gemma climbed to a dead end as the ladder reached the manhole. Her arms pushed hard against the cold dirty underside of the manhole cover. "IT'S NOT MOVING! IT WON'T BUDGE!"

Echo right behind her tried to wriggle between Gemma and the wall around them, she just about squeezed through and tried to push through with her, both hands tried in vain to move the cover.

Echo shuddered and the hysterical fear which had gripped her earlier returned. "WE CAN'T GET OUT! WE CAN'T GET OUT! OH GOD NO!"

The two teenage friends squirmed together on the narrow ladder attempting feebly to move the cover. Echo sobbed pitifully and the strength in her arms began to weaken. "CAN SOMEBODY HELP OUT THERE? PLEASE OPEN THE COVER!"

Gemma eased herself past Echo, down a few more rungs and breathed hard. "Nobody's coming, nobody can hear us."

Aphrodite was a slow climber and had just crawled behind Mitchy and could hear her sister.

"What have you done now?"

Gemma didn't even look down to Aphrodite and merely answered, "The manhole cover is stuck, we can't get out."

Aphrodite sighed and looked at her dirty outfit. "My god, I didn't realise how much of a blimp I look in this dress, you should start calling me Mitchy soon."

Echo spat in anger. "MY GOD ARE YOU FOR REAL? WE CAN'T GET OUT AND THOSE THINGS ARE BEHIND US AND YOU'RE WORRIED ABOUT YOUR DRESS?"

Gemma sighed at her dispassionate sister. "You get used to after a while, Echo."

"It cost an arm and a leg, darling," scowled Aphrodite.

Jason shouted up from below. "WHAT'S GOING ON UP THERE?"

"WE CAN'T GET OUT," Gemma shouted back. "WE'RE NOT STRONG ENOUGH TO MOVE THE MANHOLE COVER."

Norton's panicked voice was next to speak. "Are you sure?"

"NO, NORTON! WE'RE HANGING AROUND HERE 'CAUSE WE'RE BORED TO DEATH OF LIVING!" screamed Echo.

Jason felt a lump of desperation surface in his throat and he gulped hard to keep it down.

What have I done? Jason wanted to protect the girls and wanted them in front of the group and the men climbing behind, but he didn't bank on the girls not being able to lift the manhole cover, Echo's yelling made him think even more. "WHAT ARE WE GOING TO DO?!"

And then her pleas were cut off from the sounds of moaning at the foot of the ladder.

"THEY'RE HERE! THEY'RE AT THE BOTTOM," yelled Norton.

"Can you squeeze past the girls to reach the manhole, Norton?"

"I can't get to Gemma and Echo past Mitchy, there's not enough room on the ladder." Norton scratched at his ear. "No offence, Mitchy."

"None taken honey."

"Shit," Jason whispered, and then shouted out, "THEN WE HAVE TO GO BACK DOWN THE LADDER."

"ARE YOU CRAZY? I'M NOT GOING BACK DOWN THERE WITH THOSE THINGS AROUND!"

"We don't have a choice Echo, you can't move the manhole and nobody can squeeze past you, we have to go back down and switch with me, Norton or Odysseus."

"Who's Odysseus?" asked Aphrodite.

"I'm right behind you missy," he glared at her sharply. I've been with you guys all the time.

She stared blankly at him. "Charmed I'm sure."

Odysseus adjusted his grip. "Don't worry nobody remembers me, I'm used to it."

Aphrodite held her stare. "I wasn't apologising."

Jason quickly made a move down the steps, he'd thought about jumping but it was too high and the walls were too narrow; falling between them would kill him. "EVERYBODY MOVE DOWN THE STEPS NOW!" Jason's voice was growing weaker and hoarse but the others understood. One by one they slowly moved down the ladder, Jason seemed nervous and he *was* nervous – somehow he'd been made the leader of this group and now his *flock* needed him most.

"WE CLIMB DOWN QUICKLY AND SECURELY WHEN WE GET TO THE BOTTOM, WE SWAP OVER WOMEN FOR MEN AND WE'LL SEE IF WE CAN GET THAT COVER OPEN!"

Mitchy pitched in. "What about those things at the bottom? How are we going to deal with them?"

"Let me deal with those, let's just get you swapped over and let Norton, Quinn or Odysseus try and get the hatch open and quickly, we haven't got much time.

The whole group slowly made their way cautiously down, they could hear the groans of the killer humans at the foot of the ladder.

Jason looked down and saw these changed humans huddled around the foot of the ladder, they looked so small and insignificant from his viewpoint but he knew how dangerous they were, it would be him who would have to go through them first.

The smell was overwhelming, a mixture of decaying flesh and dry sweat hit Jason as he made his way down the ladder, he could hear their feet shuffling along the ground some faster than others which concerned him. He moved lower and the stench was disgusting, each step his foot touched downwards made his heart beat faster, the adrenaline raced through his body knowing that he had to storm through this bunch of shuffling monsters in order to keep his group safe.

Oh God, there's so many of them.

Jason hesitated for just a second, wiping away a trickle of sweat from his forehead, taking one last look up the ladder, he let go and fell straight into the circle of changed human killers.

He was up in a flash and pushed the nearest ghoul-like creature to the floor. A knee to the groin took down the next one.

"GET DOWN THE LADDER NOW!" Jason screamed.

The stench was very powerful and made Jason reel away in revulsion slamming up against the damp wall.

Norton was next to drop to the fall and stumbled upon landing, a creature made a move on him immediately, he rolled out the way as they stumbled forward tripping over the body of the two Jason had felled, twisting and turning on the floor like an unearthed worm there was nowhere else to turn as the creature earlier kneed in the groin by Jason flipped over and crawled on all fours towards Norton. He backed away like a crab scuttling, there was a pleading on his face and he shook his head in fear as the creature was quickly upon him. Norton put his hand out and grabbed the creature by the throat as the dried blood around the monster's mouth moved closer, Norton was terrified, knowing in the next few seconds he was going to die.

Jason didn't wait as long as the creature, he grabbed a metal bar which lay at his feet and pushed past more creatures and stood behind the monstrosity atop of Norton. Without making a sound he lifted the bar high above his head and swung hard, his eyes never leaving Norton's as the bar crashed against the creature and it's body flopped forward, pinning Norton to the floor.

"SWITCH! SWITCH! SWITCH!" Jason snapped.

"LET US DOWN"! Echo implored.

Odysseus was next to land on the floor and frantically began looking for a weapon. "SHIT! NOTHING HERE!"

"KEEP LOOKING!" Jason yelled.

He neatly sidestepped a creature and unleashed a powerful uppercut, sending it sprawling into a crowd of others, he called to Odysseus.

"Take the bar, I'll use these," he said, holding up his fists in defiance to these foul beings. He tossed the bar over and Odysseus caught it and began swinging wildly at the creatures. Norton scrambled to his feet and began helping the girls down from the ladder.

Aphrodite clambered down the last rungs as a creature took a swipe at her, it missed its target and fell clumsily to the floor.

"Amateur," Aphrodite snorted as she stepped over the fallen creature, Norton gave another creature an almighty shove and it clattered into another.

The smell of decaying flesh made it difficult to breathe in the cramped space and Aphrodite put her hand to her mouth to stifle it.

"DON'T YOU DARE MOVE, BITCH," came a stern shout behind her. Aphrodite put up her hands in surrender at the gruff tone of Mitchy's voice.

"Look if it's about those *fat* gags—"

"I SAID DON'T MOVE!" the metal bar was swung with power and it cracked a vicious young girl on the face. Black liquid vomited from the hole in her head and she fell to the ground. A shocked Aphrodite looked at the body of a teenage girl behind her. Mitchy stood holding another metal bar.

"Knew you were talking about her," Aphrodite snorted.

"But of course you did, sugar," Mitchy's grin was broad.

Gemma and Connor ran and dodged the creatures like frightened kittens. "We could really do with some guns round about now."

"NO!" Gemma scolded him. "Guns are bad, we don't need them, we just have to swap now and get up that ladder."

"There's too many of them," hissed Connor.

"Then we move now! Jason, you ready to go?"

Both Jason and Connor were surprised by Gemma's calmness under fire. Jason waved his metal bar over his head and swung hard as it slammed against the skull of a man with an ill-fitting hairpiece. The creature hit the ground and stayed still, the wig lay by his side.

"NORTON, TAKE ODYSSEUS AND CONNOR AND FORCE THAT MANHOLE COVER OPEN, MITCHY YOU FOLLOW GEMMA AND ECHO AND YOU WATCH THEM, APHRODITE YOU STAY WITH ME AND QUINN."

Aphrodite flung her hands up in annoyance.

"Who *are* these people you're talking about?"

A streak of frustration zipped through Jason's mind. "He's standing right behind you."

Aphrodite's eyes flashed open wide genuinely shocked, she pointed at him and whispered to Jason. "That guy there is with us? Seriously? I thought he was one of those things."

She turned to Quinn. "Would it kill you to wear a shirt from this century? And look at the state of it? It's like you ironed it with a hammer."

Norton knocked a couple more down to the ground and frantically beckoned to Odysseus. "You coming?"

Odysseus glanced at him. "A little help here?"

Norton turned to see some of the creatures had broken away from the main group and had now begun to stumble towards Odysseus.

"Dammit!" Norton hissed.

He eyed up the assorted creatures ambling towards him, there was a traffic warden with his usual blue uniform caked in blood, he was missing his left arm at the shoulder and a knob of bone poked through followed by a man in a waiter's uniform with swollen bloody cheeks carrying a serving tray, there was a hole in his stomach and his entrails spilled out on to the dish which he carried diligently. Norton bought up the bar and was about to swing at the warden's head. He heard the unmistakable sounds of gunshots instead.

The warden fell to the ground, followed by the waiter and also a little girl who had begun to run at him.

Norton turned to see Odysseus breathing heavy with an old fashion pistol in his hands. It wasn't a laser pistol, as they were outlawed, it was a double cartridge old style renegade pistol.

Odysseus caught his breath. "I bloody can't stand traffic wardens."

The stench of the dead filled the air making it hard to draw breath but Norton had enough energy to scream at Odysseus. "YOU HAD THAT GUN WITH YOU ALL THE TIME? WELL WHY DIDN'T YOU USE IT WHEN WE NEEDED IT?"

Odysseus stared at him nonchalantly. "Forgot I had it in my bag."

"WHAT DO YOU MEAN YOU FORGOT YOU HAD IT? IT'S A BLOODY GUN, LOOK AROUND YOU STUPID IDIOT!"

"Watch you tongue with me Norton or I'll wind up using this gun on you."

"Anytime."

Jason yelled at the pair. "GET UP THE LADDER NOW! We'll deal with this later if we survive."

Norton hesitated making Jason yell again. "MOVE IT!"

Norton snapped out from his distain for Odysseus and made his way to the ladder, confidently shoving hard to the ground any killer creature in his way. He was unable to carry his metal bar up the ladder needing both hands to climb so he reluctantly let it fall by his side and keeping his head up he began to make his way up to the manhole. Norton climbed a few rungs when he felt a slight tug on his left leg, he looked down and saw a creature clinging to his ankle.

"GET OFF ME!" he yelled.

Norton for the first time began to panic and kicked out violently, the creature reeled back with a smashed nose and slipped down a couple of rungs on the ladder, it managed to hold on and regain its slow pursuit.

Then suddenly a shot rung out and a slender hole appeared in the creature's forehead, black slime begun to trickle out before it lost its grip and tumbled down the ladder. Norton turned to see his savoir, but the gunfire immediately gave it away.

Odysseus threw the remains of the infected person from off the ladder and to the ground below.

He glanced up at the shaky figure of Norton and beamed. "You kick and scream like a girl." Norton didn't even thank him, just climbed higher.

Connor managed to dodge the creatures after him and scrambled up behind them. Jason shook his head and focused on the inhuman girl who was blocking the path for Gemma and Mitchy to the ladder. With a swift blow to her head knocked her down; he was still unsure about striking a woman, even if she did appear to be the walking dead. "APHRODITE, MOVE IT!" he yelled.

"I'm not your slave," she reprimanded him.

"NO, YOU'RE AN ANNOYING, SPOILT FREE-LOADING WASTE OF SPACE, NOW MOVE!"

Aphrodite shrugged. "Can't argue with that darling, not yet anyway."

Aphrodite watched as Mitchy made her way up, following Gemma and pulled a face as the woman's large frame struggled up the ladder. "I'm following that? Again? I mean seriously?"

The look from Jason was more than enough to make her begrudgingly move up the ladder. Quinn signalled to Jason himself to get on the rung himself. Nodding, Jason went for the ladder as Quinn charged at the creatures beginning to crowd around it. He cursed under his breath as more and more of these creatures entered the tunnel. Quinn waited for his chance and knocked them out of the way dashing up the ladder himself, eagerly following Jason.

Everyone now was climbing to the manhole, Quinn nervously looked over his shoulder. "Oh god," he whispered. He saw and heard them behind him, the creatures were grabbing at the ladder rungs and were hauling themselves up, not using their legs only their arms with enormous strength.

He opened his mouth to speak but couldn't. Fear was finally beginning to grip him. Composing himself he whispered again. "They're climbing." Nobody heard. Quinn looked down and then up again and yelled, "THEY'RE CLIMBING, THEY'RE CLIMBING!"

Jason looked down the ladder expressionless. "Shit," he mouthed silently.

5. SPIDER SENSE

"BRING HER BACK! BRING HER BACK!" yelled Ares.

A confused Big Man swung his head round to see a pained expression on his son's face.

"WHERE IS SHE? WHAT HAVE YOU DONE WITH HER?"

Big Man still in his own kind of dazed horror fumbled at the controls on his chair.

"I think this is the right button, can't really see."

He pressed it and the great wall on the left hand side of the room began to rumble and then hum as a huge flat screen slowly lowered down into view. The TV flickered into life just as the image of Melissa appeared on screen. She was sliding down through a perspex tube and the two men just caught her splashing into a large indoor reservoir.

"GET HER OUT DAD, NOW!"

Big Man pressed repeatedly at the control panel. "It's not working, I can't stop it!"

"YOU BLOODY IDIOT!" Ares screamed.

His dad's voice dropped intentionally and cleared his throat. "I think you better turn away, son."

"WHAT? WHAT DO YOU MEAN?"

Melissa bobbed to the surface and splashed around frantically. The cameras focused in on her distress. Then there was a grating sound from beneath the water as a huge door started to open. Melissa trod water, she was moving slowly, deliberately, using both hands to stay afloat silent and waiting. Then from out of the passageway swam a monster of a shark. It had a huge misshapen snout and its teeth were so large that they looked out of proportion from the rest of its body – it was a giant panther shark, a gigantic killing machine of a creature.

Ares froze in place as Big Man looked on. "Any ideas, son?"

Snapping out from his trance Ares looked at the still open trapdoor in the conference room. "No, I don't know what to do."

Running over to the hatch, Ares attempted to dive through, but he slipped on his long lab coat, propelled himself through the air and came crashing down to the ground with a sickening thud as his head hit the floor. He shook his head and picked himself up from the office floor, his head hurt and he stumbled to the TV screen instead.

Melissa caught the sight of the shark's giant dorsal fin cutting through the water towards her and she panicked and her arms started flailing.

Ares ran to the TV and pressed his hands to the screen; he stared at the image of Melissa struggling in the water as the killer shark bore down on her, his eyes fixed unmoving, the gesture did not go unnoticed. She looked at the camera and saw the image of Ares standing motionless in front of the TV. And then the screen started to disappear, frustrated and angry in equal measure, he turned to see Big Man with his finger on the remote making the TV retract back up to the ceiling, shaking his head forlornly.

The shark dropped deeper and Melissa was caught out by the deadly speed and efficiency of the giant fish and with a quick flip of its tail it had pulled her under.

"NO!" screamed Ares.

Melissa bobbed up again gasping for air and splashing in fear, the screen had all but disappeared and Ares just had time to see Melissa's shades slip and the shark knock her up into the air like being struck by a lorry. As she came down the shark locked its jaws around her torso and pulled her under, blood gushed up like a fountain spraying Melissa a smooth red.

Then the TV screen turned itself off.

Aphrodite looked at the climbers with open curiosity, while Echo regained her composure and pulled herself up faster, Mitchy huffed and struggled, Connor didn't look down, just straight up ignoring the shouts of the others.

"FASTER! FASTER!" Quinn implored.

A creature woman wearing a yellow dress stained with blood groped at his leg, she had been very attractive with fashion model features but Quinn kicked at her face repeatedly so if there was a turnaround to this epidemic and world changed back, her modelling dreams would be over after Quinn was through with her.

Gemma leaned back to hear Quinn shouting. As she did the fastening on her backpack slowly came loose. Mitchy noticed the straps beginning to go. "Gemma, your bag!" But it was too late.

A hairbrush, bikini top, shower gel, conditioner and an apple tumbled from the bag.

Mitchy ducked as the brush flew past her, Aphrodite wasn't so lucky and was hit square in the face. She raised her hand to protect herself from the apple which bounced off her wrist. "WHAT THE BLOODY HELL IS GOING ON?" Aphrodite gazed up the ladder. A swipe card also fell out of the bag and Mitchy managed to catch hold of it. Gemma panicked and wriggled the bag from off her back and tried to slide it down her arm. She caught it with her hand and the jerk made the last remaining thing in her bag fall out.

"NO!" Gemma yelped. Buckby the spider sailed past Mitchy and Aphrodite this time instinctively ducked and looked back as the arachnid fell past Jason, a smooth grin appeared on her face. "Whoopsy daisy."

"BUCKBY! BUCKBY! NO!" Gemma screamed.

The spider had whizzed past the creatures in pursuit and landed on its back at the foot of the ladder. Righting itself, the grey spider scuttled down the tunnel as the horde of creatures rumbled past him oblivious to its presence.

"WE HAVE TO GO BACK FOR HIM!"

Jason cut her off. "HE'S GONE GEMMA, LEAVE IT!"

"NO HE'S NOT!" she snapped.

"We have to keep climbing Gemma, those things are right behind us."

"But my spider..."

"...is gone, Gemma, I'm sorry, I'm really sorry. But we're not turning back for a spider."

"Jason, please?"

"No, we move on."

"Fine then."

For the first time since he met her, Jason detected hostility in the young girl's voice.

Quinn looked down the ladder and up again behind Jason, he struggled to see Gemma but could hear her protests, he cast his eye over the creatures clambering up the ladder behind him. He sucked in his breath, closed his eyes tight and mumbled. "I'll get it."

Jason struggled to hear. "What? What did you say?"

There was a moment of silence as they still kept climbing. "I said I'm going back down to get Gemma's spider."

"Forget about it, Quinn let's just keep going," Jason said.

Norton called down from the top. "CAN SOMEONE TELL ME WHAT'S GOING ON DOWN THERE?"

Jason shouted back up. "GEMMA'S LOST HER SPIDER! QUINN WANTS TO GO BACK AND GET IT."

Norton angrily replied, "LEAVE IT MAN, WE'RE ALMOST AT THE TOP!"

"JUST GET THAT MANHOLE OPEN NORTON!" Quinn shouted.

Norton angrily shouted back, "I'M NOT LETTING YOU COMMIT SUICIDE OVER A SPIDER! LEAVE IT AND COME ON!"

Gemma went quiet as the men argued over her pet. Quinn sighed as he got another earful from Jason, he gave him a steady look and replied, "I've been a coward all my life, too afraid to take chances apparently, well not anymore."

"DAMMIT! QUINN, THIS ISN'T A GAME!" roared Jason.

Quinn steadied himself on the ladder with one hand and wiped the sweat from his brow, muttering under his breath, "If I don't make it straight back, you find my daughter, you find my little nugget Macy, and you tell her that I did it, finally did it and that she was right all along." Quinn coughed hard and looked up the ladder.

"GEMMA!" Quinn shouted to get her attention and then spoke softly. "Wish me luck."

Gemma finally broke her silence. "No, you don't have to…"

Quinn slowly smiled and squinted at the creatures below him. "It's fine."

He began to climb down the ladder staring numbly and without comment. The first creature below him took a few kicks to the head before it fell down the ladder and Quinn repeatedly kicked out at everyone after that who replaced it, descending slowly down the steps, his legs perilously close to being bitten.

"QUINN, WHAT ARE YOU DOING!?" Norton shouted from the manhole cover, which he and Odysseus had now reached.

"LEAVE IT NORTON, HE'S MADE HIS CHOICE."

"BUT JASON? QUINN IS—"

"QUINN HAS MADE HIS CHOICE NORTON, NOW GET THAT COVER OPEN!"

Jason himself now looked down the ladder and Quinn was nowhere to be seen, but he could hear him kicking out which gave him some slight relief. "Let's hope he made the right choice," Jason muttered under his breath.

Quinn was close to the bottom, and below him were half a dozen outstretched arms waiting for him. Kicking hard again he managed to drop off the last rung, carefully sidestepped the bloody creatures gathered around him, he gasped shocked at how many more had now entered the tunnel. "SPIDER! SPIDER! WHERE ARE YOU?"

Dammit, what was the name of that spider again? He silently cursed as he thought he saw the spider scuttling away from him across the ceiling. "COME BACK HERE YOU!"

Picking up one of the fallen metal bars, Quinn swung wildly again at the bloody figures picking up speed in front of him, a quick strike to the head sent the lead creature sprawling to the floor.

The next figure was an old man in overalls hacking up what was left of its insides and spiting blood, it's face was pale and sick in the dim light. Quinn's pupils dilated as the infected man stumbled forward and then suddenly launched itself at him. He sidestepped the old attacker and cuffed him behind the head. "Silly old bastard."

The spider had long gone but the creatures still lumbered forward, making Quinn finally think he'd made a mistake. "FOR GOD'S SAKE WHERE ARE YOU, SPIDER?"

He stared at the drooling shuffling creatures before him and still couldn't digest what he was seeing. "Oh God," he gasped. "Oh my god."

Quinn suddenly began to sneeze uncontrollably which bought tears to his eyes, he didn't know if it was due to his hayfever or the fact that he was terrified of losing his life. Some creatures began to scream as they edged closer to Quinn and he joined them in a chorus of high-pitched panicked shrieks. Looking at their blank lifeless eyes, Quinn stumbled backwards and slipped on a loose piece of rock, dropping his metal bar as he fell. A small child in a horribly blood stained dungaree playsuit, sprang from his infected mother's arms and with terrifying speed nipped along the floor and bit hard into Quinn's leg. The group on the ladder heard him cry out in pain and just for a moment they all stopped climbing and listened. Quinn reached like a mad man for his bar and lashed out at the toddler but missed. The creature was upon him now and twisted its little hand into his side, before Quinn could scream again the child monster clambered up his arm and began scratching and tearing at his face. The stench of the child and its body gagged his chance to scream again and then its bloody milk teeth clamped deep into his neck.

Jason called out.

"QUINN? QUINN? DAMMIT QUINN, ANSWER ME!" The silence was met with groans from most of the people on the ladder. "Oh no, Quinn," whispered Norton. Jason now was the bottom man on the ladder. "No" he sighed. "Ok, let's climb and get the hell out of here."

Aphrodite rotated her head round and stretched. "We would get out darling, if dumb and dumber here could move the manhole cover."

"It's not shifting, missy," spat Odysseus. "Wanna give it a go, your royal bitchness?"

Aphrodite flashed her left hand nails at him in response, which he couldn't see in the dark anyway and shouted back, "Your royal bitchness? You're quite the ladies' man aren't you? What woman could resist your smooth charms?"

"You'd be surprised," Odysseus muttered.

"I doubt it," Aphrodite smirked.

"Can you get the cover open?" a very quiet Echo asked. "I can smell them coming."

Jason's nose twitched too, the smell of stale blood was closing in. A huge shape loomed below him on the steps of the ladder, Jason saw the first droplets of blood dripping from its mouth, it was a massive body builder his skin tight top stretched over his muscled body, there were specks of blood on his outfit and Jason knew if they didn't move fast then there would be more. He sucked in a nervous breath.

"OPEN THE COVER!" he screamed.

"WE'RE TRYING!" the men shouted simultaneously from the top. "IT WON'T MOVE!"

Jason's body stiffened with fear as the infected bodybuilder heaved itself closer, foaming through its bared teeth. The two men at the top struggled to push at the manhole cover.

"Guys, to be fair, I'm not putting pressure on you or anything, but you really have to try and get that cover open."

"It's almost there, Mitchy."

Norton huffed. "Just a second more, it's slowly shifting."

This new monster was faster than the others and was clambering past each rung at a tremendous rate, Jason tried hard not to shake but his hands suddenly gripped tightly against the ladder and he couldn't move – they wouldn't release their grip, as if somebody else was controlling them, he was scared. Scared shitless.

His hands did not obey his commands to move either, he rested his head on the ladder and began to pray and hoped for a quick death, but he knew it wouldn't be.

"GOT IT! IT'S OPEN!" yelled Norton.

"Shit yeah!" said Odysseus, helping to sling the cover aside.

The remains of the evening sun poked through the open manhole and the cool air was a joy on the skins of Norton and Odysseus.

Jason's eyes snapped open and so did the rest of his body. "OK! THE COVER'S OFF, LET'S MOVE IT!"

Connor crawled out next and was up on his feet in an instant alert and ready. The two girls scrambled out afterwards and Echo turned back and shouted down with less fear and more fury, "C'MON MITCHY, ALMOST THERE, LET US HELP YOU!"

Gemma and Echo grabbed each arm of Mitchy and pulled back with all their might to ease her out.

As Mitchy's head popped through the hole her eyes squinted, slowly getting accustomed to the light and then suddenly they widened in panic, her mouth did the same. "GIRLS! DUCK!"

Both girls tumbled forward in unison rolling tightly into a neat ball, barely avoiding the blood stained man who was creeping up behind them, Mitchy slumped back, stuck from the torso down in the manhole.

The creature was slow and clumsy, an ageing hippy corpse with wild silver hair and wraparound shades. He had now ignored the girls and stood directly in front of Mitchy.

"Odysseus, SHOOT IT!" she screamed.

Odysseus causally took his pistol from his belt and aimed it at the creature's head and then almost instantly lowered it again. "Sorry darling, it's jammed and not firing."

His unremorseful acid voice gave Mitchy a hint of anger for company to join her fear, he simply shrugged and turned his back on her, the creature's jaw snapped violently open and lurched for Mitchy. She closed her eyes tight and stopped wiggling in the manhole, turning her shoulders away to accept her fate. "Oh God, oh God! Oh God!"

"NO!" Norton screamed. He shoulder barged the hippy and knocked him to the floor and started to pound him in the face.

Still in the tunnel, Jason could hear the moans of the bodybuilder growing louder below him. "Oh shit, oh shit, oh shit!"

Mitchy was out of the manhole now, with Aphrodite quickly behind her, Jason could see the light poking through at the top but was too tired to climb any faster, the bodybuilder grabbed at his ankle, tearing his boot cut jeans. "GET OFF ME!" He kicked out, connecting with the gym guy's face but it showed no sign of pain. "PULL ME UP! PULL ME UP!"

By the time the bodybuilder had regained it's footing, Jason was scrambling out of the top. Coughing and sputtering he fell to the ground, ending up in the foetal position. "GET THE COVER ON, QUICKLY!"

Connor and Gemma carefully picked up the manhole cover and dropped it on the hole.

"I'll LOCK IT," Conner shouted, and pressed the 'secure' button on the manhole cover.

A whirring sound came from beneath the cover and suddenly four bolts shot forward securing themselves through the bolt holes just beneath the tunnel's surface.

Connor picked his hair from his eyes looking at Jason slumped to the ground, but it was Norton fighting with the hippy which grabbed his attention the most. He mumbled as he left, "Cover's secured."

As Connor walked away, Jason lay shivering on the manhole cover listening to the bodybuilder banging from the tunnel below, as he lay there motionless, the banging finally became more distant. The others had gathered around Norton, fighting with the spaced out hippy creature. They were rolling around the floor and Norton screamed with rage, gradually growing numb to the sounds of shouting behind him. Straddled on top of the creature Norton punched harder at the creature's face. "I HAD A DATE TODAY YOU BASTARDS!" Norton's eyes were a frenzy of hate, tears suddenly welled up inside. "I HAD A DATE!" Blow after blow rained down on the hippy, Norton felt its cheek crunch. "WE WERE GOING TO MEET AT A THEME PARK!" The hippy feebly tried to take a snap at Norton's face as he continued to hit it. "THEN HAVE SOME WINE."

Mitchy screamed at Norton. "HE'S DEAD. STOP IT!"

Norton ignored her cries and carried on punching. "TARA! TARA!...WHERE ARE YOU, TARA?"

Mitchy stumbled over and pushed Norton off the now non-moving creature. "I SAID IT'S DEAD!" Norton stayed on his knees looking at his blood stained hands. Odysseus hovered above the bloody remains of the creature and grinned at Norton looking at his blood stained hands. "Classy mate, real classy."

Echo pushed past him and knelt beside the sobbing Norton, his eyes were gone now and his face was splattered with the hippy's blood, so much that he could have easily been mistaken for one of the creatures. She consoled him quietly, hugging him gently, her eyes fixed on the manhole and her thoughts straying to her sister's body and the state it must be in now. She sniffed hard and wiped her nose and whispered to Norton whilst rocking slowly. "Shh, shh, everything's going to be fine, we're all going to be fine."

Between sobs Norton answered, "We're not. There's no one else left." He then pulled away and threw his head back shouting at the evening sky. "THERE'S NO ONE ELSE! IS THERE NO ONE ELSE?"

Aphrodite pulled down her sleeves, making sure her arms were still covered. She surveyed the group, whilst scratching her forearms.

She eased off her sky high heels and rubbed her aching feet, she looked at their 'leader' Jason still curled up in a ball by the side of the man hole, shaking uncontrollably, looking at him was the Goth youngster Connor studying Jason like a lab rat, his head cocked to one side.

Aphrodite probed her earlobe, fiddling with it slightly. "Where are you, Father? she whispered.

Gemma stood close by with her arms folded and eyes fixated on the manhole too, thinking about Buckby and what her spider was doing, if he was still alive. She noticed Aphrodite mouthing to herself. "Are you alright?"

Aphrodite stopped whispering. "Don't mind me darling, just talking to myself."

Odysseus was laughing hysterically at the sobbing Norton back in the arms of Echo who held him tight. He cackled like a madman pointing and then rubbing his hands with glee.

Mitchy wanted to berate him, but it was all too tiring for her and she walked to the side of the pavement and flopped down, sweating profusely and pulling at her already tight trousers, under her breath cursing quietly.

Aphrodite went back playing with her feet, rubbing the dirt out carefully from between each toe, she then suddenly jerked her head up and started to sniff the air, she sniffed the evening sky casually and then turned round to the road ahead. Squinting her eyes she could see a blur of faces closing in on them in the distance. She turned to the group and their disarray and wondered how they had ever survived and how they were going to in this sorry state. She didn't put back on her high heels, instead holding them close to her chest. "Gemma darling, we have to move now."

Gemma looked at her, reluctant to leave the spot. "Why?"

Aphrodite sniffed the air for a final time and probed her ear. "Trust me darling, we have to go." She looked up the road again to the mass of heads approaching. "And I think we need a van."

"YOU'VE KILLED HER! YOU'VE KILLED MELISSA!" Ares yelled at his father.

Big Man hesitated and then nodded. "I didn't mean to, I really thought she was a protester...I couldn't see, I guess the driving lessons you were going to give me later are out of the question?"

Ares's eyes grew large. "WHAT? WHAT? WHAT ARE YOU TALKING ABOUT? SHE'S A GIRL, NO SHE'S A WOMAN, A BEAUTIFUL WOMAN WHO YOU'VE MURDERED!"

Big Man, eager to get away from Ares backed away from his enraged son. "She looked like one of those people from the street, I swear to God, besides, do you think she's put on a few pounds recently? She does look like a geezer from some angles."

"DAD!"

"Sorry, sorry, I don't get out much."

"WE HAVE TO SAVE HER, DAD!"

"Don't think there's much of her left to save, son."

"DAD!"

"I'm only saying..."

"WELL DON'T! YOU'VE DONE ENOUGH I THINK."

Big Man's skin prickled as his son's eyes bore deep into him. "Apart from the whole Melissa thing, have I offended you in some way, Ares?"

Ares clumsily tried to grab his father. "All the time, Big Man."

Big Man easily shoved his son off him and straightened his crumpled tie. "What are you waffling on about?"

"Nothing gets to you does it, Father? You prance around like the top dog, stepping on each and every one of the people you cared for, Melissa included, it's all about the 'business'."

Big Man felt a nudge of annoyance coming from Ares. "It wasn't all business son, it wasn't all about being top dog, it was about providing for the family, ever since your mother walked out...listen all I ever wanted to do was provide for you and your three sisters."

"Two."

"I'm sorry?"

"I have two sisters, Aphrodite and we're trying to adopt Gemma, remember?"

"Yeah two girls, sorry."

"What made you say three?"

"I don't know."

Ares raised his eyebrows. "You're not lying to me, Dad?"

"No, of course not, slip of the tongue that's all."

"You sure?"

"Yes, now back to business?"

"Again with the business?"

Rubbing his greying beard, Big Man truly thought hard. "Calm down."

"CALM DOWN? THE GIRLS ARE STILL OUT THERE! APHRODITE AND GEMMA ARE STILL OUTSIDE!"

"So? They've gone swimming and maybe Aphrodite's taking Gemma for a milkshake or something afterwards, no wait, Gemma can't drink milk, see? I remembered, or was it the other way?" Big Man looked around for someone's approval to show them that he *could* remember some information sometimes, but there was nobody apart Ares, who looked at him in confusion.

"NO, NO, YOU DON'T UNDERSTAND, SOMETHING'S HAPPENED TO THE PEOPLE OUTSIDE! THAT'S WHAT MELISSA AND I WERE TRYING TO TELL YOU, THEY'VE CHANGED INTO SOMETHING!"

"Into what?"

"Something not human."

Big Man froze in place, his eyes didn't move and he didn't blink, then suddenly the realisation kicked in. "My girls aren't back yet?"

"Nope, nobody's seen them."

"This is your fault!"

"My fault? How the hell is it my fault?"

Big Man answered in a heartbeat, his voice still angry and confused. "I told you to take Gemma to the pool and keep her safe from protesters and you couldn't even do that right."

Ares wanted him to stop. "YOU ARE KIDDING RIGHT? YOU ASKED APHRODITE TO TAKE GEMMA THIS MORNING! NOT ME! YOU WANTED ME TO STAY AND COMPLETE YOUR ROBOT DINOSUAR PROJECT? EVERYTHING I DO, I DO

BECAUSE YOU TELL ME TO, YOU SAY JUMP AND I SAY HOW HIGH?"

"Really?

"YES REALLY!"

"You're exaggerating."

"I MEAN IT. DAD, SINCE I WAS A KID YOU'VE ALWAYS TOLD ME WHAT TO DO, WHAT TO WEAR, WHO TO HANG OUT WITH!"

"Dude you were a nerd, you didn't hang out with anybody."

Ares oddly enough calmed down in voice but still flapped his arms up in desperation. "You see! That's what I'm talking about, you never gave me any respect, you never trusted me, you always treated me like crap. He stepped away from Ares and began walking away. "COME BACK HERE DAD, I WANT A WORD WITH YOU!"

Big Man spun around quickly. "Get a dictionary if you want a word, otherwise BACK OFF! I need to find my daughter!"

"Daughters."

"What?"

"Daughters, plural, more than one."

"That's what I said."

"No Dad, you said 'daughter' as in Aphrodite, the only child you really ever cared about, do you know anything about Gemma? I mean why did you want to adopt her? Was it just to wind up Elias when you finally find out where he is? I mean he's been missing for years now and nobody knows what happened and do you care? Because everything to you is a game, you brought her up just to use as a tool in your little spat with her real father, but he's lost, last seen on camera hurtling to certain doom in that sky ship thanks to your stooge Jago, and he's missing too. No, Jago, no Elias, so you're stuck with Gemma aren't you? Didn't think about that did you, Father?

Big Man nodded slowly his eyebrows rising. "Well, well, well, the little chicken shit has grown some balls! Well it's taken you long enough, soft lad! In all the years I've known you."

He stopped in mid-sentence and his eyes glazed over, lowering himself into his desk chair, he paused once more. "By the way, how old are you again?"

Ares stared at him for a frozen moment and then threw his thick mane of hair back and cackled sarcastically. "Always wearing the clown shoes aren't you Dad, very funny." Big Man still looked confused and the realisation dawned on his son. "You weren't joking? Oh this just gets better and better, good one!"

"It's not my fault, your mother always took care of that stuff, nothing to do with me." Big Man sounded like a teenager, a petulant one as well.

"Maybe that's why Mum left you."

"SHE LEFT BECAUSE SHE WAS HAVING AN AFFAIR, DUMB ARSE! DO YOU REMEMBER THAT? THAT BITCH LEFT ME FOR ANOTHER MAN, DO YOU REMEMBER THAT? YOUR SO CALLED 'DEVOTED' MOTHER WANTS NOTHING TO DO WITH US, NOTHING TO DO WITH YOU, AND NOTHING TO DO WITH APHRODITE!"

Ares looked to the floor and then glanced back up at him, his temper beginning to darken. "It was all you, you and your game shows, all you wanted to do was be the biggest and the best of the TV big wigs, killing innocent people for entertainment."

Big Man looked squarely in the eyes of Ares and clapped his hands in mock glee.

"Innocent? Innocent? You think everybody who entered my game show was innocent? You really are a douche bag if you still believe that stuff man, it's all about fame and power and that's why those Z-list celebrities with their failing career and popularity all sold their soul to enter the game show and if they paid with their lives, then they should have read the small print, nuff said! Look I thank you very much for designing the Dinosaur sentry guards for me, I do appreciate it, but the Big Man always tells it how it is and you my son, are a loser, there! I said it, big deal."

"You're a murderer and a coward."

"No, I'm an entertainer, cowards only change because people want them to."

"You love this don't you? Well I'll tell you something Father, there's always a bigger fish, somebody bigger and better is always around the corner waiting to take you down, and when that day comes, I can't wait to see the look on your face."

Big Man didn't care.

"Look at this magnificent complex, laboratory, all the staff we have, look what me being me has given you through out the years. I didn't hear you complaining then, so why do it now?"

"Because you've just killed Melissa, that's why."

Big Man's self-assurance faded. "Yeah, that was an honest mistake and I'm sorry about that, she was a good worker and a good friend to me, she went through a lot of shit working for this family."

"LOOK WHERE IT GOT HER! BEING LOYAL TO YOU AND THIS FAMILY GOT HER KILLED!"

Big Man bit the inside of his lip and swallowed hard. "She knew the risks soft lad, it was her choice to stay on when everyone else bailed out thanks to that game show fiasco."

"KNEW THE RISKS? NOBODY GOES TO WORK AS A SECRETARY AND EXPECTS TO BE EATEN BY A SHARK IN AN OFFICE COMPLEX!"

"She was my PA actually."

"YOU JUST DON'T GET IT DO YOU, DAD? EVERYBODY AROUND YOU, ANYBODY WHO TRIES TO GET CLOSE TO YOU, YOU PUSH THEM AWAY AND THEY END UP LEAVING YOU OR GETTING THEMSELVES KILLED. I MEAN DO YOU KNOW WHAT HAPPENED TO YOUR FRIEND APOLLO? YOU SENT HIM TO GOMMERSTALL YEARS AGO AND HE HASN'T BEEN HEARD OF SINCE, BUT DO YOU CARE?"

"Of course I care about him."

Big Man's voice faded and he lowered his eyes, he walked to the table and picked up a framed photograph sitting on it. In the picture was himself, Apollo and Mr Tidy, his old bodyguard. "Man, I miss Apollo."

Ares's temper cooled again slightly when he heard the tone in his father's voice.

"I know you do."

"I really wish he was here with me now."

"Me too, Father."

"Besides, he owes me 500 notes!"

He causally tossed the picture aside making Ares's temper return.

"See? That's what I'm talking about, you don't even care."

"I do care soft lad and I've got dignity and a couple of morals, do you?"

Ares stopped shouting and listened. "I had some morals, I thought I knew right from wrong and I hoped I'd make a better father to my children then you were to yours, all of your kids, that went out the window growing up as your son."

The words of truth escaped Ares's throat easily as Big Man scratched his chin with concern.

"You think I'm a bad father? You think I wasn't there for you growing up? Well I'll tell you something, when your mother was working late at school, and the maid had the day off it was me who put you to bed and I used to tell you the story of *The Turtle and The Scorpion,* do you remember that, soft lad?"

Ares shook his head. "No, should I?"

"Well, I'll remind you then, there was this this storm, a vicious storm and the rivers were running wild. A scorpion wanted to cross a particular river, but the current was too strong. He noticed a turtle further up the bank about to cross the river and called out to it. 'Hey turtle! Carry me across this river on your back, I can't swim.' To which the turtle replied, 'You're having a laugh aren't you? If I carry you on my back halfway across you'll sting me and I'll drown'."

Big Man grinned and relished at his story telling. "'If I was to sting you then I'd drown too', said the scorpion, 'Where's the benefit in that?' The turtle thought about for a moment and then nodded, 'Ok, hop on board.' But halfway across, the scorpion stung the turtle on its back and as he felt the venom coursing through his veins, he turned to the scorpion and said, 'You stung me' and the scorpion said, 'I know.' 'Why? Now that you've stung me you'll drown too, where's the benefit in that?' So as they sank the scorpion whispered, 'I don't give a monkey's toss about benefits soft lad, I'M A SCORPION, IT'S IN MY NATURE, I WILL NEVER EVER CHANGE!'"

Big Man nodded his head confidently. "You're the scorpion son, you'll never change, you are and always will be a…" Big Man made an L-shape with his hand and put it on his forehead. "Loser."

Ares looked completely lost. "That doesn't make sense."

"It makes perfect sense, you're just annoyed because you know it's true."

"No, it doesn't make sense because how can a scorpion sting a turtle on its back? A turtle has a shell, so there's no way a scorpion's sting can penetrate it."

Big Man drummed away on his teeth with his fingers whilst thinking. "Wait, no, hold on it's not a turtle it's one of those things…it's um…it's a…"

"A FROG."

The voice from the other side of the room made both men jump, unbeknown to them the huge metal door had been opened and a slender figure had glided in and had been listening for a while. Black finger nailed hands struggled with a headscarf, patting down hard and struggling to tie it up, the voice spoke again, the figure had left puddles of water in their steps edging slowly forward.

"It's a frog, the story is called the *Frog and the Scorpion*."

Ares's stomach flipped over and kept flipping when he saw who was at the door.

"MELISSA! YOU'RE…YOU'RE…"

"Cold, wet, and slightly annoyed."

Big Man jumped around like jack in the box, pointing feverishly at Melissa.

"HOW DID YOU DO THAT? HOW DID YOU ESCAPE MY SHARK?"

Ares too was intrigued on how she managed to escape, but let his dad continue.

Melissa's voice was weaker. "Ask no questions and I'll tell no lies."

She turned away to remove her glasses and wipe away the water from her eyes. "Why were you playing the music so loud anyway?"

"To drown out the sounds of those protesters, they're doing my head in." Melissa turned back around with her glasses back in place. "And the rapping?"

"Because I can and have the mad skills to pay the bills." Big Man's eyes were still wide in amazement. "Well however you killed my shark, maybe you can do it to those protesters outside my complex."

Melissa shared a glance with Ares and she spoke again to Big Man. "That's what we came to tell you about."

"About what?"

She leaned forward and whispered. "They're not protesters anymore."

"Yeah I know, numb nuts over there told me about how they've changed into 'Something not human'."

Melissa paused, her mouth now dry and her heart hammering. "They're a little bigger."

6. SCRAMBLED LEGS

There were abandoned cars littered all over the road and even more crashed through the barriers by the roadside.

Many of the cars were burnt out wrecks, most of them were smeared with blood, on the windows and doors, former owners trying desperately to escape the creatures who had multiplied so quickly and had now gone past their 'violent' stage and were just concentrating on eating human beings. There was a huge hill at the side of junction 14 of the Upton motorway heading out of Olympia City. The crowd of creatures making their way from the top grew ever larger. They swarmed down like black ants without any real direction, just a hunger, a thirst for blood.

It was a squeeze for everybody to fit into the seven-seater taxi. After they left the manhole the creatures that Aphrodite saw in the distance had grown in mass and were running hard and fast towards the group.

Most of the cars dumped still had the car keys in the ignition as the drivers were usually violently pulled through the window with the engine still running. The big taxi they found was no different, the driver's side window was broken and the edges covered in blood, the passengers didn't get to their destination as the back seats were bloody too and the meter was still running.

Crammed into the black cab they headed away from Olympia. There were puddles of blood all over the road and Jason, who was behind the wheel, still made an effort to drive around them. He slowed down when he saw people moving through the gaps between the cars to check if they were ok and pick them up but then speeded up when he saw they were infected looking for more meals. They had seemed slow moving at the start but now some could run like fast like humans. Everyone in the car was in a sombre mood. Jason broke the silence first.

"Look, I'm sorry about earlier, you know, laying on the ground and that, I don't know what came over me."

"I know," said Aphrodite, her voice back to her unfeeling best. "You wimped out, basically rolled around on the floor like a gigantic baby."

"Quiet, woman," Mitchy shushed.

"Just ignore her sugar, she's scared and doesn't mean it."

"I'm not and I do," Aphrodite hissed back.

Mitchy shifted uncomfortably in her seat. "No, we *are* all scared, we don't know what's happening out there, we don't know where we're going, we just have to stick together and see what happens, we'll be safe if we can ride it out."

The greasy haired Odysseus chipped in. "Stick together and we'll be safe? You're having a laugh aren't you? Look around toots 'cause I'm sure this group was slightly larger earlier this afternoon. How many have we lost now?" He held up his fingers on one hand and started counting down with the other. "We ain't got a clue where we're going, we don't know what the hell we're dealing with and our 'so called' leader has wet himself and gone ga ga."

"That's enough Odysseus, leave him alone alright, I'm too tired for all this," Norton moaned whilst checking his phone.

"YOU?" Odysseus's voice was etched with sarcasm. "Check this out Norton, I give Jason some stick about being a punk, but credit where credit's due, he's trying to get us out alive, but you? Crying over some little girl you haven't even met yet?"

"Piss off, Odysseus."

Odysseus made kissy noises at him. "It's true though punk, the whole city, could be the whole world for all we know, has flipped up and gone crazy and your worrying about..." he mimicked Norton's voice, "TARA TARA, I GOTTA FIND TARA!"

This even made Aphrodite smirk until Jason intervened. "That's enough Odysseus, Norton is just upset, we all are."

Norton spoke again, twitching slightly nervously. "As soon as we find somewhere safe and, I know you guys will stay safe, then I'm going to go back and find Tara, I just have to make sure that she's ok, we will have our date today, that I promise."

"*That I promise?* Is this guy for real?"

"Odysseus."

"No, I'm sorry Jason, but I'm getting tired of this dickhead and his whining about his invisible girlfriend, no you go and run away like a bitch and try and find little miss non-existent but when she see's you for the chump you really are, which should take about five minutes, it took me four, tell her to come find me and I'll show her what a real man can do."

This riled Norton and he showed it. "Keep your dirty hands away from her!"

"Calm down chump, I'm just messing with you, besides I'm married."

This proved to be the biggest shock of the day to everyone, more so than the creatures outside.

Aphrodite took a breath. "You're married?"

Odysseus nodded.

"Seriously?"

"YES!"

"To a human being?"

Odysseus chuckled. "Yes, we had a bit of a row so I went out earlier today to give her some breathing space and then *this* happened."

"What was the row about sugar, if you don't mind me asking?"

"I love to stare at women in bikinis, Mitchy."

"My God! You're quite a catch aren't you?" Aphrodite's eyes narrowed suspiciously.

"Yeah I know it's bad, but I'll make it up to her."

"If she's still alive."

Odysseus returned the suspicious look to Aphrodite. "Yeah, if she's still alive."

He quickly changed the subject, turning to Norton. "You must have a picture of her on your phone, show me."

"No."

"Come on show me, I won't laugh."

"No."

Connor sighed. "Just show him the picture Norton so he'll shut up."

Norton huffed and fiddled with his phone until a picture of a blonde woman illuminated the screen. He passed it around the van; Gemma, Echo, Mitchy and Connor all had a look, head nods and smiles were the general reply, until Aphrodite had look at Norton's date.

"Is this her? Goodness me, wouldn't waste your time, I'd give her a five out of ten."

Norton snatched the phone back from her. "Five? You think she's a five? My Grandma's a five and she's dead! Tara has to be an eight."

The rest of the van gave their opinions.

"I think an eight too."

"Seven for me."

"Six and a half maybe."

"I like her hair."

"She has lovely eyes too."

Jason had a swift look as Norton held up the phone and smiled. "Even though I think rating people on their looks is quite rude, I think she's a nine my friend."

Norton beamed and was about to show Odysseus, who pulled away. "I was joking, punk! I don't want to see your woman, get that phone from out of my face."

"So you don't want to see a picture of my date?"

Odysseus smirked. "If she's agreed to go on date with you, then she's not worth it, I mean has this girl seen the gigantic gap in your teeth? You're a horse-faced loser with teeth like a urinal, your just lucky I've just been to the toilet."

Jason smiled and spoke to Norton. "I don't know how you're going to meet her, I don't even know where we're going, well I know where I was going, but that doesn't matter now, not yet anyway."

"Let's just see how it goes, mate," Norton replied, ignoring Jason's mild ramble.

"So after your date, you're going to chickulate her, right?" Odysseus asked.

"Chickawhat?

"Chickulate."

"That's not a word."

"Yes it is, when a first date goes well some people like to go back to their flat and—"

"I can guess what it means," Norton interrupted. "It's just not a word."

"How can you be sure, chump. You got a dictionary on you?"

Jason adjusted the rear view mirror and spoke too. "Odysseus, it's not a word."

"Idiots," Odysseus added softly.

The traffic was clogged up on the outgoing lanes, but the roads to the city were empty, everyone was trying to escape Olympia and now the group were going back.

"Why are we going back to the city by the way? We know there's nothing back there," Echo asked and then hesitated briefly. "Apart from Enya."

Gemma held her friend's hand, not only for support but it took her thoughts away from her lost spider.

"We can't get out of the city because the traffic is too bad, it's gridlocked, but maybe if we go back in we could try and hole up somewhere in an abandoned building somewhere and hope this blows over, maybe try and contact our loved ones to see if they're safe?"

Norton held his phone up and nodded his support as Mitchy spoke up. "Ok, let's try to find out more about each other shall we?"

Odysseus gave Mitchy a long hard look and leaned in, whispering, "Who gives a shit about where we came from?"

"It might help to calm things down a bit."

The van bumped over some potholes, shaking everybody inside, Odysseus rubbed his aching back. "Listen we can play nice when we get out of this pisshole! Alright?"

Mitchy smiled and forced Odysseus to catch her eye. "You've got quite a colourful vocabulary there, Odysseus, ever tried using a thesaurus?"

Odysseus shook his head. "Why? They're extinct aren't they?"

Mitchy's eyes flickered to the rear view mirror and caught a glimpse of Jason smirking.

Connor spoke next. "Well I'm from Billenge City, my family moved around lot when I was younger because of my dad."

"Was he in the army?" Norton asked.

"No, he was in prison, not too smart, he worked in a bank for twenty years and got sent down for stealing."

"Stealing what, sugar? Bank credits? Gold?"

"Pens. Like I said, he wasn't too smart."

Odysseus had a big doggy grin on his face. "I hate travelling, I think it's because my dad used to beat me with a globe."

He returned the glint in his eye to Mitchy who was fiddling with her top and dripping with sweat. She took hold of Gemma's other hand, ignoring Odysseus's lame comment.

"Jason honey, nobody has mentioned what those *things* actually are, they looked all bloody and oozy stumbling around like zombies."

Norton glanced at his watch and then joined in the conversation. "Like movie zombies?"

Gemma's eyes locked firmly on Norton's face. "What's a movie zombie?"

"Oh honey, have you not seen a movie before? You were born before the TV ban right?"

Gemma pivoted her head around to Mitchy and had threw her a quizzical look. "Yeah, I remember some movies I think I used to watch some with my dad."

Aphrodite glared at her. "My *real dad* when I was younger? But I don't know what a movie zombie, sorry a zombie movie is."

Connor leaned forward and touched his hand over his eyebrow ring, fiddling with it slowly. "A zombie is a corpse which has been animated and bought back to life, usually by magic or witchcraft."

Echo leaned into Mitchy and rested her head on the older woman's shoulder and Gemma leaned on the other. "How do you know such things?" Echo asked dreamily.

"I don't get out much."

"So how the hell are zombies or whatever they are walking or stumbling around Olympia then?"

Jason shook his head at Norton. "Don't know Norton mate, but if they are like the ones in the movies then I remember that they come out at night, and it's getting dark now, we should find some cover back in the city." He turned around at the group. "Agreed?"

"I just want to go home," said Echo.

"Me too honey, but I don't have a home." Mitchy's brown eyes were tired but she gave a reassuring smile to the young girls.

Aphrodite yawned. "So you're a tramp then? Thought as much."

"No Aphrodite, I'm stuck here. I'm on holiday in Olympia because today's my... well it doesn't matter and my flight was..." She looked at her watch. "An hour ago."

Gemma looked up at Mitchy, the young girl's eyebrows dropped. "Why didn't you go home? You didn't have to stay here, we wouldn't have minded."

"That's sweet honey but I was stuck in a sewer, don't think they do flights down there unfortunately."

"So what happens now?"

"Well I stay with you guys I suppose...I've got nowhere to go, Gemma honey."

"We'll take care of you then Mitchy, I promise."

Mitchy gave a tired polite smile. "Thank you Gemma. Oh! That reminds me." Mitchy gave a wiggle in her seat so she could reach into her trouser pockets, her fingers squeezed into her pocket with great effort to pull something out. "This fell out of your bag too when your lost your poor spider honey, I managed to catch it for you, what is it? A credit card or something?" She handed Gemma the swipe card.

"Oh thank you so much! No it's not a credit card, it's my swipe key to my house."

"Interesting front door key," Jason said.

"Where do you live, Gemma?"

"We live at—"

Aphrodite swiftly interrupted. "None of your business where we live."

Jason held his hands up in a mock surrender. "Hey, sorry, it's just that you don't mention your family much."

"There's nothing to know, Gemma is my annoying little foster sister and that's all you need to know."

"But—"

"But nothing, you don't need to know about our family or where we live, understood?"

Jason nodded. "Understood."

Gemma reached over and tapped Connor on his slim shoulder. "Connor, I lost my bag, could you look after my card for me?"

Connor studied the key slowly. "So this is the key to your house then?"

Gemma nodded. "Yeah it's my key to get me back inside my home. My brother Ares gave it to me, can get me in anywhere in the complex."

Connor's eyebrows rose slightly. "Complex?"

"House, I mean."

"So why doesn't Aphrodite carry a key to her own house?"

Aphrodite heard, and leaned forward flashing her nails. "Do you really think I could carry a card around with me with nails like these?

Connor chuckled slowly and put the card in his pocket. "Ok, I got it, I'll look after this key for you, I won't lose it, promise, and Mitchy, thanks for catching it for Gemma, let's try and stay alive so she can use that key to get home."

Odysseus threw his head back and let out his trademark cackle, counting down on his fingers once again.

Jason spoke up next. "I know we've lost some people, but we won't lose anymore, not again."

Jason's mood was pensive and defiant as he looked down the road. Aphrodite suddenly jerked her head up and looked around the van.

"What the hell's wrong with her?" moaned Odysseus.

Jason turned around and was quite surprised at how agitated she was. *That's odd,* he thought. "Aphrodite, are you—"

But he never finished the sentence. A tremendous thunderclap of an explosion came from behind them, the vibrations struck the road, rocking the van. Screams and shouts came from inside the vehicle as they turned with hands over their ears to see what the deafening sound was. Black smoke rose above orange flames and formed an oak tree shape into the night sky.

"WHAT THE HELL WAS THAT?" yelled Odysseus.

Jason instantly got off the car and shielded his eyes from the heat. "IT'S A REFUELLING STATION! IT'S GONE UP IN FLAMES!"

"WHAT?"

"I DON'T KNOW WHAT'S HAPPENING!"

Debris from the station began to rain down around them huge chunks of metal crashed on top of the taxi, side stepping the metal mess. Jason leaned inside. "STAY THERE! DON'T COME OUT."

Odysseus did a double take at the burning building and pushed his way out of the van.

"Sod that."

Another explosion, louder than the first made the others follow suit. "Sorry, have to see what's happening," Gemma said, squeezing past Mitchy.

Mitchy sighed as she followed Echo out of the van. "Wish I'd caught that bloody plane now."

The heat from the refuelling station was incredible and Aphrodite looked to the sky and wiped her scalp letting out a very frustrated breath. "This heat is ruining my hair."

Echo spun around wildly. "IS THAT ALL YOU HAVE TO SAY?"

"I've ripped my tights too, darling."

Before Echo could answer she noticed from the corner of her eye more debris falling from the fuel station and shifted her body out of the way. Her eyes freaked out when she saw what was actually raining from the skies and she screamed loudly.

Aphrodite's forehead dipped. "What the hell is her prob—" Before she could finish, a severed foot hit her square in the face, knocking her to the ground. "WHAT THE FU—!"

The fall made Aphrodite graze her knees and as she lay on the ground, more body parts landing all around her. *God I could do with a drink right now* she thought.

Echo was in hysterics and shook uncontrollably. "THEY'RE HANDS! IT'S HUMAN HANDS!"

The group huddled together by the side of the taxi van as countless charred limbs scattered on to the ground around them. Norton was too late covering his head as a slender female hand laden with rings bounced off it.

"This is just gross," Gemma said, shaking her head.

"Are they human parts or those things?" Norton asked, shaking his dizzy head in the process.

"Who gives a toss, stupid! It's raining an A+E unit here."

Odysseus was wild-eyed and stared at Norton with pure contempt.

"You got a problem with me, Odysseus?"

"Not that stupid are you then?"

Irritated, Jason opened his mouth to speak, but was hit square in the face by foot in a biker's boot.

Aphrodite grinned. "Couldn't have said it better myself." Jason picked himself up from the floor and rubbed his aching jaw, his lip was split. He buckled and fell down on to one knee, rubbing it hard with his hands.

The next explosion from the refuelling site was expected and more impressive than the last, the fires spread all over the road behind them.

"How did those fires start? Did those things cause it? How can they do that? Are they thinking now?"

Jason rose for the second time, his knee still aching, his eyes focused on Mitchy and his ears buzzing from her views. "Not sure on what Big Man's next move is, but he won't get us baby, we'll be safe soon, when I find you."

"WHAT? Big Man? That guy from TV? What's he got to do with it? You're talking gibberish honey," Mitchy said.

Another head shake brought some sense to him. "Why did you mention Big Man?" asked Aphrodite. She knew that many people didn't know that Big Man was her father and he went to great lengths to keep his family out of the public eye, especially since the bounty on his head from The Green Man, if the public knew she or Gemma were Big Man's daughters, they would stop at nothing to capture them and demand a ransom. Big Man wanted notoriety, but not for his family. *Why's that loser mentioning my dad?* she thought.

"Sorry, was babbling a bit there, ignore what I said," Jason mumbled.

"I already have chump, never listened to you anyway," Odysseus said.

Aphrodite glanced at Odysseus and whispered softly, "I despise the way you look, but love the way you cook."

Odysseus chuckled. "Right back at you babe."

Another terrific explosion shook the road as another fuel stack from the garage went up in flames, sending fuel-like a geyser spurting high into the air, and covering the group from head to toe with black gunge.

"AHHH! WHAT THE HELL IS THIS SHIT?" roared Odysseus.

"OH GOD! WE'RE COVERED IN FUEL, IT'S DRIPPING ALL OVER US, WE'RE GONNA BURN TO DEATH!" Echo cried.

Wobbling on his feet, Jason looked at the flames spreading across the road behind them and tried to shake the fuel from his body, he turned to Echo and her panicking. "Can't go back, we have to go forward."

Suddenly his stomach dropped and a feeling like a bolt of ice shot down his back, that sick feeling he had felt in the tunnels had returned, what he saw in the distance would be the worst nightmare ever. People would usually waffle on about having a 'Nightmare Day' when they had simply broken a nail or stubbed their toe on a dresser, but this was the real deal.

The sun was a dusty red in the late evening sky, hiding behind the newly formed dark clouds. The dying sunlight hit the road in front of them, and the group of infected humans stumbling along the road, but behind the slow moving ones appeared the new faster ones, pushing past them and running at speed like a raging river to the group.

"God no," Jason mouthed.

Echo saw what had unnerved him. She felt warm liquid trickling down her legs and realised she had wet herself, looking down at her wet black leather trousers, she whimpered. "We're going to die this time aren't we?"

The infected moaned in unison as they gathered pace. "We're trapped," Norton added. "We can't go forward."

He swung his head round frantically. "The fires are blocking us behind."

He shook himself, still soaking with fuel. Norton's head was still with his date with Tara, that's all he wanted, nothing else and no one else mattered.

"Shit," Odysseus hissed.

A large press of infected bodies grew tighter as they approached the survivors from the opposite end of the road, the second group were stumbling up behind the stampeding first, rushing fast into their direction. Odysseus was frantically trying to remove the liquid from his body. "I CAN'T GET THIS STINKING FUEL OFF ME!"

The smell of the decaying infected rapidly spread across the road, Echo gasped in horror as a number of the slow moving ones also began to pick up speed.

Aphrodite stood on one heel with her arms crossed in mere annoyance. "We can't go back or forward, eh? So it's either a choice of being mugged or burgled then."

Jason took a deep breath and scanned the road ahead, looking for anything to use as a weapon. Mitchy clocked what he was doing and put a reassuring arm on his shoulder.

"There's too many of them to fight honey, we're not leaving this one alive I think."

He lowered his head and didn't speak, he allowed himself a quick intake of breath before scanning the horizon again, straining his neck forward, Jason noticed something and his eyes shot wider.

Suddenly he launched himself forward shrugging off Mitchy's hand and began pointing frantically ahead of the charging infected humans. "LOOK, UP THERE, IN THE MIDDLE OF THE ROAD, THERE'S A

MANHOLE COVER WITH A GREEN LIGHT, THAT MEANS IT'S OPEN. IF WE CAN MAKE IT BEFORE THEY GET THERE..."

Echo shook her head, her eyes more terrified. "NO! I'M NOT GOING BACK IN THERE! YOU CAN'T MAKE ME GO BACK DOWN THERE!"

She started to shake again.

"WE DON'T HAVE TIME FOR THIS ECHO! WE'RE COVERED IN FUEL AND THOSE FLAMES ARE REACHING CLOSER, SO IT'S EITHER BURN TO DEATH, OR TAKE A CHANCE CHARGING AT THOSE THINGS."

Jason made his decision in a snap. "Screw it!" He sprinted towards the oncoming horde, each leg stride was purposeful and determined.

"Oh my God he's running towards them!" Echo shrieked.

Gemma grabbed Echo's wrist and pulled. "So are we."

"NO."

"YES!"

Gemma snarled with authority. "LOOK BEHIND YOU, ECHO." She pointed at the fuel spill from the refuelling station. "DO YOU SEE THAT? JASON'S RIGHT, THAT FIRE IS GOING TO REACH US IN SECONDS AND WE'RE COVERED IN FUEL AND WILL BURN TO DEATH, AND LOOK UP THERE..."

She swung Echo around. "THOSE CREATURE THINGS ARE GOING REACH US SOONER AND I DON'T KNOW ABOUT YOU BUT I'VE GOT BETTER THINGS TO DO TODAY THAN DIE, SO MOVE IT!"

Echo's body went limp, allowing herself to be dragged on by Gemma in hot pursuit of Jason. Some of the infected were falling down the huge grassy slope ahead of them, which shook the others into action.

Connor stared longingly at the others running away to the manhole, wishing them luck in his head, his eyes lingered the longest on Gemma.

"CONNOR!" Norton snapped.

"It's showtime people, time to move."

They were completely surrounded now, the flames behind them were fierce and there were hundreds of the infected charging from their front and rampaging down either side of the hills to the left and right.

Mitchy's eyes grew wider as she saw how far away she was from safety and how close the zombie things were in front of her. She puffed away in agony. "WE'RE NOT GOING TO MAKE IT, WE'RE GOING TO MEET THEM HEAD ON!"

Aphrodite sped past her in bare feet. "Drama queen," she muttered.

"AHHHH NOOO!!"

Jason had fallen to the ground clutching his knee. Aphrodite watched him tumble as she approached. "What's wrong with you now?" she asked him as he rolled on the ground.

"IT'S MY KNEE, IT'S GONE AGAIN!"

Aphrodite looked at him blankly and then a sly look came across her eyes. "Maybe I should leave you there?"

"DON'T JOKE WOMAN! IT'S A FOOTBALL INJURY, HELP ME UP PLEASE?!"

Aphrodite hovered like a ghost above Jason. "You look so helpless on the ground, like a little lamb ready for the slaughter."

"FOR GOD'S SAKE HELP ME UP!"

Her eyes rolled around and she offered her hand out to him. "Watch the nails please."

Jason hauled himself up and was surprised by the strength of Aphrodite. "What was that all about?"

Aphrodite pointed to the flames. "Run first, moan later."

Norton was keeping pace with Odysseus and tried lengthening his strides and trying his best not to be undone by the smaller grubbier little man.

"Trouble keeping up, Norton? I could probably beat you wearing heels. What would the lovely Tara say eh?"

Norton wheezed and then spat out his reply. "I said don't you touch her and I meant it."

Odysseus's mouth twisted into a smirk. "We'll see, I didn't see the picture on the phone but probably too damn fine to be wasted on you."

Norton's face screwed up in utter disgust until he noticed Mitchy lagging behind. "MITCHY! COME ON, MOVE IT!"

Mitchy bent forward and went down on one knee and waved Norton on as she realised he'd turned back for her. "You go on sugar, I'm holding everybody back." She wiped the fuel from her eyes and a small laugh escaped her lips. "I'm done, I can't keep up."

"No, you're not...come on we're almost there, please Mitch, you don't have to do this."

She pointed to Jason and the others who had opened the hatch in the road and were disappearing from sight, only Gemma remained in view standing beside the open cover beckoning frantically.

"Look they're safe honey, don't die on my account, you're going to burn to death or get eaten, either one

I guess is quite annoying. I didn't think I would be dying now, today of all days..."

"What's so special about today?"

"It doesn't matter honey."

Norton turned away from her, unable and unwilling to let it go, a trail of fuel was alight now behind them snaking its way up the road, burning everything in sight. Norton looked back at the flames and at the infected tearing down the road moments away from contact, he thought about his mother who he'd left to die this morning, he was a coward then, but not now.

"Mitchy."

"Yeah."

"You talk too much."

He hauled her to her feet and dragged her, mirroring Gemma's attempts with Echo. "COME ON LADY, LET'S GO."

Gemma stood by the manhole like a loyal dog tied to a post outside a shop waiting for its owner to return, swinging her head around at the marauding infected, she stamped her feet and screamed at the two, "RUNNNNN! THEY'RE COMING!" Gemma could see the look of terror on their faces as they could see past her and what was looming in the background.

Norton shouted over the noise of the explosions. "GEMMA, GET INSIDE! THEY'RE RIGHT BEHIND YOU!"

She spun around wildly and a flash of fear finally hit her face, the teenager's body disappeared into the ground, only the top of her head remained as her eyes peeked over the manhole. Holding on to the ladder she tiredly clutched onto the first rung, watching her new friends run for their lives and being completely powerless to help them.

Norton was charging like a madman towards the hole in the road, he was struggling to breathe as spit flew from the corner of his mouth as he looked to his running partner, Mitchy. She was gasping for breath and her eyes were watering and stinging with the fuel coated around them. Gemma implored them to keep running. "PLEASE MITCHY, YOU'RE ALMOST HERE!"

Norton could see the infected's eyes were now mostly bloodshot and some were black, but all were soulless and intent on causing death. His stomach seemed like it had split in two with fear.

"Don't let me down," Norton said between coughs. "I will see Tara tonight and somehow we will get you home."

Gemma was about to disappear for good down the manhole as she could see that both parties were closing in rapidly, praying for Mitchy and Norton to make it to her first, she silently mouthed 'No!' as her last sight was seeing Mitchy trip and crash to the ground, bringing Norton down with her. Her arms scraped along the ground and loose bits of the road embedded themselves in her forearm. Norton hauled himself to his feet and continued to drag Mitchy, turning to face the infected. There were hundreds of them, all charging and staring at the last remaining humans in view, eager to taste their sweet blood on their decaying lips. Mitchy choked and gasped for air.

"You're not heading for death that easy, kid," grimaced Norton.

Another explosion from behind them drew their attention and shook them both. "Get up Mitchy please, we're going to make it! We are not going to die here tonight, we've come through too much today."

Mitchy touched a finger to his mouth, cutting him off.

"Norton."

"Yes."

"You talk too much."

She picked herself up and with no time to waste was hovering over the open manhole.

Norton flew past and without a second glance at the infected who would be on them in moments, climbed down the hole, Mitchy waited for him to disappear and then positioned herself above the manhole and began to follow Norton.

"GRAB THE COVER, MITCHY!" he screamed.

Shit yeah, the cover, she thought. Mitchy craned her neck and reached for the manhole cover; her fingers clawed at the road desperately trying to grasp it. "I CAN'T REACH IT!"

The infected were running faster now, all of them could smell the blood of the survivors.

Norton was already halfway down the ladder when he realised Mitchy wasn't following.

"WHAT'S HAPPENING UP THERE?"

"I CAN'T REACH THE COVER!" Mitchy shook her head in panic.

"GET IT NOW, MITCHY!" yelled Norton from below her.

Her fingernails dragged along the road and she gasped out a cry. "I'M TRYING!"

"TRY HARDER FOR GOD'S SAKE!"

Mitchy was almost weeping. "ALMOST THERE…"

"MITCHY PLEASE!"

She felt her eyes itch and her mouth too as the fuel doused on her clothes was reaching her nostrils, knowing she would go up in flames like the fuel station. She grunted again to reach the cover. Burning oil whizzed through the air and Mitchy ducked below the surface careful not to have the oil go through her hair, she screamed her defiance into the night sky and clawed her way to grab the protective cover again.

"MITCHY!"

"I'm on it."

"HURRY!"

"I KNOW."

Her fingernails had long since snapped off in the tunnels but with an almighty resolute headshake she managed to haul the cover finally towards her. Running up quickly was a woman whose left arm had been eaten away, her hair used to be blonde, but was matted with blood and there were slash marks all across her face. The infected woman ran straight up to the manhole and a small smile of relief spread across Mitchy's face. "Not today honey." The cover was slammed shut just as the flame trail flew over, igniting the infected. The heat was unbearable, as were screams of the infected humans and the fires burning them, deafening like a jet engine.

Mitchy gingerly made her way down the ladder blocking out the sounds of the people on fire above by humming to herself. She reached the bottom and looked to see the ragged bunch of survivors she had now known long enough to call friends illuminating her way with their mobile phones. The light blinded her and Mitchy covered her eyes as Gemma ran over to hug her.

"I'm fine child, I'm fine," she whispered.

Gemma continued to squeeze. "I thought I'd lost you."

"I was scared honey, not going to lie about it." She cleared her throat. "But Norton made me think about my life and he saved it."

"Please don't leave me, Mitchy."

"I promise honey, I'll never leave you on your own."

She gently broke from the girl's embrace and wobbled slowly to Norton and hugged him.

"Thank you."

"You're most welcome," he said.

Jason also nodded his thanks to him for getting Mitchy back in one piece.

Odysseus looked around in the darkness, shining his phone to try and find something of use in the damp environment. "So we're back in the tunnel again? Seems we always end up in these shitholes, funny how things work out ain't it?"

Jason listened to the moans and screams of the infected as they burned alive on the road above and looked at Odysseus.

"Nobody's laughing."

A Lab with The Green Man: 2

"This is excellent," The Green Man breathed. "How long has it been since we made first contact?"

His assistant was unconcerned. "Has been a while… hours I think? But you do know what's happening outside, right?"

He looked up and gave her a brief nod. "I'm well aware of it, yes, but have you seen how much she's grown?"

The worried assistant bit her lip. "I have to get home, I have family, my team have family, we all want to go home."

"You *had* family I'm guessing, those creatures are everywhere." He turned to his assistant. "What is your name again?"

"Ariel, sir, my name is Ariel."

"Well Ariel, let's just think about the job at hand for the time being and think about family ties later, I'm paying you and your merry band of scientists a lot of money to be here, too much some might say." She nodded solemnly. "Has she grown any abnormalities?"

Ariel looked at her watch and then walked over to another computer monitor to see its readout.

"Only the ones that we're aware of, any more would result in cryogenic failure and kill her."

The foetus in the cryogenic tube had earlier grown into a young girl, but now in the space of mere hours had aged a few years. The Green Man looked at her features as she awoke from another nap from cryogenic sleep, she seemed to be at peace in the comforting warm water around her, she hadn't noticed that she was no longer a child.

"Are you still afraid?" The Green Man asked.

The girl turned her longer blonde hair towards him and pressed her hands against the glass chamber. "*Yes, I'm still afraid.*"

"Why is that?"

The specimen cocked her head and frowned. "*I don't know where I am.*"

The girl was a very attractive and now taller young woman contained in a cryogenic chamber; The Green Man spoke as soft as his metal mask would allow. "You're safe here with friends."

The girl writhed and recoiled after The Green Man's words. "*With friends?*"

The Green Man watched as Ariel moved another computer screen round the glass chamber, he carried on with his questions as his assistant tapped away on the keyboard.

"Yes, do you know your name?"

A dim sensation spread on the girl's face. "*I think so.*"

"What do you know?"

The girl looked across the whole laboratory and saw Ariel and her team looking back at her, some of them smiling, others concerned with events outside. Excitement crept into his voice as he repeated the question. "Do you remember anything about who you are?"

"*A little.*"

The Green Man and Ariel listened intently. "*I can remember where I was born, I can remember where I lived.*" She hesitated behind her glass chamber, her eyes big with awe and wonder. "*I can remember how I died.*"

7. Truth or Dare

Big Man walked across his massive office, parted the blinds to the window and looked down below. He was a step ahead of Ares who stood by his side – he looked at his father's face, it was a mixture of terror and pure disbelief.

The hundreds of infected people standing at the foot of Big Man's tower swayed in unison like a gentle wave washing up to shore on a bright summer's day. Big Man spoke softly, his voice devoid of any emotion, eyes focused on the humans with a manmade virus coursing through their veins, probably manmade, that's what he thought anyway. "So my girls are still out there?"

Ares nodded. "As far as I know, yes."

"Is this a pandemic now, is that the right word?"

"It's looking that way, Father."

Big Man tried to look at their faces with no satisfaction, it was too far up to make out the features, but it was beginning to look like they weren't human anymore.

"So are you certain you had nothing to do with this, Ares?"

"Why does everybody keep asking me that?"

They both turned around to see Melissa walking towards them, she stood by Ares's side and looked down also at the changed protester crowd.

"You didn't answer the question, Ares."

"No," Ares said suddenly.

"Are you sure?" Big Man looked at him sharply. "Answer me."

"Yes, I'm sure."

Ares glanced to the floor and noticed his father's feet had odd socks on, he used to dress impeccably all the time, even after his wife had walked out, but over the last few years he had just seemed to stop caring about his appearance. Big Man grew impatient and his voice snapped Ares out of his sock-related trance. "If I found out you were behind this thing, Ares…"

Ares mumbled something he failed to catch and Big Man pressed him again. "Why isn't anybody saying anything?"

Melissa remained silent.

Suddenly Big Man turned to face Ares, grabbed him by his collar and slammed him against the high-rise window. "I SAID WHY ISN'T ANYBODY SAYING ANYTHING?"

Melissa pulled him off sharpish as Ares adjusted his crumpled collar.

"I usually do what you tell me to, Father, but not this time, I didn't make the virus or whatever it is that turned those people like that."

Big Man gave a look to Melissa and calmed down. "Ok, I believe you and hopefully the girls are alright."

"Is that it?" Ares said.

"You were all concerned a moment ago and now you're saying 'Hopefully they're alright'?"

Melissa had also picked up on Big Man's sudden nonchalance and it concerned her slightly as Ares pressed him again.

"Are you trying to tell me something, Father?"

Big Man's demeanour had completely changed, he was far too relaxed now. "Check this out son, Gemma is stronger than you think and as for Aphrodite? The world could get attacked by aliens and she'd still come up smelling of roses, they're safe, probably."

Big Man's withering logic was no comfort to Ares. "Is that all you have to say about it? We have to do something, we have to get out there."

"Don't start waffling on now, Ares, it's too late for that, my girls are stronger than you think."

Melissa looked on astonished.

"You've messed things up royally with your stupid ideas, Father, if the girls are still alive, then you have to go out and find them."

"Me? Go where? How am I meant to find them?"

Melissa touched her hand against Ares's shoulder and squeezed lightly.

"Why are you saying these things, Ares? Your father is as just as worried about the girls as you are."

"You've changed your tune, did you forget that he just dumped you in a shark tank?"

Melissa took a while to digest the information and pulled her headscarf even tighter.

"I've been through worse, trust me."

Ares shook his head and nervously but gently took hold of Melissa's jaw. "You're way too trusting you know."

Big Man eyed his son severely. "Shit, I just realised something, if I bring Aphrodite back in alive in one piece?"

"Yes, Father?"

"Then I might stand a change of getting back with your mother."

"WHAT!?"

Big Man clicked his fingers in a way the young people did today which Ares and Melissa couldn't do, and to be fair, had given up trying.

"WHOOP! WHOOP! YES MATE!"

Ares's eyes bulged in disbelief.

"So the only reason you want to find Aphrodite is to try and get Mum back?"

"Shit yeah, well no, I mean she is my daughter as well."

The skin under Big Man's chin wobbled. "Your mum's going to be so pissed off with me if she finds out I had something to do with Aphrodite turning into a zombie, which I didn't by the way."

"You're serious aren't you? You want to get Mother back? She's a teacher, who left you for another teacher? And you want to get back with her?"

Big Man had a huge grin on his face. "She made a mistake and she knows it, I'll take her back."

"But nobody has seen Mother in years. I haven't, Aphrodite hasn't, nobody knows where she is."

"News travels softlad, there may be a television ban, but your mum will find out about this probable virus breakout and if she finds out that I saved the day and got back her daughter? It's a win-win situation!"

"What about Gemma?"

"What about her?"

"Well she's your daughter too, or have you forgotten about that?"

"Of course I haven't! But she's not my favourite kid."

"How can you say that?"

"Whooaahh! You're not going to trick me lad, I'm not going to say who, just to say I love my main daughter and the other one exactly alike." Ares looked at his dad, not with hate but with disappointment. "Look son, it's like saying if two of your kids got lost in the woods and your favourite made it back home, you'd look for the other one, just not right away."

"So why did you try and adopt Gemma then?"

"Well I'd thought it'd bring her real father, Elias Glaucas, back from wherever he was so we could continue our game? But that was years ago and nobody's heard from him, so that plan backfired, but I'll save her as well, I'm not a monster, Ares! Two for the price of one." Big Man clapped his hands and rubbed them with glee. "I'm going outside Ares, it was never in doubt."

Ares shook his head slowly and looked away. "You're incorrigible, Father."

"Aphrodite says that a lot, I'd agree if I knew what that meant."

Melissa stood cradling her temples, silently listening to her boss.

"How do I get out of here then? I can't go through them."

Ares tried to think straight and ran his hand through his jungle of hair. "Then you have to go under them."

"How do I do that?"

Ares made a break from the window and pulled out his phone from his long lab coat pocket, he pressed a few buttons and turned the phone sideways.

"You have to go through the underground tunnel ducts to get out, that's the only way I think, the old vertical shafts are probably safe, slip through the ventilator blades on section C and you could make your way out.

I've got a schematic read out map on my phone of the whole building it's a new app I've got, it shows all the construction and floor plan layouts."

Ares held his phone aloft and waved it like he was a conductor in charge of an opera, a dull green light slowly illuminated the spot next to them.

"You see, that's where we are now." He spun the phone with concentration until more light appeared. "And that's where you need to get to. Of course you're going to need authorisation to get out, but you're the boss and nobody comes higher than you."

"You got that right," Big Man's impatient mood was obvious. "Just tell me where to go and I'll get out of here and get my girls back."

Ares frowned and looked out the window.

"There are miles and miles of tunnels below. If you manage to make your way out of the labyrinth of the lower levels those things will tear you apart in a heartbeat the moment you step outside, you didn't see what happened to that policeman on the security video."

Ares could see his father's excitement bubbling like water in a big pot. "Don't forget Gemma, Father."

She's my kid too, ain't she? Adopted, fostered or not, I'll get her back, her and that freaky spider."

Ares watched his father lick his lips as his mouth was so dry, he was determined to get out there all for the wrong reasons.

"Do you know what suicide is?" asked Ares.

His father stared him down. "Do you know what love is?"

The younger man looked shocked. "I'm surprised you do," Ares said, jabbing his finger in Big Man's chest. "So the only time you care about your children is when it's a chance of a reconciliation with your wife."

Big Man's expression twisted. "Don't patronise me and, yes I do know what that word means and I really don't have time for this. Give me your phone for that map thing."

He reached for his son's mobile.

"No, Father."

"YOU WHAT? You out of your damn mind?"

Ares took a step back, still holding the phone in his hand, his voice was uncertain and hollow. He took a mint from his lab coat pocket and popped it in his mouth, sucking away nervously. "You can't take this phone, I mean what if the girls ring while you're away? Or what if they come back? I've got to stay here in case they do and keep the phone."

Big Man's eyes flicked back and forth between Melissa and Ares, wondering what her take was on Ares's lack of commitment or brutal common sense.

"You're not coming with me? How am I going to get out of this place if I don't know where I'm going?"

Ares raised his right eyebrow, a trick he learnt from his dad; he then turned to look for something in his father's office.

"I can send the map to that printer over there, you can use that."

"Do I have a choice?"

"At this moment in time, probably not."

"And you're really not coming?"

Ares shook his head.

"Then I'll guess I'd better be going then."

Melissa sighed, irritated.

"No, I guess *we'd* better be going then, we've got to—"

"Whoa, whoa, whoa, whoa," Big Man interrupted her with his hand raised. "You can't go with me, you're a woman." He walked over and put a comforting hand on his personal assistant's shoulder. "But thanks for the offer, I appreciate it."

Melissa shrugged off his hand with ease. "Oh please! We can deal with the sexism at work case when we get back."

A look of confusion crossed Big Man's face. "It's too dangerous for you Melissa, you would be scared."

"I just killed your shark, so I think you know that I don't scare easy."

"Oh yeah, I forgot about that, how did you do that again?"

Melissa felt her headscarf slipping and pulled it tighter, with a smirk. "Like I said, ask no questions, Boss and I'll tell you no lies."

The confused look returned to Big Man's face as Melissa kept her smile and mouthed, '*You big Jessie*' to him.

Ares jealously looked at the banter between his dad and Melissa. "Please don't go."

"I'm sorry?"

Ares stood closer to her and held her hand. "I've only just got you back and your leaving me?"

"Leaving *you*?" Melissa chuckled.

"Sorry, I meant leaving. Why are you going? You've just survived a shark attack and now you're off to face those creatures in the tunnels below."

"We're not sure they're down there, Ares."

"But why do you have to go? Stay in the complex and be safe with me?"

She looked at him, clearly puzzled. "You know what your father is like, he can't go down there on his own, he's hopeless like a puppy."

"I am still here you know," Big Man huffed.

Melissa put her hand on Ares's chest and gently pushed him away. "I have to go, if you want your sisters back safe and sound I have to go with your father."

"You mean you *want* to go, because of him."

"Are you going to start this again?" Melissa sighed.

Big Man stared at her and kept his face blank. "What does he mean?"

"Ares thinks I fancy you."

"WHAT?! THAT'S ABSURD! Wait...you don't...do you?" Big Man asked.

"Oh please! You're my boss and I think I could do a little better than you, no offence."

"None taken, well maybe a little bit."

Melissa's eyes softened behind her shades. "Ares, I appreciate the concern, really I do, but we both know I have to go and take care of your father, it's my job."

"No it's not! You're a PA! Not an adventure tour guide. Dad is a joke but I'm sure he can handle a trip in some tunnels on his own."

Big Man raised his hand. "Still here people."

"SHUT UP!" the pair shouted in unison.

"So you're choosing my dad instead of me again?"

"No, I'm choosing what's right, why won't you understand that?"

"Because I know what he's like! That's what he does, he charms you, he's very charming and you're falling for it!"

Her eyes widened at Ares behind her shades. "What's gotten into you. Ares? Your sisters are out there on their own, nobody has heard from them all day and you want to enter a pissing contest with your dad to impress me? Fine, why don't you both stay here and I'll find the girls myself."

"But—"

"But nothing, Ares! This thing is much more important than you I'm afraid."

Her words hurt him and he closed his eyes to think, he opened them slightly to allow a thin glare at Melissa.

"Fine, have it your way then."

Big Man broke the awkward tension. "You do look cute when you're about to cry, son."

"Shut up, Dad." He looked up miserably. "Ok then, now listen you two if you're going…"

"Wait!" said Big Man.

"Can't we use the Dinosaur sentries?"

Ares spoke in a voice that reminded Melissa and Big Man of who was *really* in charge of the situation.

"The sentries aren't ready to use yet and in that tight location, they'd be no good to you anyway as they're too big."

"But couldn't we just arm them and blow a hole through the lab wall and then we could get out that way?"

Ares walked back to the window and pressed his forehead against it. "The flaws with that logic, Father, are that if we arm the Dinosaurs and blow a hole in the building to get out, it would let in the infected and also, the Dinosaurs aren't in this building, they're in tower 6 and this is the Messiah's Complex, so even if they were armed and shot their way out, we'd still be stuck here."

He paused, waiting for a smartarse comment from his father, which didn't come. "Oh righty then, you two should go now, we haven't much time."

The printer had finished with the map and Ares tore it off and scrutinised it with his eyes in a squint.

"You want to take a short cut towards the toxic waste storage chamber and bypass those ventilator blades."

"Is it quicker?"

"It's a short cut, Father."

"So it's quicker then?"

"Yes, it's a short cut."

"So short cut means quicker?"

"Yes it does, hence the term *short* cut."

"And you're quite sure about this?"

"Yes." Ares tapped his head. "Touch wood."

"Guys, can you please stop messing about and let's get moving."

The two men fell quiet like scolded children as Ares meekly gave the map to Melissa. Ignoring his whimpering, Melissa snorted and tried to make sense of the map. She took charge and beckoned to her boss. "We need to get some supplies, food, torches, etc."

"Food? You're the woman, my PA, so that's your job."

She was about to snap and say something offensive, but reconsidered when she saw the worry on Big Man's face, he genuinely meant no offence, that was just the way he was and Melissa *did* do everything for him, Big Man was hopeless at everything.

Melissa smiled and ushered him out of the door, looking back at Ares.

"Take care Ares, and keep this place secure. We will be back, and with the girls too."

Ares looked thoughtful. "Find my sisters and bring them back to me." He hesitated. "Please."

Melissa nodded. "We will."

Ares watched his father and Melissa leave and stayed silent until the huge metal door was shut and locked. He reached into his pocket for another mint and popped it into his mouth. Ares felt a buzzing in his pocket and realised his phone was vibrating, the mint was a different flavour to the one before, an icy freshness entered his mouth as the phone began to flash and finally ring. Ares answered whilst his tongue pushed the mint around his mouth.

"Hello?...hey you!...yeah I'm good thanks...really?... sounds cool!...no I didn't see the football...bit's and bobs I suppose...a little bit strange...it might need some cream...what me?!...possibly...Dad?...He's not here at the moment...you mean now?...oh I see...Yeah change of plan as Melissa went with him...yeah I know it wasn't meant to happen...I know, so don't add them down the tunnels...please? I don't want them to kill Melissa...me too!...I didn't think so either but fair enough...speak to you soon...bye now." He ended the phone call and sucked the cool mint again. "Result."

"Anybody have any idea where we are?"

Aphrodite had given up on trying to keep her dress clean and just focused on keeping her arms covered, but she had heard Odysseus's question and for once had the answers.

"We're in club land or beneath it anyway, you see all these tunnels? This is the biggest club in Olympia, it's called the Labyrinth, many clubbers have got lost in these tunnels so we should stick together." She looked around and saw the sprinkler system dotted around the high ceiling. "One more thing, if any those sprinklers go off, don't ever let the water touch you."

"Why's that toots?" beamed Odysseus.

Aphrodite scratched her arms again, making sure they were quite covered. "Just trust me on this one, ok?"

Jason waited for Aphrodite to catch up and pulled her to one side. "So if you've been here before, how do we get out of here?"

Aphrodite stroked her smooth chin and studied the network of winding tunnels around her. "I think we're near Dangerfield Adventure theme park, the one that goes on all through the night? I think that's very close so we can get out there, we need to go left at this next turning here."

Jason shouted ahead. "TURN LEFT PEOPLE!"

He kept Aphrodite behind. "One other thing, back when we first got out of the tunnel and got into the taxi, when I flipped out for a bit?"

Aphrodite couldn't contain her grin. "Yes I remember, you rolled around on the ground and squealed like a stuck pig."

"Yeah, whatever, how did you know those creatures were on the way? I mean they were too far to be spotted by sight, so how did you know they were coming?"

She looked at him coyly. "I don't know, maybe I just have good eyesight."

Jason wasn't convinced and his silence allowed Aphrodite to ask her own question.

"Since you're in a probing mood."

"I wasn't probing."

"I don't care, but I've noticed something about you too."

"Go on..."

"Well, the little Goth girl Echo was clothes shopping with her dead sister, the human house Mitchy is a tourist, geek boy Connor was looking for comics, I'm guessing love sick Norton was probably trying to buy something to help hide that big gap in his teeth before he meets his date, Odysseus the charmer was letting off some steam after a tiff with his wife, and I had to take Gemma swimming, plus I'm sure the other dead ones had their reasons…"

He smiled lamely. "Reasons for what?"

"For being in town this morning?"

"Should I need a reason to go into town?"

"Well you haven't said why you're here."

"Should I?"

"Would help, darling."

He leaned over to whisper. "Off to see someone."

"Who?"

"Someone took something from me."

"So what are you going to do about it?"

"Get it back, whatever it takes and no matter the cost."

"Whatever darling."

Aphrodite grinned her white teeth to Jason's yellow ones. They walked on silently knowing that each excuse was a barefaced lie, but none had the time or the proof to do anything about it.

Norton's phone purred in his pocket and he took it out, the text message illuminated the dank tunnel.

Hiya r we still meeting then? Thought we were meeting at theme park? Phone has gone a bit funny. Ring me when you get here. Tara XxX

Norton felt a nervous knot in his stomach.

"Tara's just texted me, I really have to see her, she could be in danger."

Connor blew his nose into a much worn out tissue and wriggled it for a while, feeling something still stuck inside he blew out snot on to the ground, before eyeing up Norton.

"She's kind of desperate isn't she? Your girlfriend."

"Connor, she isn't my girlfriend, she's my date, a date who I wouldn't mind seeing before she gets eaten."

"So what you gonna do? Surely you can't go and meet her now?"

Norton closed his eyes, he was imagining meeting Tara and having a fun day out as they'd planned at the theme park only a week earlier. He'd seen her pictures on the dating website they'd both joined; pictures of her partying and having fun with her friends and some of her looking sombre and relaxed at an illegal music festival. It was those photos that had made him get in touch with Tara and her response, her warmth, the humour she shared with him, the moment they clicked, that was the reason why he had to find her, quickly.

"Yeah, I am going to meet her, and I'm leaving now, she's all alone out there and all we'd wanted was a day out at a theme park."

Odysseus scrutinised Norton's concerned face. "Isn't it a bit weird you having a first date at a theme park? I mean surely you'd want to go for a drink first or go bowling or some shit?"

Norton snapped back. "It was her idea and I don't care what you think, she's my date, my friend and I *am* going to meet her."

Odysseus rotated his neck in the dark until he pleasurably heard it click a few times. "Your funeral then chump, I won't cry for you."

Jason caught some of their conversation and hung back, gently taking Norton to one side. "Are you sure about this? Those creatures are running crazy on the surface, you could get yourself killed."

Norton was reflecting on events of the past evening and failed to answer.

"Norton?"

His eyes drifted back to Jason's voice. "Sorry, what did you say?"

"Do you think it's such a good idea to go back and find this girl?"

Jason had Norton's full attention now. "I know it's not safe up there, which is more reason to find Tara and make sure she's ok. Look the theme park apparently isn't too far from here, most of our phones are working so I'll ring or text you to let you know that I'm safe."

"It's too dangerous Norton, your gonna get yourself killed, look what happened to Tero and Quinn." He looked to see if Echo was out of earshot. "Echo's losing it, she's just a kid whose lost her sister and I don't know how long she can take being back down in these tunnels."

Norton shrugged. "What do you want me to do?"

Jason put up his hand in a 'halt' motion to Norton and called ahead. "ECHO? ARE YOU OK, LOVE?"

Echo turned around and gave a tired pathetic smile with a head nod, her head kept shaking through nerves and looked like a toy dog nodding on some car dashboard. Jason turned back to Norton.

"Do you see how she is? Help me, stay with me, I can't guide these people to safety on my own, the situation's getting worse out there, you know it is."

Norton let out a slight breath and gently slapped Jason on the shoulder.

"Jason, you don't need me man, Echo's still in shock, hopefully she'll come round soon, Mitchy seems to be clued up, well now anyway, and Gemma and Connor are good kids."

"But that's just it! They're mature for their age but they are just teenagers at the end of the day."

"And the end of the day is almost here. In fact it could be the end of the world, and they've survived it, give them some credit, dude."

Norton raised an eyebrow to Jason and whispered, "But watch out for Odysseus and Aphrodite, I don't trust them, him especially. Her...just watch your back."

They both watched the elegant figure of Aphrodite walk on ahead and were still struck by her poise even in the damp dirty conditions, they watched memorised as she neatly tucked a stray blonde hair behind her ear, Jason just about switched his attention back to Norton.

"So you're still going to go?"

"I'm not going to lie to you Jason, I'm scared, scared shitless if I'm honest, I get my first date in ages on the day the city has turned into zombie type things, you couldn't make it up really, but I'm not going to leave a defenceless girl out there all alone, I was brought up better than that, although you wouldn't know that if you'd met my mother."

Norton tried to keep his mind away from his mother's demise earlier today and his part in it.

Jason swatted his hand away from a fly buzzing around him. "Yeah, I can see you're a decent man, Norton, shame the dead have chosen to rise on your date!"

Norton's face entertained a warm smile, *Decent? If only he knew what I did this morning,* he thought. "So do you think the dead have risen then?"

"I don't know what those things are, if it's some plague, or chemical related? And I don't know if the whole world is affected, we've just seen what's happening in Olympia, but you're old enough to remember zombie movies before they banned television, those things aren't too dissimilar to them and we've struck them in the head and they've stayed down, so who knows?"

"So what are you going to do? You do know that you're not in charge anymore?"

Jason laughed and clapped his hands together and some of the group turned to see what was so funny.

"Yeah, I know it sucks that we're now following Aphrodite! But if she can get us out of this labyrinth safely then fair play to her."

Norton began to back away. "Look, I'm going to sneak off, please don't tell the others, I'm not good with goodbyes."

"Well if I can't persuade you to stay all I can give you is my luck." Jason looked up and around at the musty tunnel. "Saying that, it hasn't done that well for me."

Norton smiled at Jason's refreshing honesty. "You've done well to get us this far, well far enough, and then back again to the city!"

"At least we're not going around in circles, I hope!"

Jason noticed the group pressing ahead. "Look, I must catch up with the others."

"Yeah, I know, remember what I said, watch out for Odysseus and Aphrodite."

"I will…and you watch out for everybody!"

The two men who had become good friends as Olympia lost the plot smiled, hopefully not for the last time at each other. It was only now even in the dark that

Jason noticed the large gap between Norton's front teeth, it made his smile somehow warmer and it made Jason chuckle.

"Take care, Jason."

"You too mate, Vaya con dios."

Jason ran up to catch the others, refusing to look back as Norton disappeared into the shadows. His mind was now filled with the image of Norton getting torn apart by the infected and he shook his head to rid himself of these thoughts, he now thought interacting with the group could help and he called out to release those fears. "ECHO! HOLD ON."

The teenage girl was walking in between Gemma and Mitchy; she turned around and lowered her eyes as Jason came running up behind her. "How you holding up, sweetheart?"

"Sweetheart?" Echo's voice rose.

"Honey? Is that better? I'm not sure really."

She welcomed him with a better smile than before. "A little better thanks, it's not as bad as the last tunnel..." Her voice trailed off and she looked over Jason's shoulder expectantly. "Where's Norton?"

"He's gone honey, gone to meet his date, Tara."

Echo stopped dead in her tracks and softly moaned reverting back to a questioning little girl. "Why? Why did he go and not say goodbye?" The whole group had stopped now to hear Jason's explanation much to Aphrodite's annoyance.

"He just wanted to leave without a fuss that's all, apparently he's not good at saying goodbyes and he really needed to see Tara."

Echo wasn't convinced and kept her childlike whine. "But we could have helped him, we should have stuck together."

Jason put a consoling arm on her shoulder. "I know sweetheart, but he's a smart guy, he came this far like us, didn't he?"

She was resigned to losing the discussion and backed down. "I guess so, he was just a nice guy, that's all."

"Hey!" Jason playfully nudged her, his mouth an open grin. "I'm a nice guy too you know!"

Echo finally giggled. "I know you're a nice guy, but you've been like our boss? Didn't think you did 'fun'."

"Well I can and I am!"

"Sorry, boss."

"Come on then, let's go and piss off Aphrodite."

Echo cheekily bumped him with her bottom as they walked on. Jason quickly bumped her back.

Aphrodite's mouth twitched, a reflex action when she was deep in thought. "Hmmm." Her mouth had stopped moving and she had finished thinking. "This way, we go this way I think."

Mitchy slapped her forearm quickly as a little beetle tried to make it's home there. "To be fair, are you sure you know where you're going?" she asked, still feeling the crawling sensation on her arm.

"As sure as you know your way around a kitchen, darling."

Jason just caught the tail end of Aphrodite's sharp rebuke. "Will you stop winding her up, Aphrodite?"

"Thanks Jason, but I'm fine and little miss moody here can't bring me down."

"I don't think a hurricane could you bring you down with those legs, darling."

"APHRODITE!" Jason ordered. "Stop it!"

Aphrodite couldn't be bothered to argue with Jason's sharp, no nonsense tone.

"Oh poo! You're no fun."

"We can have fun later, Aphrodite," Connor spoke in his slow comfortable twang of an accent from Billenge City, based in the north of Olympia. "Now we have to find a way to get out of here and—"

He noticed Aphrodite's voice seemed fuller than usual and he ran up alongside her, his eyes shrunk with suspicion. "Are you eating?"

Aphrodite shook her head dismissively as Connor peered at her face in the dark.

"Yes you are! You're eating the last of the chocolate bars!" He turned around and ran back to their adopted leader. "Jason! Aphrodite's eating the last of the chocolate bars."

Jason sighed in amusement. "Rise above it, Connor and be the bigger man."

Connor turned away and shot a cheated glance up the front. "I think I can see chocolate on her lips!"

"It's brown lipstick," came Aphrodite's hard reply.

"Children please," Jason pleaded, he chanced a looked at the girl in front. "Any luck with the directions, boss?"

Aphrodite didn't even bother to look back. "You're an amusement aren't you? But we're here." She wiped her lips away from Connor's view. "If we go up and through this nightclub here there's a tunnel leading from the main front exit all the way to the street…we should be able to…well, I don't know what we're going to do and where we'd go but this is an option."

"You're sure this is the right way out?"

She nodded casually. "Yes Jason, this is one of the ways to get out."

Aphrodite fell silent as a cold feeling suddenly crept upon her. She knew this more than she had let on. Years ago she had danced on its various themed night floors in the most revealing of outfits and the highest of heels, there were times when she shouldn't have been in there in the first place, being either too young or too drunk, but she always went back to her favourite nightclub, her and stooge friend Sabrina constantly partied there, until that faithful night when her self-indulgent life changed forever. She scratched again at her arms, the constant reminder of that night.

"But even though it pains me to say so as I don't really like any of you, I've told you once and I'll tell you again, there are some sprinklers in there scattered all over the club. Some are quite visible, others are hidden well, but for whatever reason they should release their water, don't ever let it touch your skin."

"Why's that, honey?" Mitchy said, wiping her sweaty brow.

Aphrodite slightly wobbled on her high sling backs on some uneven ground before answering. "Trust me, you don't want to know."

"Is there something you're not telling us, Aphrodite? Because strange as it sounds and I think I speak for everyone here, it's the first time I've heard you sound worried."

She shook her head, making her blonde hair sway. "I don't do worried."

"Terrified maybe then?"

Aphrodite turned around, Jason couldn't make out her smirk in the faint light. "You think I don't get you, Jason? You think I don't respect you? I know I've pissed you off and I know you could kick my fantastically shaped arse if I stood out of line, but trust me, you're heading into my territory now, so just watch your step."

Jason relented.

"Fair enough, lead on."

The nightclub's lower level resembled a huge cave clearing with a giant indoor waterfall still operational. Gemma peered over the barrier and looked into the gushing waves. "I wonder how deep that water is?"

"Don't know, don't care," came her sister's short reply.

The wary group followed her up the long winding staircase until they came to a metal ladder leading them up to the club's first level as Gemma was still fascinated by the cascade of water flowing inside the building.

"How long until we get to the next level, Aphrodite?" Connor huffed.

"Not as long as you'll have to wait for your next date, Goth."

Mitchy felt a sheepish grin appear, as Connor's mirrored hers. "I'll give her that, that was a good one," he winked back. Echo moved slowly up the steps, glancing behind her and wincing. "I'm sick to death of climbing up ladders, it's all I do at the moment."

A cold draught swirled around Gemma's feet taking her away from her waterfall trance.

"Sorry, what did you say, Echo?"

"I said I was sick to death of ladders for one night."

Echo had come to a stand still and Gemma right behind her nudged at her feet. "WHAT? STOP PUSHING! I'M JUST TIRED."

Gemma under her breath swore slightly and then with a sigh arched her back and rotated her shoulders. "Wait there," she whispered to her old friend.

Gripping hard with her hands on either side of the ladder's metal bars Gemma leaned back slowly and heaved herself up, hand by hand climbing up the ladder, she crawled spider-like over Echo with an amazing effort, her legs dangled behind her as to not to disturb her friend from her place on the slight steps, Gemma was now above Echo and nestling above the tired girl reached down with a spare hand. "Take it and hold on."

Echo reached up grabbed tight as Gemma with an almighty effort pulled her up and placed her on her back.

Mitchy looked up, concerned. "You sure you can do that, honey?"

Gemma's voice strained a reply. "Wait." She shuffled Echo slightly to make herself more comfortable. "Not too tight." Echo slowly loosened her grip around Gemma's neck. "Yep, cool."

Aphrodite looked down the ladder with a stony face. "Finished? Why don't you give her a make over whilst you're at it?"

Gemma managed a huff. "Echo's tired, Aphrodite, I can't exactly call her a cab to take her away."

"You'd best call her a ambulance if she doesn't shut her noise."

"Is it chilly up there on your high horse?" Gemma said grimly.

"Wow! My little fake sister is finally growing a pair, I'm slightly impressed."

"I haven't even started," Gemma growled.

Mitchy sadly studied the tired figure of Gemma on the ladder. "Just ignore her, honey."

Aphrodite scrambled up the ladder with a smile. "Yes! Listen to our resident house, she knows it all. I'm here just trying to save all of your scrawny hides and your taking it out on me? Ridiculous!"

Jason was still not completely used to all the name calling, never had he heard such bitchiness in such a limited amount of time of meeting somebody, even with his days of being a teacher, he looked past the others on the ladder and in a routine conversational way spoke out. "Nobody is having a go at you, Aphrodite, we just need you to get us out of here."

"So you need me right?"

"Yes we need you."

Aphrodite stopped climbing and held her pose. "Say it then."

Jason, taking a deep steady breath to calm his nerves, slowly closed his eyes. "Say what? You're holding everybody up."

Aphrodite stayed still. "You know what to say."

Jason hesitated for a moment and then threw her a dirty look. "We need you more…"

Aphrodite's slender right hand left its place on the ladder briefly to wipe more sweat from her face and bit the top of her lip in expectation. "More than what, Jason?"

Jason looked below at the others and then to Aphrodite expertly hanging on to the ladder.

"More than you need us."

"That's what I wanted to hear."

Jason sighed. "Just get us away from this place, maybe we can find Norton on the outside." His tired voice stopped and then started again slowly and quietly. "Vaya con dios, my friend."

"What did you say?" Aphrodite asked.

"Vaya con dios, it's from the old language, it means 'Go with God' I think. I just hope he's ok."

The socialite beamed and licked her teeth with her probing tongue. "We're here."

The Labyrinth nightclub was an enormous complex, a purpose built underground entertainment arena within the rocks. The whole area was known as the clubbing district with many clubs built above in the city, but the biggest and classed as the best was Labyrinth. It had been forced to close down years ago, the official story was something boring like the owner couldn't get a proper alcohol license, but Aphrodite knew the truth, that her father was the reason why the popular club had to close – her dad and *those sprinklers*.

The second tier of the nightclub was an impressive sight, even in its now neglected state. Its main stage still looked bright and inviting with a mic stand alone at the front. A laminated dance floor lay chipped and cracked, unused and missing the thunder of hundreds of clubbers. Hanging from the ceiling on huge industrial suspension wires was another dance floor, with a third floor swaying slightly above it. The glitter ball in the centre of the ceiling rotated ever so slowly, covered in dust, its dazzle had long been put to sleep, the overhead lights dimly lit each of the dance floors.

Snaking their way all around the ceiling ornaments was the sprinkler system which made Aphrodite stop dead in her heeled tracks. A sad selection of cheap bottled beers still stood behind the counter of the main bar.

"Wow! Is that a swimming pool over there?"

Like the dance floors above it was a huge swimming pool suspended at each corner with suspension wires.

Aphrodite ignored the now excitable Connor as she watched silently at the sprinklers, slowly releasing a drip of water or *something* that trickled through the cracks on the floor and into the indoor waterfall below.

Her heart was cold as many people told her throughout the years, but being back in *that nightclub* had obviously shaken her and making her just a little bit human as the hairs on the back of her neck froze in tandem with her heart, she shrugged as the question from Connor finally registered with her.

"I can't believe there is a swimming pool...above a waterfall...inside a nightclub...hanging on wires! That is pretty cool!"

Jason, surprised by the uncharacteristic behaviour of the usually morose Connor, answered him instead. "Yes, it is pretty cool I must admit, Aphrodite, but we still have to find the way out of here, do you know where we're going?"

Her eyes beamed across the empty bar stools, which were always full whenever she went clubbing, but now they just played host to cobwebs and dust. "Aphrodite?"

She glanced over her shoulder at him.

"God, yes, I'm so sorry, what did you say?"

Jason was taken aback by the change in tone. "The way out? Where do we go?"

"We can climb up to the swimming pool, walk around it to the elevators off the platform or go to the right and up those ladders which would lead us to another level and then to, I think an exit? Choice is yours." Aphrodite softened even more and a short smile escaped. "Let's just go up and through the swimming pool and get out of this dump shall we?"

Jason took a moment to compose himself and nodded. "I think we'd all agree on that one."

The group made another laborious task of climbing up ladders to reach the precariously balanced swimming pool level. The people with mobile phones turned on their home screens, the batteries were low on power and the dim light barely showed up the bottom of the vending machines scattered around the pool. The water was stagnant and stank more than most of the group could stomach.

"This smell is rank."

Mitchy sniffed the air and agreed. "Something sure smells funky in here, it's probably the water, looks like it hasn't been used in years."

Aphrodite noticed a solitary sprinkler set above the swimming pool, leaking its water above the pool. Something Gemma noticed too. "That's strange having a sprinkler above a swimming pool don't you think?"

Aphrodite paused, her eyes remembering an age old grief in the club. "More than you know."

Connor looked at Jason. "Do you think we should try and get some food out of those machines? We've no idea how long we're going to be down here for."

The terrible smell had Jason distracted momentarily, forcing Connor to ask him again. "Jason? The vending machines?"

"What about them?"

"Shall I break them open for food?"

Jason was about to reply when he saw Echo's eyes slightly light up.

She had caught a glimpse of something which improved her mood, like Connor. "Oh look! They have heart sticks here." She skipped around the shaky platform of the pool and picked up the two sticks laying at the foot of the one of the vending machines, they glowed slightly and hummed as they were in Echo's hands.

Mitchy scrutinised her for a moment. "Heart sticks? Oh wait I remember."

She thought back to the quaint demonstration she'd had from Hutson in his store earlier. *"Don't you remember? Grooving with these sticks, back in the day?"*

A sad bleary smile appeared on Mitchy's smile, thinking back to the kind man. "I remember them, you go girl, you little star."

Echo grinned. "Well you're a star to me too, Mitchy."

Aphrodite cut in. "Well I think she's the same size as a star anyway."

Echo ignored her and continued, she waved the sticks in her hand and started to gyrate away, her hips rotated and she thrust and bound herself forward to the sounds of music in her head, twirling the sticks and throwing them up in the air and catching them like an over enthusiastic cheerleader, her legs nimbly moved to the left and then the right as she continued to groove away to her heart's content. Echo's neck nodded quickly, her eyes shut as she reminisced about the tunes she used to dance to before things turned to despair in Olympia.

Jason whispered to Mitchy. "What's she doing?"

"I think she's dancing," Mitchy announced. "Well I think you can call it dancing."

Jason's eyes were wide but empty. "I know she's dancing. But why?"

Echo started to attempt some back flips and she spoke out between each one. "These are called heart sticks, we use them for dancing in clubs."

"How old are you again, sugar?"

Echo had spotted a metal bar used for pole dancing and was already on it before Mitchy had finished.

Unable to make her way up the ladder to reach the nightclub, Echo had now found the energy to pull herself up the pole, her legs wrapping around it. Then she leaned backwards released her hands and allowed herself to seductively slide down the pole upside down. Her head was almost touching the floor when she finally answered. "Old enough, Mitchy."

"You dance in nightclubs, sugar?"

"Occasionally, it does pay the bills."

Aphrodite tugged at her skirt uncomfortably. "Pay the bills? How old is the little strumpet then?"

Echo held her position on the pole and glared angrily at Aphrodite. "Just because I pole dance doesn't make me a tramp and besides, you're the one dressed up like a reject from a lingerie shop."

Mitchy grinned. "Busted!"

Jason was concerned as Connor was now on the other side of the pool, kicking the front of a vending machine filled with chocolate and bottled water. Like a nervous parent he called out, "Connor, stay close to us, don't wander away."

Aphrodite pulled a face. "Have we finished with the skank aerobics class? Or are we actually going to attempt to leave this place?"

Jason beckoned to Connor but the gesture went unnoticed. Aphrodite stood with her arms crossed in indignation. "I've only been babysitting you children for five minutes and I'm sick of it already! I swear to God that potty training was easier than this."

"Can't imagine you getting your fingers dirty."

"It's a figure of speech darling, have you not heard of it? It's basically me telling someone that Jason is a dick."

Jason smiled and paused, a nervous edge crept into his voice. "Mitchy, where's Odysseus?"

Mitchy's eyes expanded and quickly darted around the cavern. "I don't know, I haven't seen him."

"Since when?"

"No idea, I honestly don't know."

"Shit."

Gemma stopped watching Echo dance, sensing something was wrong. "What is it? What's happening?"

Jason tried to hide his anxiety. "Nothing honey, everything's fine."

She held her breath in disappointment. "I'm not a kid Jason, I know something is wrong."

He didn't have time to lead her on. "We've lost Odysseus, we don't know where he is."

Gemma whirled around and retreated slowly away from her dancing friend, realising that she too hadn't seen Odysseus for a while. "When's the last time anybody saw him? Did he climb up with us?"

Echo released herself from the pole. "What's going on?" she asked.

Gemma's voice fluttered slightly. "Odysseus has gone, nobody's seen him."

Echo instinctively reached for Gemma's hand as panic began to set in. "WHERE IS HE? HAVE THEY GOT HIM? THEY'VE GOT HIM, I KNOW IT!"

"Keep it calm people, Connor, get back here now."

Connor was still blitzing the vending machine, he shouted over. "I'M ALMOST INSIDE! GIVE ME A MINUTE!"

"WE DON'T HAVE A MINUTE!" Jason yelled back.

Mitchy moved several paces towards Jason and whispered, "I don't remember Odysseus on the ladder or the nightclub."

"I know, he may have snuck out on us."

Mitchy felt a twang of guilt. "I never even missed him."

"Me neither, and that's bad, that's real bad from our point."

"Do you think those creatures may have got him?"

Jason slowly answered, uncomfortably. "There is that possibility that they've taken him and if that's the case, we're in trouble, we have to leave quickly. APHRODITE! WE ARE LEAVING!"

Aphrodite still stood with her arms crossed and huffed, "Finally."

Gemma cradled Echo and signalled to Jason. "We have to go." She began frantically pointing at Echo to remind Jason of her fragile state.

Jason acknowledged this and hustled the two girls over. "Come on you two, Gemma stay close to Echo, keep an eye on her."

"Yeah, we're fine we just have—"

Gemma's voice cut off suddenly as she studied something on the floor. "Oh my God."

"What? What is it?" Echo stammered.

"Look at the heart sticks."

The two sticks lay at the base of the pole Echo was dancing on, as all heads turned towards them, they began to slowly illuminate the poolside. Huge clumps of algae floating on the pool surface glowed red from the pulsating dance sticks. The wall behind the pole was now a crimson hue as the humming continued.

Echo broke free from Gemma and backed away fearfully. "OH MY GOD! THEY'RE HERE! THEY'RE INSIDE!" She began to shudder uncontrollably.

Mitchy turned to Echo who was close to becoming hysterical. "We don't know that for certain, honey."

"LOOK AT THE BLOODY STICKS GLOWING, WOMAN! THERE ARE MORE HEARTBEATS IN HERE!"

Jason found himself backing away from the pole, his eyes alert. "Be quiet for a moment, Echo."

"BUT THEY'RE HERE!"

"Please, just for a moment, everybody just stay calm."

The group did what they tried to do from the very start of the afternoon, and listen to Jason. "If those things are in here, we need to be quiet."

The heart sticks continued to glow rapidly in the silence which began to unnerve Jason more than he let on, most of the far end of the pool was illuminated by the red glow of the heart sticks – the only noise that could be heard in the entire complex was Connor on the other side of the pool still trying to ransack the snack machine. Jason called to him through gritted teeth. "Connor! Get over here now."

"I'm almost in."

"I mean it!"

"But—"

"NOW!"

Connor was so close to breaking in the machine, he sighed and took a step back and glared at Jason.

"I was almost in there, I could have got some food and fresh water for us."

Jason knew the truth in Connor's words but knew time was probably against them, he checked the increasingly glowing heart sticks and it convinced him even more.

"It doesn't matter Connor, we have to go."

Connor straightened his back and rubbed his foot, the one which had done all the bashing to the front of the machine. "You know I can see people's death, right?"

A headshake from Jason convinced Connor to continue and raise his voice to the whole group. "Well, they're coming," he informed them purposely.

Echo's ears pricked up. "YOU SHUT YOUR MOUTH!"

The sticks continued to glow and now began to vibrate off the stage as the heart rates continued to increase. "Just thought you'd like to know, I can feel death coming."

Echo screamed at him. "WHY ARE YOU SAYING THIS?"

Jason was beginning to lose his patience with the Goth. "CONNOR, STOP IT AND GET OVER HERE NOW!"

Connor licked his lips. "So when they come for you and catch you, they'll feast on you, what are you going to do?"

Echo raced over to him, nimbly sidestepping the dancing pole and around the swimming pool she hurled herself at his slight frame, the slap she sent to his face shocked everyone watching. "WHAT THE HELL IS YOUR PROBLEM?"

Connor gazed sadly at her whilst rubbing his jaw.

"I'm only saying...some of us are going to die."

Echo slapped him again, prompting Jason to run over to the pair. "Will you two just cut it out please?"

The heart sticks were throbbing with a purpose now as Jason tried to separate the feuding teenagers. The three stood by the foot of the pool arguing and pushing one another. It was only Gemma who noticed at the corner of her eye a section of the water rise. She pulled away from Mitchy and screamed with authority to the trio. "RUUUUUNNNNN!!"

The stinking water of the swimming pool had come alive and shapes reached out and grabbed Echo, Jason and Connor.

"IT'S THEMMMM!" Mitchy roared.

The weed covered creatures leapt from the waters and pulled down the closest three at poolside. As they fell the water from the pool splashed up and hit Gemma in the face and chest; she fell back as the filthy slime sat in her hair and turned streaks of it green. Churning waters were beginning to sweep everybody to the centre of the pool as the infected held on to their prey.

Mitchy raced to the poolside as Aphrodite waited and held back. Weeds hung off the creatures as they lurched from the pool. Jason, Echo and Connor were completely submerged as Gemma wiped the slime from her eyes and hurled herself at the foot of the pool to pull one of them out. "ECHO! GRAB MY HAND! She reached into the pool as Mitchy ran over and hovered above her.

Aphrodite noticed pool activity with her sister and for the first time slightly showed some emotion, she concentrated on her sister. "Don't touch the water, darling!"

But it was too late, the young girl reached into the pool and with Mitchy holding her waist, managed to haul out the shivering Echo. She collapsed on the side, shaking and holding her throat, gasping for air.

"IT BURNS! MY BACK IS BURNING! IT'S BURNING ME! HELP ME PLEASE, FOR GOD'S SAKE!"

Whatever was in the water it ate through her clothing and chewed rapidly through flesh and tissue, her back was exposed and the slime seeped in.

"THIS WASN'T SUPPOSED TO HAPPEN," she screamed.

The black hair she proudly sported was being overtaken by a new bright red strand, no black on her head remained as the red completely took centre stage. Echo's body convulsed violently by the poolside.

"GRAB JASON! GRAB JASON!" Mitchy screamed to Aphrodite, who was staring at the higher deckings of the whole nightclub. Level two was swaying freely and movement from the upper tier she kept her eyes focused and carried on looking as something from the top burst through the exits above, she watched them as they scuttled forward.

"Here they come," she muttered.

The infected creatures were high above dance floor level three. They clung upside down to the platforms and pipes, crawling like bats sniffing out their would be prey, the heart sticks were beating in a frenzy as suddenly the infected paused for a brief moment, and then simply dropped. Figures fell from the extremely high ceiling and on to the platform below. As they landed, some of their legs broke on impact, bones pierced through skin as they crawled closer.

Many shapes dropped straight into the pool, green water splashed up everywhere as Aphrodite did her upmost best to avoid it. More and more humanoid shapes emerged from the pool, covered in green slime.

The support wires swayed dangerously with all the added weight.

"WHERE'S JASON? WHERE'S CONNOR?" Mitchy yelled.

"THEY'RE STILL IN THE POOL!" Gemma's eyes diverted from the trembling Echo to the thick water.

Aphrodite calmly pointed to a spot in the water. "There's Jason."

Gemma moved quickly again and this time jumped into the pool.

"Don't," Aphrodite whispered, but it was too late.

She waded in, fully aware of the infected people making their way towards her. Mitchy waited by the edge.

"I CAN'T SEE CONNOR! CAN YOU?"

Gemma didn't answer, her actions spoke for her, she held her breath and dived under to where she had roughly last seen him.

"GEMMA!"

But she didn't reply to Mitchy, who was nervously looking around at the infected making their way around the platforms towards her. "GEMMA! WE HAVE TO MOVE NOW!" There was no sign of her. "GEMMA! WHERE ARE YOU?"

Mitchy tried hard to control her breathing and kept on repeating to herself in her head

Please don't be dead. Please don't be dead. The woman who had come to Olympia for a holiday could only see the infected clumsily shifting in the water. Gemma still hadn't resurfaced and Mitchy shot a worried glance to Aphrodite. "Still no sign," she whispered, her gaze worriedly shifted back to the pool.

Then Mitchy heard a splash close to her, she turned towards the sound and saw Gemma finally breaking through the water's surface with Jason in her hands, struggling desperately to make it back to the edge with the added weight. Mitchy refused to let Echo pass out and shook her whilst keeping an eye on Gemma, the young girl spat out green water and coughed hard. Mitchy's hands left Echo's side and pulled Jason out from the slime. He too shivered like Echo, completely covered in foul rancid water. Gemma ignored Mitchy's outstretched hand and looked back deep into the pool's centre.

"I STILL CAN'T FIND CONNOR, I'M GOING BACK IN."

"NO! THEY'RE TOO CLOSE."

The pool was well over its weight occupancy and the wires began to show it. Infected humans were well past the centre and were closing in on Gemma, they couldn't swim but simply drifted towards her.

Then something far more sinister hit Mitchy, the waters began to bubble and churn and something else, something bigger began to make its way toward Gemma. At the dimly-lit poolside Mitchy couldn't start to comprehend what it was, all she could see was a glimmering apparition rising silently from the water behind Gemma.

A fluttering of giant bat-like wings unfurled and cut through the pool; Mitchy stood rooted to the spot as a shiver coursed through her body. *What the hell is that?* she thought briefly.

Mitchy bit her lip, trying to quell her thumping heartbeat until she saw the crest of the wave and finally saw the horror of what was chasing Gemma – writhing and twisting like a giant snake, its head poked through the surface.

"No, no no," Mitchy repeated.

Gemma, oblivious to the creature, bobbed back up to the surface, still unable to find Connor. Mitchy whimpered a warning. "Gemma swim." The girl couldn't hear and Mitchy repeated herself, her voice shaking with fear. "Please baby, swim."

Aphrodite stepped back onto the landing stanchion and noticed Mitchy mumbling. "Listen you, we really have to get going, those things are dropping from the—"

She stopped and ignored the slumped bodies of Echo and Jason, her eyes were now fixed on the shape looming in view towards her little sister. She studied it and then suddenly recognised the bulk of the creature; she had seen it before, its scales, its markings and for a moment, its eyes. "GEMMA! SWIMMMMM!!!"

The pure emotion coming from the Aphrodite shocked herself and Mitchy, who managed to clear her head began shouting at the top of her voice too. Gemma made the big mistake of glancing behind her and took on water, eyes wide in panic.

More of the infected humans writhed around in the pool as the waters were doing something to them and mutating their DNA into something far more horrific. The pressure on Gemma's lungs was agony as she struggled to breathe, Mitchy roared instructions, urging her on. "DON'T LOOK BACK BABY, SWIM AS FAST AS YOU CAN!"

She kicked frantically, her strokes becoming more erratic, as the powerful new creature began to catch up with her. Even Aphrodite began gesturing, unbothered that her arms were now on show as her sleeves moved up. The teenager was tired and began to slow down.

"NO! BABY DON'T STOP!" Mitchy screamed.

Panic had well and truly set in as Gemma looked back again and saw huge shiny fangs in the water, looking as if a grin had emerged as they were almost on her, she screamed involuntarily and all the air from her lungs was spent. Gemma took on more water as she struggled to swim. Both Aphrodite and Mitchy reached out their hands as Gemma slowly inched closer to the platform around the swimming pool.

The platform remained still but the pool was close to collapse, there was a gap in between the two which Gemma would have to jump across to be safe, her eyes stung with slime, burning it's way through the water, she bobbed up and saw how close she was from the support platform. She reached out with her hand, but something huge and inhuman had a hold of her ankle, she managed to claw a hand to the platform, but before she could grab hold of either her sister or new friend a massive leathery wing, not dissimilar to a large bat, and had completely engulfed her little body and pulled Gemma still kicking and screaming below the murky water.

"NO!" Mitchy screamed.

Aphrodite looked hard to follow her sister's descent and whispered towards the pool. "Gemma? Gemma?"

The swimming pool rocked soundly as the winged creature thrashed around in the water, two of the support wires snapped with the added weight and the whole pool created a mini tidal wave effect.

"MOVE!" Mitchy shouted.

She managed to pull Echo and Jason from off the poolside and onto the flimsy walk around platform. She shouted again. "APHRODITE! IT'S TOO UNSTABLE! WE HAVE TO JUMP!"

Aphrodite casually turned to Mitchy and offered her hand to her, Mitchy climbed up wildly and gasped in horror as the two remaining metal wires began to groan and twist themselves free from supporting the pool's sides.

The indoor swimming pool built inside a nightclub, which itself was built within a rock face was unable to support the various creatures inside and finally snapped.

It fell through the various club levels and headed towards the waterfall canyon below, the winged creature managed to find its voice and roared a horrific angered war cry as it dropped. Aphrodite tried to scream but couldn't, her throat wouldn't allow it, she simply watched the entire swimming pool containing her foster sister Gemma, the Goth boy Connor, countless infected humans and now this gigantic horrific silhouette of a creature plummet and vanish into the waves below.

Aphrodite in some people's eyes was too posh, a bitch, gorgeous, ruthless, stuck-up, and an ice queen, but it wasn't until she heard the swimming pool finally crash into the canyon that none of that mattered and only a whimper left her lips. "Gemma."

Mitchy leaned over and shook Aphrodite more in concern than frustration. "We have to go, those things are coming."

A flood of the infected humans were making their way around the platforms and closing in fast, Mitchy moved forward boldly. "Grab Echo, I'll take Jason." Aphrodite's lips moved to reply but no words came out. "We have to move now, quickly!" Mitchy reminded her.

Aphrodite swallowed hard and began to drag the unconscious body of Echo to the nearest exit. Mitchy grabbed hold of Jason and followed suit, she was thinking of the swimming pool and its plummet towards the waterfall below. "What the hell was that thing in the water?" Aphrodite mumbled something unintelligible whilst trying to find the best way to drag Echo. Mitchy eyed her through tired lids, unable to comprehend the mumblings from Aphrodite. "What did you say?"

Aphrodite rolled her blonde head and suddenly focused. "It was a dragon, it was a dragon in the pool."

8. SHE'S GOT ISSUES

Norton found himself climbing his way out of the labyrinth faster then he'd expected. The many tunnels and ladders which had clubbers lost for nights on end and if rumours were to believed around Olympia, sometimes more, hadn't troubled Norton at all. People around the city whispered and rumoured about the caverns of the nightclub holding weary dancers, trapped there and unable to escape from its catacombs, he didn't really believe that story, no matter how many gullible people tried to tell him otherwise.

He was surprised how easy it was for him to get out though and thought Aphrodite was exaggerating on how hard it was to actually leave the nightclub. His throat was thick with dust as he mounted yet another ladder. *Almost there* he hoped more than thought.

The lighting was minimal in the tunnels and Norton's eyes were very used to the darkness, he had been underground for the most of the day now and it was a murky grey in front of him instead of the pitch black he'd started with.

Norton's phone buzzed again in his pocket and he felt a wave of excitement wash over him as he had a pretty sure feeling of who it was, but then he cursed aloud as his hands were busy gripping to the rungs on the ladder.

He stopped climbing and tried to get his body into a comfortable position on the steps, once satisfied as he shifted his weight, he reached into his pocket and took out his phone. In anticipation he realised he was still holding his breath and slowly released it as he read the text on the phone.

Where r u?
R u still coming to meet me as I'm getting worried.
Ring me when you get here.
Txx ☺

Norton's stomach churned as he had a feeling he was close to finally meeting Tara. He replied with skill as he fiddled his answer with his free right hand and gripped tightly to the ladder with the left.

I'm going through hell to meet her, he thought, and a slight smile followed. Norton was closing in on the manhole cover which he'd seen far too many of for one day, he kept climbing with new determination and squared his shoulders ready to push hard against the metal cover. With his hands placed firmly on the cold plate Norton strained hard and nudged the cover open. The new fresh air whipped soundly around his face and Norton held firm to truly appreciate the feeling of escape from the labyrinth, he stayed there steadying himself on the ladder with the cool wind flying around his face until his brief moment of solace was interrupted. "Dude, you're like coming up from the ground man, what's up with that?"

As Norton suddenly felt woozy, a man with smooth brown skin and bright blonde hair and a dirty green tracksuit looked at him with hazy eyes and a dazed out girlfriend with equally bad fashion sense on his arm. "Dude, it's crazy man. You just rose from the ground like a groovy snake, and it's like wild man."

The man's female companion swayed as he spoke. "Babes? Did that man just come up from the ground?"

"The dude just appeared like magic."

The girl could barely stand and leant on her partner for support, Norton thought he could smell alcohol on them.

She steadied herself and continued rambling. "Are you a magician or something?"

Her boyfriend answered slowly, "Dude, he's a cool magician."

"Excellent."

"Most excellent."

"I know."

"I know you know."

"I know you know I know."

"I know you know I know you know."

Norton had begun to clamber out of the manhole whilst this meeting of the minds continued. He swore softly as he tried to get a word in edgeways. "Do you know where I am?"

The man laughed and nuzzled his girlfriend who giggled warmly. "Dude, you're in a manhole, man!"

Norton drew a haughty breath as he finally pulled himself free. "I mean where is this place?"

The girl clapped her hands together. "This is Dangerfield Theme Park, babes, open all day and night."

Relief finally came to Norton, brushing himself down he took out his phone and rang Tara. When he heard her voice on the other side, his heart skipped a beat with excitement. Her voice seemed genuinely pleased and relieved to hear that Norton was ok, they spoke and finally arranged where to meet up. The couple smiled meekly and the boyfriend craned his neck to try and listen in on the conversation. Norton spun his back around when he thought he was in earshot. Ending the phone call, he caught the slick eyebrows of the girlfriend furrowed together.

"Everything ok, babes?"

Norton beamed a strong hard grin as he turned to leave, fighting excitement. "Everything is great!"

He was in mid-stride running off, when he hesitated and turned back to the loved up couple. "Thank you so much for your help."

As the two watched him shoot off into the fast becoming foul smelling breeze, the corners of the boyfriend's mouth lifted slightly. "Dude, is most welcome."

"Babe's, he is so polite!"

The boyfriend shifted his gaze towards his partner. "He's gone now, you can drop the act."

The girl quickly slid free from the man's arms. "Is that him?" she asked. The man just nodded as he felt her eyes studying his expression, he spoke only to divert her attention. "It's a shame that he's the one though, seems so nice."

His girlfriend sobered up immediately, her expression tightened. "I know, but we have a job to do unfortunately." She pecked him on the cheek. "Plus we can stop playing 'boyfriend and girlfriend' now."

The man laughed. "Bit creepy wasn't it?"

Her mouth moved again but no words came out, a frown appeared instead. "Do you want your scarf?"

"Yeah, best give it to me now," he replied.

The girl reached into a bag and handed him a long silk-like scarf. "Are you sure we're doing the right thing?"

He looked at her quizzically. "Why do you have to say that? It's what Dad would have wanted, we owe him that much at least?"

"But is this the right way? We're going to be hurting so many people."

The man looked to the skies and closed his eyes hoping to find some solace in the dwindling rays of the afternoon sun. But it was late evening now and the full moon illuminated the sky along with the lights of the theme park. He ignored her comment and simply snaked his arm through hers. "Come on you, let's go to wa—"

The girl pulled him back. "What did you say?"

"Let's go to work, I said."

She eased up a little. "Sorry, for I moment there I thought you said 'Let's go to war'."

The man smiled and allowed himself to be led by the girl. "Aren't they the same thing?"

She tilted her head slightly towards him. "Guess we'll soon find out."

As the couple began to head off towards the centre of the theme park, they failed to hear the sound of metal scraping against the road as the manhole cover was removed again as another figure emerged from the labyrinth.

The shifty character wiped dust from his eyes and like Norton earlier, breathed hard to appreciate the cool fresh air, even the slight waft of decay didn't bother him. Odysseus arched his back and stared at the departing couple. *What the hell is going on here?* he thought. He covered back the hole in the road and stealthy followed them, just has he'd done with Norton. But as he left to enter the main theme park, the manhole cover was moved aside for the third time and the wafting pungent smell of the dead became much worse as some decaying figures found their way out to the surface, this time the manhole cover wasn't replaced.

Big Man studied the map and looked back to Melissa, and then back to the map again, she anticipated what was coming next. "I don't get this, I don't know where we are."

Melissa screwed up her face and told him to wait as she snatched the map from him and mimicked his map reading, she handed it back to him. "We're lost aren't we?" she said.

"Do you think so?" Big Man's voice was laced with sarcasm.

"You're a pompous piece of trash," she muttered.

"What did you say?"

"Oh, you heard that! You didn't hear me say 'turn left ten minutes ago' or 'we're going the wrong way'?"

Big Man gave an impertinent shrug of the shoulders. "Just thought you were moaning."

Melissa gazed in wonder at him, taking in the sheer stupidity of her boss's comments.

"You haven't seen me moan yet sir, try getting dumped in a shark tank."

"You going to get all upset again?"

Melissa lowered her head. "Believe me sir, you've never seen me very upset."

Big Man wiped his eyes from the strain of map reading and listening to Melissa, he mumbled beneath him. "It's like being married all over again."

"What did you say?"

"I said I wish I carried a pen! You know to mark where we're going?"

Big Man's personal assistant put her hands on her hips and slowly cleared her throat as Big Man supposedly took charge. "So I think we have to go *that* way."

"You positive?"

"Yes."

"You're still very calm for someone missing two kids."

"I'm sorry?"

"I said you're still very calm."

Big Man fiddled with his ear. "Sorry, I can hear you now."

"Are you really taking this seriously?"

With his thick eyebrows wriggling like a couple of hungry caterpillars, Big Man drew close to her and finally acknowledged what she was saying. "What? So you're saying that I don't care about my kids?"

"Don't get all defensive with me, sir."

Melissa's eyes burned behind her deep shades. "It's just that you are incredibly relaxed for someone in this position."

Shaking his head dismissively, Big Man grunted. "Aphrodite can take care of herself, she's a big girl now."

"So what about Gemma?"

"Gemma is cleverer than you think you know, give her some credit."

"Of course she is, her father is a school teacher."

He covered his face with both hands and slowly dragged them until his head was clear, a sigh came next as Melissa watched and waited for a reply.

"I'm her father now by the way, did that slip your mind?"

"But it's obvious your not her real father, you still move your lips when you read a newspaper."

Big Man gave a short shrug. "Alright, you may have a point, I might have bitten off more than I could chew, but I've got a funny feeling that everything is going to work out fine and the girls are going to be ok, we'll find Aphrodite and Gemma Wylde very soon, just you wait."

"Thought she was keeping her name as Gemma Glaucas?"

"Yeah, well we're working on that, might bribe her or something, buy her a new spider."

Melissa jutted her lip. "She already has a spider doesn't she? Buckby I believe."

"Oh yeah, right, forgot about that."

"You're not all there, I think you're knitting with one needle!"

Big Man smiled thinly. "Sounds familiar."

As the two cautiously went in this new direction, Big Man noticed Melissa studying the map which she still held, straining hard to see the directions as she still wore her shades underground. "Why don't you take your shades off?"

"With all due respect, why don't you drop dead?"

He baulked at her reply. "You know I am *still* your boss?"

"Then act like a boss and show me some respect, sir."

Big Man knew he'd upset her and would have to be very careful from now on, the thought lasted just for a moment. "I was just wondering why you *always* wear those shades, you can take them off now you know."

Melissa felt another wave of anger wash over her. "Really? After all these years you've still no idea why I wear these?"

Clueless, he shook his head. "Should I?"

Melissa sighed softly and let her anger subside. "No, it doesn't matter, sorry for snapping at you."

Big Man blissfully carried on looking around, uneasy if to ask Melissa if they were travelling in the right direction. "It's fine," he said meekly.

They had been walking beneath the tunnels of the apparent indestructible fortress for ages now as Melissa's eyes trawled over the many lines over the map. Big Man studied the girl who although had been in his employment for many years, he still knew almost nothing about, always dressed in black and always in her trademark headscarf and shades, she was punctual, polite and until that outburst recently, no temper.

He turned and kept his eyes front, but then turned back to Melissa. "You know what we need? We need a day out at a theme park."

Melissa blew out an exasperated puff of air.

"Ok, seem to remember having a reasonable time there."

Big Man stopped walking. "Actually I was thinking we should go now."

Melissa flapped her arms wildly in frustration. "ARE YOU OUT OF YOUR MIND! YOUR KIDS ARE MISSING AND YOU WANT TO GO TO A THEME PARK? I MEAN WHAT THE HELL IS WRONG WITH YOU?"

Second time she's lost it today, Big Man thought.

"We've been wandering round these tunnels forever to find *your* children so you can queue behind a bunch of useless, over-privileged, allergic to everything, spoilt brats?"

"Pretty much," Big Man said hastily as Melissa caught her breath.

"You know what? I don't know why I bother working for you sir, you're 'up yourself', quick tempered, rude and you're as stubborn as a herd of mules."

Her words meant nothing to him and he carried on.

"So you'll come then to the theme park with me? See if the girls are there?"

She released a heavy sigh and gave a disgusted snort. "You're incorrigible."

Melissa's words finally stopped him cold and a smooth smirk spread across his face. "I know what that word means now."

Gemma knew the sound of water only too well, her dad, her *real* dad, Elias Glaucas, had made sure she was able to swim as soon as she was old enough. She vaguely remembered days out with her dad *and* mum, going to the local swimming baths and then an afternoon picnic, this was when her family had spent time together, before her dad became a headmaster, before the arguments over coming home late and neglecting both of the women in his life happened, and before her mother left them.

Water was what kept her happy, obviously apart from her dad, Auntie Kay and her missing beloved spider Buckby, it was nice to splash in its cool inviting arms, even her new family made an effort to take her swimming every now and then, even though her foster sister Aphrodite couldn't swim.

Aphrodite would stay by the poolside, dressed as always in her evening attire oblivious to her sister's wave thrashing and keeping her eye on the lifeguards dotted around the pool.

That was the *old* water, the water she splashed around in on bath night, the water she dipped her pet spider in to frighten the poor creature, the water she playfully ran zigzagging through the rain. This new water wrapped itself all over her, was inside her, this water was trying to kill her.

Gemma was swept up on the rocky shore aggressively by the water, it spun her body around and tickled her lungs again before leaving her alone at the very bottom of the water cavern.

The teenager managed to haul herself from the water and coughed up the rest of the water from her lungs, sick quickly followed the flow of water from her mouth and a creamy new texture swiftly sat on the water's surface. She clambered onto the jagged rocks, cutting her hand in the process. Holding her injured hand she watched coldly as the blood oozed from the cut. Making her way slowly back down the to the water's edge and she dipped her hand in, the cold flow of water cleaned the wound as Gemma shook it some more, this was the type of helpful water she was used to, she forced more blood out and looked around, the mighty waterfall in front of her particularly grabbed her attention.

"HELLO? ANYBODY THERE?" The strong waterfall surged powerfully over her cries. "ANYBODY? I'M DOWN HERE!"

Gemma rubbed the still bleeding wound with the thumb from her other hand, she coughed some more, still remembering to cover her mouth, something Elias had taught her from a very early age, she winced as her closed fist wrapped around the cut as she coughed into it. Panic hadn't set in just yet, she knew she was lost, alone and had no idea if the others were still alive. She wobbled on the rocks and felt a bit light headed, her arms began to itch, Gemma scratched them vigorously – it was as if an army of ants were inside and gnawing away at her bones. Her arms felt hot as she tried to get rid of the itching, wading back into the water she rubbed them hoping the burning sensation would stop. Gemma caught her reflection as she flailed around, making her stop dead, she peered long and hard and felt her hair and pulled strands slowly between her fingers. *It's green?…my hair is green!*

The right side of her hair had turned a shocking green, she flung it back and shook her head, but the green still stood. She caught herself giving an irritated look via a reflection in the water. *Can this day get any worse?* she thought.

The low rumbling ominous growl she heard in the distance confirmed it could. A sour stench wafted over from the middle of the water as something rose from the remains of the swimming pool which had crashed down from the upper night club floors above. The smell grew strong and hit Gemma like oily rotting meat and she put her hand to her mouth as what appeared from the pool drew utter revulsion and finally from her, a surge of fear.

A huge black dragon stood in front of her, its underbelly had a line of perfect scales, its long snake-like body shifted on four armoured muscular legs, the hind legs were stumpy and smaller than the long front ones. It preened its huge bat-like leathery wings as it studied the teenage girl in the distance, on the back of its neck it had a row of razor-like quills and a crest of muddled flesh bent into a fin on the top of its head which glimmered in the soft light. A massive spiked tail splashed around nonchalantly in the water.

Gemma's eyes grew wide and she cursed under her breath, her first dad would have been disapproving of her swear word, the second one would have loved it but given the gravity of the current situation, Elias would probably let this one slide.

Silver razor-sharp teeth appeared in gaping jaws and the dragon seemed to smile as it now began to approach her. Gemma heard herself whimper and knew the dragon could now see the slow fear on her face. *Ok, it's a dragon, a big dragon, a dragon with sharp teeth walking towards me.*

Her face changed from uncertainty to confusion in seconds, her eyes began to twitch like a beheaded chicken. She looked around quickly and noticed a cave opening to her right, looking back at the dragon, she slowly started walking backwards keeping eye contact with the great beast.

The dragon seemed to have cottoned on to what the girl was trying to do and released a slow guttural snarl in contempt.

Smoke began to appear from out of the dragon's nostrils and the creature rocked its enormous head from side to side and rose on its hind legs unsteadily whilst releasing a jet of flame from its nose high into the early levels of the nightclub. A huge roar came out of the creature, echoing all through the labyrinth, Gemma covered her ears at the deafening noise, the creature only stopped as it dropped back to its four-legged stance, breathing heavily and thick black smoke leaving its hot nostrils. It bellowed once more and twisted its long neck over its shoulders, taking its reptilian eyes off of Gemma – which was the chance she needed. With a blast of confidence and adrenaline Gemma turned and bolted towards the cave, struggling in the now knee-high water. The dragon cocked its head and roared in defiance, it allowed its prey a few shaky steps before releasing a flame burst from its nose.

Recognising the sound of intense flames from the exploding fuel station earlier, Gemma fell headfirst into the water, the flame burning her clothing and searing her exposed back. "AGGRRRHHHH!!" Gemma screamed in agony and spun around to let the water at her back.

She could now see the dragon edging towards her, trying to ignore the dreadful pain on her back she was on her feet again but it was making it harder to reach the cave opening.

Despair shot through her as the pain in her back was too much and she knew she wasn't going to make it, for a despairing moment she turned to look at her pursuer, who was almost upon her.

Gemma was forced to face the truth that after everything she had been through today, now in the most bizarre of circumstances, she was about to get eaten by a giant dragon.

She struggled to lift herself back up and looked again at the cave mouth, frantically trying to see where she could climb up for safety. With the water in her eyes, Gemma struggled to see ahead, but something crouching on the cave entrance made her stare in disbelief, she breathed heavily again and tried to take in what her eyes were showing her.

Something huge and barely camouflaged crawled gently down the rock face. Eight long giant segmented legs scuttled across the face of the cave, covered in grey hair, the legs probed their way around the rocks, unsure on where to go. Gemma watched mesmerised at the giant spider crawling around the cave entrance. The dragon had also noticed the huge arachnid and gave a growl of discontent, quickly growing louder. It started to edge slowly towards the spider, with Gemma caught in the middle.

She continued to try and run away from the dragon as the water crashed against her knees, one wave knocked her off her feet and she fell in the wrong direction.

Laying on her back she looked at the spider making its way along the cave face. Gemma spat out water and looked behind at the dragon and then quickly back to the crawling spider, a huge relief washed up alongside her and her eyes focused again, she was ashamed at her fright earlier and stood in defiance against the waves trying to knock her down. The eight eyes of the spider saw the confusion fade in the young girl's face and witnessed Gemma stand tall. She stood rebellious in front of the dragon and butterflies took over her stomach, her face went numb and she mumbled some words under her breath towards the spider, eyes fixed on the giant arachnid. The spider stopped moving when it heard the girl's whisper but nothing else. The black dragon moved slowly towards both Gemma and the spider and the teenager took one last look behind her and again to the spider and through gritted teeth spoke again with confidence and held out a outstretched hand to it. "Come baby."

The spider dropped down into the water, its fat hairy body sat tense in the water.

Its tail thrashing around wildly in the water, the dragon roared again and swayed its head from side to side baring its teeth and stomping its front legs, ready to attack.

With its fangs on show the fat spider raised its legs in a defensive position, with every step the dragon took, the spider's pose changed.

Gemma ducked under the surface as the dragon took to the air and made the first move. Even beneath the water its roar was still deafening and she resurfaced quickly, it flew over the spider and knocked it back with a strong tail whip. Crashing back into the rocks behind it, the spider regained its composure and kept its legs up.

The dragon was fascinated by the size of the spider and circled around it a few times before landing close by. It didn't growl or grunt, just sized up its opponent.

Gemma lifted her head from the water and saw how close she was from the dragon, the giant jaws of the monster were open, just near her tiny face, and then it charged. It raced like a greyhound towards the spider and collided with it sending it sprawling back into choppy waters, Gemma watched as the dragon moved on to the collapsed spider and started to hammer it with its forelegs, the spider gave no resistance as the rain of blows rained down on its body, one of its legs was crushed to a pulp by the repeated blows and was torn from its body.

With the spider seemingly lifeless, the dragon turned its attention to Gemma who dipped her head back into the water trying to stay submerged, but realised she couldn't tell where the dragon truly was and poked her head back through the surface. She had to run away now and started to splash away from the glimmering dragon. Huge feet began to stamp after her, fanning its mighty wings as it ran. There was no way she was going to outrun this monstrosity and her legs began to falter. Gemma was resigned to her fate and simply stood still as the dragon moved in, its jaws slowly descending on her.

A cloud of noxious fumes swarmed around her head from the dragon's mouth making her bend over double and retch, she closed her eyes and waited for the end. Maybe it was the sight of the little girl quivering beneath it that made the dragon hesitate for a moment, Gemma opened one eye and looked over to the crumpled body of the spider and waited for the bite to come, it never did and this was her chance. "BUCKBY!" she screamed.

The spider flipped back onto its now seven legs and crawled with extraordinary speed towards Gemma, the dragon reared up like a startled horse and spat out a jet of flame at Buckby.

This *was* her pet spider, the spider she thought was lost in the tunnels, the spider which had remarkably grown enormous in size maybe due to the water, the spider which was scampering quickly to save her, with incredible ease the giant spider side-stepped the shot of flame which enraged the dragon more. It was uninterested in Gemma now but almost trampled on her as it squared up to Buckby once more. Another burst of flame left its mouth but Buckby flipped over allowing the fires to miss again.

Shifting its huge bulk the dragon lined itself up for another fire shot but the spider was faster and twisting its thorax in the air a fine jet of webbing left its behind as if it had been shot out from a gun, the force from the webbing smashed the dragon right in the mouth, breaking teeth as it hit its target.

Eyes wide with primal fury the dragon shook its head desperate to free itself from the sticky substance. Gemma heard the snorts and squealing of the monster as it tried to chew through the webbing. Unbeknown to the dragon Buckby was already on the move and darted up onto the dragon's shoulder. Long fangs repeatedly broke through the dragon's armour and sunk into soft flesh.

There was a blur of motion as Buckby struck again, biting hard. The titan twisted its back and roared with pain struggling to shake off the spider, fangs embedded deeply.

It was becoming more difficult for the dragon to move its arms and legs as the spider's venom coursed through its veins, it began to stumble as its eyes grew weary.

Twitching and jerking it finally succumbed to Buckby's poison and slumped into the water. Gemma stood up in the water and hoped she felt safe for the first time. She looked at the giant spider which had climbed down from the dragon and stood motionless.

Looking at its battered body a gooey mess pumped from the stump where its eighth leg used to be.

Its eight eyes were dark and oily and she sucked in a deep breath as the eyes didn't move as she moved cautiously towards her now huge pet. It looked old and horribly scarred and its white fangs stood out like a beacon in the dark.

The dragon wasn't dead just unconscious, its heavy breathing almost drowned out the sound of the waterfall.

The spider raised its front legs again and Gemma froze where she stood, she lifted her head and looked around slowly, there was a gnawing in her stomach as she realised that the dragon was standing up again. An utter roar of rage came from the enormous beast. Before she could move a shot of excruciating pain struck her neck, her skin had been punctured and her body began to spasm. "Buckby, what you—"

She failed to complete her sentence as the venom took hold, the pain was becoming too much and she let out a choked cry more with shock as her spider had betrayed her, she feebly tried to beat off the spider throwing her arm across the spider's many eyes. It's legs picked her up from the water and began to encase her up in a sticky mess of fine webbing.

Her pet was too big to sit on her back and was now hovering above her held by single strong web strand. It hung on to Gemma tightly as it continued to wrap her up into a little parcel. She couldn't even scream out in agony anymore, even though the pain was unbearable her face was completely covered in webbing. Her fingers and toes grew numb and her final thought before she passed out was *I don't want to die*. Only the blood from the puncture marks from her neck could be seen, she was covered from head to toe.

The dragon looked on, shaking its head to rid itself from the efforts of the spider venom.

Buckby carefully placed Gemma's body in it's front legs, taking complete care with it's load as the dragon stomped and grew more agitated. Panting heavily it staggered a step towards the spider. With Gemma securely wrapped up in its cobweb, Buckby simply watched from the other side of the rocky shore, its eyes sensing alarm, it started to turn around and scuttle back into the cave.

With an almighty effort the dragon took to the air again with Buckby in its sights, the underground cavern was filled with the sound of the dragon shrieking.

The plump round body of Gemma's pet crawled quickly through the cave, the dragon's steely eyes were fixed on it, the creature didn't flinch, it didn't blink, just spat out another flame burst at Buckby. The flame hit an underwater heating pipe which immediately exploded. Its aim was true as the force of the blast propelled the spider through the cave. Buckby's legs burned in the heat and snapped forward in unusual directions. Another leg was lost due to the violent unnatural movement caused by the explosion.

A roar of triumph came from the glimmering beast and it stayed in the air and made its way up into the higher levels of the nightclub, completely disinterested in the carnage it had left behind.

The flames danced all around the squashed body of Buckby, but they couldn't penetrate the webbing which was still wrapped tightly around Gemma.

The spider fought for control of its package but the flames were too much. Buckby made a vain attempt to push Gemma's web compartment to safety but a huge cauliflower of flame still hung in the air as the fires illuminated the sides of the cavern. Gemma was unaware of the flames hissing around her protective shell, she was also unaware of the body of her great spider sinking slowly beneath the waves.

Aphrodite stopped for a moment and leant against Mitchy, with her back pressed into her like a club dancer on her pole. She breathed heavily as she dragged behind her the stricken body of Echo, whilst Mitchy had hold of Jason. Mitchy sat with her legs wide, back to back with Aphrodite, and sighed softly, "I don't believe this."

"What? Has the price of chips gone up again?"

Aphrodite's reply was met with a quick roll of the eyes from Mitchy. "No, I meant that we're lost again, I thought you knew your way around these tunnels?"

"I do know my way around these tunnels, just as you do around a cake shop."

"You've used that gag already tonight, you're losing your touch."

Mitchy turned and gave Aphrodite a soft punch to the shoulder. Even in the poor light Mitchy could just about see a smile on the posh girl's face. It was ended as soon as Echo screamed again. "PLEASE HELP ME! MY BACK IS BURNING, OH GOD, HELP ME!"

Mitchy placed her hand on Echo's forehead.

"She's burning up, she's got a really bad fever, that water obviously has affected her."

"What shall we do then? I mean apart from being passed out and an idiot, Jason seems fine, I prefer him this way actually."

"Well we can't stay here, it's not safe, not with those creatures still lurking around, Echo's shivering so much it's like she's going cold turkey."

"I suppose any turkey is good for you, cold or hot."

Mitchy raised her eyebrows as Aphrodite's grin returned. "I believe that's a new gag, still got it!"

"Indeed."

Mitchy turned her attention to Jason. "Jason is out for the count like you said, don't know what the water has done to him."

"Hopefully it'll give him a personality."

"Honey, this is serious."

"I'm not joking."

Mitchy shook her head soberly. "Well, I'm not staying here, we have to find the others and get out of here."

Aphrodite stared back at her, with a look as sharp as a blade. "Others? What others? Everyone has left us or died on us."

"That's not true."

"Really? Norton, gone…Odysseus, gone…"

Aphrodite shivered slightly and paused. "Connor is dead and, so is Gemma."

Mitchy detected more emotion then ever coming from Aphrodite, the loss of her foster sister had affected her more than she'd let on.

"We don't know that for sure."

"You may be the size of a small house, but even I had put you down for having some common sense."

"But..."

"BUT NOTHING. MITCHY! NOTHING COULD HAVE SURVIVED THAT DROP, GEMMA'S DEAD... END OF..." She had a guilty look in her eye. "Daddy's going to be so mad."

Aphrodite brushed her hair behind her ear and rubbed it slowly and then frantically began to scratch her arms.

A second of confusion flashed across Mitchy's eyes. "You ok, honey?"

Aphrodite shook her head clear. "Of course I am darling, what was I thinking?"

"I'm sorry about your sister."

Aphrodite held her head up. "It's funny, after all these years, she was just finally becoming ok."

"You ok yourself? I mean you were the only person I've seen since this stuff kicked off today who has remained remarkably calm I guess."

"Didn't plan on losing Gemma though."

"I know honey, we didn't plan on losing anybody."

"I've lost my sister."

Mitchy reared her head.

"Did you actually acknowledge her as your sister even once?"

Aphrodite shrugged and went to stand up. "This will be the first and only time."

A groan from Jason made them both turn their attention to him.

"Jason? You ok, honey?"

He looked around sluggishly and rubbed his arms. "My arms itch."

"They will for a while," huffed Aphrodite.

Mitchy's eyes flashed a glare to her.

"I mean that's what I heard, apparently..."

Jason sat bolt upright. "We're still in the tunnels, aren't we?"

"Yes honey."

"I can remember being in the water."

Mitchy felt uneasy recollecting what happened. "We came under attack from 'you know what'."

"Did we lose anybody?" There was no reply from anybody. "I said who did we—"

"GEMMA!" Aphrodite cut in.

"We've lost Gemma and the little Goth boy."

"Connor," Jason said, his voice rough with tiredness and now touched with grief.

"I'm sorry, Aphrodite."

"Not your fault, you're still in the lead, we followed you, we lost four or five people? Following me, we only lost two."

Mitchy's lips made a disgusted sound. "That's uncalled for, honey."

"No, she's right, I blindly led you people out and then back through all sorts of tunnels today, with each time losing more of the group."

A trademark shoulder rub came from the larger woman. "You didn't force us to come, honey, you rescued us."

"You certainly did," Aphrodite added.

"You're a real knight in shining armour."

Jason wiped down the back of his neck and sighed. "I see your sarcasm hasn't gone away."

"Seven on a scale of one to ten, darling."

"Missed you too."

"Looks like I have a compassion thing for losers, who knew?"

He looked over to the teenage Echo, laying shivering next to Aphrodite. "Is she alright?"

Mitchy narrowed her eyes slightly. "She had a worse reaction to the water then you, she's burning up and her back is red raw, we have to get both you and her to a doctor, what's your doctor's name?"

"I don't know."

Aphrodite caught his tired eyes. "Darling, you don't know your doctor's name?"

"Listen I don't even know my dad's name."

She threw him back a fierce grin. "Typical."

Struggling to his feet Jason looked around worriedly. "We can't stay here for too long, not with those infected zombie things down here, but we take care of Echo and try and find Norton and Odysseus on the surface, and are you really sure about Gemma and Connor?" Mitchy's sad eyes gave him his answer as he continued. "Then I guess we should get moving, 'tough times don't last, tough people do'."

Aphrodite's shoulders tightened and a feeling as if someone had stuck their hand in her stomach and pulled out her insides and began to force feed them to her, she couldn't breathe, she felt sick and couldn't move.

"What did you just say?"

"Excuse me?"

"That saying, about tough times not lasting, where did you hear it from?"

Jason winced at the sudden sharp tone in her voice.

"I don't know, just a saying I heard."

"From where?"

"I don't know…just…around I think one of the guys from work maybe?…Why do you ask?"

Aphrodite stroked her perfectly formed and covered abs before standing. "Just wondered I guess."

Aphrodite's eyes grew curious and it unnerved Jason, she held his face softly with both hands and gave him a peck on the cheek. "I'm sorry, didn't mean to frighten you."

Jason looked away nervously. "Ok, well no it's fine I guess."

"Is there anything else I should know?"

"Yeah, we also have a dragon chasing us."

"A DRAGON?! Like in the fairy tales?"

"Yes, just like the fairy tales."

Aphrodite's face furrowed and she let out a reluctant sigh. "Mitchy darling, could you please pick up Echo? We really must be leaving now."

Jason wasn't satisfied and wanted more answers, he sucked in his breath and gently grabbed her arm.

"So a dragon was in the water too right?"

Aphrodite took a deep breath as well and tried to collect herself.

"Listen, we really don't have time for this, I suggest we move along quickly."

"Wait, what with everything we've been through today and you're going to leave me hanging on about a dragon?"

Mitchy instantly jumped to her feet, a struggle in her tight-fitting trousers, her voice was quavering.

"Aphrodite?" she protested.

"Yeah, I know, I'll take Echo."

Jason still wanted information. "So this dragon, where did it come from?"

"I'm not sure," said Aphrodite, quickly ushering Echo along the narrow pathway and carried on until they came to an giant entrance, which opened the cavern up.

Jason shook his head and looked perplexed. "What did it look like then?"

Aphrodite suddenly turned around to him, hands on her hips in an annoyed stance.

"It's black...black armour-like skin with beady red eyes, one eye is bleeding and it's got a silver, glimmer thing on it's head like a crest."

"A glimmer fin?"

"No, a glimmer thing, as in 'thingy me bob'," said Aphrodite defensibly.

That sounds familiar, she thought. She carried on quickly. "Its teeth are razor sharp, with a few missing."

"That's quite a description," Jason said with eyebrows raised. "How did you remember that?"

Aphrodite looked at him blankly and then said, over her shoulder, "It's standing right behind you."

Norton would have loved to been able to jump on the rides at the theme park. He had never been to one before and looked on in awe at the different shapes and sizes and the cool movie-like name each ride had. He wasn't aware if these film names were relevant or recognisable to Olympians as new movies were banned and had to go underground, the new government were slowly coming around to the notion that 'Nobody actually dies in a movie', unlike the game shows in Olympia where fatalities were part of the entertainment and were encouraged, but it was a baby government, so baby steps had to be implemented.

The Dangerfield theme park stayed open all day and night and was the only park in the district to do so, plus, with the ban on television as well as movies, the park was more popular than ever. Families, big and small, old and young swarmed on all the rides and lapped up all the excitement as Apology Day drew to an end.

The plan was for Norton *and* Tara to enjoy the rides together, his date – his first date in ages, a date who he'd been looking forward to seeing all day, this day which was rapidly falling to crap around him which had started with his mother.

He hadn't spotted any of the dramatically changed bloodthirsty human type things and seeing that the screams from the people in the park were from having their stomachs turned from the intense rides and not from having their intestines ripped from inside of them, Norton knew he still had some time to find Tara.

Norton looked up to the darkening sky and exhaled in exasperation at the time showing on his phone. He had climbed out of a manhole in the centre of the park and Tara was apparently waiting at the entrance.

He glanced at a large map to his left and saw an arrow pointing to where he was and where the entrance was *supposed* to be. After a pause Norton burst out laughing and spun behind him, he started to run as he could see the entrance and became overwhelmed with nerves, the crowds were still pouring into the theme park, but he could see sitting on a bench just left to the huge Dangerfield sign was a pretty blonde girl; she wore a little blue skirt and a white top, a long multi-coloured chain hung around her neck which she idly played with.

Her hair was short and blonde and as Norton silently approached her, he could see her toenails were painted a bright orange and poked out from her sandals. Norton couldn't take his eyes off the beautiful creature as she neatly crossed her lovely legs and gave one a gentle scratch. He gazed across the entrance gates between the hordes of people coming in and leaving, but the little blonde firmly stood out, waving and smiling at toddlers tumbling over in front of their parents.

His sharp brown eyes were wide with intrigue and they took in every movement she made, she was really enjoying herself, which was in quite contrast to the texts he had received from her earlier.

Eventually, his gaze met hers through the crowd and Tara stood up from her bench as he moved closer.

"Norton? Norton is that you?"

Norton's eyelids rose with excitement and a nervous smile emerged. "Tara?"

Tara leapt from the bench and threw her arms around Norton. It was a while before she let him go and stood back. "Where have you been, Mr? I've been waiting here for ages!"

"Sorry! Wait...so you don't know what's been happening downtown?"

Tara's nose wriggled in a cute way as she thought and Norton liked her even more. "No, why? What's been happening downtown?"

Norton studied the cute dimples on Tara's face and her perfect white teeth, her eyes looked up questioningly to his. She was innocent, full of life and completely unaware of the horrors that Norton had been dealing with all afternoon, she continued to press him.

"Norton? What's wrong?"

Norton looked to the sky and tried to smile back at his date. "We can't really stay here Tara, it's not safe."

Tara snaked her arm through his much to his surprise and enjoyment. "So why can't we go inside, mister? I've been looking forward to this all day and you *are* late, so you owe me some time in the theme park, young man."

She shook her finger at him in a comical manner. Norton looked around nervously, there didn't seem to be a sign of the infected entering the park and he did owe it to Tara as he was horrendously late for their date.

"Ok, let's have one ride, maybe two? And then we have to get out of here, really."

Tara squealed with delight and pecked Norton on the cheek. "Come on then, Mr late! We're going on the ghost train first, your treat!"

She broke free from their arm lock and did a cute little twirl which made Norton chuckle.

Tara was a free sprit, a fun girl who loved life, the manner in which she danced around in front of him was a joy to watch and as Norton saw her spinning around in delight, there was no way he could disappoint her this evening. He broke up her little dance routine, only to hold her hand and finally enter the theme park.

"Ok missy, let's have some fun shall we?"

"I don't know why I didn't think of this before."

Big Man was in fair spirits as he and Melissa finally found an exit that hopefully would take them to the theme park. The reduced light was sufficient enough to show them that they had reached another long ventilation shaft which seemed to lead to the main generators of the park.

"If I knew all I had to do was crawl through other people's shit and piss to get out of my building, then I would have done it ages ago."

Melissa wiped her mucky hands on her leather trousers; excrement stained her shades. She turned her back from Big Man to take them off, her eyes were closed tightly, not even attempting to open them as she blindly wiped her shades on her leg. With her eyes still shut, Melissa felt her shades with her fingers, they were clean enough to put back on her face, which she did so quickly. Big Man looked on indifferently. "All spiffy clean?"

Melissa blew her nose to the floor.

"It's hard to know when you're being sarcastic."

"I wasn't actually, have you any idea what it's like to be a prisoner in your own home? It's ok for you, you can come and go."

"So?"

"So I don't have that luxury knowing that a hitman may put a bullet in my head."

"Big baby."

Big Man baulked. "What do you mean?"

"You brought it on yourself, you and your silly game show? You're responsible for this and all the lives you ruined and ended, you've got nobody to blame but yourself."

Big Man looked genuinely shocked. "That's a bit harsh, isn't it? What brought this on?"

Melissa went quiet and merely showed him her shit-stained clothes with a wave of her hand.

"Oh yeah, I see what you mean."

Melissa shook her head, refocusing on the moment. "I think you take things too far, Big Man."

"Sometimes it's better to go too far than nowhere at all."

She sighed a low hiss like sound.

"Besides, what bought this on? Like I said earlier, you knew the crack? You could have walked away when all this stuff was going down years ago, but you didn't, you just stayed on the payroll and got your cash when innocent people were dying."

He was finding his flow now. "Besides, none of those people who entered my games were innocent, they were all fame hungry nobody celebrities who wanted a piece of the action and died because they were too stupid enough to figure the shit out or too weak to fight."

"So what about the kids from the school?"

"THEY WON! THEY WRECKED EVERYTHING, THEY GOT ALL MY SHIT CLOSED DOWN! AND A BOUNTY ON MY HEAD! I DON'T FEEL SORRY FOR THEM, FAIR PLAY FOR KNOCKING ME OF MY THRONE AS IT WERE, BUT THEY DESERVE WHAT THEY GET."

"Kimberley?"

"Listen, you going to start that again? I didn't want the girl to die, not yet, she and the others were meant to escape from Gommerstall prison and Jago was meant to delay them just for a bit until the next stage in the game was being prepared, then Jago went loony tunes and blew the ship up and it crashed somewhere, so everybody is dead as far as I know."

"But *could* be alive? The ship that stolen from Spizer Airport was one of yours anyway, hence that's why we knew what was happening inside with our cameras and Jago's feedback, but don't all your flight ships have cryogenic chambers, so they could be alive?"

Big Man lowered his head to his knees and scraped some more mess from his suit. "Why are you so bothered about them anyway? It's not like you knew them or anything?"

"Elias Glaucas used to be my teacher, he was a good man."

"I didn't see you come to his aid when he was being dragged around my stadium all those years ago, and you do know he destroyed my prison?"

Melissa ducked as they began to walk passing low beneath the main ventilation shaft. "We don't know how the prison got destroyed, but I'm sure it wasn't my teacher."

"*My* teacher now, is it? You've certainly changed your tune."

She barely looked in his direction. "Just bored I guess, this is all dragging on a bit."

"Well I'm sorry if my girls going missing and the whole city apparently turning to crap is an inconvenience for you."

Behind her shades Melissa's eyes rolled around in her head. "No, I didn't mean it like that, what I'm trying to say is that I want things to go back to normal, like things were before." Melissa pressed her fingers on her hair beneath her scarf. "But that's never going to happen now is it?"

"Nope, those days are over," he said reluctantly. "The only way things will get back to normal is if I wasn't here."

"But you're not here, you've been a prisoner in your complex for years."

"It's not enough though is it? The whole city want me dead, even if I did hand myself into the police, that wouldn't do anything, the police are more corrupt than me, hell I used to own those bastards until they sold me out, no...prison isn't the answer."

"Then what is?"

"I can't change what's happening with that infection or plague or whatever it is up top now, but when it comes to a city wanting their television back, their movies back, then you're going to have to kill me."

If there was ever a time that Big Man wanted to see the true colour of Melissa's eyes, then it was now.

"Are you serious? Are you kidding me?"

Big Man tried to be patient and remained strangely calm. "All I'm trying to do is to live my life, but I can't thanks to the mess I made, and you're right, this *is* my fault, I did this and the only way I can put the city right is if I was dead."

"You're talking gibberish."

"Am I? What's the bounty on my head now?"

"You really want to know?"

"Yes."

"I think it has gone up to seven hundred million credits to see you dead."

He pulled a stubborn face. "Really?...I'm only worth seven hundred million? Holy shit!"

"It goes up regularly, every minute or hour you remain alive, the amount goes up."

Big Man scratched his chin leaving remnants of faeces on his greying beard. "So how much?"

"I'm sorry?"

"How much would the amount have to rise to for you to turn me in?"

Melissa slapped a hand to her mouth to cover her laughing. "Why do you keep asking me that? I told you before, I won't do that!"

The former TV executive walked ahead of Melissa and stopped dead in front of her, with his back blocking her face.

"So go on Melissa, what's it going to take?"

She took a deep breath as Big Man held his hands aloft in surrender. "Seven hundred and fifty million enough for you? My back is turned, you can knock me out and take me in for the money."

Melissa smiled in the dark. "If I was to 'knock you out?' how the hell would I be able to drag you up this ladder by the way?"

Big Man paused briefly. "My shark, remember? I think you're strong enough."

"Oh yeah."

"So go on then," he protested.

"Besides seven hundred and fifty million is not enough money for me to turn you in."

The pair had reached one of the ladders beneath the main generators to the theme park, Melissa looked up to the top.

"This is the way out, we climb up here and we get out, probably to the theme park." She reached up to the step. Big Man tried to tighten his shit stained mouth, but couldn't and blinked profusely.

"HOW MUCH, MELISSA?"

Melissa stepped down from the ladder and walked over to her boss, she wiped some more mess from his face and gave him a peck on the cheek.

"I'm adaptable."

"So more than seven hundred and fifty million?"

"Much more, remember I did say eight hundred million earlier but until then you're my boss."

"You know you are quite the little bitch, Melissa."

She smiled and gave him a one-fingered salute. "Well go on then chuckles, get your fat behind up that ladder."

Big Man began to climb as Melissa then followed. He chuckled, "Cheeky cow."

"But seriously though, the only thing I don't get is why we're heading towards a theme park to find the girls when surely it would have been easier just to simply stay in the complex and let them come to us?"

Big Man pulled an excited face, getting ready to explain. "I thought the very same thing at first, why leave the complex when they both have their entry cards right?"

"Yes, makes sense to me."

"Well…"

Before she could finish an infected human, faster than the others appeared from the dark, rushed at Melissa and pulled her down. "OHHH SHITTT!!" she yelled.

"MELISSA!" Big Man shouted.

More of the infected emerged from the shadows and swarmed over Melissa. "GET OFF ME, YOU BASTARDS!"

She continued to yell as she was dragged to the floor as more of the infected stumbled out from their hiding places of the tunnels.

"GET OUT OF HERE, SIR!"

Soon the tunnels were filled with the infected. Big Man tried to make his way higher up the enormous ladder and gave a backward glance to Melissa, the fear in his gut stung him hard as she was finally overcome with infected humans biting their way through her skin.

"FOR GOD'S SAKE, MOVE YOU DICK!" That gurgled demand was the final sound that came from his personal assistant's mouth. Melissa was now buried beneath a mountain of the infected. A woman with her top bloodied teeth poking through her mouth made a grab for Big Man's leg, he kicked her away with anger and force, the woman looked suspiciously like one of his former dates.

You're not getting a second date with me, he thought. He slowly climbed the ladder as the infected rounded the tunnels and reached for the steps. *Don't do it...don't do it*, he thought again as he saw a mass of arms reaching for the ladder, his heart sank as one of them managed to haul itself up and clumsily begin to climb up. *Shit!... you're doing it.*

A Lab with The Green Man: 3

"Can you get rid of it?"

"Get rid of what?" Ariel replied to her boss.

The Green Man watched the beautiful blond creature move around her containment tube, her movement was limited as the tube was small and she was growing bigger by the hour, she twisted more as she listened to the other people outside.

"She has retained some of her memories, we have to get rid of them," The Green Man said. "Listen Ariel, I don't want her to remember anything from her past, her memories must be wiped, can we do that?"

"Yes, I'm sure we can."

Ariel's eyes were focused on the girl's growing form, her hair, legs and even breasts caught the attention of The Green Man's assistant. She mopped her brow and pressed up her glasses.

"So you want all past connections disconnected? I mean the readouts are perfect, why ruin it?"

"Anything connected with the past I want erased, I want complete control over the specimens."

"Specimens?"

"Yes, specimens."

"Plural?"

"I'm well aware…"

Ariel threw her boss a sideward glance. "We only have the equipment to sustain one life form here, we don't have the technology to produce more in these labs."

"Not here, but the facilities in the Messiah's Complex should be more than adequate," The Green Man assured her and signalled to Ariel's team, who seemed to be more clued up than their team leader, to start dismantling the equipment.

"You're moving her? You can't move her! We have no access to Big Man's complex and what makes you think they have suitable laboratories there?" The specimen blinked lazily, unaware of the chaos her presence was causing.

"I think we'll have access to the Messiah's Complex fairly soon."

Ariel's hands fisted slowly by her sides. "Why wasn't I informed of this? I am in charge of this project, remember?"

"I can snap your neck like a dry twig, remember?" The Green Man replied.

Ariel shifted uncomfortably in her heels, taking a breath and holding it. "I just want to be kept in the loop, that's all, this is my project as well."

"That was a bit rude of me about the 'neck snapping' I'm sorry."

The satisfied noise coming deep from The Green Man's mask made Ariel relax slightly.

"Just have some faith in me sir," Ariel sighed.

His huge fingers tenderly tucked a strand of hair behind her ear. "And you with me."

"Thank you."

Her gaze shifted as she tossed more hair from her eyes. "Are you ready for your own test? Your own treatment? the huge Green Man asked.

Ariel grimaced, her eyes locked now firmly to the floor. "Will it hurt?"

The Green Man stared at his young assistant hard and then casually answered. "Yes, immensely."

9. Fifty Shades of Grey Fur

Gemma slowly opened her eyes, not too sure of her surroundings. A few more blinks bought some memories back, she remembered the fight between her spider and the dragon, but didn't know what had happened to Buckby, she tried to move her arms but found them stuck. She had been cocooned in Buckby's webbing, the dragon fire had died out and Gemma was unaware of the protection the webbing had served.

It was damp now and felt like sticky honey, she pulled hard at the fine strands to free herself, transfixed at the webbing as she fell to the ground, Gemma crawled away from the messy sack ending with her back to the rock wall.

"BUCKBY? BUCKBY, WHERE ARE YOU?"

She swung her little head with its new green streaks from side to side, determined. "BUCKBY PLEASE COME..."

Gemma shuffled her body as close to the wall as she could and wiped away a tear forming in her eye. "I need to...I want see you," she whispered.

The rock face was high and Gemma glanced at the waterfall, slowly remembering how she made it to the bottom. The teenager moaned and dragged her hand down her face. *How am I going to get out of this place?* she thought.

She turned around and placed her little hands on the rocks, sighing hard. Her dour thoughts turned to frustrated words. "HOW AM I GOING TO GET OF THIS PLACE?"

Gemma's thoughts were broken with sudden shrieks of terror coming from beyond the rock face above her, the voice was familiar to Gemma, she shouted back.

"JASON! JASON?"

She had visions of what was happening to Jason, she remembered what the dragon could do and it made her body shiver. The cry shocked Gemma's hands away from the wall momentarily and then with a deep breath she placed them back and began to take hold of the jagged edges, her feet tried to find foot holes in the stone too.

Looking up at the huge rock face, her mind flicked back to her earlier question on how she was going to manage the daunting task of climbing it, another scream from above made her mind up and the young girl gritted her teeth and answered the question out loud. "Quickly."

"Oh for goodness sake, you even scream like a girl," Aphrodite grumbled steadily to Jason as the group tore down the tunnels with the glimmering dragon hot on their heels. Jason huffed back.

"THERE'S A DRAGON CHASING US, APHRO-DITE! HOW DO YOU EXPECT ME TO SCREAM?"

"Like a man probably, just a thought?"

Mitchy was at the back struggling with the still poorly Echo. "He has a point honey, you seem strangely calm for someone being chased by a dragon."

Aphrodite allowed herself a sneaky smile, reminiscent of the similar Cassandra Paintshark incident years ago.

"You get used to it darling, these new dragons are getting slower and slower if I'm honest."

Jason flashed an unsure look back to Mitchy who replied with the same perplexed stare as they watched Aphrodite with her heels in her hand scampering down the tunnel. The gleaming gnashing teeth of the dragon made their hesitation brief.

"WHERE ARE WE GOING, APHRODITE?, THE DRAGON IS GAINING ON US!"

Aphrodite replied in a controlled calm voice, "We followed you all over the city's underground network this afternoon with no complaint."

"HEY!" Mitchy shouted.

"Ok, maybe a little complaint from me and you managed to lose half the group, the girl who calls herself my sister included, so have a little faith in me."

"You're out of line, honey," snapped Mitchy.

"No, what I am is gorgeous, that's a fact, I'm not boasting about it, that's the rules, do you fancy me, Jason?"

"WHAT THE HELL?" Jason yelled.

She smiled and accelerated, not even out of breath. "Anyway, I think we should head to the Messiah's Complex, the home of that TV guy...Big Man?"

"I was going there anyway," Jason replied.

His answer intrigued Aphrodite. "Why were you going there?" asked the ice queen.

"Well the building is impenetrable so I thought if we headed there, we'd be ok."

Aphrodite wasn't convinced. "We have to be able to get in first in order to be safe, why the sudden change in plan, you didn't say boo to a goose about your plans earlier, so now you want to head off to Big Man's tower?"

"Things change Aphrodite, things change." Aphrodite sucked her finger slowly and smiled.

"So would going to his tower take your mind off of me then?" Jason's eyes stopped blinking in shock. "Don't worry about it Jason, don't feel embarrassed, you're only human, everybody falls for me after a while, it's inevitable."

"This isn't the time, honey."

"MITCHY'S RIGHT, WOMAN!" Jason said, trying desperately to glide up to Aphrodite and her new cross country running abilities. "I don't know why you're saying these things, but it stops now!"

The dragon rocked its head from to side to side, roaring in desperation as the tunnels began to get smaller and its huge frame struggled to fit through them, it managed to squeeze through, but was tired, and the effects of the spider's venom still hung around making it slightly groggy.

"Aren't you going to kiss me, Jason? Aren't you going to save me from that big nasty dragon?" Aphrodite slowed down to run beside Jason. "Let's stop now and imagine ourselves together! We'll let Mitchy stay still in the tunnel as that dragon will take ages to get around her, we could have some fun together."

Jason stopped completely and grabbed Aphrodite by her arms, slamming her against the wall, she gasped with relish.

"What are you going to do to me, Jason? Are we getting kinky now?"

Jason rubbed his temples in frustration and went back to rubbing his itching arms, sucking in a tired breath.

"Look, I don't know what's got into you Aphrodite, but I don't fancy you, I don't want to take you out."

Aphrodite gave a look that suggested otherwise. "Really?" She began to rub his shoulders with her still covered arms. "Are you sure I can't tempt you?" She licked her lips seductively. "You do know I want you... don't you?"

Jason pushed her away forcefully. "GET OFF ME!"

Her luscious lips screwed up. "Is that how you really feel about me, Jason?"

"I HAVE A WIFE, APHRODITE! A WIFE WHO I LOVE AND I WILL GET BACK HOME TO SEE TONIGHT!"

Aphrodite finally relented. "As you wish, lover."

The dragon gave an exasperated snort as it desperately tried to scrape through to reach the fleeing pack, it had now stopped roaring and was grunting as the tunnel got smaller.

Echo looked back and spoke dreamily about her pursuer. "Maybe we can try talking to it? It might stop chasing us."

Mitchy struggled to keep her up and gave an audible sigh.

"Oh dear, she's delirious. It's a dragon sweetheart, if it doesn't like you, it'll eat you...end of."

The tunnel was getting tighter as the dragon tried to claw its way forward. Jason prodded Aphrodite distrustfully. "Have you finished talking rubbish now? Are you going to stop coming on to me you stupid woman?"

"I don't think you really mean that, lover."

Anger still brewed from the pit of Jason's stomach and he was finding it hard to ignore her, Mitchy still kept up the rear, sweating hard.

"This tunnel doesn't seem to be heading anywhere honey, you sure this is the way out?"

Aphrodite showed a knowing smile. "You finding it a struggle to get through, Mitchy darling? With all the running we've done today I'm quite surprised."

"I'm in great shape, sugar."

"What shape is that? A circle?"

Jason spoke reprovingly. "We're running out of time and space, Aphrodite. Where are you taking us?"

"This is where the nightclub meets the theme park, we'll be out soon, lover."

"STOP SAYING THAT!" he yelled.

Aphrodite wasn't sweating at all, not a bead was on her forehead, she just calmly twisted and turned gracefully around the tight catacombs with ease as the others lagged behind.

She increased her speed, clutching her sky high heels. The tunnel then cut into intersections with crossing corridors. Aphrodite easily weaved her way through and was quickly disappearing further down the dark corridor.

"HEY WAIT UP!" Jason called, he hung back to check on Mitchy and Echo and Aphrodite was already out of sight. The three at the back zig-zagged through the new network of dimly illuminated tunnels. The inadequate light didn't seem to trouble Aphrodite as she was now nowhere to be seen.

"APHRODITE! SLOW DOWN, WE CAN'T KEEP UP!"

Echo stumbled to the ground as she struggled with the pace. "My back! It's burning so much!"

Mitchy gently picked her up and gave a hurried look, she couldn't see the dragon but could hear the sound of its huge legs breaking down the walls behind her. "We have to go, sugar."

"But my back?"

"I know it hurts baby, let's just get out of this place in one piece and I'll take a better look."

Jason stood in the centre of the tunnel, motionless now and his face drew a blank.

There was a low rumbling sound ahead of them.

"Did you hear that?" Mitchy asked.

"Yeah, sounded like a train or something?" Jason said, straightening his shirt.

"An underground train? Didn't think that would work?"

"We're in a cave with an underground nightclub and you can't believe they could have a train down here too?"

"Not really."

"Don't you have underground trains where you come from?"

Mitchy stretched her arms and groaned. "Nope, never heard of it." Jason eased a smile and continued.

"Anyway we've lost Aphrodite, she ran on ahead and left us."

He was standing underneath one of the corridor lights and Mitchy could see the drawn out lines of his cheekbones and his eyes were worn and tired now, the dragon's huffing near them kept him alert.

"Come on," he said.

"We'll try and catch her up, let's go."

A rush of cool air blew through the tunnel and the three breathed it in before thinking of setting off again.

"Do you think we'll catch her up?" Mitchy asked.

Jason shrugged uncomprehendingly. "She's running very fast isn't she?" he murmured.

"Plus that dragon thing is still behind us too," Mitchy continued.

Jason reached over and smoothed his fingers over Mitchy's wrist.

"We're going to be fine, come on."

The big woman who collected ceramic elephants, key rings and told the best 'dirty' jokes smiled back in the poor light. "Let's run, sugar."

Aphrodite was nowhere to be seen as the three tried to follow where'd she just been.

With certain death pounding down the tunnel walls behind, they all built their strides into a tidy rhythm, Echo was the first to slow down due to her condition and her companions gestured to her impatiently. Jason's gaze narrowed as he divided his attention between the women and a presence in the distance, he was completely oblivious to the sound of the dragon tearing up the rear, he spoke softly but firm.

"Aphrodite? Is that you?"

Mitchy wiped more sweat from her brow. "What is it, Jason?"

He paused before answering. "I thought I heard something, something is around the corner."

"Is it Aphrodite?"

"I'm not sure, hopefully it's her."

His nerves oddly slipped up making him shout once more, he froze and tried again. "Aphrodite? ANSWER ME!"

Mitchy already had a hold of Echo and then she reached out to pull on Jason's shoulder. "All right, Jason, let's go."

He caught her agitated stare long enough to know it was time to leave. The tunnels switched from rock to metal now, but the groaning sound of them being torn apart behind them wasn't as close as they'd expected, the dragon was slowing down which gave the three a chance to find and catch up to Aphrodite. None of them looked back, afraid of what they might see behind them.

With their eyes well-accustomed to the dark, they carried on moving swiftly forward.

Jason's eyes noticed something and he stopped the group abruptly.

"Damn. This tunnel marking looks familiar, I think we've been here before."

Mitchy's heart sank, but it was Echo warily raising her head who spoke.

"We've been running around in circles then?"

"It looks that way I think," Jason sighed.

He horned his hands to his mouth and shouted, "APHRODITE? YOU THERE?"

Jason tried a new tactic and put his fingers to his mouth and gave a tremendous wolf whistle. The sound was magnificent in the cramped space and the group waited. They looked around and listened for a response, something else *did* hear the whistle.

On the low ceiling was a shape, long and grey, it had an elongated humanoid body and its arms stretched out, probing along the mix of jagged rock and metal along the tops of the tunnel. Its clawed hind legs gripped steadily and hung on tight like a trapeze artist making a swing. The creature seemed to be covered in fur and it was a dull grey-like colour. Its head wasn't as visible as the rest of its body, the creature's speed was incredible and it clambered quickly out of view but not before Echo caught full sight of the beast and threw her little head back and screamed a horrific cry of terror.

"WHAT THE HELL WAS THAT?" Mitchy yelled.

Jason watched wide-eyed as the grey apparition climbed out of sight. His eyes stayed glued to the spot long after the creature had left and it was a while before he was able to speak. "I've no idea what that was."

He arched his shoulders and rubbed the bridge of his nose with his fore finger and thumb. "Just add it on to the rest of the strange shit we've seen today." He looked back to Mitchy. "Is Echo ok?"

"Echo's right here," the girl answered in the third person.

Jason looked up, mildly surprised. "Yeah, sorry for missing you out, how are you?"

Echo twisted her body towards Jason. "My back is numb, but the burning has stopped."

"That's a good thing, right?"

"Hopefully."

Echo's knees were still trembling. "What was that thing on the ceiling?"

Jason gave a long wistful look to the spot where he last saw the creature. "You know what? I've been running away from things all day, all my life some might say, well I'm sick of it. That thing got in here, so it might know the way out, we're going to follow it and see if it leads us out or at least to Aphrodite."

The rumbling sound came into their earshot again.

"There's that train sound noise again, why don't we follow it? It may be a way out?

Mitchy listened to Echo's idea. "That doesn't sound half bad Jason, to be fair I'd rather follow a train then a big crawly monster thing."

"Do you know you say that quite a lot?"

"Say what a lot?"

"To be fair," Jason continued. "You say it all the time."

Mitchy looked surprised. "Do I?"

"I've noticed it too...to be fair!" Echo made a funny joke, even though the numbness in her back was spreading.

Mitchy laughed, a sound that bubbled deep from her inside. "Must be a 'Strallen City' thing then."

There was no sign of the creature as they pressed on and the train noises grew louder. They followed the sounds and finally emerged from the cramped conditions of the winding tunnels. Most of the walls now were metal, with only the high ceiling now formed of rocks. A final maze-like bend seemingly lasted for ages as they walked through.

"Do you hear that that?" Jason's eyes rolled around suspiciously.

"Sounds like voices, it sounds like people talking."

Jason looked seriously at Mitchy. "Ok let's keep moving, I want to hear this."

Sounds of music playing joined the voices, Echo even began mouthing the words to the song. The tunnel ended and the immense underground installation finally opened up as a huge wind whipped around what stood in front of them. A massive theme park ride was directly in their path, a long line of people queued all around the carts on a long and winding track. The ride started out in the giant underground clearing and the track twisted and turned and continued through the rock face, probably heading back up to the surface.

Couples, parents and best friends stood in the queue laughing and giggling, eager to move on and take their place on the fantastic ride.

Echo exhaled in pure relief as the realisation hit home. Jason scratched his head in bemusement. "What the hell is this?" he asked.

Mitchy put her hand over her mouth as if she was desperately trying not to laugh at Jason's outburst and their possible salvation. Jason let out a sharp series of desperate laughs and began to shake nervously and the day's events took their toll on him for the second time but he didn't go into meltdown like before, this time he just simply snapped, "WHAT'S THIS CRAP? HOW LONG HAS THAT RIDE BEEN HERE? WHO ARE YOU PEOPLE? DIDN'T YOU HEAR ANYTHING? DIDN'T YOU HEAR THE DRAGON CHASING US?"

The people at the back of the queue heard Jason's outburst and turned away embarrassed, they made drinking motions with their hands, thinking Jason's behaviour was due to alcohol.

Mitchy calmly rubbed her hand on Jason's shoulders again, it wasn't the first time she had done this today, and it usually had the desired effect. "Look honey, I don't know how this underground theme park ride got here but if they can have underground train systems? Then this is nothing new!"

Jason frowned uncertainly, until a smile finally broke through. "You got me there Mitchy, let's get the hell out of here."

With Echo slowly perking up, the three made their way to the back of the queue and tried to blend in, but the smell from spending hours in dank tunnels and wet clothes from the pool made them uncomfortable to stand with; a tall skinny man with a long grey scarf that touched the floor twitched his nostrils.

"Dude, what's that horrendous smell?"

Jason felt a little sheepish, but was glad of this new human interaction. "Sorry friend, laundry day." The man simply huffed. Jason looked around in awe at the massive rail device.

"So what's this ride thing then?"

The man in the scarf glanced up with eyebrows up. "What is this? Dude, this is the 'Excavator' the first underground theme park ride. It's brand new, man, it goes through the nightclubs and then back up to the surface, goes upside down and everything...everyone's talking about it man, don't you know about it? Where have you been recently? Living in a tunnel?"

All three shared a grin.

"That's a good one," Jason whispered to Mitchy.

"So are you going to give it a go?" the man asked.

Jason felt a tingle of safety hit his spine, he relaxed his shoulders and smiled, – after all that had happened over the last few hours, this could finally be the way out.

"Yeah why not? Would seem rude not to."

Mitchy came forward and took Jason aside. "Look I know we may have a chance of getting out here, but what about Connor, Gemma and Aphrodite? They're still down here somewhere, are we going to come back and look for them?"

Jason respected Mitchy's deferential tone and gave a quiet reply as it deserved. "Look, we get out of this place, we get Echo and me probably as well to a hospital and when we're fit and healthy again, I promise to come back and find the others. Norton and Odysseus too, but look at us Mitchy? We're in no fit state to look for anybody right now, let's just get out, rest for a while and take it from there."

Mitchy looked at Echo, struggling to keep up with the others in the fast moving queue.

"Ok, I see what you mean, we'll get out and regroup, we don't even know if those creatures are still up there."

"Exactly," Jason agreed.

Mitchy took hold of Echo and held her close in the queue, Jason stood in front and for the first time in the day, all three felt somewhat normal, just like everyone else in the queue who seemed to be oblivious to the infected human events that took place earlier. There wasn't anybody screaming and running around in a blind panic, nobody stumbling around with torn or missing limbs, it was just a simple queue for a underground ride at an all day and night theme park. The three blended slowly into the queue, the hushed whispered tones from the others in the line aimed directly at Echo began to stop.

Echo tried to stand upright on her own and threw up as she arched her back to do so, her arms and shoulders screamed with pain. She took a few more steps, each one was agony as the pain in her back returned.

"Woaahh! Wait til you get on the ride to be sick, man!" the man in the scarf moaned. Mitchy cradled her and Echo looked on behind her. Something caught her eyes and they widened in a dreamy fascination.

"Gemma?"

"Gemma's gone sugar, she's not here," Mitchy rubbed her back some more.

Echo didn't stop. "Gemma's coming."

Mitchy sighed. "Jason, Echo's gone back babbling and shaking, she thinks she can see—"

Jason turned and finished her sentence. "GEMMA!!"

From the far other end of the tunnel sprang the little teenager, running as if her life depended on it, her newly formed green hair swished in the slipstream of the rollercoaster as it flew past her. She carried on running and didn't look back, but the others could see why she daren't.

Jason screamed, his voice echoed like a snow avalanche. "FOR GOD'S SAKE GEMMA, RUN! RUN AS FAST AS YOU CAN!"

In unison Mitchy and Echo's eyes shot wider when they saw what was chasing her. The big grey creature that occupied the ceiling in the tunnels plunged towards the floor and was giving chase to Gemma. Its nightmarish hairy figure bounded towards the fleeing child. The people towards the end of the queue clocked the beast and roared with approval, thinking it was part of the ride, the man with the big scarf punched the air.

"DUDE! THEY HAVE A DOG TYPE THING AS PART OF THE RIDE! HOW COOL IS THAT?"

Jason shouted back. "IT'S NOT PART OF THE RIDE, IT'S REAL!"

Jason did notice what the man had said, the beast did look like a huge wolf hound but he didn't care. He just wanted Gemma to run. "GEMMA! KEEP RUNNING PLEASE!" Talons and huge claws closed down on the girl. The creature had a slimline canine body with slick grey hair which gleamed in the now artificial lights of the roller coaster bay.

Its head was wide and filled with sharp teeth, a long bushy tail hung behind its back. The wolf creature resembled a sled dog, running just as fast, but twice as big. The crowd still whooped and cheered as the huge wolf creature gained on Gemma, the howling wind drowned out some of the people's shouts but not all. It barked savagely and louder with each closing step. Jason screamed at the man controlling the roller coaster. "YOU! GET THIS MACHINE GOING NOW!"

The man simply ignored him and looked back to witness the chase with Gemma and the giant wolf. "That special effect looks pretty bad ass! Don't know why my boss didn't tell me about it."

"START THE RIDE NOW, MISTER!" Mitchy shouted.

The controller looked on in awe oblivious to the shouts of Gemma's friends. Gemma breathed calmly and steadily, her pursuer was gaining on her and despite the cries of Jason and Mitchy the rollercoaster wasn't moving.

Suddenly the wall opposite the rollercoaster began to rumble, there was a hole big enough to allow the cart through, but that was the only gap, the massive rock face wouldn't stop crumbling. A couple of youngsters standing in front of the man in the scarf watched with curiosity at the ever-decreasing wall, the rapidly melting ice-creams they held in their hands fell to the floor.

"WOW!" the children exclaimed in unison.

Bursting through the rock was something big, tearing it down with ease. Emerging from the rubble of the wall stood the irrepressible form of the giant black dragon, its glittering silver mane sparkled in the new light. Roaring and rising impressively from the midst of the rubble, the dragon made both the wolf creature and Gemma halt immediately in their tracks. The sight of the huge monstrosity had split the people waiting in the queue, some still cheered thinking it was all part of this fantastic ride, whilst others stood nervously, watching the beast with gritted teeth and urine-stained clothes.

A man standing with his new bride sidled up to the controller and stammered slowly.

"Please start the ride, I don't know if it's fake, please I don't want to stay anymore."

The controller frowned back and spoke with a meritorious tone. "People, you've got to stop moaning! It's part of the ride, relax."

The dragon stood magnificently surveying the crowd. Gemma glared at the dragon behind her.

What did you do to my spider? she thought, breathing heavily, fear finally beginning to roll around in her stomach. The dragon thumped the ground in rapid succession with its huge claws, this act was familiar to Gemma, it was going to charge.

"Oh no," she whispered.

"Oh shit," Jason added.

The wolf hound barked frantically at the monster. Adrenaline replaced fear and Gemma made a dash towards the rollercoaster, the wolf gave a departing yelp to the dragon and ran in the same direction. Both progressively increased their speed towards the rollercoaster. The dragon's wings remained folded, not even attempting to gain flight, if it was going to catch Gemma, it was to be on all fours.

"SOD THIS!" Jason cried.

He left Mitchy with Echo and ran to the front of the queue.

"WHERE ARE YOU GOING?" Mitchy screamed.

"I'M GOING TO START THIS THING TO GET US OUT OF HERE!"

Mitchy trembled with frustration, concentrating fully on Gemma. "COME ON GIRL!"

The wolf was almost on Gemma, and a nervous glance over her shoulder revealed it to be directly on her heels; she began to tire and slow down. What Mitchy saw wasn't encouraging.

"GEMMA! DON'T STOP HONEY, PLEASE!" But the wolfhound wasn't giving up as the dragon chased it too, Gemma was going to be mauled by a giant dog and then eaten by a dragon. It was no use, a pitiful cry came from Echo, Mitchy watched wide-eyed as the huge jaws of the wolfhound enveloped the fleeing girl.

"NO!" Mitchy screamed.

The huge teeth secured a grip around Gemma's tiny waist and yanked her off her feet. Then, suddenly and quite unexpectedly, the dragon stopped. Still with Gemma hanging from its mouth it turned to look at the charging dragon...and then flipped Gemma upwards towards its back. She landed face down on the smooth fur and scrambled up and clung hard to the wolfhound's neck. Bounding away from the dragon with Gemma swinging wildly from its neck, the wolf accelerated towards the stationary theme park ride.

"What the fu—?" Mitchy looked on in shock. *Didn't expect that,* she thought.

All of a sudden Mitchy became a dog lover and urged the hound closer. "HERE BOY! COME ON, THERE'S A GOOD BOY!" She shouted past the people in the queue to Jason. "DO SOMETHING!"

Jason acknowledged this and leapt up to join the ride controller on his platform.

"YOU HAVE TO START THIS THING NOW, MISTER!"

The laid back controller wasn't pleased with his new company. "Sir, you can't be up here! You have to get back in the queue."

"START THIS MACHINE NOW!" Jason shouted.

"No, way sir, you have to get down and stay in the line, you can't push in."

Jason looked back and saw the dragon, gaining ground on the wolfhound and Gemma despite its huge bulk.

"THIS ISN'T A GAME! START IT NOW!"

"Sir, you need authorisation to start this machine."

Jason looked the controller square in his dazed eyes and then punched him in the nose, knocking him off his platform.

"Will that do?" Jason asked dryly. He leapt over to the control panel and his fingers hovered over the keyboard. The dragon let loose a flame burst which Gemma recognised as the signature snort and ducked instinctively.

The fires sailed overhead and hit some generators above embedded in the rocks above Jason controlling the 'Cheese Factory' and the 'Tug Boat' rides in the theme park. The blast from the explosion staggered Jason and knocked him off his feet. He took a big blow to the head which felt like a sledgehammer. Regaining his footing he lumbered forward towards the controls which still seemed alien to him.

Jason nervously pressed a few buttons on the keyboard, itching for something to happen – nothing did.

"DAMN!" The dragon's roar took his shout of despair and carried it away.

Gemma and the hound were closing in on the ride, but the dragon was closer.

"JASON!" screamed Mitchy.

"ALRIGHT!"

"QUICKLY!"

"I KNOW!"

Another wall of heat from the dragon sailed over Jason's head, the flames were closer and more intense, his face was slightly blistered and his eyes closed in pain. Vomiting on to the platform, the smell of it didn't even register as he frantically played with the control panel, none of the controls did what he wanted, his vomit-splattered clothes leaked slightly on to the keyboard and he vomited again this time, coating the laptop with sick. Puke seeped through the cracks on the board and sparks flew out. The brand new theme park ride began to slowly move forward, its engines rumbled and then spluttered and the wheels on the track began to turn faster.

Mitchy's mind was working overtime watching Jason fight with the controls and Gemma and the wolfhound dodging flame bursts from the glimmer beast. "MOVE IT, JASON!"

Jason tried to clamber off the control panel onto the ride which was picking up speed, but hesitated until he could see Mitchy and Echo safely on board.

The entire queue surged forward still amazed and cheering at the fantastic special effects on show and the tremendous acting of the apparent child actress feigning terror on top of a giant wolfhound. The crowd hurriedly and excitedly strapped themselves in as the Excavator gathered pace.

Mitchy's legs turned to rubber as she barely managed to put Echo in the final cart, her heart was set to explode with the effort, she threw Jason another advisory look and then tried to strap Echo into her seat.

"Dude! Don't leave me!" cried the man in the scarf.

"GET IN, SUGAR!" yelled Mitchy.

Scarf Man dived head first into the cart, his feet wriggled like a worm on a fishing rod. "WHOOAAHHH!! THIS RIDE IS AWESOME!"

Jason waited impatiently as the carts of the Excavator went past him into the tunnel, the groaning of the wheels on metal grew faster and he had to time his jump just right or he would end up a bloody mess onto the tracks.

The effects of the contaminated water were now giving Jason more problems than he needed, he felt ill and giddy and the intense heat from the dragon was becoming unbearable. He ground his teeth and swayed as the carts tumbled by. *Hold on Jason,* Mitchy's shuddered thought came. "Just hold on." She said it out loud this time.

With the sound of the fantastic ride ringing in his ears, Jason fell forward, just in time to land in the final cart and bounced out towards the track before Mitchy could grab hold of him.

"JASON!" Mitchy roared.

"Not today, dude."

The man swung his scarf with sublime effort and it neatly wrapped around Jason, he spun him around and then hauled him up to the cart. "Dude, should I have done that? Not sure if that guy falling on the tracks was part of the ride? Would the theme park company sue me?"

Mitchy reached over and hugged the man who was unwrapping his scarf from Jason.

"This is not a game sugar, everything is real, you've just saved his life!"

"For real?"

"Yes, for real."

Scarf Man rubbed his chin and looked over to Gemma and the wolfhound still bounding behind the cart. "So the girl on the dog is not an actress?"

"No she's not," Mitchy said hoarsely.

"So I take it that's a *real* dragon chasing us then?"

"I'm not kidding, sugar," Mitchy huffed, her eyes locked straight back to Gemma continuing her steady speed on her wolfhound mount.

"And if it catches us, it'll will probably eat us?"

"YES!"

The laid back man peered down at the sick body of Echo, now joined by the still Jason.

"Is he dead?"

Mitchy checked Jason's pulse. "He's alive, barely."

"Result."

Mitchy kept her full attention on Gemma now, the Excavator ride was now speeding towards the main tunnel and Gemma and the wolf hound were beginning to fade, it was struggling under Gemma's weight.

"COME ON, GEMMA!" was the frequent shout from Mitchy.

The dragon emitted a low snarl and let out another flame burst close to the ground, the hound nimbly cut a sharp right as Gemma almost lost her grip around its neck.

The ground continued to churn from the intense heat of the dragon and the tracks began to rise as the tunnel loomed ahead which would take the Excavator ride through the night club and up to the surface. It was now or never for little Gemma.

"LITTLE DUDE! KEEP RUNNING!"

The volume from the man in the scarf even surprised himself, Mitchy kept her voice on par with Jason's rescuer. More flames swooshed over the ducking teenager's head.

"Come on, boy," Gemma whispered to her new furry friend, she kicked her legs against its shaggy hide as if she was riding a horse. She hadn't ridden a horse before and had never seen one on television, even less chance now as televisions were banned, it just seemed instinctive and it had the desired effect.

With supreme effort the wolfhound picked up speed. Mitchy noticed and flashed a quick look behind her at the dragon and then forward to the tunnel looming ahead, time was running out for them, both the dog and the dragon were on the tracks, now nimbly moving along the gaps like hamsters on their wheels.

Gemma's dog had caught up with the last cart and Mitchy, Scarf Man and now the revived Echo frantically egged Gemma to make the dog run faster.

The dragon's huge head bobbed up and down, shaking the glimmering mane, suddenly it stopped in its tracks, which happened to be the theme park one. It threw its head forward and starting hacking frantically like a cat with a hairball.

"Dude, that doesn't look good," the man with the scarf observed.

The dragon's fin began to pulse repeatedly and a sudden burst of white plasma flew from it's mouth, it blew a large crater in the ground just to the dog's right, it stumbled but kept it's footing.

"DO IT NOW, BABY!" Mitchy roared.

With its tongue flapping wildly the wolfhound took a single tremendous leap and landed onto the last cart, winding Mitchy in the messy process.

"WAY TO GO, DUDE!" yelled the scarf man.

Gemma tumbled off the dog and Echo reached out to stop her from falling over the side.

"DON'T LET ME GO!" Gemma screamed, panicking for the first time.

"I've got you," Echo whispered.

The cart whipped to the right, suddenly throwing both Gemma and Echo to the floor.

"Missed you," Gemma whispered back to her best friend.

"Love what you've done to your hair," Echo commented through gritted teeth.

Another plasma shot was brewing up inside the black dragon. The Excavator ride roared underneath a rocky manmade high bridge as the tunnel grew closer. A tired dragon released a vicious plasma burst underneath the rising track. The sound of the explosion was thunderous as the force made the lead cart tip onto its left, the whole convoy of carts behind it were heading that way as well.

Stunned and thrown back by the force of the blast, Mitchy managed to shout, "LEAN THE OTHER WAY!"

For a second she expected a wisecrack from Aphrodite about her weight and not letting the cart tip over, but that wasn't going to happen as she was missing too. If the cart continued to lean to the left, everyone who had just come out to enjoy a ride on the new underground ride would be a mess on the floor below or a smeared mess against the walls of the upcoming tunnel.

The majority of the people in the carts still believed the dragon and chase to be a part of the theme park, the others who kind of thought that 'No special effect can be *that* good', simply held both hands to the safety bar and whimpered smoothly.

"DUDE, WE'RE NOT GOING TO MAKE IT!" Scarf Man yelled.

"KEEP LEANING," Mitchy screamed.

"DUDE?"

"LEAN!"

"DUDE!"

"NOW!"

Screeching around the final corner before the tunnel entrance, the Excavator dropped to the right and all its wheels returned neatly to the tracks and roared through the tunnel.

"YEEEEEHHHAAAA!! WAY TO GO, DUDE!"

Racing into the rock tunnel deep underground, the Excavator sailed on its tracks and then dropped and swooped, shaking the riders and giving them the adrenalin rush they had waited and queued up most of the evening for.

The onslaught of the dragon slipped from their minds, holding on for dear life as the ride continued to try and hurl them from its seats.

Mitchy had Echo and Jason strapped into their seats securely, Jason's head was clamped in his hands which was being flung left and right from the bumpy ride. He didn't attempt to hold on to the safety bar, but just allowed his body to get whipped round with each turn.

Echo's back was in agony and her mind was going into meltdown with the pain. With each shake and jolt from the cart came a tumultuous cry of anguish from her. Gemma sat by her side, unable to comfort her due to the force of the ride, the stream of tears flowing down Echo's face continued.

Mitchy and Scarf Man tried with difficulty to hold onto the wolfhound and keep it calm; they had the maximum capacity of people in the cart but it wasn't designed for giant dogs.

The hound struggled in Scarf Man's arms, he had such a tight hold on it that he thought he was crushing the dog and doing it harm.

"Dude, I can't hold on to this dog much longer!"

"Don't let go of it, sugar!" Mitchy shuddered as well as the dog was becoming too much for her as well.

At every dip and turn of the ride, the hound struggled to break free from both Mitchy and Scarf Man's grasp. Suddenly it stopped fidgeting and began to pant heavily.

The panting continued as the dog began to feel different in Scarf Man's arms, it's tongue lopped out the side of its mouth, each pant made its fur recede, the smooth grey fur was disappearing before everyone's eyes as well as the bulging muscles on its huge back.

The rush of turbulence from the ever-increasing ride drowned out the sounds of the dog's bones cracking as they reformed themselves.

"Dude, what's happening?" Scarf Man asked, but nobody replied.

Its gums bled profusely as its huge fangs shot back up and new teeth stretched in its mouth. As the hair disappeared and its hind legs shrank, what was left in its place was a human body dripping in sweat and shivering.

Dirty blonde hair flapped around wildly and the girl now lying in the dog's place looked at the shocked faces in front of her.

"HOLY SHIT, DUDE! IT'S A GIRL, IT'S A GIRL!"

An icy stare with shockingly blue eyes bore deep into Scarf Man, ignoring his cry of astonishment. She still had his arms held tight across her naked body, the girl raised an eyebrow and suddenly a voice as sharp as the toughest diamond hit and shocked Scarf Man like a slap in the face.

"Happy to kop a feel are we?"

Scarf man immediately withdrew his hands from the girl's breasts.

"Cretin," she hissed at him.

"IT CAN TALK! IT CAN TALK!"

"I can also ride a bicycle, you oaf."

Scarf Man looked around at the others, their initial shock began to subside. "WHY ISN'T ANYBODY SAYING ANYTHING? DUDE, WHY ISN'T ANYBODY SAYING ANYTHING? IT'S"

"APHRODITE!" Gemma squealed in delight, cutting him off.

"I THOUGHT I'D LOST YOU!" Gemma grinned.

"As did I, no such luck on that front."

Gemma chuckled at her would-be adopted sister's dry sense of humour. The cart took a sharp turn, flinging everybody right and then back again.

"Love what you've done to your hair," Aphrodite pointed out to Gemma's green streaks.

Gemma shot a look at Echo who grimaced a smile through the pain.

"Yeah, I get that a lot."

"Welcome back sugar," Mitchy smiled.

"Cheers chunky," was the reply.

"Ohhh Jason, you're all sick," Aphrodite said with a baleful stare to him.

"And you're a dog, figures," he rasped.

"DUDE, IS NOBODY SHOCKED THAT THIS GIRL WAS A DOG A FEW MOMENTS AGO?"

Aphrodite raised her voice as the ride sped up through the tunnel and addressed the man in the scarf.

"SO I SEE WE'RE STILL PICKING UP WAIFS AND STRAYS, WHAT IS THE NAME OF THIS DELIGHTFUL STONER WHO HAS JOINED OUR MERRY BAND?"

Mitchy thought for a moment, on her face would have been a look of perplexity if it wasn't being attacked by the extreme wind, whatever she was thinking the others were doing exactly the same.

"YOU KNOW WHAT, SUGAR? WE DON'T EVEN KNOW YOUR NAME?"

Gemma threw her a glance and regarded Mitchy with a serious look beyond her teenage years.

"WAIT? YOU DON'T KNOW THIS MAN'S NAME?"

"DUDES! NO NEED TO WORRY, LET ME INTRODUCE MYSELF."

He let the next bump from the ride flip him over and he huddled quickly next to Aphrodite. "THE NAME IS PICKINGS, SLIM PICKINGS, PLEASURE TO MEET YOU, MA'AM."

Aphrodite's face tensed as she struggled to shake Slim's outstretched hand.

"Charmed," she huffed.

"SO DUDE, IF NOBODY ELSE IS GOING TO ASK YOU, HOW THE HELL DID YOU MANAGE TO BECOME A DOG?"

Aphrodite pushed hair out of her eyes with her free hand.

"SO YOU'RE NOT AFRAID TO TURN DETEC-TIVE, BUT SOAP STILL SCARES YOU, RIGHT?"

Slim could only lift one arm to check for body odour, he grinned when his nostrils proved otherwise.

"IN A NUTSHELL? THE SWIMMING POOL YOU ALL FELL INTO HAD 'SOMETHING ELSE' IN IT."

"SWIMMING POOL?" Slim shouted.

Aphrodite put a finger to his lips to silence him with a dry smile. "Be quiet darling, I'm being intelligent, yes?"

She went back to shouting. "IT HAD A SOLUTION IN IT, AN ABOMINATION OF A FLUID WHICH AFTER CONTACT WILL USUALLY TURN YOU INTO, A DIFFERENT BEING, I TOOK A SHOWER IN THE GHASTLY STUFF YEARS AGO AND LO AND BEHOLD...I'M A DOG, WELL MANY DOGS ACTUALLY."

The penny finally dropped for Gemma. "ARE YOU DOG THAT DAD USED TO HAVE? THE SCRUFFY ONE?"

"GOLD STAR FOR YOU, DARLING," Aphrodite quipped loudly. "THAT SCRUFFY LITTLE MUTT WANDERING AROUND THE COMPLEX YEARS AGO WAS ME, DADDY LIKED TO HAVE ME AROUND TO KEEP HIM COMPANY, AND IT'S AMAZING WHAT SECRETS YOU CAN FIND OUT ABOUT SOMEONE WHEN, FOR EXAMPLE, YOU'RE HIDING AND PEEING BEHIND THEIR COUCH."

"I take it you're not in human form when you do your business behind the couch sugar?"

Aphrodite simply grinned at Mitchy.

"WHAT SECRETS? AND DID HE KNOW IT WAS YOU?" Gemma asked.

"SECRETS? NOT TELLING AND...DID HE KNOW IT WAS ME? DOUBTFUL DARLING."

Fear flared up in Echo's heart. "SO WE'RE GOING TO TURN IN TO DOGS THEN?"

Aphrodite nodded dumbly as the ride shook everyone again.

"OH ECHO ISN'T IT? I SHOULD REALLY KNOW YOUR SILLY NAME BY NOW AS I'VE BEEN STUCK WITH YOU FOR ALMOST THE WHOLE DAY, NO NOT EVERYBODY GETS TURNED INTO DOGS."

The ride spun around throwing them to the left and back to the right, Aphrodite slowly continued. "I'VE SEEN ANOTHER DRAGON, RED BY THE WAY AND MY BEST FRIEND HAD GREEN SCALES AND THERE WAS A GIRL WHO BLEW UP MY DADDY'S TELEVISON EMPIRE BY TURNING INTO FIRE, SILLY CREATURE."

"So we're going to turn into dragons?" Echo whispered.

As the cart whipped around another sharp bend, Aphrodite held tight onto Mitchy with one hand, whilst checking her now beaten nails with the other, she sighed heavily as she replied.

"MAYBE NOT DRAGONS."

Aphrodite noticed Echo scratching her arms.

"BUT YOU WILL TURN INTO SOMETHING DARLING, I PROMISE."

"Oh my God! Oh my God! Oh my God!" Echo quietly panicked, ignored the searing pain in her back and held the safety bar tight across her chest. Aphrodite tried to steady herself for a moment with the cart flying around too many bends for her liking. Forcing herself up, ignoring the pain of her transformation Aphrodite stared at everybody. "YOU DON'T SEEM TOO SURPRISED THAT I CAN INTO A DOG."

Gemma left Echo's side, reassuring her with a kiss on the cheek she then unlocked her own seat belt and sidled up to Aphrodite who was still clutching hard on the safety bar.

Gemma unlocked her hopeful sister's belt and crossed it over the pair of them.

"So far today I've seen zombie people running around trying to eat us, my Buckby turned into a giant spider, my hair has turned green from being dipped in some funny water, my arms won't stop itching and now there is a dragon chasing us on an underground theme park ride, and I'm sure that dragon killed my beloved Buckby, so I'm actually not surprised you can turn into a dog."

The track beneath them shuddered violently, all part of the special effects, but everyone spun around to see if it was the dragon. Gemma nuzzled up closer to her naked foster sister. "All I wanted to do was go swimming today, why can't we be a normal family like everyone else?"

Aphrodite allowed Gemma's head to nestle in her chest, her ears pricked up as she heard the sound of the dragon's feet hammering at the tracks behind them as it still kept chase and smiled at Gemma's comment.

"Normal?...now where's the fun in that?"

10. Fairground Attraction

"Come here you."

Tara pulled Norton closer towards her and kissed him strongly, she squeezed his thigh playfully and he yelped and pulled away laughing.

"Wait! Wait! Slow down a little, you haven't even told me if you're involved with anybody?"

Tara giggled and slapped his thigh – the same thigh she had earlier squeezed. "Don't be silly! Would I join a dating site if I already had a boyfriend?"

Norton pulled a comic annoyed face and looked past her, making sure she'd seen it first.

"You'd be surprised at people having affairs these days."

Tara relaxed back into her seat on the ghost train ride. It was billed as the 'ultimate ride in terror', it was a maze set in an old dark industrial building where a miniature train ride travelled through various rooms. The rooms had plastic torture instruments littered all around, with dim lighting, and a cheesy rock soundtrack playing in the background. Actors hid in the dark and jumped out in horror costumes at various intervals to scare members of the group. A sign hung down from the top of each room.

Please refrain from punching the actors.

"You really didn't have to come on this ride if you didn't want to?"

Norton looked back at Tara with a loose smile on his face. "It's fine I don't mind, I love riding on ridiculously fake ghost trains with jobbing actors attacking us!"

"You are funny," Tara beamed. She threw her hands around Norton's head. "Funny guys are so sexy, I love funny guys."

She began to kiss him again, only coming up for air to mention something. "Besides you owe me for making me wait around all evening for you, I was so close to bailing out, it's only because you sounded so nice on the phone I stayed around."

Norton's shoulders stiffened slightly, thinking about events over the afternoon and the people who had lost their lives against the infected zombie people. He tried not to let Tara see his sadness and over-compensated by nodding like a maniac.

"I know, and I'm so sorry about keeping you waiting around for so long."

"Do you have a reason? You didn't say."

Norton studied her accusatory raised eyebrow. "I'll tell you later, I promise."

"You'd better."

"I will."

Tara beamed at him and squeezed his bottom, pulling him closer and kissing him fiercely. The ghost train rumbled through the rooms as the actors jumped out and tried their best to scare the kissing couple.

"Ohhhh, I'm soo scared!" Tara mocked. "Big strong man is going to save me from these nasty little ghosts, aren't you?"

Norton playfully puffed his chest out.

"Stick me with me, honey, I won't let anything hurt you, if these suckers try, things will get very, very ugly!"

Her arms snaked around his waist. "My hero."

"Oh for god's sake will you two please get a room!"

Tara released Norton and looked behind to see where the voice was coming from that had stopped her from her embrace.

A large man who had filled out most of the seat leered at them with an ill-fitting grin, his teeth not being able make up their mind how to fit in his mouth. Next to him sat a slightly younger woman shifting herself away from him what with little space she had in the cart, her body was long and graceful, with huge breasts and jet black hair.

She lit a cigarette with the butt of another, blowing the smoke on to her large companion. Her voice was husky and low like Tara's. "Don't be so mean, let them have their fun." She blew a smoke ring at Norton and Tara. "That's how he used to be to me before he had a 'fun transplant'." She pointed to Tara with her cigarette hand. "Just ignore this tub of lard sweetie, you and your gorgeous man just keep on doing what your doing, it's lovely and fine by me." She prodded the big man. "Why can't you do that to me?"

The man wheezed softly. "Because you charge too much." The woman punched him in the arm playfully.

"Stop trippin' stupid!" She leaned into Tara and spoke quietly. "I'm quite cheap really."

The large man shook his head otherwise. "Don't mind her, she's just annoyed that she can't find someone to feed her cats."

Further back in the train of carts was another figure, crouched down out of sight and hidden, was Odysseus. He had been following Norton since he'd left the tunnel and kept watch from a safe distance. Odysseus had never got on well with Norton, but knew he had to keep an eye on his sparring partner since he was waffling on about meeting his blind date. Odysseus could only make out a mop of blonde hair kissing Norton's neck so he assumed it was Tara, he sank lower down in the cart, and as a strange noxious odour wafted over him, it made Odysseus uneasy, keeping him from showing his face to his strained friend; he held his bag close to his chest and remained quiet.

Norton elicited a bleak smile as Tara went back to cuddling him – something had distracted him from Tara's kisses, and even the large man's comments. The strong revolting smell drifted in from the back of the current room the ghost train was in. It was like rotting flesh, which made Norton's nose and memory tingle, he pulled away from her neck nibbling. "That's odd." He put his hand to his mouth and coughed.

"What's wrong?" Tara asked.

"That stench, I've smelt it before today, we can't stay here."

He pulled at Tara's hand, which she resisted. "Listen here mister, you were late for our date today, very late! So you're going to make it up to me by staying on this ride."

The large man turned to Tiffany, his gorgeous companion. "Looks like they're having a lover's tiff, honey."

The woman sighed. "I suppose you want to show them something to remember?"

"Damn straight."

Tiffany leaned back into the cart and allowed the large man to start kissing her awkwardly, her eyes shut with displeasure.

She complained about the smell as well now. "God, can't you smell that, Lee? It's bloody awful."

Lee, the large man carried on. "It's just the smell of my animal magnetism, baby."

Norton was still trying to get Tara to leave. "Tara please, we have to go."

Tara playfully shook her head and turned her attention to the couple behind them. "They're having fun so why can't we?"

Norton just held his nose and looked around nervously.

"Lee, that smell is disgusting," Tiffany protested.

Lee carried on kissing her as some figures moved in behind him.

"Oh wow I can totally smell it now, I think it's these actors, they're made up to smell like the dead."

He completely ignored the shapes like the sign above them had stated. Tiffany shifted awkwardly beneath Lee, her eyes still closed.

"Well it's working, that smell is killing me, let's stop this, Lee and go somewhere else."

In the poor light of the room, Tiffany felt a cool liquid trickle through her fingers.

"God baby, you're sweating like a pig." Not a sound came from Lee. "You ok babes? Lee? Lee?"

She felt the liquid again on her fingers, with the fearful realisation that it wasn't sweat, but blood. Tiffany gingerly lifted Lee's head, it was limp and his mouth was open wider than usual as a bloody fist poked through it. Her voice dissolved into a scream as the infected humans swarmed around her cart. Pinned underneath by the huge bulk of Lee, Tiffany never stood a chance as the zombie creatures made her their next meal.

"Shit," Norton whispered through gritted teeth. He yanked Tara from the cart. "We're moving."

"But—"

"NOW!"

Tara looked at Norton with a smile and a shrug and allowed herself to be pulled away, unaware of the perilous situation they were in.

"MOVE IT, TARA!"

The infected had found a way into the theme park and their first target was the ghost train. The actors in their scary outfits would have longed for only a punch from these new visitors. But it wasn't to be as the sea of creatures swarmed in and tore the actors apart. Many of the people in the ride remained in their seats thinking that it was all part of the show, they were causally slaughtered before they had even a chance to move.

Odysseus stayed hidden in the cart, the infected ran past him attacking the people in view instead.

Norton ran with Tara, leading her to the ghost train entrance. She allowed herself to be towed and wasn't panicking, she felt alive as she ran from the chasers and into the now night air.

"STAY CLOSE TO ME," Norton shouted.

Tara's eyes scanned the night sky and the packed crowds at the theme park.

"You'd better stay close to me," she whispered back to Norton.

He replied with a faint smile and looked to the moon, which was illuminating the sky. He had been running around for the best part of the day in the tunnels beneath the city and the dark wasn't new to him, Norton's eyes adjusted to it quickly. The howls and screams of the infected behind shook him out of his trance.

"Come on," he said to Tara.

They mingled easily with the fun-loving crowd and but kept up their long strides looking for the main exit.

The entrance of the ghost train rapidly filled with the infected, the overflow was like water filling a bathtub. Some charged at the crowd, others staggered forward, but it was all types of people, men, women children – all infected with this strange bloodthirsty disease which lay siege on the theme park attending public.

An old lady with a blood-stained nightgown grabbed a teenage boy with horrifying speed and pulled him to the ground, his ear was ripped off and swallowed in one swift gulp, the boy screamed as the flesh was stripped from his neck like cheap nail varnish.

A father out with his family for the day struggled frantically with an infected policeman, the officer bought him down with a rugby tackle and had already bitten deep into the dad's leg and back, they rolled around on the floor as his wife screamed her fear out loud with her two young children in her arms.

Her husband could only watch in vain as he saw his wife struggle with the youngsters in her arms and try and run away, his last sight was to see his young wife fall with their children still clutched tight. He didn't even blink away the tears forming in his eyes as his family were torn apart before his eyes.

Odysseus remained quiet in the cart, he had heard the others in the ghost train crying with terror and fleeing for their lives, he heard too many die as well. His face had lost its colour and he couldn't feel his feet with the numbness of lying down in that cramped space. He took a deep breath and got to his feet, his legs shaking with each step to bring the feeling back. Grabbing his bag, Odysseus maintained his composure and slowly followed the screams to the ghost train entrance.

Norton weaved his way between the crowds who were in the dark running around bumping into the infected...apologising and then getting ripped apart for their clumsiness.

In the dark, the lights of the rides didn't move as nobody rode them, but the screams associated with theme parks still could be heard in the air as the infected made their way through Dangerfield theme park. He looked at the infected pouring out of the ghost train.

"Did you get a map of this place when you came in?"

Tara pulled her gaze from the sky, nodded and reached into her bag and handed him a crumpled piece of paper.

"I bought it whilst I was waiting for you."

"You're full of surprises aren't you?"

Tara glanced at Norton and returned her gaze to the sky.

"You've no idea," she smiled as Norton pulled her away.

One of the fastest rollercoasters in the park 'The Grand Slammer' was stuck in mid-ride. The ride controller had been killed and failed to bring the carts down from their highest point of the rollercoaster, and so there were people stuck right at the top, unable to get down as the point was so high. The infected gathered around the construct and sensed the human meat stuck high on the ride. They huddled around the foot of the ride and began to climb on each other's backs. Like ants they swarmed higher and higher onto the rollercoaster, forming a pyramid of the dead. The people from atop the ride leaned over the edge of the carts and saw the rise of the infected loom towards them, only the deluded few thought that this was still part of the ride and whooped and cheered at the coming onslaught of the supposed dead.

A newly married couple looked at the infected climbing up towards the ride. Crying uncontrollably the woman turned to her husband. "WE'VE NOWHERE TO GO, HAVE WE?"

Her husband's face continued to look over the edge as his wife's cries grew more desperate. "This isn't a game honey, I think this is it."

"WHAT ARE WE GOING TO DO?" she wailed.

The concern on his face grew as he saw the other people in the cart scream and try and wriggle free from their seats as the climbing infected grew closer. He turned to his wife and mouthed silently, "I love you." Then he slung his arms around her neck and guided them both off the tower, the two quietly sailed off the high rollercoaster still in an embrace to their doom on the ground below.

The infected were running riot and charging hard now, the ones who could still find their feet were rushing various rides, their mangled, battered bloody faces overturned small theme park rides and feasted on the youngsters inside.

On the ground of the theme park lay the chewed up bodies of people who went to the park just for a fun day out.

"FOR GOD'S SAKE HELP US!" a woman cried as she tried to unsuccessfully shield her children away from the rampaging infected, her body jerked up as she swung her kids around looking for safety, it was to no avail as her children were dragged from her arms.

Norton zipped through the oncoming crowds as they tried to find an exit.

"There's nowhere else to go is there?" Tara asked.

He glanced down at the very many manholes scattered around the theme park. "We're not going underground, I've spent all day down there."

"Really?" Tara asked.

Pausing slowly he looked past her. "Shit," he swore quietly. "There are more of those things coming."

"Just keep me safe, babes."

Norton could only emit a slight smile. "Always."

The killings were happening in full swing. An infected human charged at Norton, he reached quickly to the ground and picked up a rock and smashed it through the creature's jaw, it was softer than he thought it'll be and the rock came out easily. The creature staggered back only to head towards Norton again.

"Norton?" Tara's voice was confident.

"I got it," he replied quickly.

He shoulder barged the bloody human to the ground and picked up the very same rock that had earlier gone through the creature's jaw, this time the rock was used with force to smash its skull in.

Tara looked at the twice dead creature on the ground and turned to Norton, who was breathing heavily.

"So going by what you told me about these things, if they found a cure for it and managed to reverse all these crazy creatures? You've just killed someone."

Norton ran his hand through his hair in desperation trying to figure out what she said amongst the noise and confusion.

"Seriously? You're taking the moral high ground now? Will you take a look around Tara, this thing isn't going to change, it's gone too far for that now. It's them or us."

Tara rested her hand on his shoulder. "I've just seen you kill a man a little too easy for my liking, honey."

Norton straightened his head and dusted himself down. "Like I said, it's them or us."

Tara nodded and kissed him lightly on the cheek. "I know," she whispered. "Now come on and make me safe."

Taking his hand Tara led him on a mock ballroom dance, Norton tried to pull away abruptly from this merry dance that she was leading, he knew now she was a complete eccentric, but now wasn't the time. "Tara, what are you doing?"

She pulled his body close to hers as they danced around in a circle, people's screams were heard in the background, completely oblivious to Tara as she swung Norton softly.

"WE DON'T HAVE TIME FOR THIS!" his voice raised now, more alarmed than anger.

"But you'll look after me won't you, Norton?"

"YES! BUT WE HAVE TO LEAVE NOW!"

He was double checking all behind him nervously. "There's a storm coming, my lovely and I'm going to stay with you until you keep me safe."

"I'LL KEEP YOU SAFE IF YOU STOP DANCING AND COME WITH ME!"

Tara smiled and relented. "You're sweet, my lovely man, your face is perfect. You've got more expressions than a ferret's got fleas."

"SO WE CAN GO NOW?"

"Let's go."

Most of the theme park was overrun by the infected and the crowds of people out for a fun night out had no defence. Norton had seen this before, earlier in the day when most of the group were hiding underground and decimated by an attack from the then newly formed virus. He and Tara were now squatting down in the 'Dinosaur Safari' ride.

It was a children's ride, just a walk in some tall grass and fake trees populated by life-size dinosaur statues.

Earlier in the day kids had jumped and swung like excited monkeys on the models, but now only blood splatters adorned the monsters now. Norton didn't even want to entertain the thought that the blood could have been from children, he just kept his head low with his hand gently pressed on Tara's head, as she was still too excitable and kept popping her head up to view the situation.

Norton squinted in the darkness.

"I think we're fine for the moment, none of those creatures are at this ride right now."

Tara rested her head again on his shoulder, still talking too loud for his liking.

"So what's the deal with those things? Do you know why they're attacking people and eating them?"

Norton closed his eyes, still running on adrenalin he thought back to the tunnels with Jason, Aphrodite and even Odysseus, like a feverish dream. *Maybe they were right,* he thought. What with the eccentric excitable Tara bound to give away their location to the infected, he should have stayed with the others, he may have stood a chance with them, but now things were different there was the strong possibility that staying with Tara, the date he had looked forward to meeting all day, could get him killed.

Norton looked at her for a moment or two longer toying with the temptation to make a break for it and head back underground to find the others, to find his 'family'. But he had to stay with Tara, no matter how carefree she was finding the situation, it would be inhumane to leave her behind to be eaten, he shook his head clean and answered her earlier question.

"I've no idea where these things came from or what they are, but yeah, they are eating people and again, I don't know but I'm not sticking around here to find out."

Tara nuzzled up closer to him.

"You're a good man my lovely, and goodness is a gift. I'm so glad I chose you."

"Thanks."

"So...we going to go on second date?"

Norton should have felt uncomfortable but he didn't, he saw the look of trust in her eyes and grew confidence from their gaze.

"So even though the whole city is now churning out zombie creatures for fun and you still want to go on a second date?"

"Of course I do, you funny sexy man, I didn't think you could top coming to a theme park for a first date? But running for our lives from creepy munchy people beats it hands down!"

Tara playfully touched her finger to his nose. "So thank you very much, lovely Norton."

"Thank me when we get out of this place alive."

"Well I think you're—"

Norton quickly cut her off, throwing his hand over her mouth to quiet her, her eyes wandered around quizzically until she realised why; a man was stumbling past so quietly that Tara had completely missed him, he was walking with his stomach open and hands trying to keep in his intestines. The obviously dead man was trying to eat what was left of them, struggling to scoop them up in his hands and feast on his own insides.

The unified moans of the 'creepy munchy people' as Tara called them hung out across the theme park landscape as well as the terrified screams of their victims. Norton had been used to cramped conditions all day, he wasn't used to open spaces, even though it would give him the opportunity to run and fight if needs be, he was used to the growing reality that this infection was spreading and that the little fun he had with Tara was coming to an end. He kept his hand over her mouth and whispered, "Don't say a word, it might ignore us." She began to point frantically to something on the ground beside them, Norton ignored what she was pointing at and was fast losing his patience. "Could you stop doing that for one second and look at me please?"

Tara's sparkling doe eyes looked up innocently at him, but he refused to move his hand from her mouth. "Please honey, you really must be quiet or he'll hear us."

Suddenly there came the sound of a huge thump underground followed by a click and a whirling noise. Both Tara and Norton stood up and looked at a manhole cover which was slightly covered with some broken ferns.

"See? I did try to tell you, sweetness," Tara said, wiping her mouth where Norton's hand had once been.

He threw his hands up in the air with exasperation.

"This just gets better and better!" he grumbled.

The manhole cover was pushed aside and two gloved hands appeared, probing away on the soft grass. Finally latching onto some solid ground they managed to haul up their tired owner. A man with greying blonde hair and a thick scarf wrapped around his head emerged from the hole in the ground and wormed his way out.

The man emitted a quiet curse as he looked around at his new surroundings and rubbed his head. He took out a small pocket watch and flipped it open, checked the time and beneath a muffled voice thanks to the scarf, looked up at Norton and Tara and then back down to the manhole.

"Oh Melissa, oh Melissa, you poor girl, I'm so sorry." The man wiped at his nose and composed himself, looking back up to Norton. "I believe I'm at Dangerfield theme park?"

Norton stared at the man dubiously. "Can we help you?"

The man with his face fully covered removed the crap-stained scarf from his mouth.

"Enjoying our date are we, Officer Norton?"

The face scarf was completely removed as Big Man took in his new surroundings. A confused look swept over Norton's face.

"Boss?"

"That's right."

"What are you doing here?"

"Well I'm going to be running for my life in about thirty seconds, I suggest you and your lovely companion join me."

A hideous chorus of shrieks came from beneath the man hole cover as Big Man let out a sigh and looked at his watch again. "Better make that ten seconds."

"MY BACK, IT'S BURNING! FOR GOD'S SAKE HELP ME!"

"Could someone shut her up please? Apart from having the personality of a corpse, her moaning is really beginning to get on my nerves."

Mitchy's stare rose at Aphrodite. "Echo is hurting honey, can't you see that?"

Aphrodite raised her tired head, arms still clutching onto Gemma. "Nope."

The Excavator ride hurtled along the rails nearing the end of the cave, the dragon still in pursuit.

"There's something pouring out of your back, Echo."

Gemma shifted herself from Aphrodite and inspected her friend's back, her leather jacket already had holes in from when the water first burnt through it, but now

a creamy substance like liquid soap seeped down her coat.

"MY ARMS KEEP ITCHING! WHAT'S HAPPEN-ING TO ME?"

Mitchy leaned over and felt Echo's forehead. "She's burning up, we have to get her a doctor."

"Listen ginormacous, we've said it time and time again and you've heard it before, there is a chance that those ghastly little creatures have taken over the city, we've nowhere to run, nowhere to hide, because there's no one like us left."

"Remind me to book you for a motivational speech, dude," quipped Slim Pickings.

"I also do funerals darling, would love to speak at yours."

Slim turned his attention to Echo and her weeping back.

"Dude! That shit looks nasty. BOOOOOMM!!"

"That isn't helping, Slim," said Gemma, her voice slightly defeated.

"Sorry dude, just looks sick."

"Sick meaning good?"

"No, sick meaning bad."

"Right." Gemma sighed. "Glad we straightened that up."

Jason began to come round as Mitchy held his body close to the cart.

"What's happening?"

"It's bad dude, giant dragon is still chasing us."

"Oh is that all? Thought you said it was bad!"

Jason gave a weak smile to Mitchy, the two and the whole group bar Slim had bonded from what they had experienced earlier in the day, it was a day of horror, constant running, despair and the loss of friends.

But Jason knew that this little group of travellers were now survivors and no one else was going to die today, not if he could help it, even though he couldn't move any part of his body at that precise moment.

Aphrodite raised her head from the cart floor and looked behind. "I think you should take a look at this, people."

All heads swung around to view Aphrodite's glance as the air whipped around her face.

"Oh no," Gemma grumbled.

The dragon somehow had gained ground on the cart and between the sharp flapping of its wings and somehow huge bounds from its stumpy little legs it was almost on the rollercoaster cart.

Mitchy looked on, fascinated by the dragon's nimble foot touches along the rail, bounding closer to them. "You know this is really quite a magnificent creature."

"Sorry, I don't share the same sentiment," Aphrodite moaned. "Especially as it's trying to eat us."

Aphrodite grinned her perfect white teeth to Mitchy.

"I'm actually shocked that it's not *you* chasing us with a mind for a meal."

"Dude! That's totally not cool."

"Thanks Slim," smiled Mitchy. "But you get used to it after a while."

Two more severe jolts shook the cart as it headed for the cave exit.

"Was that the dragon?" Gemma asked.

"No, just part of the ride and it's cool! I gotta do this Excavator next week without the dragon, dude."

"I'm sorry to offend you, Slim Pickings, darling," Aphrodite shuffled. "But I'd rather go on a theme park ride without being eaten?"

Slim struggled to wrap his scarf further around his neck as the cart rattled towards the cave opening.

"Good call your highness, might give it two weeks then."

The new darkness from the night sky hit the group as the cave exit loomed, trapped underground for most of the evening the group were about to taste a new kind of darkness, illuminated only by the lights of the theme park.

"Thank God we're getting out of this cave," Gemma peered up through the slits of tired eyes. *I miss my spider,* she thought.

Slim leaned inquisitively toward Echo. "Dudes, should she be glowing like that?"

Whilst being shaken to their bones by the extreme rattling of the cart, the group managed to stare at the quivering body of Echo. A blinding white light pulsed from her, Mitchy shook the teenager, shielding her eyes from the glare.

"ECHO! ECHO HONEY, YOU OK?"

The girl was unresponsive as Mitchy had to finally advert her eyes from the glow.

"WHAT'S HAPPENING TO HER?" Gemma shouted.

Echo suddenly cut out Gemma's question as she began gasping for air, her body stopped convulsing but splayed out at an awkward angle.

"Dudes, she doesn't look right."

"Your views on the obvious are quite magnificent, darling," Aphrodite purred, struggling with her position in the cart. "It's obviously the effects of the water darling, she's changing, quicker than I'd thought but she is changing into something."

"WHAT IS IT?" pleaded Gemma.

Aphrodite sniffed the air. "Not sure, but not a wolf anyway."

"Dudes, we're heading outside," Slim said in the uneasy silence.

Aphrodite rose her head again and looked behind the cart and the chasing dragon as everyone was focused on Echo, her eyes were alight with intrigue and squinted furiously. "Forgive me people as such little things I forget from time to time as I was a wolf for a while, but when a blue light appears from this charming dragon creature's mouth, what does this mean again?"

Surprisingly, from beneath a blinding light and growing pain and confusion it was Echo who groaned a reply. "Dragon's going to shoot...darling."

Aphrodite took a deep breath and turned to the group. "Does anybody have a working phone I can use?" Without even looking at her, Slim gave her his phone and continued to look at the glowing Echo.

"Dude, you can try, but there's no signal down here."

Aphrodite tapped on the keys and waited for a response. "It's ringing thank God."

She had the whole group's attention now and they all voiced their concerns. "CALL THE POLICE!"

"RING AN AMBULANCE!"

"Oh hello, this is Miss Wylde, I'm afraid I'm going to have to cancel my 4.00pm manicure for tomorrow... Why?...well it seems I'm about to be roasted by a giant dragon...what? Can I do 5.00pm?...I'll let you know, thank you." Everybody stared at her wide-eyed.

"What are you all looking at?"

She raised a finger in warning. "Do you know how hard it is to find a decent manicurist in this city?"

Finally the last cart which they occupied left the confines of the labyrinth cave. The gigantic ride vomited out the tunnel with frantic speed, snaking its way higher and higher up the magnificent construct tilting at various angles and rolling consecutively.

Mitchy looked over the cart at the people on the ground, they were as small as ants now but as the wind rocked her face it seemed that some ants were eating others. "I think something hideous is happening down there, I think those creatures have reached the park."

"Expected really," Gemma said, chewing her bottom lip. She tried to sound confident but it wasn't working. "Those things are everywhere, I just hope they haven't reached home yet, hope my dad is ok."

"*My* dad!" Aphrodite spat.

"Our dad," Gemma spat back, her confidence restored.

Aphrodite stared at her for a moment longer, then finally shook her head. "Whatever."

Velocity built up fairly fast and Aphrodite held on to her stomach, trying to keep what little food she had in, the ride did another loop and rolled furiously with further speed. She peered behind again and this time raised her voice as the wind whipped her hair around.

"REMEMBER WHAT I SAID ABOUT THAT SWIRLY BLUE THING COMING FROM THAT DRAGON'S MOUTH?"

"What about it, honey?" Mitchy asked, her voice with obvious concern.

"Believe me darling, you might want to duck."

With a furious roar of anger the dragon released a gleaming ball of blue fire from its mouth. The fireball struck the cart with force erupting it into flame, the impact tearing it from the rest of the roller coaster train and spinning through the air. Echo was flung from the ride and sent hurtling to the ground.

"NNNNOOOO!!" Gemma screamed.

She held onto her harness with a death grip as the cart went into freefall.

The dragon ignored the rest of the Excavator ride and had to choose between which of the plummeting things to catch – Echo or the cart.

"I WON'T LET YOU FALL! I WON'T LET YOU FALL!" Mitchy screamed.

She caught glimpses of the terrified look on Gemma's face as the cart spun faster towards the crowds below. Echo still had her glow as she fell, it was like watching a small meteorite falling to earth, she didn't scream, she knew it was helpless, but her glow was so beautiful and so calm, lighting up the night sky.

The weird taste of death was almost upon her as her vision began to shudder, the bright image burned her retinas so Echo just squeezed her eyes shut, the glow pulsed and sounded like a cat's purr of satisfaction. The trembling of oncoming death for Echo was probably soon, her back had stopped burning now but that seemed neither here nor there at that moment. Falling was so relaxing to her, there was a strange smell in the air too as she noticed that she was now spinning out of control, the purr became louder and sounded so sweet to her...it was a shame she was going to die because falling down felt so cool.

The dragon soared elegantly through the air and in a graceful freefall, making its choice of which of the two falling objects to follow, it fired off a series of concentrated energy blasts at the rollercoaster cart.

The three fireballs all missed their target and headed off to the infected people growing closer on the ground.

"I TAKE IT BACK, THIS ROLLERCOASTER IS PRETTY LAME IF I'M HONEST!" Slim yelled.

Aphrodite remained quiet and remarkably calm, even though she was struggling to hold on to the metal side of the cart. The only thing going through her head was, *At least I'm going to make a fantastic looking corpse, such an ineloquently bastard way to go.*

Mitchy still managed to have a secure hold of Jason and saw that even though she could see that Gemma was terrified, she was at least secure in her harness. But it didn't matter as even though they were strapped in and wouldn't fly out like Echo, they were about to smash into the ground and die.

"DUDE! I KNEW I SHOULD HAVE GONE ON THE GHOST TRAIN RIDE INSTEAD." At least

Slim had changed his tune, clinging on bat-like to his harness.

Mitchy saw the tops of the other rides now, the Excavator ride was the biggest in the park and now they were approaching the second biggest, and then the third. She was going to actually countdown to impact, she knew she could do it, and probably time it just right, thinking that today of all days she really should have stayed in her home city of Strallen. *So far, so good*, she thought as the ground loomed up. She wondered how much the impact would hurt.

"Oh my god," Gemma mumbled. "We're dead."

Mitchy mouthed, "I'm sorry." She was about to yell goodbye when the screaming people from the ground could be heard.

Everybody could hear the shouts of terror as they accelerated to their doom.

They could also hear a low purring sound, which grew steadily louder and louder, a blinding light soon followed and suddenly the cart was yanked upward with such violent force that Aphrodite was finally flung from it, landing unceremoniously on a heap on the ground, she didn't fall as far as she thought she would but it didn't matter, she rolled around naked on the ground covering her eyes from the light.

"WHAT THE BLOODY HELL IS HAPPENING?"

The final cart from the Excavator ride was gently lowered to the ground, there were no infected people around that part of the theme park, just confused and intrigued humans standing in a circle, some cheering whilst others looked on open-mouthed.

Gemma opened her eyes with a start, her heart still hammering, the light dazzling her. She and Mitchy reacted simultaneously.

"What just happened?"

Breathing heavily, still dizzy, standing by the cart she had just caught, was Echo. She stood with an amazing glowing light circling her body, it sparkled in various colours like lights around a village pub advertising happy hour. But what completed this amazing transformation was a pair of glimmering protrusions which had appeared through her shoulder blades and two more which had burst through her skin and from her back, they hung from the holes in her leather jacket almost touching the ground.

"YOU'VE GOT WINGS!" Gemma pointed excitedly to her best friend's back.

Four wings like a pixie or dragonfly had sprouted from Echo's back, they buzzed and purred like a contented kitten, she stood with her red hair flapping from the beat of her wings and her torn leather jacket and trousers. She gave a nervous and polite wave and took a step back from the cart which she had just heroically caught, wobbling slightly as her balance and centre of gravity was offset.

"Hello there."

"WHAT HAPPENED TO YOU?" Gemma squealed.

"Silly bitch threw me from the ride," Aphrodite moaned.

"Not you, Echo I mean," Gemma muttered.

"So what are you now? An insect or human?"

"Aphrodite! Leave her alone," Mitchy warned then turned still in astonishment to Echo. "What *did* happen, honey?"

Echo shrugged her shoulders and gave a tired smile. "I'm not sure, one minute my back felt like it was on fire and then I fell from the cart. I was falling but it felt like

I was falling for ages. But this light? It soothed me and calmed me down, I can't explain it but I knew I was going to be safe...and these wings...I just can't explain it..."

Aphrodite wasn't impressed. "Like I said before darling, it's the water, that's what it does, it turned me into a wolf, and you into a bug."

"Do your arms itch?"

"A little."

"Bingo!"

Gemma piped up, "But we were all in the water and all I got was this green hair, what about Mitchy and Jason?"

"Well if Jason's new power is to drool like a baby and talk bollocks, then I think it's working."

Echo noticed Aphrodite was still naked, looking stunning but still naked, she folded her wings with a fantastic effort and struggled to take off her leather jacket. With help from Mitchy she managed to get it off and hand it to Aphrodite.

"Take this."

"It's not my colour."

"I SAID TAKE IT!"

Everybody looked at Echo, wide-mouthed at her outburst, she even shocked herself.

"Wow, sorry, don't know where that came from, just feeling so confident all of a sudden."

"Rude as well," Aphrodite huffed, examining the holes in the jacket.

Slim got out of the cart and leaned closer to Echo, smiling mischievously. "Dude, those wings do look pretty bad ass!"

Gemma bounded over and inspected the wings, chuckling and shaking her head. "So what happens now then?"

Echo bit her lip and fluttered her glorious wings, the purr sounded beautiful. "Looks like I'm keeping them."

Jason stumbled out of the cart, still groggy. "What's happening?"

"Echo's got wings and can fly," Gemma clapped her hands excitedly.

"That's nice." He collapsed into Mitchy's arms.

"He's still not right in the head."

"I could have told you that," Aphrodite winked at Mitchy with satisfaction, shuffling her shoulders awkwardly with Echo's jacket, her ears pricking up suddenly.

"Incoming by the way."

Mitchy looked up, narrowing her eyes.

"What's that, honey?"

"You still remember there is a dragon circling above our heads don't you? And nobody listens to me when I shout duck."

"Duck?"

"DUCK!" Gemma screamed as a huge streak of blue light hit the ground next to them and flipping the cart on its side, the dragon's fireball was so hot that it burnt its way through the ground. The group struggled to find safety as the black dragon with the glimmering fin spun around for another attack.

Echo ushered the others away and stood up defiantly, she spoke to Gemma without even looking at her friend's face, her voice oozing confidence.

"Gemma, take the others and stay in the shadows, keep out of the light as those creatures could still be around, I'll come and find you. Mitchy, you and Slim take care of Jason and if possible try and find Norton and Odysseus, they're here somewhere too and Aphrodite, two things for you to do, number one, look after my jacket and number two, if those creatures do attack…"

"What?"

"Bite."

A worried look crossed Gemma's face.

"What are you going to do, Echo?"

"Whatever it takes."

She made sure everybody was out of the cart, and gripping the sides tightly she began to lift it with ease. "If you'd excuse me…"

Her light blinded everyone again and her wings purred louder then ever, her eyes glowed too and then she suddenly shot up in the air like she had just been fired from a gigantic catapult.

The glittering shape of Echo flew towards the dragon and like a cannonball she struck the dragon with full force with a swinging attack with the cart to its mouth, the dragon reared back and howled in protest, Echo swung around for another attack, screaming, "COME ON YOU DRAGON SLAG! LET'S SEE WHAT YOU'VE GOT!"

The dragon dropped below, avoiding her attack, and showed a surprising burst of speed by catching up and launching a fireball at Echo. She sensed the attack immediately and jerked up higher into the air as if someone had pulled her up by puppet strings attached to her shoulders. The fires missed their target but hit the 'Junior Jungle Bus ride' below instead.

The mini ferris wheel for children shattered into a million fragments and within seconds was reduced to ash.

Echo let out a squeal of delight as she flew up unnoticed and clattered the dragon with the cart again in the mouth.

"She's doing it! She's really doing, she's winning against that dragon!" Mitchy studied the glittering flying figure that was hanging around in the air.

"What good does it do us, Gemma if it gets her killed?"

"She's biding us some time, Mitchy and that's all we need to get out of here."

"Dude, no offence but where are we going to go? Shouldn't we stay here?

Aphrodite shook her head in fake revulsion.

"Why don't you crawl back under the rock where you came from, Slim Dickings?"

"Dude, I'm only saying we should stay here and find your two dude mates who I don't even know."

"Oh that would suit you wouldn't it, Slim...to stay around a circus of freaks, home from home for you isn't it?"

Gemma clenched her teeth as she answered.

"Why are you being so rude? He saved Jason's life."

"Your point being?"

Mitchy kept her eye on the fight in the sky before speaking to Aphrodite. "Do you still think we'd be safe in this Big Man's tower?"

"I can't see why not? The Messiah's Complex is impenetrable. Is that a word? Never mind, well nobody can break in or out, hooligans and hitmen have been trying for ages."

"And he'll let us in?"

"Can't see why not."

"Seriously?"

"Yes, seriously, where have you been for the last few years?"

Mitchy felt a flicker of irritation. "Strallen City."

"And they have televisions there?"

"Yes, but we don't watch them all the time."

"You really should."

Jason rose to his feet unsteadily like a newborn foal, he collapsed on Mitchy's shoulders before trying to speak. "I think we should stay here and wait for Norton and Odysseus."

Aphrodite's eyes fixed securely on Jason.

"Really? Is there a reason why you don't want to go to Big Man's tower?"

Jason stared back at her, stalling for time. "Look, we don't even know if Big Man will let us in, I mean why should he?"

Gemma tried to intervene but Aphrodite pushed her away.

"Why shouldn't he? We're people who are in need of help because the rest of the city have turned into ridiculous fighty bitey people."

"But—"

"But nothing Jason, we try and find the sad sack on his date and the little guy with anger management issues and then we go to Big Man's tower, agreed?"

Mitchy spoke with a touch of impatience. "Jason honey, listen..." Echo smashed the cart hard against the dragon's mouth momentarily drawing Mitchy's attention away, she shook her head and carried on. "Maybe we should just stick to the plan of finding Norton and Odysseus and head off to Big Man's tower."

He replied with a pout. "You're not from Olympia Mitchy, you have no idea of what he can do, or what he has done to some people, especially to the ones you love."

"We're not idiots from Strallen City honey, we know all about Big Man's game shows and the game show to end all game shows called remarkably enough 'Game Show' and how it affected the whole city."

Mitchy turned to Gemma.

"Television still banned here, sweetheart?"

Gemma nodded vigorously. "You betcha."

"We have nowhere to go Jason, we need to be safe and maybe this is the only way, can we please go there?"

Jason just looked at her, his face said it all. "You really think that Big Man will help you?"

Gemma's head nod carried on. Jason stopped as the realisation hit home – everyone wanted to go the mighty tower of Big Man. "Guess that's it then," he muttered.

He began to get motivated again, but with a touch of desperation, which most of the group noted.

"Why don't we go to Strallen? With you, Mitchy?"

Mitchy didn't want to be too hard on Jason, he'd taken a nasty blow to the head and had almost drowned in the waters of the labyrinth cave, but he had been such a strong young man earlier in the day and commanded respect, so why now was he spouting off ideas so nonsensical?

"We haven't seen any planes since this whole thing kicked off, we don't even know if it's a pandemic and Strallen could be infected too. Honey, I would love to go back home right now, truly I would, today of all days especially…"

"What's so special about today?"

Mitchy shook her head in a slight refusal. "Doesn't matter."

The more Jason thought about it, the greater the certainty that going to Big Man's was a bad idea, but the group seemed determined to go. "Well let's find the others and then we'll take it from there." He shook his head trying to shake off his dizziness. "Ok, let's move people."

As Jason slowly moved away he noticed that he was the only one doing so. He stopped in his tracks, swayed lightly, and hesitated slightly. "Guys?"

The newcomer Slim Pickings stood in front of Jason, his eyes grew wide with terror, a look which Jason had unfortunately seen too many times from today's events.

"J-Jason?" Slim stuttered.

With an inner wrench of fear he answered, "Yes?"

"Dude, whatever you do, don't move."

Dammit! Jason thought. *Sometimes when you ask someone not to move, it's like putting a sausage on a dog's nose and telling them not to eat it.*

"Please tell me what's wrong?" he asked.

Jason slowly glanced around, and caught some movement out of the corner of his eye, he fixed his gaze on two people in front of him, a man and a woman whose eyes were a milky white and completely lifeless, both had blood-smeared faces and terrible looking shirts which were caked with mud as if they'd been rolling around in it, the mud helped their terrible taste in clothes.

The smell of decay hit Jason next, it should have hit him sooner but the night-time breeze had carried it in another direction, away from the group.

A third person who was infected appeared and then a fourth and a fifth.

"Oh shit," he said.

Jason looked around the grass verge and realised that there was no place to hide, just a theme park filling rapidly with the infected.

Slim tried to get the attention of Jason.

"Dude we have to leave now, quietly."

Aphrodite looked at the entire scene of oncoming infected looming towards Jason. She wiped her heavy eyelids and played with her false eyelashes.

"I think Jason's going to die, can we leave? Bored now."

As the infected edged closer to Jason she shrugged and gave him what she'd thought would be his final smile to see.

"Bitch," he mouthed silently.

An infected zombie creature was dragging itself slowly towards Jason, its legs were missing and its lower torso left a trail of dirty blood behind it, the creature must have been caught in a fire earlier on as its face was blistered and melting, its clothes burnt and unrecognisable.

Another infected being ambled Jason's way, it was a man in his fifties, completely naked with a bloated stomach that covered his nether regions.

Jason thought, *Where was he attacked? The shower? Changing room at the gym maybe? Probably the first one really, but he could go to the gym...why am I being so judgemental? In fact, why am I thinking this? I'm going to die any second now and this is what is on my mind?*

The infected humans were coming in rapid succession and were almost upon Jason, the others couldn't help him from their now increasingly distant viewpoint.

"JASON!" Gemma screamed.

Jason looked to the sky, closed his eyes and expected his death to be horrific, but just a second before the horde closed in, he opened them.

Echo was still fighting with the glimmer dragon in the skies; she had plunged into a nose dive, accelerating straight towards the ground, glittering fiercely with the dragon attacker following.

The infected stopped in their stumbling tracks and stared hard at the glowing teenage firefly. Something in their minds, which were decaying and in some instances torn slightly from their heads, had made them halt their stampede and stand in awe at the beautiful glitter that was Echo.

They were mesmerised by the bright lights, the pure brilliant lightshow flowing from Echo had caught their attention and for the moment had stopped their bloodlust.

Echo came out of her dive and spun forward, knocking some of the infected down with the rollercoaster cart, they collapsed like bowling pins, falling in all directions.

"STRIKE!" Echo yelled, the grin on her face grew wider as she actually made a joke – unfortunately the infected were her only audience on her comedy debut.

She had only been flying for a little while but as she climbed higher into the night it was if she'd been flying for years, she illuminated the dark with elegance and felt alive again, the first time since her sister's death that there was something to live for, if anything the dragon pursuing was merely a hindrance and nothing danger-ous, she gave the creature a mighty uppercut with the cart and another shout if simply to reiterate her point.

All the remaining eyes left in the infected human heads followed then surged forward brushing Jason aside, they pushed past him like passengers doing their daily commute on the Olympian underground.

He stayed perfectly still as everyone in the theme park, infected and humans watched in awe at the tremendous fight between Echo, a teenager with newly acquired pixie wings against a giant black dragon which emerged from the waters of the labyrinth cave network.

Jason tried something, he began to move backward and push himself through the crowds of the rushing dead, his mind flashed back to the early encounters with the creatures in the tunnels below Olympia, the situation he found himself in that afternoon and the other survivors he came across looking for salvation below the city of Olympia.

He spent the whole day trying to avoid these strange creatures, running from them, hiding and trying to stay safe and protect his new friends from this new unremarkable horror. But now they were amongst him, uninterested in his scent and blood. Gemma made a dart for it and ran nimbly across the short grass and threw her arms around Jason for a quick hug.

"Time to go, matey."

Taking his hand she led him slowly through the occupied infected, their eyes were fixed on Echo fighting in the sky, Gemma swallowed hard and kept her head down, her eyes darted from left to right as she tried hard not to bump into them, thinking that they could at any time forget about their Echo fixation and easily revert back to type and tear her apart.

"Where are the others?" Jason whispered, unable to see the group between the crowded dead.

Gemma glanced in the indicated direction. "They're over there, just watch yourself, ok?"

"Shouldn't I be telling you that?"

The girl with the green hair lifted her gaze from the infected and smiled. "You've taken care of me all day, taken care of all of us really, it's my turn to look after you for a change."

He closed his eyes and put his hand further up Gemma's shoulder for support.

"Thank you, Gemma."

"Come on, let's go."

Jason's group of survivors ushered the two of them closer. As they approached Aphrodite glared at him with piercing blue eyes. "Never getting rid of you are we?"

"Not yet."

A demoralised expression sat on Aphrodite's face. "We'll see."

The group now reunited with Jason and Gemma moved quickly with their eyes roving around to see if the infected were still occupied with the glowing Echo in the sky. All of them were, which made the survivors' run to the exit of the theme park easier.

"I'll be so happy when all this running is over," Mitchy huffed. "The amount of running I've done all day must be enough to start a new weight loss plan!"

Her head snapped back in an instant, directed right at Aphrodite. "Don't you say a word, sugar."

Aphrodite looked at her, eyes blazing with mischief. "You said a mouthful already, darling."

Slim Pickings made a fake gasp and clutched his hand on his heart. "Dudes, we're almost there at the exit, finally time to say goodbye to zombie park."

Jason wheezed and stumbled slightly, looking up at the new member of the group.

"You sound sorry to see it go, Slim?"

"Dude, just liked the whole theme park, the world's end kind of vibe you know was pretty cool and intense in there, don't you think?"

"I'm sorry, but I don't agree with you," Jason cleared his throat. "People are dying out there, it could be my family, it could be yours, are you not worried about that? Not really my idea of cool, my friend."

Slim Pickings smiled and wrapped his scarf tighter around his neck. "Sorry dude, just get carried away sometimes."

"No problem."

Jason looked to the dark sky, the glittering Echo was still holding her own against the dragon, battering it with aplomb, still using the cart from the Excavator ride.

"Well Echo still has that dragon creature under control and the zombie things are still mesmerised by her, this is our chance to get out of here and head to Big Man's tower."

Aphrodite raised a well-trimmed eyebrow. "You *want* to go there now? What changed your mind?"

"I'm exhausted and hurt, everyone has been running all day and they're tired and scared."

"Dude, have you been living under a rock for the last few years?" Slim became animated with his arms.

"The dude has been holed up in his tower for ages now, there's a bounty on his head from this dude dressed in green with a fedora hat. I've seen the dude, he's massive and there's tanks and helicopters and snipers and battering rams trying to get in, but dude, they never do."

"Well I think," said Gemma, fluttering her big brown eyes, "I think if there was a world record for the amount of times somebody can say 'dude' in a sentence? you'd probably win."

Everybody swung around and looked at the now very embarrassed teenager's face, she began to blush, Aphrodite started a slow hand clap.

"Well, well, well, Gemma made a funny! Good for you, couldn't have said it better myself."

"I know, and that's the worry," Gemma beamed, the first time since her spider disappeared.

"Ok," Aphrodite added. "All afternoon when this delightful bunch of nobodies asked where you were heading off to, you always said 'nowhere', but as we're in such esteemed company, zombies et al., where were you really heading? Now I know because you told me earlier, but enlighten our merry group if you would?"

Jason shuffled slightly in his well-worn shoes.

"Ok, you want the truth? I didn't want to get you people involved but…"

He looked around uncomfortably, not even worrying about the infected around him. "I was going to Big Man's tower anyway."

Aphrodite spoke next quick and sharp, without enthusiasm.

"Why are you going to Big Man's tower Jason, we'd all love to know."

Jason looked at the others for a while and nervously blinked several times rapidly.

"I didn't want to involve you people, you're a good bunch and it doesn't concern you…"

Gemma took a deep breath, concerned at how the man who had saved her life on more than one occasion today had issues with her foster father. "Why do you want him?"

Aphrodite looked on and a small smile crept on to her face as she realised how well her 'little sister' was handling the situation, she spoke next, surprisingly supportive.

"Answer her, Jason."

He growled a response. "He took something from me and I'm going to take something back from him."

Aphrodite blew out a tired noisy sigh. "What would that be?"

"He took away my—"

Before Jason could finish a tremendous bang like a thunder clap could be heard followed by a shriek of bright light which sizzled through the sky illuminating the night; the group followed the light until it found it's target – Echo. The beaming projectile struck her like a speeding locomotive, knocking her out of the sky in an instant. Her glittering frame was extinguished as she fell at speed back to earth, unmoving.

"ECHOOOO!" Gemma screamed, this becoming a habit for her, watching her best friend in peril yet again in the same day.

The smoke from the missile left a trail all the way back to a very tall ride in the theme park, it was called the 'Sonic Detonator' and was the second tallest ride next to the Excavator. Perched precariously on top was a male figure dressed head to toe in a high tech battle armour suit, his still smoking grenade launcher strapped firmly over his shoulder. The man pulled out a small walkie talkie from his suit and whispered a message to someone. When he was finished he adjusted his thick-rimmed glasses and began his long descent to the bottom.

Ares smiled and shifted his glasses once more as he watched Echo disappear from sight.

"Bang baby!…you're dead."

"Oh God no," Mitchy whispered.

"Echo's gone, the light is gone!"

Slim nervously looked around at the confused infected, wondering where the glitter in the sky had gone.

"Dude, shit just got real."

The group were surrounded by the stench of decaying flesh, the smell hadn't bothered them as much when the infected were preoccupied with Echo, the infected weren't hungry when the glitter woman hummed in the sky, but now Echo and her glow had gone and their bloodlust had returned. There were more of the zombie people than the living at the moment in the theme park.

Gemma had never seen so many of the infected in one place, it seemed unbelievable that they could stand there and not attack, until now, the yellow eyes of the infected turned towards every human being in the park.

"WE GOTTA MOVE NOW!" Jason screamed.

In a flash the infected turned on the theme park crowd, pulling them to the ground and feasting on their brain tissue, bloody hands ripped open soft skin of the party goers and snapped their bones clean from their bodies. Frightened yells came from all directions, people elbowed each other out of the way and scrambled towards the exits, yelling and fighting with each other to escape. The ground from the Dangerfield theme park was flattened under the mass trampling feet of the infected, they stumbled through gate after gate and picked off every living creature in their path.

A weakened Jason was pushed to the ground easily by the stampede of scared humans, surprisingly it was Aphrodite who helped him to his feet. "No time to dawdle you strange little man, time to leave."

He looked around in a panic. "WHERE ARE THE OTHERS?"

"Not here, I think we've been separated."

"NO! WE HAVE TO FIND THEM."

The whole scene was complete confusion. Gemma looked around frantically for her foster sister.

"Mitchy! I can't find Aphrodite and Jason!"

"Damn it! Listen sugar we can't stay here, look they know where we're heading."

"Big Man's tower?"

"Yes, stay close honey and lay low, Slim, stay close."

Slim Pickings stammered a response. "Dude, I'm going nowhere."

As the startled crowd fled for their lives, a heavily disguised Big Man pushed his way towards the exits, followed by Norton and his date Tara; they hid behind a big hot dog stand, the owner lay chewed up at the front.

Odysseus struggled to keep up with them, he didn't want Norton to spot him but couldn't risk losing them in the melee, he knew the girl must be Norton's date but had no idea who the other guy was dressed in old rags, he watched them duck behind the hotdog stand and held back.

"You didn't tell me what you were doing here sir, you shouldn't be out of the Messiah Complex, you know I'm not on duty at the moment," Norton asked Big Man, unaware he was being watched.

"What is this? Twenty questions, Officer Norton?" Big Man's heart was like a jack hammer and he kept telling himself his girls were ok. "Look I know I shouldn't be out of the complex and I hope me being here isn't ruining your date."

Even with all the carnage happening, Tara was still smiling and shook her head playfully, still clinging on to her man. "It's just that..." He pulled Norton towards him and whispered in his ear, eyes keeping up with the trouble around them and away from Tara. "It's just that my girls are still out here somewhere and these bastards mean business, they've just killed Melissa, tore her apart in front of me."

"Melissa? Your PA?"

"Yeah, in the tunnels beneath the city, we went under the tower as all the protesters out front have turned into those creatures, I just had to get out to find my girls."

"I know where they are, sir."

Big Man grabbed Norton by the collar. "YOU'VE SEEN THEM? WHERE ARE THEY?"

"I've been with them all day, we were travelling underground for safety and I left them to find Tara."

Big Man tightened his grip. "YOU LEFT MY GIRLS ON THEIR OWN? UNDERGROUND WITH THOSE THINGS?"

Norton struggled free. "We weren't alone sir, there is a group of us, three other guys and two girls at last count."

"Last count?

"Well there were more of us, but you can fill in the blanks sir, obviously from the first moment I saw Aphrodite I had to be professional and we couldn't let the others know that I knew who she was. I'm your head of security and she knows that, but the others didn't."

Big Man's expression was grim as he tried to keep his head down from the marauding horde. "So you leave a group of people to go on a date with a piece of skirt you don't even know?" He pulled away and turned to Tara. "No offence."

"No idea what you're talking about, you funny man."

"Cools." He leant back to Norton who nodded. "Well I would have done the same thing, but my girls are involved."

"Sir, didn't you always tell your girls that if they were in trouble or something horrible kicked off in the city much like this, shouldn't they find somewhere safe to hide?"

"Yes I did."

"So no offence sir, but where is the safest place in Olympia?"

Big Man slowly stared at each of them in turn and threw his arms up in the air in frustration and then ducked down again, remembering the situation. "They've gone back home haven't they?" Tara and Norton nodded simultaneously. "So I should go back and see if they're there, right?"

"If we can sir, as you can see in a heartbeat it's all turned to shit right now, and I think we've finished our date for tonight." Norton looked knowingly at Tara who nodded her response. "So can we come with you?"

Big Man should have felt uncomfortable, but felt lifted in knowing the girls were probably heading back home. "Agreed, let's get moving."

He stopped abruptly and pointed to the sky. "By the way, is that a dragon flying up there?" Both Norton and Tara nodded. "Not a part of the theme park?"

"It's killing people sir, so I doubt it," Norton replied.

Big Man huffed. "I've seen bigger."

Odysseus watched them leave and quickly followed, keeping his eye on the dragon and holding his bag tightly.

Jason covered his ears from all the screaming, he and Aphrodite crouched down in their new hiding place in one of the carts in the ghost train as a new type of scream entered the fray, with the loss of Echo, the beaten up dragon continued its reign of terror on the theme park, bright blinding streaks of blue fireballs fired indiscriminately at everybody on the ground, smashing into the zombie-like infected and humans.

Various body parts were sent hurtling through the air, limbs were sliced off in an instant and heads rolled along the candyfloss covered floor.

Jason shook his head and screamed with his hands still clamped to his ears.

"STOP IT! STOP IT! IT'S KILLING THEM!"

Aphrodite cautiously raised her head from the ghost train cart. "I had noticed, darling."

The screams from the people were deafening, as the dragon soared through the gaps between the tall rides and unleashed volley after volley of flame bursts on the crowd. They were running blind, hightailing it away from the dragon's fires and bumping into the infected, death came from all sides.

People's skin burned from their bones as the dragon's flames grew more confident with each swoop.

"WE HAVE TO GET OUT OF HERE!" Jason tugged hard on Aphrodite's hand.

"You have a remarkable knack of noting the obvious."

"TURN INTO THE DOG AND GET US OUT OF HERE!"

She responded with a smile that oozed pure wickedness.

"Can't honey, too tired for that, we have to make a break for it."

The noise of people howling in pain was becoming too much for Jason, the strong leader in the tunnels beneath the city earlier in the day was all but gone, just a shivering wreck of a man shook in his place.

Aphrodite stroked his hand gently with her now broken nails. "We have to go back underground my darling and make our way to Big Man's tower, are you up for it?"

His tired eyes looked back at her sparkling blue ones and accepted the challenge with a nervous nod. Aphrodite hauled him to his feet. "Ok darling, well any tunnel will be safe at the moment, you ready for this?"

"Let's see," Jason replied wearily.

She pulled him back into the startled crowds as they started a run towards the nearest manhole, her grip tightened as they edged nearer to safety, the manhole they chose in the distance was clear.

"We're going to make it," Jason said, slowly satisfied.

"Seems that way darling," Aphrodite replied, her voice more icy than usual.

"Thank god we're almost...OHHH NOOOO!" Jason collapsed in a heap clutching his knee.

"OH GOD NO! NOT NOW! PLEASE NOT NOW!"

Aphrodite stopped and bent her head in a quizzical manner. "You ok darling?"

Jason shook his head violently in a blind panic. "MY KNEE! MY KNEE HAS GONE AGAIN, HELP ME UP PLEASE!"

"Oh my dear, we can't have that can we?"

Before Jason could answer, one of the many infected broke into a sprint towards him, talons quickly grew from Aphrodite's hand and she slashed at the man, slicing his arm off at the elbow, but the loss of its arm did nothing to deter the creature and it turned around and charged again.

"Fair enough," Aphrodite sighed.

Her talons stayed out as in a blur of a motion they cut deep into the creature's neck, its head rolled off its shoulders as momentum carried the creature spinning on into the coconut shy.

"No interruptions please."

She retracted her claws and turned to Jason and slowly walked towards him.

"Now where were we? Ah yes, we need to have a chat right now."

"APHRODITE! WHAT ARE YOU TALKING ABOUT?"

She shuffled her shoulders in Echo's ill-fitting jacket. "When I was a little girl and whenever I got scared of anything, if I was being bullied at school or father was ignoring me, my mum would come into my room and say that 'Tough times don't last, tough people do' now she was the only person I ever heard say that, until I heard you say that exact thing earlier, now where did you hear that?"

"I DON'T KNOW WHAT YOU MEAN?"

Aphrodite remained calm and neatly sidestepped another infected man rushing her, before backhanding it with a single blow. As the creature fell she returned her attention to Jason.

"I think you know exactly what I mean."

"MY KNEE HAS GONE, APHRODITE PLEASE!"

"You heard that from Hannah Wylde, my mother."

Jason's eyes couldn't open any wider. "What did you say?"

"You're the man my mother left my father for, you're the teacher she had an affair with, yes Hannah is my mother, tell me it's true."

Jason spoke in a broken voice. "My Hannah?"

Aphrodite ran at him and held her right hand around his throat, claws slightly out drawing blood, she snarled complete contempt at him."

"No, *my* Hannah! And you took her from us, you took her from my father, you took her from ME!"

Barely a whimper came from his lips. "You? Big Man is your father? You're one of his daughters? She didn't tell me about you, I swear I didn't know your name, she told me she had left your father before I came on the scene."

"How old were you? You must have been a boy for god's sake, you're disgusting."

"I DIDN'T KNOW ABOUT YOU, I PROMISE! LOOK, SHE TOLD ME IT WAS OVER BETWEEN YOU AND YOUR FATHER, I SWEAR TO GOD!"

"Not good enough."

"IT'S THE TRUTH! ALL SHE TOLD ME WAS THAT BIG MAN AND HER HAD FINISHED LONG BEFORE WE MET AND THAT SHE HAD TWO DAUGHTERS AND A SON, BUT SHE DIDN'T TELL ME THEIR NAMES, SHE DIDN'T TELL ME YOUR NAME!"

"That's a lie darling, Gemma is not my mother's she's adopted or fostered or whatever, she's not my real sister, you know I had to lie to my father when I said I'd gone to visit her? I said I knew where she lived and went off on my own sat for hours on my own in some greasy café and then came back home having bought myself a gift claiming it was from her."

Jason rubbed his knee and tried to stand. "What did you say?"

"I said I had to buy my own gifts and—"

"No, before that, I know Gemma is adopted or soon will be, you told everyone constantly in the tunnels, but you have another sister, somebody else…"

"You lie."

"I'm not."

"I SAID DON'T LIE!"

Jason's focus sharpened directly on Aphrodite and gave a fading stare. "Am I?" Her grip tightened, drawing more blood.

"Where is my mother? WHERE IS SHE?"

"I DON'T KNOW! THERE WAS A KNOCK AT THE DOOR SOME TIME AGO, HANNAH ANSWERED AND SOMEONE CAME IN AND TOOK HER."

Aphrodite paused before she replied, calm again and ignoring the chaos over her shoulder.

"Is she alive?"

"I'm not sure."

"Who took her?"

The fear in Jason's face was replaced by anger.

"WHO TOOK HER? WHO TOOK HER? WHY DON'T YOU ASK YOUR PRECIOUS FATHER WHO TOOK HER?"

"Is that why you were heading to my father's tower?

"Yes, didn't want to involve you guys, that's why I kept quiet. I know he has her, I know he wanted revenge, I know he has my Hannah."

"So if you think he has her, which he doesn't by the way, why are you only making your way to my father's complex now? Surely that would have been your first port of call?"

"Don't you think I know that? Every day I went to the complex and every day I tried harder to get in, but I couldn't, nobody can get into that complex, it's too heavily guarded and impenetrable."

"I know it is doofus, I live there."

"So I met someone, I met a man who said he could get Big Man out of the tower, all I had to do was to look after some people after the 'Turning point' began, that's what he calls this madness, he said to lead them on a merry dance but make sure you make it to the Dangerfield theme park, I didn't know you were Big Man's daughter."

"What was his name?"

Jason's sudden laughter caught her off-guard. "He didn't tell me his name, just told me to 'say nothing and save something'."

"What are you going to do now then darling?" Aphrodite asked.

"You don't get it do you? I'm going to kill him, I'm going to kill your father for taking my Hannah."

Inside Aphrodite exploded with anger, but on the outside she remained calm.

"The Hannah you stole from my family in the first place, right?" Aphrodite shook her dirty blonde hair and cleared her throat. "So what you're saying is that I have another sister and my mother has been kidnapped by my father?"

Jason almost taunted her in a response. "What do you think?" he said more animated by nerves than confidence. He spoke again. "I guess you're going to kill me now? The man who is your mother's lover?"

Aphrodite stretched out her gorgeous legs and rubbed them softly. "I was going to kill you, Jason," she said dead pan. She pointed at the oncoming rush of infected in front of them. "But I don't have time to queue."

Jason saw this new bunch of infected who had now spotted them and reached out with an outstretched hand, imploringly.

"MY KNEE HAS GONE, APHRODITE, YOU HAVE TO HELP ME!"

Aphrodite kissed him on the cheek and shuffled her shoulders again, starting to get used to Echo's jacket and brushed the hair from her face. She began to walk away as Jason exploded with anger overtaking the nerves.

"FOR GOD'S SAKE HELP ME PLEASE! I CAN'T WALK!"

Aphrodite watched the crowds of infected stumbling closer and took a step back towards Jason.

"Help you like you helped yourself to my mother?"

"WAIT, THAT'S IT! I'VE SEEN HER, I KNOW WHAT THEY'VE DONE TO HER! PLEASE HELP ME UP!

Tears were streaming down his face, he was scared, more scared than he'd ever been since this day had started.

"PLEASE DON'T LEAVE ME! I KNOW WHERE YOUR MUM IS!"

"Don't lie to me, you moron."

He was screaming for help now and began to crawl to the first available manhole, as the infected came lumbering towards him, they moved so slowly but Jason knew each step would lead closer to his death if he didn't make it to the tunnels. Aphrodite rolled her beautiful head round to him and wiped her nose as the full stench of the infected hit her.

"What were those words you told me earlier in the tunnels that meant 'God be with you' in the old language again?"

Before he could answer the infected had already toppled on to him, Jason kicked out feebly as they moved on him, but it was to no avail, they tore into his back easily with eager hands and teeth. Still crawling, Jason was almost over the manhole leaving a bloody trail behind him.

His fingernails had split open as he tried to make his way across the ground.

An infected glamour model dressed in a PVC nurse's outfit walked forward in a series of bizarre twitches, her enormous fake breasts rested easily on Jason's chest as he turned to face her, she ripped open his cheek with her whitened teeth with ease. Blood streamed down from Jason's nose as more creatures bit eagerly into his face. His hair was torn apart in different directions by the infected with dried blood in their mouths, eager to taste the new blood from this fallen victim.

"H-Help m-me," he pleaded.

Aphrodite tapped her temple with her fore finger, mocking a deep thinking expression.

"Can't think of those words you know, was it 'I was a spoilt, freeloading waste of space?' Well I can recall them being said but those aren't the words I'm looking for, now what are those words?"

Jason had stopped panting with fear, his face was wet with sweat and tears – what was left of it. His face was opened up again and his attempt to remove the manhole cover was made harder as he was struggling to keep his intestines from spilling onto the ground. He could feel the creatures tugging on his legs, he steadied his mangled torn up arms and with a rasped cry moved the manhole cover and attempted to crawl through it, he was losing his left leg below the knee in the process, eaten away by the infected.

Aphrodite smiled as Jason's pleading turned to a blood curdling gargling sound, his eyes had already changed colour from brown to a milky white, what was left of his shredded body tumbled through the manhole and into the waters below the city as the current took his bloody body through the nightclubs of Olympia. Many of the infected that had gathered around the manhole to feast fell into the hole too and were also washed away by the strong waters flowing beneath the city.

Aphrodite walked over to the hole in the ground, pleased with her efforts, people were still screaming and running for their lives around her as she calmly bent down, replaced the man hole cover and wiped her hands on Echo's coat. She rose and shook her golden mane of hair with a hidden grin. "I remember those words now my lovely." She blew a kiss towards the manhole. "Vaya con dios."

11. How to Ruin Your Love Life

"I CAN'T SEE HER! CAN YOU?"

Mitchy found it hard to hear Gemma, let alone understand what she was saying, she guessed it was concern for her sister and tried a reply. "I DON'T KNOW SUGAR, BUT YOU'VE SEEN WHAT SHE CAN DO, SHE CAN LOOK AFTER HERSELF."

So many people just going out for a day of fun at a theme park had been pulled apart to their deaths by some who only this morning were 'normal' but now had been infected by a bloodlust virus and feasted eagerly on the insides of those trying desperately to escape. The wounded screamed all over the park and dead bodies were dropping everywhere.

Spinning through the air with a mouth flashing with flames, the dragon had set most of the theme park alight with many people stuck on the rides burned along with them too.

Mitchy saw the pain and despair in Gemma's eyes, something she had rarely seen through spending the day with her. Gemma had calmed herself down and turned to Mitchy.

"Everybody keeps leaving us...Tero, Quinn, Norton, Odysseus, Connor, Buckby, Echo, and now Jason and Aphrodite."

"Now I miss them too, truly I do, but we don't know if Norton and Odysseus are dead? Even Connor?"

"Connor drowned," Gemma sighed.

Mitchy cocked her head and her brow furrowed. "Yeah, I know."

Gemma's usually alert brown eyes were still dull and Mitchy knew she had to try hard to get her back on track. "Listen sugar, I've met some arrogant people in my life, but Aphrodite is the biggest bitch ever! She is mean, rude and disrespectful and doesn't give a toss about anybody but herself."

"But—"

"*But* Gemma, she is the strongest person I've met, ever since these dreadful creatures appeared today and we all came together, whatever has been thrown at us and whoever we've unfortunately lost, she's always been there with some sort of insensitive quip, she'll be fine, she's stronger than all of us put together."

A figure crept up behind them with amazing stealth. Slim Pickings noticed but the two women didn't. The figure switched their slender weight to one hip and folded their arms and then spoke with words which were characteristically direct.

"Darling Mitchy, you're fatter than all of us put together, who knew?"

"APHRODITE! Gemma squealed.

She leapt from her hiding place and flung her arms around her foster sister, Aphrodite stood with her arms now by her side and spoke with her sister's green hair in her mouth.

"How many times have we done this today, darling?"

Gemma didn't move but kept her grin. "Enough."

"Aren't you bored yet of hugging me when I always come through?"

"Nope."

A small smile eased onto Aphrodite's face.

"Good girl."

Mitchy walked over and patted her hand on the small of Aphrodite's back, looking around for somebody else in the process of welcoming her back.

"Where is Jason?"

Gemma removed herself from Aphrodite and moved back to Mitchy, waiting for a response.

Aphrodite's tongue probed all around her front teeth.

"Jason is dead, the infected thingies got him."

Slim Pickings rubbed his head and then shook it. "Dude, I just saved that guy earlier."

Gemma shook herself and tumbled into the arms of Mitchy as Aphrodite continued. "Yep, he went out quite embarrassingly actually, crying and screaming like a baby."

"How many more will we lose?" Gemma moaned.

"Hopefully that annoying idiot will be the last," Aphrodite huffed.

"A little tact please, Aphrodite?" Mitchy glared back, holding a distraught Gemma.

"Jason was our friend, he saved our lives so many times today, is that all you've got to say?"

Aphrodite gave her trademark gorgeous yet icy blue-eyed smile.

"Yeah pretty much, not wasting anymore time on that waste of space."

Mitchy tenderly stroked Gemma's green hair.

"Honey, have you always been this cruel?"

"Pretty much, and this is good for me, haven't made a 'Fat' gag in ages."

"How can you keep this up, honey? The stone cold attitude?"

The icy smile stayed. "Like I've always said, it's down to breeding darling, immaculate breeding."

Gemma wiped the tears from her eyes for Jason and looked around nervously. Slim was unusually quiet.

"How did you find us?"

Aphrodite looked at her broken nails and gently placed some hair behind her ear. "You forget that I'm sort of a dog now and some of the perks of this canine carry on is that I have a tremendous sense of smell, works wonders for a new shoe sale, anyway I sniffed you and the human house out easily."

Mitchy raised an eyebrow. "Human house?"

"Sorry darling I did try…so as I was saying, I found you and the little rug rat quite easily."

She sniffed the air again. "That loved up fool Norton is close by as well as that psycho midget Odysseus."

Gemma left Mitchy's arms her brown eyes flashed wide with anticipation.

"THEY'RE ALIVE? REALLY?"

"I'm afraid so."

Aphrodite sniffed the night air again.

"Yes, it's definitely them as well as…" *No, it can't be him!* Aphrodite thought. *What's he doing here?*

Aphrodite suddenly turned to Gemma. "We have to go, NOW!"

Before Gemma could react her foster sister grabbed her hand and pulled her into the fleeing crowd, her breathing heavy, Gemma looked to Aphrodite. Both faces were in complete confusion.

"What's wrong? Why are running this way?"

"I smelt somebody, someone who's not supposed to be here."

"Who is it?"

Aphrodite's grip tightened as they bumped into the rushing crowd.

"Tell me," Gemma pleaded.

Aphrodite stopped abruptly and cupped her hand over Gemma's mouth and looked back at the tired pursuing Mitchy and the spaced out Slim Pickings, and whispered slowly, "Father...father is here."

Before Gemma could answer an explosion knocked them both off their feet. Something had taken out the Excavator rollercoaster, a blast not from the dragon. As the debris came falling back to earth with loud thuds and the smoke began to clear, Aphrodite picked herself up and wiped the dust from her eyes and Echo's jacket which she was now becoming quite attached to.

There was a huge crater in the ground and Aphrodite's eyes left it and followed where the smoke was coming from. Her eyes noticed something big moving awkwardly in the dark and her ears and pricked up to attention. She turned to Gemma who was slowly making her way to her feet and then turned to Mitchy who had finally caught them up, coughing heavily. For once it was Slim who lagged behind.

All three women held their necks high into the night and focused on had what caused the explosion. They stood poised and stared at a new gigantic construct which had no right to be at the theme park. Gemma watched as the smoke finally cleared from two large cannons in the distance, she nervously bit her lip to stop it from trembling and ignored the pain her body was in.

Staring at the new massive object in the theme park she folded her arms tight across her chest and had now stopped panting with fear, she took a deep breath and closed her eyes, hoping that the massive thing would be gone by the time she opened them again. She waited a while and then opened her eyes slowly to find the two gigantic cannons still pointed in her direction.

"Oh for fuck's sake," she sighed.

A sound of grinding metal and whirling gears cut through the air, the three women and slim covered their ears from the clanking monstrosity.

The tremendous hulking machine Tyranadroid loomed into view, the sentry robot was in full operational mode, with weapons online.

The monolith moved closer giving the people of the theme park something else to worry about as well as the infected. Aphrodite grabbed Gemma and ran off again.

Tyranadroid emitted a low hum which caught the attention of the circling dragon, its huge mechanical head aimed the sonic beam directly at the dragon, the sound had a calming effect on the creature.

It roared louder than it had ever done and circled around the robotic monster before nestling onto its shoulder, much like a parrot on a human.

A voice boomed out from the machine, a metallic sound which everybody recognised.

"THERE'S A GOOD GIRL." The voice of The Green Man came quite clearly from loud speakers attached all over the gigantic frame of Tyranadroid. People who hadn't fled the attack of the infected trembled slightly.

"GOOD EVENING LADIES AND GENTLEMEN, PLEASE FORGIVE MY THEATRICAL ENTRANCE, BUT WE HAVE A SPECIAL GUEST IN THE CROWD AND I KNOW FOR CERTAIN HE WOULDN'T WANT TO MISS THE MAIN EVENT!"

Tara held on to Norton's arm, her eyes transfixed on the giant robot. "This has to be best date I've been on – ever!"

Norton had seen the sentry robots before, he was a security guard at the towers and had seen all various types of robotic designs resembling animals and dinosaurs, built to defend the Messiah's Complex from attack, but he'd never seen any of them active, he was too shocked to reply to Tara.

Big Man shifted uncomfortably in his heavy disguise standing close by to his security man, he knew nothing good would come from this, even though some good ideas for some new game shows had entered his head from seeing the walking mechanical dinosaur.

Aphrodite had smelt her father out fully now and was edging closer towards him, eyes fixed on what was ahead of her and not above. *Some of these scents are familiar,* she thought.

"It's the bloody apocalypse!" Mitchy gasped, finally catching up with the other two girls.

Gemma had somehow wriggled free from Aphrodite's grip and slowed down her pace.

"It's going to get much worse than that, trust me," the teenager said, eying her disapproval at the machine.

"What makes you say that, sugar?"

"Just a feeling," came the solemn reply. "Bad things happen at night."

Massive flashlights beamed down from Tyranadroid, sending the humans scattering like spiders from a bright light switch.

"DON'T BE SHY, BIG MAN!"

The Green Man's voice followed the lights. "IT'S TIME FOR YOUR PENANCE, TIME FOR THIS DAY

OF RECKONING TO END, YOU MAY HIDE
AMONGST YOUR FLOCK LIKE A WOLF IN SHEEP'S
CLOTHING, IT'S TIME FOR THE PEOPLE YOU
HAVE WRONGED TO STEP OUT AND SHOW THEM-
SELVES, ONE BY ONE THEY WILL COMPLETE
THE TURNING POINT AND SEE WHO YOU REALLY
ARE AND NOW THAT YOU ARE FINALLY OUT OF
YOUR TOWER, YOU ARE AS DEFENCELESS AS A
SARDINE IN THE SUN, AS ARE YOUR SECRETS."

Aphrodite was so close to her father, as soon as she
heard The Green Man utter the word 'secret' she
quickened her pace. Curiosity finally got the better of Big
Man and he threw off his disguise.

"COME ON THEN SOFTLAD! STEP OUT OF MY
GIANT TYRANADROID, WHICH I NAMED BY
THE WAY, AND LET'S GO!"

The Green Man flicked a switch on the control panel
and turned to another person lurking in the back. "Do
we have sound now?"

The person in the shadows nodded.

"RIGHT, WE HAVE SOUND, WE TOOK THE
NECESSITY OF INSTALLING MICROPHONES AND
LOUDSPEAKERS AND DOTTED THEM AROUND
THIS THEME PARK, LET'S TURN A FEW OF THEM
ON SHALL WE?"

Big Man's rants suddenly became audible to the entire
theme park.

"OH THERE YOU ARE, BIG MAN," The Green
Man purred with a metallic twang.

The crowd around Big Man remembered the bounty
on his head and forgot their fear of the infected, beginning to rush the former TV executive.

"NOT YET, NOT YET," The Green Man hit another switch on the front panel. A flame thrower from the dinosaur's side released a jet of fire towards Big Man, the fires burned into a circle, separating him from the crowd as well as Norton and Tara.

Aphrodite finally arrived to see her father surrounded by a wall of flame. His eyes glowed when he saw his daughter stop sharp at the fire.

It had only been hours since he'd last seen her, but after everything that had happened today he was so happy to see her alive, and slightly confused that she was seemingly naked apart from a black leather jacket, he had taught her to be cold and aloof and even though his heart crashed against his chest to see her again, a respectful head nod was what she received from her father through the flames, which she replied to with the same. There were no tears, but she looked unhappy, her blue eyes bright in the new flame light. Gemma ran up next and saw her foster father in a ring of fire, her knees almost buckled with delight.

She went to call him but Aphrodite clapped her hand around the younger girl's face and whispered through clenched teeth, "I don't know what this creature wants with Father, but let's just wait to find out, he holds the cards now and I think he knows we're here."

For the second time today Gemma squirmed free from her sister, she glared back and frowned.

"That's our father in that fire ring!"

"Would you keep your voice down? People still don't know that's our father out there, I also know that for the first time in years he's outside the Messiah's Complex... something or someone got him out and I want to know why."

Gemma's little ears listened intently to Aphrodite's well-spoken voice.

"I just hope I know what you're doing, Aphrodite."

For the first time since Gemma came to live with her family, Aphrodite had to agree with her foster sister.

Mitchy spotted Norton on the other side of the flame circle and waved her hands frantically.

"NORTON! NORTON! OVER HERE, HONEY!" She got Gemma's attention and pointed in Norton's direction. "LOOK IT'S NORTON! HE'S ALIVE! HE'S ALIVE!"

Gemma flicked a glance over and relief swept away the anger on her face, her back was still sore from the dragon's flame in the water earlier and she moved awkwardly and then joined Mitchy with the waving.

"HE'S NOT WAVING BACK, HE CAN'T SEE US!" Gemma's smile slowly faded. "HE CAN'T SEE US, MITCHY!"

Mitchy grabbed her hand. "COME HONEY, WE'LL RUN ROUND THE FIRES TO GET HIM."

More of the infected were shambling around the fires, the flames startled them and they were disorientated, but still tried to pick off the humans close by.

"WHAT ABOUT THE INFECTED? THEY'RE ALL AROUND US!" Gemma yelled.

Mitchy took a long and assessing look at the infected blocking their path, her mouth curled. "Just let one of those bastards try and stop me." She turned back to Gemma. "You coming, sugar?"

Gemma turned to Aphrodite who was preoccupied with Big Man, her eyes drew back to Mitchy.

"Let's go get Norton."

She let Mitchy lead her through the crowds of infected and humans, trying to make their way round the flame circle to Norton.

Aphrodite and Slim Pickings stayed still, just waiting for The Green Man's move as Mitchy and Gemma ran around the huge flame circle to reach Norton.

Lurking behind Norton was Odysseus, still keeping an eye on proceedings, he saw Gemma and Mitchy running around the flames to probably meet Norton and a small smile crept on his face to see them alive. He stood up from his hiding place and shouted too but neither Norton nor Mitchy could hear him. He too began to push past everybody to reach Norton.

Tara stared hard at Big Man surrounded by the biting flames, then quickly back to her date, scratching her arms as she went to hold him.

"Dance with me Norton, hold me close."

"WHAT?" Norton blurted.

She took his hands and pulled him towards her swinging him around ever so gently. Confusion swept across Norton's face and he tried to struggle free but Tara's grip was surprisingly strong.

Big Man watched intently behind his firewall as Norton shouted, "WE'VE GOT TO GET OUT OF HERE, TARA!"

She calmly put a finger to his lips. "Shush my love and just hold me."

"TARA, WE HAVE TO GO NOW!"

Mitchy and Odysseus were running towards Norton from opposite ends still trying to get his attention, shouting and waving. Tara kissed Norton's neck tenderly and continued to lead him. "Remember what I said about a storm coming to Olympia, my lovely? Well it's here and there's nothing you can do to stop it."

"WHAT ARE YOU TALKING ABOUT? WE HAVE TO LEAVE!"

"I know you're scared." She scratched her arms again and quickly put them back around her date. "I know you're confused but it will go away, I can take it away for you, I can make it so you will never have to be scared again."

Tara with her sweet lips bit softly into Norton's neck, calm instantly shot through him as his date nibbled gently, his eyes rolled softly in a sweet euphoria. "I came to warn you earlier today, I came to tell you to leave Olympia because the storm is on the way, I wanted to tell you to pack what you could and flee before the chaos began, do you remember, my love?"

Norton didn't respond, his lips curled into some type of bliss. "I really did like you, my love, even after what you did, I wanted to make sure you would be safe, so I ran to you early in the morning when you were at work doing your security for the Big Man? I came to tell you that things are getting hot and to get out, and what did you do, my love? You struck me in the face and knocked me down, do you remember? From the protest?"

Norton's legs had gone soft, there was nothing in them as Tara held him up and stopped talking to simply keep her teeth nibbling on to his neck, her kissing was so gentle and calm that Norton didn't even reply to her.

Odysseus was closing in on them and Norton was still in the embrace of Tara, he should have heard him shouting, but the warm arms and tender kissing of Tara were enough to cancel out the shouts from the little man.

Tara removed her lips from Norton's neck, she spun him around, watching her feet against his, trying not to upset the dance routine.

"Tell me," she said in a beautifully seductive tone. "Would you let me save you?"

Odysseus was in view and he noticed Mitchy running from the other side.

Tara went back to Norton's neck and bit again, harder this time. He felt the tiny warm drip of blood trickle down his shoulder as her smooth lips latched on to his skin.

Unbeknown to Norton, Tara's teeth had grown; they were long and smooth and had broken through Norton's neck, she sucked and kissed him tasting his own blood. Norton was in a wound of desire, the sensation was beautiful as Tara drew his blood and swallowed deeply.

He pulled in a breath trying to speak and that was when Tara's teeth clamped harder on his neck and pulled part of it out. A small fountain of blood sprang from the hole in his neck and Norton collapsed in a heap.

"NOOOOOO!!" Mitchy screamed.

She reached Norton as he lay spread-eagled turning the ground around him scarlet.

The big woman shoved Tara out of the way and cradled her wounded friend as Odysseus followed.

"WHERE WERE YOU?" she howled.

"I was following him."

"WHY DIDN'T YOU DO SOMETHING!?"

"It's not my fault, she was fine, she was human."

Norton's body was splayed out at an awkward angle, Odysseus bent down and held his head along with Mitchy, he tried levity but knew it was too late.

"What have you done here, mate? Got yourself in a bit of a mess."

Norton's eyes were wide with fright, he was panicking as his life ebbed away, he recognised Odysseus and tried to smile, gurgling up blood as he did so. Mitchy turned his head and the blood trickled to the ground, she tried to stem the blood flow from his neck but it was too great.

Odysseus's mind worked furiously, trying to figure out what to say next. "Told you that girl would be trouble, mate."

Gemma blinked back the tears as Norton struggled to reply. "D-d-didn't c-c-hick ulate her."

He gasped for air and his body began to shake, the desperation in his voice made Odysseus hold his hand.

"Shush mate, don't speak, we're going to get you out of here."

Finding it hard to look at Norton, Odysseus felt a gentle squeeze on his hand.

"I s-s-should h-have s-stayed w-with…"

"Don't speak honey," Mitchy said, her voice quivering.

Tears rolled down his cheek as he became frightened again. "I'm s-sorry, I'm s-so sorry."

"Listen you, you're tough and you're going to be okay." Odysseus gazed at the wound in Norton's neck and finally looked away from it, hoping Norton couldn't see the despair in his eyes.

Norton shook and twisted his head, smiling through blood stained teeth. "Liar." His head began to nod now and he tried to say something else but he died first.

Mitchy stood back, wiping the tears from her face. "What do we do now?"

Odysseus looked at Norton and then up to the towering Tyrannosaur machine, The Green Man inside had remained silent throughout Tara's attack.

"I'm not sure what to do."

Tara picked at her long vampire-like teeth and caught Odysseus's glare.

"Oh it's you! Hey babes!"

Odysseus squinted against her soft eyes. "What have you done?"

Tara walked forward and the flames of Big Man's circle illuminated her face.

"God no," Odysseus whispered.

"It's me babes, from the bus stop this morning?"

Odysseus dropped to the floor holding his stomach, he couldn't contain the sick that sprang from his guts and vomited all along the ground, the realisation too much to bear.

"Whoopsy," Tara smiled.

"Thank you so much for letting me take your seat on the bus by the way, I wouldn't have made my 'business meeting' otherwise, with your friend Norton."

"YOU BITCH!" Odysseus spat.

Tara waved her fore finger from side to side. "Now that's not very nice is it, babes? And remember…?" She reached into her bag and pulled out a silver coin. "Heads I win…tails you lose."

Odysseus roared a guttural cry of anger and leapt at Tara, she caught him in mid-leap by the throat with ease and held him there, his feet twitched like marooned fish.

"PUT HIM DOWN!" Gemma cried.

"Not yet, babes."

Her head turned quizzically, studying Odysseus. "Why did you come here? Norton told me there was no love lost between you."

Odysseus groaned in Tara's grasp. "You didn't have to kill him."

Tara switched to look at Norton being cradled by Mitchy and Gemma. "Technically speaking babes, you killed him, all for being too polite and too stupid, now why were you here again?"

"Was trying to keep an eye on him, keep him safe."

Tara turned to the still body of Norton. "You've done an exceptional job, babes."

Odysseus squirmed in her vice-like grip.

"I'm not finished with you, lady."

Tara grinned through her massive teeth. "Yes you are." With a calm flick of her wrist and with terrifying ease, Tara hurled Odysseus into the fleeing crowds of humans still trying to escape the infected.

She turned her attention to Big Man and slowly walked through the flame circle, his eyes grew when he saw her teeth and invulnerability to fire.

"What are you?" he asked.

Tara's mouth was mixture of blood and deep red lipstick, her lips quirked into a cool smile.

"It's more like 'who am I?' don't you know, Big Man?"

"Should I? I know you're one of those freaks with powers."

"Yes I am."

"The little maniac was right, you shouldn't have killed Norton, he did nothing wrong."

A lopsided smile appeared on her lips. "It's not nice losing someone you care for is it?"

"I wouldn't go as far as that, I mean we played poker a few times but that's it."

"Always joking aren't we, Big Man?"

"I get by lady, but like I said, you didn't have to kill Norton."

Big Man's nose twitched as Tara's beautiful scent wafted closer as she approached him.

"Norton was doomed from the start the moment he was employed by you, he had a chance to leave but forfeited his life by striking me earlier today."

"Is this going anywhere?"

The Green Man's huge voice boomed from the dinosaur cockpit. "LISTEN TO HER, BIG MAN, YOU MUST LEARN."

Big Man looked up to the robot and tapped his watch towards Tara.

"Tell me Big Man, do you know what a condolence package is?"

His eyes rolled in his head slightly.

"Oh yeah, it's a hamper I think? It's what my company send out to the relatives of people who have been injured or killed in my service."

Tara's voice grew tense for the first time today, her smile was gone. "Flowers, sympathy card usually, am I right?"

"Yep, pretty much."

Tara wasn't feeling strong or confident, she looked down at her pale hands and they were shaking, she was unmoved when she killed Norton but was finding it hard facing Big Man. Norton's blood had dried up already in her mouth and she licked her lips slowly running out of spit, breathing in, she lifted her eyes and focused hard on Big Man.

"Does the name 'David Davis' mean anything to you?"

"Nope, should it have?"

Tara gnawed gently on her bottom lip, keeping her stare with Big Man.

"Think back to a few years ago then, you were having a board meeting about how to get more viewers for your show *Leviathan?* Well one of your employees gave you some suggestions on how to improve the show and you disagreed with his comments, so what did you do? Did you tell them that you respect their views but don't agree with them? Did you ask them to politely leave your company? No, you see there was a young man who offered you some advice years ago on your game show and you disagreed with his comments, so what did you do?"

Big Man smiled broadly in his response. "I think I remember, but remind me anyway."

"You choked him to death."

"YES, THAT'S IT!" Big Man clapped his hands. "I remember now! Threw him against a rubber plant as I recall? Anybody you knew?"

A blast of anger shuddered over her, Tara breathed in and her eyes narrowed. "He was my husband."

Big Man exhaled in a rush and stood back, mouth open. "Really? Wow! I did not know that."

Tara's eyes were busy scanning Big Man's reaction. "Yes, we met at college, dated for a while and moved in together, money was tight but we were young, loved each other and decided to get married, work dried up for both of us until David got a job working for the 'Mighty' Big Man at the Messiah's Complex, the money was better, so much more that we moved from Utopia City to Olympia City, he was happy, we were happy, until you killed him."

"Wait! I didn't know Davis was your husband."

"So that makes it ok, does it? It's ok to go flinging people across the room into rubber plants after choking them to death?"

"I didn't say that."

"Did you ever think about your aftercare for grieving relatives? I mean how could we survive on flowers?"

"We?"

Tara couldn't fake a cool response this time and simply spat her reply. "My son!"

"Oh, I'm so sorry!"

"Really? Are you really sorry? Or just annoyed that you got caught, have you any idea how hard it is to survive in this city bringing up a child on your own? After you took away his father that is."

The microphones picked up the entire conversation and the crowds which remained from the passing of the infected booed and hissed. Gemma drifted back to Aphrodite and tugged on her jacket.

"Did you know about this?"

"Oddly enough no, the little hussy has balls though I'll give her that."

Gemma grew agitated. "What shall we do?"

"We keep waiting."

Tara walked forward, her breath quickened. "You look pale, Big Man and quiet, what's wrong? Cat got your tongue?"

"Look I didn't know about your son, and I'm really sorry about that, but I'm not the same guy I was years ago! I'm different now, I've changed, where is your son by the way?

"With my parents, safe back in Utopia City."

"Well I have changed."

The icy glare from Tara made him shut up. "A leopard never changes his spots, Big Man."

"No offence but that's just a saying that morons use to say that people won't change but people change all the time, that's what we do, that's what humans do, we have to in order to adapt and to survive."

"Adapt and survive?" Tara had her smile back.

"Is that what you think you are? The dominant species? Well humans used to be, but…"

Her front teeth grew to a sabre toothed tiger's length. "Those days are over."

"Excuse me?" Big Man asked.

Tara clutched her handbag tight as the flames around them grew more fierce. "You see, I was in a state as you could well imagine and it was all your fault, I wrote to and called you and your company for financial aid and nobody replied." She pointed up to the metal dinosaur. "That was until that man in the green coat up there found me and offered me a chance to turn my life around, offered me, sounds corny but revenge on the Big Man corporation."

"Revenge on me? Ok I get it, expected in your case." He pointed at her teeth. "So how did you get your unique talent?"

She kept her finger pointed at the dinosaur. "He introduced me to a few new tricks, but there were some I already knew."

"Will you play those tricks on me then?"

She didn't answer for a moment, then her eyes narrowed.

"No, not me, somebody else will."

Big Man stretched his arms and yawned. "So young lady, you're a single mum who's a super villain right? Now that's what I call multi-tasking."

He looked around at the growing fires trapping him. "Listen, I'm sorry for what I did, again, but why did you bring Norton here? Just simply to kill him?"

A short, sharp laugh followed from Tara. "My friends had an issue with him, I'll let them tell you themselves, whoops that reminds me." She ran back to the body of Norton and rummaged through his pockets. "Ah ha, got it!"

It was Norton's entry key card to the Messiah's complex. Tara examined it and put it in her bag and ran back to Big Man, taking it out to show him. "Got your key, babes."

"My pass key to the complex? This is what it's all about? You could have taken that key from him at anytime without killing him."

"I know babes, but this way was much more fun and besides, Norton had it coming, you'll find out soon enough."

Tara put her thumb and a finger in her mouth and blew an almighty wolf whistle.

Slim Pickings scratched his nose softly and turned to a still distraught Gemma. "Whoops that's my cue, later dudes."

"WHAT?" Gemma yelled.

"YOU'RE WITH HER? SHE KILLED NORTON!"

"Dude I know, was all part of the plan, well the plan was to include Jason in all of these proceedings but I don't know what happened to him."

Aphrodite heard Slim and a smile flickered across her face. *Never saw that one coming,* she thought.

Gemma ran ahead and tried reasoning with Slim. "WHY ARE YOU DOING THIS? I THOUGHT WE WERE FRIENDS?"

"Dude we are friends, sort of, but this is a family matter." Slim stopped running. "Which reminds me..." He screamed into the crowd. "SISSSSSSS!!"

His voice was loud and direct and the human crowds parted and let a beautiful black haired girl walked through, her eyes big and brown like Gemma's, her skin a smooth cream chocolate, her strides were graceful and confident.

Her arms glowed, they pulsed with an energy that flowed throughout her body, with each beat of her heart her arms followed suit. The girl walked calmly up to Slim and kissed him on the cheek, eying up Gemma.

"You took your time, bruv."

"You got away lightly with what I experienced earlier in the tunnels dude, a giant dog and a dragon."

The girl sighed. "You do know that a dude is a man right?"

"Yep," Slim nodded, his face serenely calm.

"You sure you wasn't dropped on your head as a baby?"

Slim tapped his head. "Hard as rocks, Sis."

The girl stood with her brother outside the flame circle and looked at Gemma. "Gotta go sweetie, love your hair by the way."

She took her brother's hand and they walked through the flames to join Tara and Big Man, leaving Gemma on the outside, the teenager ran back to Mitchy, shoving past people, the infected were feeding on the fallen theme park crowds and for once since Echo's glow were not interested in the live ones.

Aphrodite stood near and Gemma glared at her and went straight to Mitchy.

"What do you think they're going to do with Big Man?"

"I don't have a clue," Mitchy answered back quite firmly.

"But why do you care about him anyway? You heard what that 'Dinosaur thing' said about him and I know what he did in that game show years ago, so do you really care about what happens to him, honey? I certainly don't."

Gemma's eyes closed down on Mitchy. "That's not like you, why are you saying that?"

Mitchy rubbed her arm slowly. "Things change honey."

Within the flame circle Big Man grunted as Slim Pickings and his sister entered, he saw the girls arm's glowing and smiled grimly. "Great, more freaks with an axe to grind, let me guess, I stole your lunch money at school or some shit?"

The girl turned around and looked at the flame perimeter, even though the flames didn't harm her, she still shielded her eyes from the bright light, blinking profusely when she opened them.

"You murdered our father."

"How?"

"You made him blow himself up."

Big Man's eyes went huge and then small again. "There's a lot things I don't remember, my kids' birthdays, my kids' names, even optician appointments have got me in trouble today, but blowing up your dad? That's something I think I would recall."

The girl pressed her fingers against her forehead.

"Norton was a security guard for you, as was our father, Norton wanted to change shifts with dad as he had a date, a girl he met on a dating website, apparently he was hooked on those sites, wasn't he bruv?"

Slim Pickings nodded quickly, eager to hear his sister's storytelling as she continued.

"He had been trying for years to meet someone throughout various websites we were told, but to no avail. Nice guy according to reports and he did finally get a date with someone, but he was working nights so he asked to switch with my dad, let him work that night and giving him the night off so he could have his date, which he did, so my dad worked that night and came home the next morning shattered. He was meant to take us to school but was too tired, so our mother drove us instead, which was cool, I liked when Mum drove us, as she told stories, the best stories! I remember that morning, Mum was looking for a ring she had lost and was desperately trying to find it before she put us in the car, it was a birthday gift from dad." She stopped and released a long, slow breath. "So we were on the way to school, listening to Mum tell us a story, what was it again bruv?"

"The Frog and the Scorpion," Slim Pickings said, for the first time today he was deadly serious.

"Ah yes, The Frog and the Scorpion. Loved that story, so Mum is telling the tale and her phone starts to ring, she puts it on speaker and it's my dad who had just finished work and rang to say 'Hi'."

The girl suddenly wiped her eyes as a genuine feeling of sadness hit her, slowly sniffling and looking up to the pitch black sky, Slim Pickings went to console his sister and she gently pushed him away. "No please, I'm fine, let me do this." She composed herself just enough to carry on. "Mum was speaking to Dad on the phone and then I saw something glittering on the floor of the car, I picked it up, and it was her ring, her birthday ring. I was so excited and wanted to show her right away that I'd found it and I did, I shoved it right in her face to make her happy." The tears were forming again and her eyes dropped to her hands. "Mum's face was a picture, it lit up like the moons above, her eyes smiled as she looked at me and I saw the joy in her face and I'll remember that smile, because a builder's truck took it away from me."

She tried hard to stop her tears and her limbs were turning to jelly. "Mum wasn't looking at the road, she was looking at me when a truck crashed into us. Mum died instantly whereas my brother and I were kept on a life support machine in hospital."

Big Man didn't move. He whispered, "Oh shit, oh shit, I know who you are."

Turning to the dinosaur, the girl shouted, "CAN THEY HEAR US?"

The Green Man's voice followed swiftly. "THE CROWD CAN HEAR YOU, AMBER ACE."

Amber acknowledged her name with a nod and continued her story. "My brother and I were in hospital recovering, but you didn't tell my father this."

Big Man shifted uncomfortably in his shoes. "Listen, you don't have to do this, you don't have say anything, nobody needs to know."

Amber kept up her icy glare.

"No, you didn't tell my grief-stricken father that his two children were alive in hospital, now why was that?"

The surviving crowd heard everything and began to boo whilst keeping an eye out for roaming infected.

Amber began to revel in the constant booing and gave her voice even more confidence.

"Our father was in pieces, ladies and gentlemen, believing that his children were dead, he slumped into a downward spiral of alcohol bingeing and throwing himself in his job, all the while being consoled by his 'friend' Big Man, but you had an ulterior motive, didn't you?"

"Don't know what you mean," Big Man shrugged, his bravado faltering.

"I think you do," Amber replied, her voice determined like a police sergeant interrogating a prime suspect. "You knew exactly what you where doing when you kept us from our father."

She turned around quickly to the crowd, just barely able to see them as the flame circle grew. Amber threw her hands in the air, egging on the remaining theme park people.

"YOU SEE, LADIES AND GENTLEMEN, AND..." She paused and threw a blank smile. "Sod it, INFECTED AS WELL, THE REASON WHY BIG MAN KEPT US AWAY FROM OUR FATHER WHEN HE WAS IN BITS AND PIECES OVER HIS WIFE'S DEATH, WAS BECAUSE OF THE GAME SHOW!"

Big Man clapped his hands slowly in a mock applause. "You stupid girl."

"Ok then, shall I continue? Is that alright with you, Big Man? No? Well let's get going anyway, you decided not to tell my father about his kids surviving the car crash because you wanted to tip him other the edge for a new idea you had for your game show programme, to keep him hooked on booze and on the brink of despair and then give him a job in a hospital caring for the sick whilst intoxicated with a film crew following him around, and you were going to call it 'Drunk and Disorderly'."

The crowd upped their booing as Big Man shook his head with a smirk.

"Oh you're good, you're really good, who told you that?"

Amber Ace simply pointed to the metal dinosaur.

"Ah I see, you again, the infamous Green Man who knows a lot about me yet I know nothing about him."

He made a glance at Tara and Amber and then back to the dinosaur.

"Well that's two I owe you now."

He then spoke glumly to Amber Ace. "So Nayan was your father then I take it?"

"Correct, gold star for you, mister."

"That's strange, I thought Nayan had two boys...are you sure he's your dad?"

Amber was struggling to keep her temper down.

"I *am* his daughter, he used to call me his little 'Tom boy'."

Big Man picked at his teeth, oblivious to the chants of the crowd as he'd heard it all before.

"That would have made a bloody good show too, he was just about ready to be filmed I think, until he went off behind my back and rescued that Kimberley girl, funny how the girl he went to rescue ending up killing him."

The hairs on the back of Amber's neck slowly raised.

"I know what you did, you captured him and sent him to Gommerstall prison, but he was strong willed and planned an escape and died being a man sacrificing himself to rescue his friends."

Big Man thought for a moment before answering. "Fat lot of good that did him if 'being a man' means you end up getting killed, then you can stick it! Now I'm guessing you got your powers as well from that green buffoon up there right?"

"Yep."

"What can you do?"

"Wait and see."

The crowd's wild response still didn't faze him and he rubbed his eyes with the ball of his thumb. "Listen, I'm bored shitless standing here, so whatever you're going to do, just get on with it."

"Like I said, wait and see," Amber said sternly.

As the fire continued to burn brilliantly, keeping him prisoner, Big Man continued his chat as Slim and Tara looked on.

"Listen Amber? Is it? I can tell you are still pissed off with what happened with your dad, right?"

"What do you expect?"

"What *you* should expect, young lady, is that is what I do." He signalled over to Tara. "Listen jaws, I am sorry for what I did to your husband, I shouldn't have done what I did and I know words from a dickhead like me won't bring him back."

His voice was on automated with hardly any emotion. "But Amber, what can I say? You've obviously grown up into a fine looking woman with your father's death hanging over you, so you've probably trained for most of your adult life with revenge in order, waiting for the right time to get me, which should be easier with your new freak powers."

"Maybe," she mumbled.

"Amber, this is what I do, or used to do before the TV ban, which I guess was down to me, but I made television shows back in the day, bloody good ones too. It's all about the ratings, it's all about money."

"Check this out, we live in a violent city, a violent world, look around you, there's people eating other people and we're watching it, we're taking it in because that's what we do, people love it so I gave them what they wanted."

"You're a monster," Amber spat.

"No, I'm a businessman and made money. Fact. And as for your father and my friend Nayan? His great escape from my prison? I'm sorry, I only vaguely remember it."

"You don't remember?"

"I'm sorry my dear, I think we ordered a take away when we watched it, I'm not sure."

Amber's voice deepened with rage. "What are you saying?"

"For you, watching your father's death on TV must have been the most terrible event in your life, but for me?...it was pizza night."

"BASTARD!" Amber screamed, her right hand glowed fiercely as she leapt towards Big Man. Before her arm could connect with her target, Slim Pickings let his scarf wrap itself around her waist and pull her to the ground.

"WHAT ARE YOU DOING?! HE KILLED OUR DAD!"

Slim Pickings began to unravel his scarf from his sister's midriff and pointed to The Green Man's robotic dinosaur.

"Dude, I know the Big Man killed our pops, but you know the rules, we don't do anything until the dude in green says so."

Amber still struggled in her brother's scarf as he slowly pulled it off her.

"SO YOU'RE JUST GOING TO STAND THERE AND DO NOTHING WHILE HE TAUNTS US?!"

"Until the man in the dinosaur says otherwise, Sis, we do nothing."

Big Man chuckled and hovered between Amber Ace and Slim Pickings. "Your slacker brother has a point you know, I want to know what exactly mutton chops in the dinosaur has in store for me." He looked up to the dinosaur. "MATE! IS THAT IT? LOOK, I'M SORRY ABOUT KILLING DAVIS AND I'M SORRY ABOUT NAYAN GETTING BLOWN UP, I'VE DONE A LOT OF SILLY STUFF, YEAH I GET IT, I'VE SENT GLAMOUR MODELS AND FOOTBALLERS TO THEIR DOOM IN VARIOUS GAME SHOWS, I'VE KIDNAPPED STUDENTS FROM A SCHOOL, FORCED THEM TO TAKE A SERUM WHICH GRANTED THEM SPECIAL POWERS TO FIGHT HORRIFIC MONSTERS FOR ENTERTAINMENT AND I SENT MY BEST FRIEND APOLLO TO GOMMERSTALL PRISON AND HAVEN'T HEARD FROM HIM SINCE...BUT THIS IS WHAT I DO, SOFTLAD, IT'S BUSINESS, NEVER PERSONAL."

The Green Man sighed and swivelled around in his chair in the dinosaur cockpit, he peered down at the fire circle, viewing the people inside the flames; he made sure his microphone was working.

"SHALL WE MAKE IT PERSONAL THEN NOW, BIG MAN? OR SHOULD I CALL YOU ZEUS WYLDE?"

Big Man frowned a little bit, annoyed that the crowd now knew his surname. "Call me what you like, I still don't give a monkey's about you."

Mitchy eyed up Aphrodite with a disapproving look. "Didn't you say your surname was Wylde?"

She answered back with a voice softer than usual. "Wylde is a popular name in Olympia." Aphrodite's finely plucked eyebrows rose. "Like 'Porkins' must be popular where you come from."

Mitchy rubbed her arm slowly, oblivious to the remark. "Why did you want to get us to the Big Man's tower anyway? Is it because he's your father?"

"Big Man's Complex is virtually indestructible, so that's why I thought it'd be a good idea to head there, ok?"

"Whatever honey, I'm keeping my eye on you."

Aphrodite smiled with half her mouth. "For what? To eat me maybe?"

"Tables have turned now honey, you're the wolf now." Mitchy slowly smiled. "Let's hope you don't choke on me, eh?"

Aphrodite didn't reply and looked on into the fire circle and unbeknown to everybody except Gemma, stared hard at her father and his apparent captors.

He grew more anxious as the night wore on, Big Man looked at his watch as a blustery gust of wind made him pull his wasted disguise of a coat closer to his chest and he spoke to the dinosaur.

"Listen pal, could you please hurry this along? Things to do and people to see."

"SO THAT IS ALL YOU HAVE TO SAY ABOUT THE DEATHS OF DAVIS AND NAYAN?" boomed The Green Man's voice.

Big Man gave him a sheepish look.

"Yeah, kinda."

"WELL LET'S MAKE THIS PERSONAL SHALL WE?"

Big Man's voice hovered with uncertainty. "Yeah go on then, knock yourself out."

12. The Wylde Child

Gemma stood back up close again to Mitchy and Aphrodite, her head bobbed up and down cautiously looking around for the stray infected, the ones who hadn't tucked into the theme park people and were still a threat ambling around. Casting her eye over the flame circle she tried hard not to feel increasingly vulnerable, for her sake and her father's.

"I still can't believe Slim Pickings turned against us, why would he do that?"

Mitchy mumbled a small angry voice.

"Big Man sent Slim's father to prison and then the poor man got blown up I take it? That would pretty much ruin anyone's life, let alone their day."

Gemma was concerned by the change in Mitchy's usually upbeat attitude, as Aphrodite took her eyes off her father to speak to the pair.

"I always knew that beatnik hippy freak was going to betray us, I could just tell by his awful attire."

"Never judge a book by its cover," Gemma whispered.

"No, judge them on their criminal record which I'm sure that useless degenerate has." Aphrodite focused on the circle. "Now shut up and let me concentrate."

"LET ME ASK YOU ZEUS WYLDE, WHY DID YOUR WIFE LEAVE YOU?"

Through his metallic voice, it seemed as if The Green Man was trying to hold back a giggle.

"You don't want to go there, mister."

"OH BUT I DO, BIG MAN, I WANT TO KNOW WHY A WOMAN WHO WAS MARRIED TO A SUCCEFUL BUSINESSMAN LIKE YOURSELF WOULD TAKE OFF AND LEAVE HER CHILDREN IN A HEARTBEAT."

Big Man waved a finger angrily at the robot dinosaur.

"I don't know who's feeding you this shit mate, but it ends now."

"HAVE I TOUCHED A NERVE? SURELY THE PEOPLE OF OLYMPIA MUST KNOW WHY THEIR GLORIOUS LEADER OF TELEVISION TURNED OUT THE WAY HE DID? AND WHY HAS HE HAD A VENDETTA AGAINST TEACHERS FOR YEARS?"

"None of your business."

"BUT I THINK IT IS, BIG MAN. NOW YOU HAVE ALWAYS STATED THAT YOUR BELOVED WIFE, WHO WAS A PRIMARY SCHOOL TEACHER HAD AN AFFAIR WITH ANOTHER TEACHER AND LEFT YOU, AM I RIGHT?"

Big Man looked at the dinosaur in a challenging manner. "Yes she did."

"WHY DID SHE HAVE AN AFFAIR?"

"I'm not sure."

"I THINK YOU KNOW WHY SHE LEFT YOU FOR ANOTHER MAN."

"Fell out of love with me maybe?"

"SO THAT IS THE STORY YOU TOLD, AND THE ONE YOU'RE STICKING WITH I PRESSUME?"

Not a sound came from Big Man.

"VERY WELL, TELL ME, HOW MANY CHILDREN DO YOU HAVE, BIG MAN?"

When he replied, it was very slowly. "I have three children."

"OH YES, I KNOW OF YOUR CHILDREN; ARES WYLDE, APHRODITE WYLDE AND YOUR FOSTER DAUGHTER GEMMA."

Who is he? And how does he know who we are? Aphrodite wondered.

"WHY IS IT BIG MAN, THAT SOMETIMES, ONLY SOMETIMES, YOU LET SLIP OF ANOTHER NAME, ANOTHER CHILD KNOWN AS ATHENA, WHO IS SHE, OUR MIGHTY TELEVISION LEADER?"

Gemma tugged hard on Aphrodite's sleeve. "I wondered that sometimes," she whispered.

"Be quiet, child," Aphrodite hissed. "People will hear you."

Mitchy expelled a breath of annoyance. "Too late honey, so Big Man *is* your father then eh?"

"Like I said…Wylde is a popular name in Olympia."

"DON'T LIE!" Mitchy shouted. "Why didn't you tell me that he was your father?"

Aphrodite spoke softly, her demeanour was that of a child with their hand caught in the cookie jar.

"We didn't know if we could trust you."

"TRUST ME? AFTER EVERYTHING WE'VE BEEN THROUGH TODAY? YOU DIDN'T THINK TO TELL ME THAT YOUR FATHER IS BIG MAN?"

"Why should I have done? You don't even live in Olympia, why should it even bother you? The aim of this day was survival, not parental matters, the whole city is after my father for the bounty of 'whatever' million that *thing* has put on his head and I—" She looked at Gemma. "*We* couldn't take that chance with you."

Mitchy's anger increased and she looked at Gemma too.

"*We?* Were you part of this too?"

Gemma copied her sister's stance. "Aphrodite mentioned something about not telling you."

"So you went along with her? I thought we were friends, honey!"

"We *are* friends Mitchy, but she's my sister!"

"SISTER?!" The woman swung her broad frame around and jabbed her finger angrily at the increasingly vulnerable teenager. "You're no sister to her, I know you're fostered now, but to her you're just some stray who wandered in off the street! HOW COULD YOU EVER THINK IT WAS ABOUT THE MONEY, GEMMA!"

The venom in Mitchy's voice was unforgiving and tears formed in Gemma's eyes. "Why are you saying these things, Mitchy? Why are you being so cruel?"

"Cruel? You call me cruel? Take a look at your 'sister' and how she treats you, all day she's insulted you and made you feel like crap, I thought I could trust you?"

"You can trust me, please Mitchy," Gemma implored.

"You're no better than Aphrodite, at least she doesn't pretend that's she's not a bitch."

Even Aphrodite thought the surprising bile coming from Mitchy was a tad extreme and butted in.

"That's what sisters do, Mitchy darling, we take the piss but help each other too."

"How do you possibly help her?"

"I lift my feet up when she's vacuuming, can't always rely on the maid you know."

Mitchy sucked on her lips.

"Always joking eh, Aphrodite?"

Aphrodite returned her focus to the flame circle and her smirk disappeared.

"Not all the time darling."

Big Man swallowed a couple of times before composing himself.

"Like I said, I think you've got your information wrong."

"EVEN FROM ATOP HERE AND IN THE DARK, I CAN SEE YOU NERVOUSLY SWEATING."

"I'm surrounded by flames dickhead, what do you expect?"

"I EXPECT THE TRUTH FROM YOU, YOUR TIME OF DECEPTION IS UP, LET ME TAKE YOU BACK YEARS AGO, YOUR WIFE WAS PREGNANT, YOU ALREADY HAD A BOY KNOWN AS ARES AND SHE WAS ABOUT TO GIVE BIRTH AT HOME TO YOUR SECOND."

"Aphrodite was my second."

"NO, YOU HAD ARES AND BEFORE APHRODITE WAS BORN WITH HER TWIN BROTHER WHO SUPOSEDLY DIED SOON AFTER BIRTH, YOU HAD ANOTHER CHILD."

Big Man's fists shook with rage and hurt.

"HOW DARE YOU! YOU BASTARD, I LOST A CHILD! APHRODITES'S BROTHER DIED DURING CHILDBIRTH YOU SICK PRICK!"

Gemma looked to her foster sister. "Did you know you were a twin?"

Aphrodite shook her head, she stammered her reply, nervously for once. "I didn't know, father didn't tell me, why didn't he tell me?"

The Green Man's expression tightened in the dinosaur cockpit and his voice lowered even more.

"Suddenly you care about your offspring, Big Man?"

"I ALWAYS DO," Big Man snapped back.

"Really? Your loving wife finally gave birth after a long and painful labour to a girl, or what you thought was a girl, but she wasn't a girl was she, Big Man?"

"COME DOWN HERE AND SHOW YOURSELF!"

"Not yet Big Man, but as I was saying she wasn't a girl, she was born a mutant or had a mutation? Is that better for you? Now according to the dictionary a mutation is some sort of change in genetic build up which could be passed on to future generations? And your new daughter had that mutation didn't she? She had a genetic defect passed down from you or her mother which made her slightly different and gifted from other babies, when you saw her for the first time, when the doctor held aloft your new baby to you and your wife, it disgusted you, it's long teeth, it's red skin but most importantly, her tail…"

The Green Man smiled wickedly from beneath his mask.

"Her tail, that was it? A baby born to the network king of Olympia with a tail couldn't be allowed, what would the public think? A man so high in the public standing with a deformed child could never live it down, so you had your advisors take her away, away from her pleading mother who begged and screamed for her baby, she implored you for her to keep her daughter and sunk to her knees in tears of pain and protest, but you didn't, no sooner than the child's umbilical cord was cut you had her shipped out and hidden from the public whilst your poor wife, Hannah Wylde screamed her heart out on the floor as you took away her baby, she stayed with you for a while, more out of than duty than love."

The Green Man's thoughts froze for a moment as he heard Big Man starting to sniffle and then he continued as the crowd's boos urged him on.

"So your wife *did* leave you Big Man, and there was another man waiting for her, but that wasn't the reason why she left you, her heart had shattered long before her affair.

Before Big Man could answer Aphrodite changed instantly to her werewolf form and leapt from her spot from Gemma and Mitchy, her power took her easily over the flame and landed in the centre of the circle.

Aphrodite grabbed her father by the throat as Tara, Amber and Slim Pickings looked on as father and daughter exchanged looks. Her eyes stung Big Man's as her huge canine head stayed firm, the voice was gritty but surprisingly calm for a girl with a wolf's head.

"WHAT THE HELL ARE YOU?" he cried.

"What the hell am I? I'm a liar that's what I am! I was wearing the same jacket earlier and you acknowledged me, don't you remember? I used to lie about seeing mother when I was younger, I used to pretend to go off and see her but spend hours in coffee shops alone, I used to buy myself fur coats and say they were from her but then say she wasn't ready to see you yet remember? I am a liar."

"GET OFF ME!" Big Man squirmed in Aphrodite's grip.

"GET OFF YOU?" her wolf's head rasped.

"Don't you recognise my voice? I'm the one who lied for you, remember? I'm the one who told you which students to take from my class to use for experimentation for the game show remember? I'm the one who betrayed her best friend Sabrina to you, after she confided in me about her condition, remember? I'm the one who has taken care of your dirty little secrets since I was born, remember? I'm the one who snuck out years ago and went to a rave and got showered with your serum filth that turned me into 'this'.

Something you don't remember."

She pulled him closer and whispered through gritted sharp teeth, "Also I've just taken care of Jason, your wife and my mother's lover for you, remember that."

Aphrodite pulled back slightly.

"Do you really want to know who I am, Zeus Wylde or Big Man? Let me show you."

She shook her head and it immediately changed to another dog, and then another and another.

"WHAT THE SHIT?" yelled Big Man.

"Do you remember this dog?"

The next dog that Big Man saw was the scruffy mutt that used to wander the floors of his complex years ago, he remembered it instantly.

"YOU'RE MY DOG!"

Aphrodite stopped changing and her own face finally emerged.

"No, I'm your daughter."

Big Man broke free and made a garbling noise at the back of his throat.

"Aphrodite?"

Her voice was cold but clear. "Yes Father, it's me, your daughter Aphrodite, another one of your dirty little secrets."

"What happened to you?"

"*You* happened to me, Father, I was at the nightclub years ago when you showered us with your miracle juice, which turned me into this wolf *thing*!"

Big Man stepped forward, trembling.

"I didn't...I didn't know, why didn't you say anything, why didn't you tell me?"

"So you could put a *freak* like me into one of your games? Or send me to Gommerstall, I think not, Father."

"I wouldn't do that to you, you're my daughter."

She stiffened, trying to bottle up her remaining anger as her jaw began to clench.

"Like the one you gave away perhaps?"

Aphrodite chuckled, a breathy snort followed as she turned to The Green Man's dinosaur.

"YOU UP THERE! WHAT HAPPENED TO THE OTHER CHILD?"

The Green Man turned his head at an angle, intrigued by Aphrodite's question, as was everybody else who'd heard her thanks to the loud speakers, and they wanted to know too. Beneath his metal mask, The Green Man grinned and took a wheezy breath.

"I will not bark out what happened to the little one, just merely speak the truth, before she was torn from her grasp her mother had just enough time to name her daughter, she chose Athena, which means 'Wisdom' in the old language, but because Athena was born with a mutation and a probable embarrassment to her father and his empire she was taken away by Big Man's advisors, screaming her heart out."

"HOW DO YOU KNOW THESE THINGS? WERE YOU THERE?" For once it was Big Man asking the questions and not Aphrodite, but she sided with her father just for that one question.

"ANSWER HIM!"

"I was not there, but I have my sources, I know that after she was hastily taken away from her mother she was placed into care, but you didn't want to know anything about her progress did you, Big Man, is that why you're trying to make amends with the girl Gemma Glaucas I wonder?"

Big Man failed to answer.

"Athena was adopted by a family here in Olympia, she grew up in a loving household unaware about her true background and her mutation remained latent until her teenage years, she went to your school, Aphrodite and you shared the same form tutor who also served as the headmaster, Elias Glaucas, the same one whose school you tried to take over if I remember?"

Gemma's eyes widened with wonder and whispered slowly when she heard his name.

"What does he mean?"

"Nothing," Aphrodite shut her up abruptly.

The Green Man failed to hear the girl's voice.

"She was a clever girl, was doing well in her classes. The girl went to a nightclub with her friend some years ago, you remember don't you, Aphrodite? Because this was the same nightclub which your daughter previously spoke about, everybody was showered with your serum and knocked out, as they awoke hours later, they did so with itchy arms and new strange abilities, abilities you wanted to use on your game show programme. So you kidnapped and drugged a few of them and they were indeed welcomed to the carnage."

Big Man rubbed a sweaty hand over his short grey hair, he looked to Tara and Aphrodite, the blood draining from his head in nerves, he was still shaking. "W-what do you mean?"

"I'll explain it to you through a limerick shall I?"

"The girl's parentage was kept in the dark
Her features gathered awful remarks
Kidnapped and battered, her spirit now shattered
Poor little…Cassandra Paintshark."

Big Man stepped back, shaking his head.

"No!"

"She apparently hated limericks too, but yes, the girl who you infected with your designer serum, the girl who you captured and drugged and put to fight for your entertainment, who you sent to prison for a year and who after her escape with her friends was sucked out from a hole in their plane and seemingly fell to her death? That was your lost long daughter, and chances are, you killed her."

Big Man threw back his head and screamed, a gut wrenching scream of anguish which was amplified by the speakers and raised the hackles of all the remaining theme park crowd who heard it. He fell to the ground on his knees clutching his head.

"Secrets, those little slices of death, how I love them," The Green Man said softly.

"You see, the ironic thing is, Big Man, Cassandra's body had control of her mutation, it had done for years and she never even knew it existed, it lay dormant until you sparked her dragon form into life just to get some more viewers for your show, I guess you made the wrong call on that one, my friend."

Big Man staggered backwards, catching the glare from Aphrodite and the others in the circle, he struggled hard to contain his cries.

"You're not my friend, you bastard!"

"Oh but I am Big Man, I am the truth, I am your reckoning."

Big Man got up to his feet and clumsily fell down again.

"YOU'RE A LIAR!"

"Am I really? Did you hear what Tara said? Did you hear what Amber said? Why would they lie? And why would I lie?"

Twitching in his disguise outfit, Big Man wiped his eyes and pointed an accusatory finger at the dinosaur.

"YOU! YOU SON OF A BITCH! COME DOWN HERE AND DEAL WITH ME, YOU BASTARD! YOU'RE A LIAR! YOU'RE A GOD DAMN LIAR!"

The Green Man smiled with his metallic teeth showing fully now.

"You know what? I will, but not yet..."

The black dragon, which everybody had seemed to have forgotten about, stretched its huge wings and yawned. Shuffling slightly to adjust its position on the shoulder of the robot dinosaur, the dragon went back to keeping an eye on the proceedings and possibly listening.

Tears of grief were on the face of Big Man, a sight nobody had ever seen before, not Aphrodite, Gemma or the gathered city folk who in the past had spent years watching his grinning face on the television, mocking the victims on his game show.

"Well, it would seem I have finally found a chink in the armour of the mighty Big Man, I think I will continue."

The Green Man, ignoring Big Man's anguish, politely raised his hand like an inquisitive student.

"Do you mind?"

Big Man failed to answer, still in a great pain from his loss.

Aphrodite shouted up at The Green Man. "HEY MONSTER!, WHY DON'T YOU TAKE THAT FACE BACK TO THE SECOND HAND SHOP AND LEAVE HIM ALONE?"

The Green Man was quiet for a moment and then stood from his cockpit chair.

"Oh the ever loyal daughter Aphrodite, even after what you just heard you blindly still defend your father, what will it take for you to finally think your dad is a bit of a dick."

"We'll deal with him in-house." She threw her father a disappointed look as The Green Man cupped his hand to where his ear should have been, and adopted the pose of a confident stand up comedian. "What? You want more family revelations? Ok, you got it." He was grimly calm. "When's the last time you saw your mother, Aphrodite?"

"Are you deaf as well as stupid? You heard me say I haven't seen her in years."

"Ah yes, she walked out on you when you were a mere child, am I correct?"

"You seem to know all my family's history so I'll take your word on it."

His lips behind the mask curled up into a smile. "Indeed, your mother left you in bed with a monster in the closet."

"How did you know that?"

"You should know by now I have my ways, did the this creature have a name?"

The woman wriggled her noise in thought. "It's the Glimmer... thing"

"Glimmer fin?"

"Glimmer thing…as in 'thingy me bob'.

"Oh I see…Glimmerthing."

Aphrodite stopped and then groaned through her teeth. "This conversation sounds familiar, very familiar, are you my mother?"

The Green Man let out a mock shocked sounding breath.

"That would be all too easy, wouldn't it? No, we took care of your mother ages ago, paid her a visit no less."

Aphrodite looked down at her hands; without knowing it her fists were clenched and began to tremble.

"What have you done with my mother?"

"Well she was incredibly hard to track down but we managed to find her and we wanted her to take part in this little family reunion but she surprisingly didn't want to come with us, so we had to make her, she was very stubborn and put up a good fight, something hard to do… in her condition."

"WHAT DID YOU DO TO MY MOTHER!?"

He laughed a strange rusty sound.

"Wow! Wow! Where did that come from? A second outburst of emotion from the ice queen Aphrodite today? I must be doing a great job." He stopped and thought for a moment. "Where's Jason? He was supposed to be here? He was spotted at the park earlier by my spies, still never mind, he's done his job bringing you here, but a shame as I wanted to tell him where your mother is, funny thing is, he really thought it was all down to Big Man who abducted her? But it wasn't him… it was me! Are you sure you don't know where he is?"

Her mouth was a mixture between human and wolf and she growled slowly. "Where is my mother, you son of a bitch?"

"Son of a bitch? That's not very nice Aphrodite, but are sure you don't know where Jason is? He was one of your companions today wasn't he? Did you know I found him trying to break into the Messiah's Complex? And obviously I knew what he looked like from his house when we took your mother, so I offered him the chance to get his partner back, obviously blaming Big Man for her disappearance, if he brought a group of people together and brought them here. What happened to him, Aphrodite? My spies tell me you were the last one to see him alive, what did you do? What did you do?"

Aside from Aphrodite, Mitchy and Gemma were the last remaining members from the group present, nobody moved and nobody blinked, until Gemma walked forward and spoke loudly so her foster sister could hear in the flame circle.

"JASON WAS YOUR MOTHER'S PARTNER?"

Aphrodite threw a rebellious look through the flames to Gemma.

"ANSWER ME!" Gemma cried.

"YES, HE WAS."

"HOW LONG DID YOU KNOW THIS?"

"NOT LONG, NOT ALL DAY, LOOK ARE WE ACTUALLY DOING THIS NOW, GEMMA?"

Visibly furious, Gemma pressed Aphrodite further.

"YOU SAID THE INFECTED KILLED HIM."

"YEAH, LIKE I SAID EARLIER, HE WENT OUT LIKE A BITCH, CRYING AND SCREAMING LIKE A BABY."

"YOU COULD DO NOTHING TO HELP HIM THEN?"

"NOPE."

The Green Man's eyes rounded on Aphrodite and waited for Gemma to calm down before speaking.

"Well that's a shame as chances are Jason probably guessed where your mother is."

Aphrodite looked panicked. "What did you say, monster?"

"I said her partner may have finally out figured what happened to your mother, did he tell you where your mother was?"

"No," she said firmly.

"Well no, of course he wouldn't, he was keeping his relationship with your mother secret, he didn't even know who you were, so if something happened to him untoward whilst he was in your charge, you would never know where your mother is, now are you sure you didn't do anything?"

Aphrodite's guts twisted and she discreetly held her stomach, Big Man knew what she had done even before she whispered it to him.

The Green Man smiled with metallic teeth fully showing now.

"Good, I couldn't imagine how you would feel if you could have found out her location before killing him."

"I didn't kill him."

His smile stayed.

"But of course you didn't, Aphrodite."

"Anyway, you didn't answer my question, where is my mother?"

Big Man stepped forward to support his daughter; she shrugged off his arm.

"Answer her, you dick."

Tara and Amber fidgeted with boredom. "Are we finished yet, boss?"

"Soon my lovelies soon, in fact let's speed this up a little because I'm getting bored too. In fact, if they were writing a book about this sorry event and they came to this scene, I'd be bored shitless! Anyway I'm coming down."

The mouth of the huge dinosaur opened wider and booster rockets fired up from behind its head, the cockpit turned into a small ship and separated from the dinosaur's mouth.

Sounding like distant thunder the ship fired its reverse thrusters and then slowly lowered to the ground below, it's engines sounding like metal rain.

The dragon flapped its wings in protest but still remained on the robot's shoulder.

The dinosaur's small escape craft landed directly in the middle of the flame circle, everybody inside the fires stood back and let the ship settle. A side door slowly opened with jets of landing steam flowing from beneath the ship. The landing ramp slid open and the intimidating figure of The Green Man emerged. His green fedora tilted to one side and his face was a battered robotic sight.

The green mac he wore tried hard to cover his huge frame, it was stretched along the arms and the legs; he turned slowly to admire the now ruins of the theme park.

Aphrodite snapped forward angrily and changed into her full wolf form, leaping towards The Green Man's throat. Big Man's eyes rolled in shock as he watched his daughter transform into a wolf and jump into the air, leaving behind Echo's leather jacket.

The Green Man easily caught Aphrodite in mid-leap by the throat.

"Well, well, look at what we have here. *Canis lupus* in the old language but translated I do believe it means grey wolf." The wolf hung helplessly in his grasp. "Stay there Big Man, you cannot help your daughter now."

Aphrodite started to wiggle and then turned herself into a Chihuahua dog and slipped through his fingers. The little dog trotted beneath the feet of The Green Man and changed into a giant wolf hound, knocking him off his feet.

As The Green Man lay flat on his back, Aphrodite retuned to her human form and straddled him. This time it was her who had her hands around his metal throat, talons from her fingers crept along his metal mask, his guards lifted up their ponchos and pointed their guns at her and Amber Ace's arms glowed, ready to release a microwave blast at Aphrodite.

Waving them to stand down, The paused and rolled his head over towards her.

"You do know your sitting on top of me naked, right?"

"I do."

"This is kind of awkward."

"Why's that?"

"I'll explain later."

"I won't ask you again, where is my MOTHER?"

"So what you're saying is you have no clue whatsoever on what happened to your mother?"

Aphrodite's talons slowly began to penetrate the throat guard of The Green Man, an act that surprised them both.

"Do you want me to continue, monster?"

"If I'm honest, I'm going to have to say...no."

He shifted uncomfortably beneath Aphrodite.

"Your mother loved you very much before she left, didn't she?"

"Yep."

"Did she ever tell you what happened to your twin brother?"

"Yes," she said warily. "He died at childbirth."

Big Man walked over towards the pair and stood at the side as The Green Man tried to strain his neck free from Aphrodite's claws.

"Is this creeping you out, Big Man? Your daughter sat naked on top of me with her claws at my throat?"

"A bit distracting actually, yes."

"Ok, I'll rush through this, your twin brother was very ill when he was born, Aphrodite. Nobody knew what was wrong with him and he was taken away, again by your father's advisors and his dodgy doctors. But here's the thing, the little boy didn't die, he was ill yes, but he didn't die, understand? The illness he had was a growth defect, even as a baby he was growing at an alarmingly fast rate. So one of Big Man's advisors took the baby away for further tests, but told you he died, to give him more time with the baby."

Big Man interrupted him.

"You're lying, we had a burial for my son."

"No, you had a burial for a dummy, pardon the pun, but the advisor drugged the baby and that was what you and your wife saw at the hospital, no home birth this time, but as soon as you left he switched them and took yours home with him for further tests."

Big Man looked into his metal eye.

"I still don't believe you."

"Well the boy grew up not knowing about his past and he grew up rapidly, he had a mutation as well which seems to run in your family, by the time he was ten, he looked twenty, and when he was twenty he looked forty, and so on and so on.

He could delay the ageing process but it would take a tremendous about of energy to slow it down.

"Anyway he got a job with you years ago and like I said, he didn't know who you were. He was about twenty maybe, but looked forty. Can you guess who it is yet?"

Confusion rained in both Aphrodite and her father's eyes.

"Ok, I'll show you."

Knocking away Aphrodite's hands, The Green Man twiddled with a release valve underneath his mask, the water in the tubes flowing from his nose and all over his head stopped and he slowly removed the metal face appendage. Beneath the mask was a human face, a face that Big Man and Aphrodite slowly recognised. It was scarred and battered and looked much older than when they'd last seen it – the eyes were too dark and his skin was a pasty white.

He cracked a small smile when it came off. "Ta dah!"

"Apollo?" Big Man asked.

"Is that you?" Aphrodite continued.

Apollo ran his tongue over the inside of his right cheek, his 'Green Man' disguise had ended. "How do you like them apples?" he asked.

Aphrodite rolled off of him quickly and collected her jacket, doing it up embarrassedly.

"You see where I was coming from, feeling a little odd having my sister on top of me? A tiny bit weird." Apollo rose to his feet and completely discarded his mask, he spoke with a nervous giggle. "Oh thank God for that! That mask is a killer."

"What trickery is this?" Big Man demanded.

"What trickery is this?" Apollo mimicked.

"Why are you talking like a dick? That's not the same Big Man who used to crack open a few beers with me back in the day when we'd watch glamour models get torn to shreds by giant squids, saying that I have to apologise for the way I was speaking whilst wearing that mask, holy shit! It was like I'd just stepped out from one of those old classical movies!" He spread his arms in a theatrical manner. "All of this 'MY BROTHERS AND SISTERS OF OLYMPIA' and 'THE TURNING POINT HAS BEGUN'? Please! What a load of bollocks, as my sister Cassandra used to say...apparently."

Apollo grew in confidence.

"God and how I spoke in the battle of Gommerstall... 'STOMP ON THEM' and 'SMASH THEM, YOU OAF' and what did I say to that kid called Felcey? 'WASTED HEROIC NONSENSE FROM A NERD'...was I on drugs or some shit? Did anybody remember that?"

He looked around at his audience.

"Nope, none of you were there and everybody else dead probably, ho hum."

Big Man was still confused.

"Ok check this shit out," Apollo began to pace up and down. "After Mum gave birth to Athena and gave her away for having a mutation, a year later she fell pregnant again with Aphrodite and me, thought I died at childbirth and was buried, however, this was because one of your advisors took me home to raise him as his own son."

"What was his name?" Big Man demanded.

Apollo wriggled his finger at him cheekily. "No, no, no, matey! Not going to give you that information so easily, Dad, now let me finish please? So my 'other' dad brought me up and funnily enough it was him who got me a job at your place. Thanks to my age condition I looked older than I was, so I must have been around seven but looking around twenty-ish? Now stay awake as this gets confusing with my 'two dads'.

"Now I have no idea why my advisor dad wanted a seven or eight-year old to work as a guard at his boss's house, but I was fairly intelligent for my age and he was there watching me. You, Big Man, had this idea of making super bodyguards for your children, remember? So you had that scientist Dandridge and his nut job crew runs tests on me and that other guard, Streaky? The serum they designed had been tested on animals but not humans, so we volunteered. Streaky turned into a cannibal and began eating people and I apparently turned into a psychopath with heightened intelligence and agility, and by the way I didn't kill anybody in the house, three people died in a lab explosion and I got the blame, but by that time it was too late and you contained me and Streaky and tried to destabilise the remaining amounts of that serum shit in our bloodstream and it worked."

"I don't know whether it was my mutation as well as the serum, but over the years I calmed down, to the point that you gave me another job. I was hired to be a babysitter to your kids, and I loved looking after Aphrodite and Ares, that was freaky, babysitting your brother when he's older than you? I was there the night Hannah, I mean Mum left, she knew she was about to leave and called me in. Ares was in a right state and I was there to look after him."

Anger and frustration briefly flashed upon his face.

"Do you know what it's like looking after two kids who you adore and then only years later finding out that they're your brother and sister? Anyway for some unknown reason you promoted me to act as your enforcer, a muscle man, you paired me up with another guy called Mr Tidy, who by the way you treated like crap, so what if he sold your mum a pogo stick which made her break her leg, and forgot where he parked your fish and chip van, he was a good worker, if slightly dim and I miss him."

He wanted to laugh but tried desperately hard to keep it in, turning serious in a heartbeat.

"Even as an enforcer I was talking like an idiot, trying to act older than my years."

Apollo wiped his brow slowly. "You made me do some terrible things, making me burn down the houses of certain people." He threw a look at Gemma, but she couldn't see through the flame circle which was finally starting to die down. "Now this is what gets me, even though I still didn't know that you were my true 'Old Man' I did a lot of illegal stuff for you, and how did I get repaid? Without warning you packed me off to the prisoner city of Gommerstall to watch over the teachers you sent there and they escaped, yeah I tried to stop them, me and Sabrina as her reptile form called 'Hammersmith'."

Apollo turned to Aphrodite and winked. "Wasn't she your best friend who you betrayed? Good one." Hesitating for a second or two, his smug smile continued. "So after the teachers managed to escape with my sister Athena on the plane…" he shook his head in a fake loss of memory. "…Sorry, with my sister Cassandra on the plane, I woke up after being knocked out by Sabrina to find everybody had gone, the prison was destroyed and it was just me and loads of giant crabs trying to cross a beach for company, and I thought, 'When am I going to be picked up?' 'When am I going to be rescued?' And you know what? Nobody came, not you or your guards, heck I even thought Mr Tidy might make an appearance to take me home! But none of you bastards did." Offering the best reassuring smile he continued. "So as I made my way back to Olympia, and as I made my way back to home, I thought, 'Wow! Nobody really cares about me, nobody gives a toss about who I am, oh wait…"

He slapped his hand playfully on his head. "Where are my manners?" Apollo reached into his armoured pocket and pulled out a bag of sweets. "Sweet anyone?"

Big Man shook his head. "Are you for real?" he asked.

Apollo nodded. Aphrodite walked over to him gingerly. "Are these sweets fattening?"

"Nope honey," Apollo said, popping one into his mouth.

Aphrodite sighed and ran a hand through her dirty blond hair. "Thank you."

"You're welcome, Sis."

Aphrodite raised her eyebrows as Apollo swung his head round.

"Let's see now, so as I'm making my way back to Olympia, I meet someone on the way, someone who I know quite well and this guy is mustard! And he tells me the truth, the truth about where I came from? And this geezer lets me know about everything, and I mean everything about my real mother and father, and how they abandoned both me and my other sister, how my mother only really cared about Aphrodite and not me and Athena, even my brother Ares didn't get a look in."

"Who was this man you saw?" Big Man asked.

An instant of anger came from the pit of Apollo's stomach. "It doesn't matter who he was, what mattered was that Ares loved his mother, he loved his father, that's you Big Man by the way, and both Mother and you ignored him, ignored us, so when I finally got back to Olympia, I thought how could I get back at my parents for abandoning me! How could I make them both pay for not knowing who I was? Didn't you even think about the name 'Apollo'? You have a son who dies called Apollo and then years later a guy shows up at your place with the same name? Didn't it even click?"

Big Man rubbed his chin.

"Apollo was a popular name and it still is, we didn't know you were still alive, son."

"Too late daddy-o! So I had an idea, an idea to mess with you and mother, wait hold on…" He signalled to the cockpit of the dinosaur. "Could you turn the microphones off please lads? This is very private."

The amplified sound of the speakers around the theme park slowly quietened, and Apollo continued.

"So I thought the only way I could mess things up for you was if your precious daughter Aphrodite was in mortal peril, but how could I do that? What could I possibly do to mess up your precious city of Olympia? I mean you messed up my life and everybody else's in this circle?"

"I didn't know you were my son."

"It doesn't matter Father, it doesn't matter, anyway I needed to get rid of you for a bit, have you in one place so I could keep an eye on you."

His eyelids fluttered.

"So I thought 'What if I come up with a shady character who the city of Olympia would love? And who would turn the city you love against yourself? What about the 'Man in the Green Hat' or 'Green Man' whatever you want to call him, but that was a book I used to read to Ares to send him to asleep when I used to babysit and he loved it! The city had almost let you off for the whole game show debacle with your stupid 'Apology Day' rubbish and I wasn't standing for that, so that's when I put the 500 million credit on your head or is it 600 million? I forget, anyway I and made you turn tail and hide in your little tower for all those years, but here's a little secret, Father…"

Apollo glanced around to see if the microphones were still off and whispered into Big Man's ears with a glorious smile etched on his face. "I'm absolutely broke."

Big Man angrily pulled away from him. "Oh yeah, I haven't got a pot to piss in. Yet I managed to convince all these Olympian simpletons that I was loaded, result! Obviously I knew none of them would breach your impenetrable Messiah's Complex so it was win-win for me, but that wasn't all, I needed something else to threaten your family and bring the city to its knees, and that's when the virus idea came up, what about a disgusting virus creating a blanket of rage and bloodshed across your precious home, turning Olympians into bloodthirsty infected freaks?"

Apollo's excitement returned.

"This possible pandemic of a disease is quite bad isn't it? People turning into murderous savages unexpect-edly in front of you, father against son, mother against daughter, neighbour against neighbour, boss against employee, the city of Olympia has turned into your worst nightmare, traffic completely gridlocked, only a few phone lines working…"

Gunfire still slapped the air like a distant thunderclap.

"Do you hear that, Father? Your beloved city of Olympia is a war zone, the sound of this theme park tries hard to drown out the fire engines and ambulances but the city is a dead zone, no children play out, no dogs bark, just a touch of death due to this infection that plagues the city. Now that was my idea and obviously it's working, but you must be thinking to yourself 'How did he do it?' 'How did this handsome bastard create this virus which has wiped out half of Olympia?' Well I can't take all of the credit for that…I had help, but since you fired my last partner in crime, Mr Tidy, I had to find somebody else, I'll introduce him to you…"

Apollo turned around and wolf whistled towards the craft. "YOU CAN COME ON OUT NOW."

Aphrodite sniffed the air. "Smells familiar."

Big Man strained hard to see as the fires went out and he looked into the lights of the ship. The figure in a full high tech battle armour walked into view and a wall of despair flooded Big Man as he recognised him. For the second time that night Apollo used his mock fanfare call for attention.

"Ta dah!"

"Ares!" Big Man gasped.

"Alright Dad," Ares calmly responded, pushing up his glasses from his nose bridge.

"WHAT ARE YOU DOING? YOU DID THIS? YOU MADE THIS VIRUS? DO YOU KNOW WHAT YOU'VE DONE? DO YOU KNOW WHAT YOU'VE DONE?!"

"I have an idea, yes."

"WHY ARE YOU DOING THIS? THIS VIRUS IS YOUR DOING? LOOK WHAT IT'S DONE TO THE CITY!"

A smile appeared on Ares's face, which turned into a guffaw.

"Really? This 'Great' city that allowed my mother to walk out on me as a child? this 'Proud' city that let me get bullied at every school I went to because I was a little bit smarter than the other kids, this 'Beautiful' city that made every girl I've ever met treat me like something they've stepped in? So if I'm really honest? I couldn't give a shit about this city."

Big Man shook his head forlornly. "What happened to you Ares?"

Ares walked down the landing gear of the escape craft and joined his brother, facing their dad. "*You* happened to me, Father, I can remember when I was growing up, soon after Mother left, you never knew I existed, it was all Aphrodite and nothing else, and nothing has changed, she was the one who got showered with gifts, not me, she was the one who you paid babysitters to take to the park and to the funfair, not me, I was the mistake of the family, I was the nerd who built things for you and that's it, I was the laughing stock of this family, and now I know I wasn't the first one."

His eyes in the dark stared hard at his sister who let out a short harsh grunt.

"So this is what this whole sorry turn of events today is about? You feel neglected?"

She walked purposely towards her father and stood confidently by his side, but she refused to look at his face. "Well build a bridge and get over it you annoying little dick! I mean for god's sake, that's the reason? Mummy didn't give you a hug as a baby so you go all fruit loops on us and make a virus to kill all of Olympia? Have you ANY IDEA WHAT I'VE BEEN THROUGH TODAY?! LOOK AT THESE NAILS!"

"That's what I mean, Aphrodite, I've turned the whole city into a walking dead war zone and you're still thinking about yourself, you've ruined my life you little tramp."

"Can I ask why?" Aphrodite purred.

"WHY? I'LL TELL YOU WHY, YOU LITTLE WHORE! FROM THE MOMENT YOU WERE BORN EVERYTHING TURNED TO SHIT FOR ME, YOU SURVIVED AFTER APOLLO APPARENTLY DIED, YOU WERE THE MIRACLE BABY AND I WAS THE PAINFUL MISTAKE THAT PLOPPED OUT A YEAR BEFORE, YOU GREW UP LIVING THE BEAUTIFUL DREAM OF A FIRST BORN, WHEN IT WAS ME! I'M YOUR OLDER BROTHER AND GOT NO RESPECT FROM ANYBODY, YOU LIVED THE DREAM OF BEING THE DAUGHTER OF ZEUS AND I GOT SUCKED INTO THIS FUCKING NIGHTMARE OF BEING A NOBODY!"

Aphrodite blew her nose and wiped her eyes, still smiling. "But I always have been Daddy's favourite and always will be, Ares! Why are you so shocked? I am a bitch, you know that I am."

Ares calmed down when he replied. "Indeed I do, Sis, but I didn't have a mummy growing up, she left me thanks to *him,* and one other thing Dad, you had a baby son called Apollo who 'died' and then years late a guy turns up to work for you called Apollo too, didn't the alarm bells start ringing then that there was a chance you could be related?"

"Haven't we already been through this?" Big Man sighed.

Ares pointed to Big Man and held his finger at him for a while like a football linesman with their flag raised aloft for an offside decision.

"The revolution has begun now, Dad. You and Aphrodite had better be ready, no mummy to hide behind now sis, she left me."

"My mother is your mother you silly boy, she left all of us, but I didn't go turning the city into freaks because she did."

Big Man spoke next. "How did you know?"

Apollo raised an eyebrow. "Excuse me, Father?"

"Don't 'Father' me, I'm not talking to you. Ares, how did you know that Apollo was your brother?"

"Let me answer that for you, Father."

Big Man looked angrily at Apollo. "Did I stutter, dickhead? I said I wasn't talking to you."

Apollo backed up a little. "But I can explain it better, so as I was saying, I've finally got back home to the Messiah's Complex and there's no welcoming party, nobody around to welcome back the weary soldier – no boss, no friends and no new sister called Gemma to hug, so my swipe card still works so I get in to the place and the first person I see is Ares. We slap hands and when you have the uncontrollable urge to tell anybody that what you thought was your life was a wretched lie and that the strange absurdity of your existence was all down to your father being a little bit thick...you might want to tell someone about it, so I did. I told Ares everything that the stranger told me and obviously he didn't believe me, so to show faith I gave him my swipe key. Who has it now, Ares?"

Ares froze for a moment in thought, and slowly answered.

"I gave my entry card to Gemma I think? She's responsible."

"Yes, so our 'would be' adopted sister has the key to get into the complex, as well as, who else, Ares?"

Ares thought. "Um? Gemma has one, Norton, the head of security had one..."

Apollo butted in. "...Which Tara now has, right?"

The vampire girl waved her key in the air and shouted to Apollo. "JUST SWIPED IT FROM HIS POCKET, MY LOVELY!"

Apollo smiled back and carried on.

"Good call honey, right so my mother had a key and we've taken care of her."

"WHAT DID YOU DO WITH HER!?" Big Man shouted, his eyes pain filled.

"Like I said, Mother has been taken care of, she like you, abandoned Ares and me as children so we tracked her down, took her key and she now isn't the woman she used to be."

"WHERE IS MY WIFE?!"

"Mother has gone, softlad and I doubt she's ever coming back," Apollo gleamed.

"So as I was saying ages ago before I got side tracked, I told Ares the truth about my past and to his credit he wanted proof, so I told him to check the blood samples because our family has an unusual blood type. The stranger told me to ask about this, and that's when I found out he already knew about Cassandra being our sister."

Big Man cautiously spoke. "What do you mean?"

Apollo glanced back at his father with his face still pleasant, he quickly looked over to Gemma who was checking to see whether she could make it over the dying flames; he spoke quickly before she would hear.

"I mean, when you closed down the school of Elias Glaucas and put some of the children in your game show apparently we took blood tests of all the contestants and one of your young researchers realised he had the same blood type as one of them, the girl Cassandra." Apollo's lips stretched to a cruel smile. "The researcher happened to be your son Ares, he knew all along that the girl Cassandra was related to him."

Big Man roared at the pair. "IS THIS TRUE, ARES?! YOU KNEW THAT CASSANDRA WAS YOUR SISTER AND YOU LET HER FIGHT IN THE GAMES?"

The answer came back straight from the horse's mouth.

"Yeah I knew, I was just wondering if you did."

"OF COURSE I DIDN'T!"

"Well I knew, and I watched, I watched as you and Apollo laughed at the poor girl struggling for her life at the cottage with that cannibal Streaky and his kids, and then as she was shipped off to Gommerstall and she's now missing presumed dead."

Apollo moaned. "To be fair I didn't know we were related when I did that and yeah, I do regret it."

"WHY DIDN'T YOU DO ANYTHING, ARES?" Big Man barked.

"Aphrodite was the real reason, Father."

"What? I didn't have anything to do with it!" his sister spat.

"I know," Ares added.

"But it was the way Father treated you, the way he loved you and not me, he made you turn your classmates in, he made you turn your best friend Sabrina in to his games and you didn't bat an eyelid."

Aphrodite gave both brothers a look with empty eyes. "Really, is that it? You found out you had a new sister and you turned into to the games because you were jealous of me? Fair play brother, but I am bored now."

Big Man cut in, mumbling angrily, "You're a heartless freak, Ares, you killed your own sister."

"Nope, you killed your own daughter, how does it feel?"

Ares took off his glasses and wiped them with his fingers. "So after Apollo revealed himself to me and told me that our father didn't even attempt to get him from Gommerstall we both thought 'wow, our father doesn't give a toss about us really', so we thought the only thing he really cared about was his city Olympia, and his daughter Aphrodite. So let's take both of them away from him, so Dad, if I'm honest I lied to you earlier today, I did know about the virus, because I created it."

"You bastard," Big Man said quietly.

"Do you know what you've done?"

"Yep, I know exactly what I've done. I've taken away your beautiful city, made it a wasteland of violence and shit."

"Why would you do that?"

"Because I'm a nerd, because I'm nothing to you, because you have made my life a living hell since I came into this world, you made me work on your projects, your robots, your serum, you didn't care about me or anybody else for that matter, apart from your TV show." Big Man looked weak and fragile as Ares continued. "So we rounded up the loved ones of everybody you hurt, everybody you had killed and given them the serum, given them powers to take their revenge on you. So we tracked down Tara, we tracked down Amber Ace and Slim Pickings, you took away members of their family for enjoyment, so we're going to take away your most precious thing, your city, hell we even had Jason, the guy Mum left you for unknowingly involved."

"You made the virus, Ares?"

"Certainly did Dad, and loved every moment of it, just to mess you up."

Apollo looked up at the night sky and turned back to his father.

"Enough already, I'm tired now of explaining this bullshit." He laughed out loud. "Ok so let's get the checklist out, we've done the whole big reveal thing, Dad knows it was us who started the virus, right? What else haven't we told him?"

Apollo turned to Ares.

"So Father, you've found out today that you had two extra children, one of which grew up to be probably killed by you in your pathetic game show and the other grew up to be me! So can I finally reveal my swipe card gig? Ok so we've got the cards from Norton, mother, who else had a card?"

"Melissa," Big Man said sternly.

Her name made the butterflies in Ares's stomach return and his eyes rose as he looked around. "Where is Melissa?" he asked.

Big Man raised his grey head. "She's dead."

Ares looked up sharply. "What did you say?"

"Oh I'm sorry, wasn't that part of your plan?" Big Man swiped. "Did you not prepare for that?"

Ares trembled slightly, the words coming through terribly clear. "You're lying."

Big Man sidestepped and presented him with an empty spot. "I'm lying? You've been lying to me all day, I'm not the deceitful one here, then where is she, son? You saw us leave together and she isn't here."

"WHAT DID YOU DO TO HER?" Ares demanded.

"What did I do? You're the one who made the virus, so it was *you* who killed her really."

"YOU LET HER DIE!"

"Are you deaf? I just said that it was you who made the virus that turned people into savages which killed your friend and my best PA and why? Just to get me outside of the complex? I mean why?"

"SHE SHOULD HAVE STAYED WITH ME!"

"But she came with me to find my daughters, your sisters because she was a good person, unlike you."

It was maddeningly hard for Ares to think through his grief. "How did she die?"

"How do you think? She was protecting me and got torn apart by those savages."

"Did you see her die?"

"Yep."

"Well, if she survived your shark, she'll survive this, I know she's alive."

Big Man pulled an awkward face.

"I don't know, those tunnels are quite intense."

It was Ares's turn to pull a face.

"Wait? Tunnels? You got attacked in the tunnel?" He turned angrily to his brother. "I told you not to fill the tunnels with the infected, I said to keep them free so Father could reach the theme park easily, the whole map thing was a ploy, you may have killed Melissa."

Apollo silently straightened up. "Really? Oh sorry, I forgot about her, stuck up cow. If I'm honest I'm kind of glad she's dead."

"DON'T SAY THAT!" Ares roared.

"Oh dear, is there trouble in paradise?" Big Man smirked.

Aphrodite moved closer to her father. "Do you think she's really dead?"

Her father shrugged. "Hope not, do you know how hard it is to find a decent PA in this city?"

"You haven't changed a bit, Daddy."

"It's only been a day sweetheart, but Daddy's back."

Apollo cocked his head and frowned a little. "Ok people are we done here? Time to get this show on the road, we'll talk about Melissa later, Ares."

"But of course."

The flame circle had completely died and the infected were finishing up with chewing up on the dead bodies of the theme park crowd and had begun to grow hungry again.

Gemma saw her chance and skipped over to the middle to meet her foster father and brothers, she looked dizzy but tried to be focused.

"Hello Ares," she said calmly.

"Gemma! I'm so glad to see you!"

He walked over and gave her a hug, Gemma shifted uncomfortably as his body armour was awkward to hold.

"Your hair is green now?"

"Yep, parting gift from the waters below the city."

Ares stoked Gemma's hair tenderly. "Where is Buckby?"

"Buckby is dead Ares, that dragon over there killed him."

"Your spider is dead? I didn't mean this to happen, Gemma."

"You didn't mean a lot of things to happen today Ares, but they still did and I just don't get it?"

"Gemma wait."

"No, you wait, I didn't hear why you did what you did as the microphones were off, but I got that you made that virus that killed most of the city? Why would you do that?"

"Because of my father, he had to pay."

"Pay for what? What exactly did he do?"

"He lied to me, he lied to all of us."

Gemma could barely look him in the eye.

"Ok, I only got a part of that, but whatever he did, surely you could have gone into a quiet room and discussed it? Why wipe out half of the city because you have a gripe with Dad?"

Apollo walked over and butted in.

"Hello Gemma, I don't believe we've met, I'm your 'sort of' brother, Apollo."

Gemma thought back to when she was with her real dad Elias, and how not to be rude when you meet someone.

"Hi. I've heard a little bit about you."

"A little?"

"Yep, obviously more about you now after what happened tonight of course."

"Well you are a delightful and polite young woman, and a credit to your father, your true father."

Gemma's eyebrows rose slightly in the dark. "You knew my real dad?"

"Yep, I met him a few times, I actually went round to see you both a few years ago, my associate Mr Tidy and

I, but you weren't at home, you were visiting a friend of yours called Echo, I presume?"

Gemma swallowed hard, finding it difficult to think about her friend and what happened to her in the sky, she missed her glitter.

"What did you want with my dad?"

"Just to throw a business proposition to him, that's all, but it doesn't matter." He cleared his throat. "I'm sorry about your loss, about Elias Glaucas and what really happened to him."

"What really happened to him? What do you mean?"

Aphrodite rumbled a low growl as Big Man shuffled nervously.

"She doesn't need to hear this Apollo, not now."

Apollo returned to his theatrical side. "Oh but Father, are we all not family now? I just wanted to tell my new 'sister' how her real father died as I don't think the poor girl knows."

Gemma shook her confused head. "I know what happened."

"Do you?" Apollo asked. "Really?"

"Yes, he died in a car crash."

"A car crash?"

"Yes, he died and his best friend Zeus, I mean Big Man sorry...looked after me."

Apollo could practically hear his father's ears perk up. "His best friend? Do you remember seeing this 'best friend' as a child?"

"No, he was away on business when I was growing up."

"Ok so what happened to your Auntie...Kay, isn't it?"

Gemma wriggled her nose in anger, a trait from her new family.

"She left me, she went travelling around the world and didn't come back."

"The world is a huge place."

"Her heart was bigger, well it used to be until she split."

"Is that what Big Man told you?"

"It's the truth, Auntie Kay left me, even knowing my first dad had died my Auntie never wanted to see me again, I loved her and I don't know why she won't come back."

Apollo shot a suspicious look at his father. "No, me neither." He turned his attention back to Gemma. "So Big Man told you your real father died in a car crash and your Auntie had abandoned you, right?"

Gemma nodded, as Apollo paused and looked at Big Man, seeing his father sway nervously.

"Were you going to say something, Father?"

"Please don't."

"Please don't what, Big Man? Tell Gemma how her father really died?"

Big Man blinked slowly. "You don't have to do this Apollo, we can work this out."

"Sorry Father, I just have to tell her how you lied about the death of Elias and how he wasn't killed by a car at all, and how you should have told her the truth."

Gemma tensed her shoulders and sighed at her foster father.

"What does he mean, how did my father really die?"

Stammering slightly he began to answer, until Apollo interrupted. "He wasn't hit by a car...it was a large jeep," he said smoothly.

"That's it? That's the truth?" she asked. Apollo shot a quick look to Big Man, their secret safe for the time being. "I thought it would have been worse then that if I'm honest, I mean I'm still sad he's gone and I miss him dearly, but a jeep? That's not what I was thinking."

Apollo's laugh had little humour in it.

"Sorry about that Gemma, it was a jeep."

He shook his head impatiently. "Anyway let's finally get this party started shall we?" The dragon still perched on the robotic shoulder of the sentry guard let out a series of wheezed huffs of annoyance and frustration towards anybody below it. "You see my friend up there is growing restless."

Aphrodite didn't like the look that crossed Apollo's face as he walked over to their father, he grabbed Big Man by the collar.

"WOW! I DIDN'T TELL YOU WHAT MY POWER IS, WHAT I CAN DO?"

Before either of them could react Aphrodite had transformed into her werewolf and leapt at Apollo again with the same result as last time.

"We've danced this dance before my sister and you still fail to learn the steps."

He casually flung Aphrodite out of the circle and crashing into a few remaining spectators. "As I was saying, Father, I have a mutation too with my genes, like all your children there was something 'inside' us which was bought out by the serum, the serum you had your son Ares put into all those schools and nightclubs showers when he was...how old was he? Seventeen? Eighteen maybe? The funny thing is he never took the serum himself, so we have no idea what his 'gift' is but mine is so cool, check this out."

Apollo's skin began to ripple like someone was skimming stones in a lake, under his green robes his arms began to lose their hair, the hair on his head began to disappear and the small mole on his face vanished. Apollo was shrinking in front of Big Man's eyes, his bones were reshaping at an alarming rate, until all that remained of Apollo was a little toddler.

Big Man picked up the child smothered in his massive green robes, his eyes wider than they had ever been in his life as he looked on at the child with a streak of blonde hair.

He looked on in amazement at his son, now a small child. The audience behind him gasped in wonder.

Gemma accepted the strangeness of it all after everything she'd seen today, Aphrodite made her way back to the circle, scrutinising Apollo's transformation.

Big Man held the child close to him and whispered. "Oh my son, what happened to you?"

The little Apollo grabbed at the collars of Big Man and attempted to pull himself towards his father's ears.

"Ahhhh, you cute little baby! Do you want to speak to Dadda?"

"Damn right I do, pops."

"BLOODY HELL!" Big Man shrieked.

Big Man dropped the child on the ground and it landed heavily inside his green robes, Apollo started to wail uncontrollably, the crowd roared their disapproval and began to make their way forward.

Picking the child up quickly Big Man hurriedly began patting the crying baby in his arms.

"You can talk?"

"Damn straight I can, Dad," Apollo whispered.

"I can decrease my age at will, I do age faster than my true years, but I can turn into a toddler for a limited time, that suit keeps me at a certain age, all thanks to Ares, that boy is a genius."

"Son of a bitch," Big Man murmured.

"Well if I'm a 'son of a bitch' that's slagging off my mum and your wife if I recall?"

"Oh yeah, sorry about that."

The crowd behind couldn't hear Apollo, they could only see him nibbling at his father's ear.

"One last thing, Father as it's about to kick off in a minute."

"Why?"

"Well, Gemma is a great kid and completely pure and I'm so sorry for playing a part in her father's death, but she will come after you and she will attempt to rescue you and that's when I'll tell her about what we did to her father, both of us. She no doubt hates me already, but you? It will crush her, how you lied about everything you did to him and I know if I don't kill you…Gemma definitely will."

Snot dribbled down from Apollo's nose and he sniffed. "But I have one more trick up my sleeve, well two actually." Apollo nibbled more on his father's ear.

"What?"

Apollo smiled guardedly and leaned back and turned his head to release a giant ball of spit right between the eyes of his dad; the spit stuck firmly.

"YOU LITTLE BASTARD!" Big Man yelled, he lifted Apollo high above his head and flung him towards Tara and Amber, he landed heavily and theatrically rolled a number of times on the ground. Apollo opened one eye and scanned the shocked expressions on everyone's faces behind him and tried hard not to allow a smile creep on to his face before he spoke again, he paused briefly and then opened his mouth.

"WAAAAAH!"

He continued to roll around on the ground continuously crying.

"BASTARD!" most of the crowd cried.

"YOU SICK SON OF A BITCH!" others screamed.

The theme park crowd surged forward shouting. "HOW COULD YOU HIT A BABY?" they screamed.

By the time Apollo had up-righted himself, the theme park crowd who had avoided the infected were already close to Big Man.

"Bingo," Apollo said with a cute smile.

He threw up both hands to be picked up by the vampire Tara, which she did so easily, his little hands and mouth moved to her breasts for a feed. She grinned. "Stop it you little perv."

"Worth a try I thought, wait until the old man gets a few kicks and then we'll grab him." Apollo's voice tried to be commanding but sounded so innocent and childlike when he spoke.

The crowd ran through the circle and took Big Man down without breaking a sweat. Ten men punched and kicked at the TV boss in a rage, angry that it was him who was the cause of the television ban and the fact that he had just thrown a baby onto the ground, the fact that there was a bounty on his head didn't seem to matter. The men were quick and rained blow after blow onto the body of Big Man, ribs were bruised and his face was taking a battering.

In a sequence of bounds Aphrodite in werewolf form leapt at the men with a predatory speed, taking down five of them. She kept her claws sheathed and punched and kicked out. Her reaction time was greater than all of them and with a few kicks more, all of them lay flat on the ground.

"All too easy," she purred.

Suddenly she was hauled to the same ground where the unconscious men lay, something tight and strong was wrapped around her neck, it was Slim Pickings with his whip scarf.

"Dude! I am so sorry about this, but orders are orders."

Aphrodite managed to stand up and pulled hard at the cord around her neck, the almighty yank sent Slim flying over and landed at her feet, she gently picked him by the scruff of his neck and gave him a mighty head butt.

"Apology accepted darling," she said as he fell to a crumpled heap.

"SLIMMMMM!!" Amber screamed. "GET AWAY FROM MY BROTHER, YOU BITCH!"

Amber's arms glowed an impressive red as flames covered them both. Aphrodite felt her stomach beginning to tingle with anticipation as Amber threw back her right hand and unleashed a fireball at the wolf.

"Gladly," Aphrodite spat as the flame ball soared above her head.

Amber unleashed more fireballs at Aphrodite, this was obviously her mutation, the ability to control and manipulate flame.

She could also fire pure concentrated blasts of pure microwave energy, but was still learning to control that particular part of her genetic make up and stuck to the flames.

Amber and her brother had gone for revenge on Big Man for the loss of their father and the lies he told afterwards, they had taken the serum and gained these added powers. The flames didn't stop her arms from itching and she scratched them in between flame bursts. It was unclear how the serum had affected her brother, but the whip scarf he was given by Ares was a suitable weapon, unfortunately it couldn't protect him from head butts from werewolves. Aphrodite jumped from every fairground ride as the fireballs flew all around, just because Amber could produce flame she still had a very poor aim. The dragon, still perched on the dinosaur's shoulder, remained motionless at the activity below.

"GEMMA!" Aphrodite roared, her voice more feral in her wolf form. "FIND FATHER AND GET HIM OUT OF HERE!"

"HOW?" her little sister yelled back.

"IMPROVISE!"

Gemma pulled at Mitchy to come with her. "Come on we have to get to my dad."

Mitchy rose from her hiding place from the infected, slowly and out of breath.

"You ok, Mitchy?" Gemma looked back at her friend concerned, and had already forgotten about her previous outburst. Mitchy just nodded and clutched hard to the teenager's arm, making Gemma wince slightly.

Apollo's men in ponchos grabbed the beaten up body of Big Man as some of the theme park crowd still rushed in and took opportunistic punches and kicks.

Tara held the infant form of Apollo as Gemma and a wheezing Mitchy ran up to them.

"LET DAD GO, APOLLO!"

Tara turned Apollo towards Gemma, still holding him gently. "No can do my little sister! Daddy has to pay for being a bastard."

It was odd hearing foul language from a baby's mouth, but Gemma stayed firm.

"Aphrodite is as useless as an inflatable dartboard, and I didn't see you grow up, but our brother Ares has said nothing but praise for you, so just walk away while you can."

Gemma shook her head. "Let's just go home and talk about it."

"I don't have a home, I haven't had a home in years, all thanks to our father, well today is the day he will pay for his crimes. Step back Gemma, we're taking him back to the Messiah's Complex for the final stage and you can't follow us honey, you can't get in without your pass key."

"Oh really?" Gemma looked for her bag.

"Lost something?" Apollo asked sarcastically.

Her bag and key were beneath the city in the nightclub labyrinths, with Connor who had apparently drowned.

"You can't get in and you can't stop us Gemma, and your friend looks ready to keel over."

Mitchy failed to respond, looking more tired by the minute.

Apollo looked to his poncho guards. "Put Big Man in the shuttle, boys."

As Aphrodite dodged the fireballs from Amber further into the park, the henchmen of Apollo dragged Big Man up the landing ramp of the escape shuttle.

"Please Ares?" Gemma tried her other brother, the one she knew and spent the last few years spending time with.

"I'm sorry Gemma, you just don't understand."

"Well tell me then!"

Ares looked to Apollo and the little baby drew his lips back.

"Ok sod it! I'll tell you the truth." Still in the arms of Tara, he wriggled in her grasp and motioned to her to move closer towards Gemma.

"Years ago after my associate Mr Tidy and I paid a visit to your father Elias in your house, your lovely precious home, we beat the crap out of him, we beat him senseless to get him to sign over his school to us, and when he didn't, do you know what we did? We set the place alight and watched it burn, burn as he begged us not to take his young daughter away. Luckily you were away at a friend's house, Echo is her name apparently? You were meant to be at home but you snuck out for a sleepover.

So we dragged him out and he was put in prison for a while and forced to watch his fellow prisoners suffer and die at the hands of the deadly cockatrice birds, then it was decided he'd be taken and shackled behind my horse and dragged around an arena for entertainment and even when that didn't kill him, he and many others like him, teachers I believe, were flown hundreds of miles away to the prison city of Gommerstall. After spending a year in stasis, your father made the gallant or rather foolhardy idea to escape, along with Nayan the father of Amber Ace and Slim Pickings; they managed to escape in a stolen flight craft, piloted by your Auntie Kay".

Gemma's eyes never left her brother as he began to rock in Tara's arms excitedly.

"There was a mole placed on the ship called Jago, he had a bomb which ripped a massive hole in the ship's side, which eventually caused the ship to crash, and that was years ago, did anybody send you a text? Nope? Because everybody is dead."

Tara stroked Apollo's bald head. "Do you want to know who was behind this? Who was the brains behind the whole operation, who let your family die for a quick buck to be made on his TV empire?" Delight flittered in his baby eyes. "Big Man."

Her knees went wobbly as she stared at Apollo.

"YOU BASTARD LIAR!" she screamed.

Gemma ran towards Big Man, only to be held back by the poncho guards, she yelled to Big Man.

"IS IT TRUE, ZEUS?! THAT'S THE NAME YOU SAID I COULD CALL YOU WHEN YOU BEGAN TO ADOPT ME? IS THIS TRUE?!"

Big Man groaned in the arms of the guards. "Gemma..."

"ANSWER ME!"

His head was bowed and beaten, his eyes black and beginning to swell. "Forgive me"

"YOU! YOU KILLED MY DAD!"

Big Man began to twitch in the arms of his captors. "We didn't know how it was going to end."

"WE? WHO IS WE? WHO ELSE KNEW YOU KILLED MY DAD?"

He nervously whimpered, "Olympia...the whole city watched."

Gemma buckled and the poncho men quickly gathered her up.

"GET OFF ME!" the venom in her voice made even the most senior guards look to Apollo for advice. He called to his guardsmen.

"Not yet boys."

She fell to the ground again, her ears filled with the reverberating sound of a baby laughing.

"SO MY WHOLE LIFE WITH BIG MAN WAS A LIE?"

Apollo stopped laughing, hesitated for a moment and then started the hysterics again only to stop to blurt out some more. "He lied sweetheart, he lied to everyone, he lied to you, he lied to me, well technically speaking he didn't lie to me as he didn't know I existed, but it sounds way cool to say."

Big Man was still on the landing ramp with the guards as Gemma struggled with her own, she shouted out to him.

"SO WHY DID YOU WANT ME? GUILT FOR KILLING MY REAL FATHER?"

"It wasn't like that, I know Elias will come back for you, then we can complete the game, he's the only one to beat me, he's alive I know it."

Both Gemma and Big Man were oblivious to everything around them, the infected and Amber's flames were the last thing on their minds.

"COMPLETE THE GAME? SO MY LIFE WITH YOU WAS NOTHING BUT A GAME? A TEST TO GET MY DAD BACK?"

Big Man took a breath to answer as Gemma screamed again. "ANSWER ME!"

His gaze jerked down unable to look at her expression. "Yes."

Her once placid brown eyes had gone, replaced by hurt. "Then you're dead to me."

"No Gemma!"

With an almighty effort she broke free from her guards and surged forward only to be caught at the foot of the landing ramp feet away from Big Man, her actions more visceral.

"LOOK AT ME!" Feeling her eyes on him, he failed to do so. "I SAID LOOK AT ME!"

Big Man finally did as Gemma's own eyes began to well up.

"Wherever you go, I'll find you, you won't be able to hide from me, and when I do...I'm going to kill you."

Uncannily those words were similar to the ones her real father uttered to the traitor Jago years ago in the escape from Gommerstall. No words came from Big Man as he was finally dragged into the craft. Apollo smiled.

"I think I'm going insane with all this revelation stuff that's going down today, I'm as happy as shit that nothing can stop us now."

Gemma's whole body was vibrating with rage, before she could answer, she raised her head with green streaks to the air to see a figure descending quickly from out of the sky.

All eyes looked to see someone in a very tight brown leather jacket and a white blouse.

Smooth muscular legs under a little black dress landed confidently in the circle. Before anybody could speak, the figure punched and kicked at the guards holding Gemma captive with the greatest of ease and sheer ferocity, the men soon fell to ground, knocked out completely.

The person under a face of bright make up offered a salute to Gemma and the others.

"Howdy," the voice rasped after a smile and a roll of their eyes. High heeled shoes didn't make a sound as they treaded softly onto the dry grass. Revulsion hit most of the guards as they saw the made up face, whilst others giggled like school children.

Gemma peered hard at the person's face as Apollo shrieked as a baby should. "WHAT THE BLOODY HELL IS THAT?!"

The figure smiled and brightly coloured fingernails fiddled nervously with a handbag.

Amber stopped throwing fireballs to take a breath, as did Aphrodite who leapt in closer towards the circle to take a look, still in her wolf form she chuckled.

"Words can't describe what I'm seeing right now, so I think I'm just going to throw up instead."

"CAN ANYBODY TELL ME WHAT THAT 'THING' IS OVER THERE?!" Apollo struggled in Tara's arms. She recognised the figure and a broad grin emerged on her face, showing her magnificent front teeth.

Gemma threw an evil look to Aphrodite before turning back to the figure. "That is my friend," Gemma defiantly said to her foster brother.

"You know that freak?"

"It's not a 'freak', let me introduce you to…Odysseus."

Odysseus ran his fingers through his brown wig. "What's the matter boys? Cat got your tongue?"

"IT'S A GEEZER! IT'S A BLOKE DRESSED AS A WOMAN!" Apollo yelled.

"THAT THING IS YOUR FRIEND AND YOU DIDN'T KNOW HE WORE WOMEN'S CLOTHES?!"

"Nobody knew," came Aphrodite's voice in mid-air. She landed close by and sniffed at him. "You look better as a woman."

"You look better as a dog," came the quick reply.

"WHERE DO YOU BUY YOUR CLOTHES FROM THEN? DRAG QUEENS R US?" shouted Apollo.

"Actually I buy them from women's clothes shops, who'd have thought?"

Gemma ran over to him under the watchful eye of the guards and gave him a hug, Mitchy managed a tired smile."

"So that's what you had in your bag all this time, honey?"

"Spot on Mitchy."

"So is that's the reason you and your wife fell out?"

Odysseus turned to Aphrodite, unconcerned he was now talking to a werewolf.

"You got it darling."

Gemma left Odysseus and went to her sister. "I forgot to give you something."

She opened her palm and slapped Aphrodite hard in the face, forcing her upward.

"That's for the lies you told me every day of my life."

The slap was barely felt by Aphrodite in her wolf form, it was just the shock of it coming from Gemma that made her rub her fur-covered face.

"I didn't know anything about this, I swear."

Gemma gave a wicked grin, much like her sister's.

"Oh please, looks like this family has played me like a trombone for years, you're the queen of lies, you know everything."

Oddly enough, Aphrodite felt the hope sink inside her as Gemma glared at her. Like Odysseus, she was unbothered she was talking to a wolf.

"I only wanted to be your sister, I only wanted to be like you, but that wasn't enough was it? You put me down daily, you made me feel like crap every day since I came to your family. Mitchy was right all along about you, you're a mean girl, Aphrodite and I want nothing to do with you."

Gemma walked away and went to tend to a tired Mitchy.

"Wow, I never heard her talk like that before," said Odysseus.

"That's because I've never let her down before," replied Aphrodite sadly.

Tara stepped forward flanked by armed guards. She handed Apollo over to Ares and he kicked out wildly, already missing her breasts.

"Hello people, can we get back to us please?" She grinned and spoke directly at Odysseus. "So when you said you were in the dog house with your wife because you stare at women in bikinis, it was in fact *you* who was wearing the bikinis, right?"

Odysseus's expression changed to a scowl.

"You and me have issues darling, after what you did to Norton."

"Ah yes, I killed the man you couldn't stand and you're now being mean to me, you were much nicer at the bus stop this morning."

Odysseus mimicked her voice. "Ah yes, the bus stop this morning, you really threw me for a loop then girly, shouldn't have given you my seat should I?"

Tara shook her head as her eyes lit up followed by a smile as Odysseus continued. "Looks like you're a vampire now, one who can walk around in the day?"

She fluttered her eyes and nodded.

"But as I recall, a vampire doesn't have a reflection and their image can't be caught on film and you still want to become an actress? Good luck with that."

Tara shot him a disappointed look and merely grunted.

"So just because you now dress up in women's clothes you think you're some sort of hero?"

"The clothes give me my strength, give me confidence, that's what my wife couldn't understand."

"Well let's just hope she understands when she's at your funeral matey, because the funny bitey people aren't the only ones with teeth around here."

"Sorry to disappoint you, babes," he said, changing his stance to a fighting one.

"We'll see."

Tara's speed was faster than Aphrodite's; she knocked Odysseus down on his back and he immediately flipped her over his head with his legs as he landed on his back, she neatly rolled on the ground and got up still with a grin. "That was fun, let's say we do it again!" She charged at Odysseus and the two exchanged blows, Tara's with a smirk of true purpose.

Apollo yelled at his troops. "TARA'S TAKING CARE OF THE LADY BOY, BIG MAN IS ON THE SHIP SO LET'S GO!"

He turned to Amber. "HOW YOU FEELING?" Amber coughed slightly and gave him the thumbs up. "GOOD, THEN TAKE CARE OF MY SISTER."

Amber glowed up again.

"Oh for goodness sake," Aphrodite growled.

She hid behind a carousel, but darted out the way as Amber detonated it with her intense flames.

The poncho men had Big Man in the ship and its engines began to hum.

"ARES, PLEASE DON'T GO!" Gemma screamed.

He shook his head as the landing ramp began to rise back up to the ship.

Ares turned to go back into she ship when he noticed some more of the infected had finished their theme park meal and were about to turn on Gemma and Mitchy; they noticed their prey was close and began to charge.

"GEMMA! LOOK OUT!"

He flicked a switch on his armoured wrist. The laser cannons on the shuttle purred and the roared into life, Gemma ducked and covered her ears from the thunder of the guns as they picked off their inhuman targets. Thanks to Ares and his remote control, they swung round locked onto the infected until none stood close by and then they finally stopped.

Ares looked back to his sister with Apollo in his arms and smiled, she raised a small smile back and checked on Mitchy.

"We're leaving, brother," Apollo said and reached over and fiddled with the wrist control. "Let the dragon take care of them now, nobody can follow us."

"What are you doing?"

"Turning the dragon's rage factor to ten baby! It's going to go into meltdown."

"Is that wise? That dragon still has to play a part in our plans you know even after everything is done."

"Don't you worry about that dragon, brother."

"But what about Tara, Amber and that Slim guy? They helped us get what we wanted."

"Yes, they did brother and I'm grateful for that but we've got what we came for and we're done with the hired help."

He quickly turned to his poncho guards. "Not you guys, you guys are cool...in fact..." Ares and Apollo exchanged glances. "What was that extermination operation Father spoke about years ago? The one for which the dinosaur sentries were made?"

"Operation...Abolish and Dominate it was called," Ares replied.

"Well I'm starting it now."

He went back to the wrist control on Ares and calmly fiddled with some buttons.

"There."

"What have you done?"

A little mischievous grin crawled on to Apollo's baby face. "The other little 'project' we were working on? Well I think it's time."

"What about our sisters?"

"They survived a day with the infected chasing them, so I know they'll turn up at the Messiah's complex."

"What about the other guards down there?"

"Collateral damage."

Apollo wriggled free from Ares's hands and dropped to the ground, catching the look of his poncho guards.

"Not you guys, you guys are cool."

He walked unevenly to the shuttle seats and attempted to climb on. "A little help here?" One of the guards strapped him in securely. "Cheers chuckles."

The pilots gently lifted the shuttle of the battlefield, its warning lights cut through the dark and lit up the battle below. Flying in at an incredible speed, the dragon released a flame burst, eliminating a good chunk of poncho guards and the infected. Amber ducked and screamed to the sky.

"WHAT ARE YOU DOING?!"

The glimmering dragon turned around for another dive.

"WHAT'S HAPPENING?" she cried.

Aphrodite landed out of breath next to Amber. Tara and Odysseus still fought savagely, neither one willing to give up. She swung her slender arm at him, catching Odysseus with a clothesline to the neck.

This knocked him to the ground and she followed up the move with an elbow to his chest. Wheezing horribly, Odysseus rolled to his side to try and catch his breath.

With one hand, Tara lifted him above her head and sent him crashing onto her knee first and the ground later.

"Did you really think you were a match for me, babes?"

Odysseus groaned and held his sides. "I'm just getting warmed up, lady."

"Oh no you're not, my sweetie."

She lifted him off his feet, as Odysseus punched her repeatedly on her back. "Oh that tickles babes!"

Odysseus flinched as her voice showed she really was enjoying it and his blows were merely a mild irritation to her, he puffed some words to the vampire.

"You know there are 90% of actors unemployed in the city of Olympia, even more so as the rest of them are now zombies, but I'd rather hire a brain dead zombie than a skank like you."

"You're really hurting my feelings, babe."

She brought her feet with the lovely orange nail polish crashing down on his side.

Wheezing horribly he tried again to speak.

"So I take it you took that serum stuff everybody's talking about? To turn you into an even bigger bitch?"

She bent down and whispered into his ear. "Here's another little fact babes, I've *always* been a vampire, really I have, there's loads of us, but not as powerful as me. We've been living among you guys for generations now – peacefully. We don't want any trouble, but I did take the serum babes, it made me so much stronger."

"So you really could have killed Norton at anytime and got revenge on Big Man whenever?"

"Pretty much babes, but Apollo loves the theatrics as do I, and this way was much more fun."

Odysseus got to his feet and shuffled the pain away to throw some more punches at Tara's ribs, the dress gave him more power than he'd ever had in his life, ordinarily he would never lay his hands on a woman, but Tara was more than a woman, there was a tremendous shock of contact as the combination of blows from Odysseus would have felled the greatest of heavyweight boxers, but Tara was completely inhuman.

Pausing for breath and bent forward, Odysseus was exhausted.

"You finished babes? Tara mockingly asked.

Before he could answer Tara swung a perfect uppercut, sending Odysseus flying through the air and landing in a crumpled mess a short distance from her. "Bored now babes, time to finish you off I'm afraid."

Odysseus scampered crablike on his back like a wounded animal, tired and his energy spent. He tried one last time to reason with the girl he'd thought was so nice at the bus stop earlier.

"Listen kid, you can't win this, look at those two girls, Gemma and Aphrodite, bickering all the time but they love one another because they're a family, look at the big unit Mitchy over there, she's the one who held us together and after what we've been through because we're a family."

Tara looked at him and shook her head. "I forgot how funny you are babes, that dragon looks like it's going to roast Aphrodite for dinner, and Mitchy is it? I think her running days are truly behind her, face it babes you've no more friends left."

Odysseus looked around for a weapon, but there wasn't anything he could find to use against Tara, his scanned the ground and then the sky, and held his stare for a moment, stunned, before looking in front to Tara who was walking forward for her kill.

"WAIT RIGHT THERE," Odysseus shouted as Tara huffed and folded her arms.

"Babes, why delay the inevitable? You will die alone, with no friends to help you."

"One question, did you and Norton ever get to go on that ride 'the Excavator' roller coaster by any chance?"

"No babes, no time, why do you ask?"

"Well 'babes' I do have more friends and judging by the big red theme park ride cart which is about to land on your head courtesy of the cool winged girl Echo, I'd say my friends have just turned up."

Tara had just enough time to look up. "WHAT THE FU—"

The Excavator ride cart which had been used to batter the black dragon by Echo, came crashing down on Tara, it was thrown with such force that the vampire was buried under cheap machinery. Echo hovered in from above, still glimmering but one of her four wings was broken due to the cannon hit from Ares. It was a tremendous effort flying with a clipped wing and a roller coaster ride in her arms. Her remaining wings lowered her down to the battered body of Odysseus. "Nice dress," she said.

"Nice wings," he replied gruffly.

"What's the situation?"

Odysseus clicked his neck and looked to the sky.

"Big dragon back, Big Man captured, Norton dead."

"Shit no...Norton?"

"Yeah, that was his date Tara, she killed him, long story."

"Who's left?"

"Aphrodite, Gemma and Mitchy, Slim Pickings is now a bad guy and unconscious."

"Groovy."

Gemma cradled Mitchy on the ground, looking up at the dragon spitting flames at Amber and Aphrodite.

"We have to go Mitchy, we have to get out of here."

Mitchy joined Gemma in looking at the night sky. "I didn't think it'd end up like this honey, today of all days."

"Why today?"

Mitchy shivered and scratched her arm. "No reason honey."

Echo flew in like a diving hungry hawk and landed in between Gemma and Mitchy.

"Miss me?"

"ECHOOO!"

Gemma's body trembled with delight as she threw her arms around her friend. "I THOUGHT YOU WERE DEAD!"

"One wing down, three still buzzing, you can't keep a glimmer thing down."

"Glimmerfin?"

"No 'thing' it's what I'm going to call myself if we survive this day."

Echo turned to Mitchy and hugged her. "You're a bit quiet, Mitchy, you ok?"

Mitchy patted down her leg and looked up to Echo, her eyes were tired and drained, making a smile was a struggle. "Hey there honey, good to see you too."

Both girls could hear the strain in her voice.

"You ok?" Echo asked, her wings were beginning to hum again.

"Just tired."

The remaining infected were drawn to Echo's glow. "Here we go again." The dragon was still flying around the theme park, spitting flames at Amber and Aphrodite. Amber's flames and already burnt her grey fur and she was in no mood to have anymore singed, she had an amazing acrobatic agility which was keeping her alive and she knew it.

She landed next to Amber, still wary of her glowing arms.

"Darling, I would slap your face right now for trying to burn me, if I didn't want to get a handful of whore paint."

Amber frowned at the growling wolf. "Bitch, I don't know why Apollo let that dragon loose on me, but I'm going to kick its ass if it tries to burn me again."

"Not nice being burned is it?"

"Shut your mouth!" Amber snapped.

"Such ardour," Aphrodite mumbled but continued to speak. "Can't strictly speak for Apollo as he was merely my father's head lackey and not my brother when we last met, but Ares has always been a screw up, always has and always will, whatever plans he has for our father... they won't work."

The night was again lit up by the dragon's impressive firepower, making the two girls dive for cover again.

Amber turned to Aphrodite. "Watch over my brother please, lady? It's about to get very hot around here."

"Please? That's a first, I'm rather shocked, so I take it we're done fighting?"

The heat from her power swelled all around her olive skin, she was now orange all over from her flame, only her jet black hair remained and her lovely white teeth as a smile emerged.

"Done fighting with you? For the time being yes, but for this big old dragon bitch? I've only just started, grab that lot as well."

She pointed to Echo, Mitchy and Gemma. Aphrodite beckoned frantically to the others and they all scrambled over, including a groggy Slim Pickings. Aphrodite spoke to Echo.

"I thought you were dead?"

"Sounds familiar," Echo quickly huffed.

Echo looked at her jacket on Aphrodite, full of burn marks.

"What did you do to my jacket?"

"It was her," Aphrodite pointed accusingly at Amber, "she burnt me."

"I'll burn you again if you don't shut up."

The dragon swooped in for another flame burst. Amber rolled her orange eyes as the fire blazed within them.

"Ok I'm getting sick of this."

She threw her arms back and waited for the dragon to pause between flame bursts, as it got ready for another attack.

"GET BEHIND ME! GET BEHIND ME!"

The glimmering dragon hurled twin blasts of fire at the group. Amber parried with a wall of flame, protecting everybody from the intense heat. As she poured all her concentration into her own fires, Echo sidled up to her.

"Your name is Amber, is it?"

Amber could hardly draw a breath as she looked to Echo. "Yeah it is, um? I'm kind of busy right now?"

"When the dragon pauses, drop your flame for me please?"

Amber shot a glance at Echo with open curiosity. "Hey your wings are massive up close."

"Yeah, I noticed."

"Did you take the serum?"

Echo clicked her neck. "I took a dip in a swimming pool full of the stuff."

"Cools."

Amber was now distracted by Echo more so than the dragon. "I can't see when the dragon is about to pause, my flame shield is too big."

The barriers of flame from Amber kept the dragon's fires at bay, but it was tiring her out.

Echo gave a simple flap of her three remaining wings and rose skyward through the flames without a mark on her.

"On my mark, drop your shield."

The dragon climbed higher in the night sky and let out an ear-splitting howl as it unleashed another volley of flames. Amber's shield held firm, all the people behind her ducked down as her own flames kept them safe.

They would all have been incinerated by now if it wasn't for Amber, many of the infected and theme park people had perished in the dragon's lethal assault.

It was a beautiful sight in the final hour of the night, the glittering form of the winged Echo above the double flames of Amber and the glimmer dragon.

After its last onslaught the dragon drew back its head and circled, roaring hard for another attack.

"Steady, hold tight Amber," Echo said, her skin impervious to the heat.

True to form, an even greater flame attack left the creature's mouth.

"NOW?" Amber asked through gritted teeth.

"NOT YET" Echo shouted back deep in the flames.

A cascade of pain ripped through Amber as she struggled to maintain her terrific flame shield against the dragon's flames. "I CAN'T HOLD ON!" she cried.

The rest of Echo's clothes had been burnt away from the dragon's flames, only her glitter protected her modesty.

Dangerfield theme park was in flames, most of the new rides were now smoking ruins, but the glimmering dragon hadn't finished, the group huddled together as the heat burned the hairs on their arms and made them sweat profusely.

"I'VE GOT TO DROP IT!" Amber's legs began to buckle.

"WAIT FOR IT!" Echo replied.

The dragon exhausted its current blast of flame and whipped back its head, breathing ready for a new assault.

"EVERYBODY CLOSE YOUR EYES," Echo called to the group.

As the dragon's mouth began to glow again with the production of flame, Echo swung her head back to Amber.

"DROP IT NOW!"

Amber dropped her arms exhausted, and stumbled backwards into the arms of Gemma. With the shield gone Echo threw her arms back and unleashed a wall of glittering light at the dragon, the light was brighter than the sun and caught the dragon off guard and blinded it. With its wings flailing the dragon lost control of its flight path and headed at a tremendous rate spinning uncontrollably towards the group.

"MOVE IT!" Gemma cried.

The giant blinded body of the dragon arced into the night air and bounced off the soft grass, it skidded on its back, its legs wriggling like an upturned tortoise until it finally came to a halt. It breathed slowly but didn't move – exhausted and spent.

Slim Pickings was conscious now and turned groggily to his sister. "Dude, have I ever told you how brilliant you are." Amber shook her head. "Well I'm seriously considering it!"

She got slowly to her feet, her own orange flame was gone, only her smooth olive skin stuck out like a beacon in the night, she gave a thumbs up followed by delicate little coughs.

"Is it dead?" Amber asked between coughs.

Aphrodite reverted back to her human form, Echo's burnt jacket just about covered her up.

"Unconscious I think darling, so what do we do now?"

Gemma snapped back angrily at her. "Did you say 'we'? I don't care what you do, but I'm going to the Messiah's complex, that's where Big Man is probably being kept and I want words with him.

Feeling slightly exposed, Aphrodite stretched the jacket across her breasts.

"So how do we get there then, Gemma?"

"Not 'sister' anymore?"

Aphrodite didn't look at her.

"Nope, those days are over."

"Expected."

Echo dropped down from the sky on a column of glittering sparkles.

"What are you guys talking about?"

Her wings made a soft hum which was soothing to the ear, she was handling her new ability like it was second nature. Gemma shielded her eyes as she answered, knowing how the dragon felt.

"We're going to the Messiah's Complex, for Big Man."

Odysseus pulled at his skirt. "How are we going to get in, sweetheart? We don't have any keys to get into the tower and besides how are we going to get there?"

Gemma immediately turned to Echo, shielding her eyes as a precaution. "Could you fly us all over there?"

"All at the same time? There's six of you, it might get pretty uncomfortable up there, no offence Mitchy but it might be more difficult for you."

Mitchy stood to her feet with difficulty and Gemma went to help her, the older woman eased her words out.

"It's fine honey, I'm not going with you anyway."

"Why? Gemma asked, her voice reverting back to that of an innocent child.

Nobody had noticed that Mitchy had been covering up her forearm for ages, she took her left arm away to reveal why.

"This is why I can't go with you, honey."

Mitchy showed Gemma a nasty bite wound on her arm, from the infected, a bloody puss filled mess.

"It happened when we rushed to get closer to that flame circle, one of them got me and that's why I shouted at you honey, I'm so sorry, I didn't mean to, I was just scared, but I'm not anymore."

Gemma stood back and shook her head, tears immediately welled up in her eyes.

"No, please no, Mitchy not you, please no!"

Mitchy stepped back from her. "I'm sorry Gemma, I have to stay here."

The rest of the group looked on sadly as Gemma protested. "No, Mitchy please don't leave me, I'm sorry for what I did, please don't go, I can help you, I know I can."

Mitchy rasped a chuckle.

"You can't help me honey, but you can help your sister and the others."

"She's not my sister!" Gemma cried.

"You have to get going, honey, I don't think I have much time left."

"But you have powers! You were in the swimming pool with me so you must have powers! They can save you, please don't go, Mitchy!"

"Whatever power I have honey it's probably the reason why I haven't turned yet."

"But you might not?"

"Everyone who gets bitten turns, honey, it is what it is."

Gemma continued to cry and spluttered out mixed up sentences between tears.

"I can help you, please don't leave me, God no!"

Mitchy hugged Gemma and now Echo, who was fighting back the tears herself.

"You have lovely wings, honey."

Echo didn't reply, just nodded her head as tears now streamed down her face. Gemma's tears made her turn angrily to Mitchy.

"YOU PROMISED YOU WOULDN'T LEAVE ME! YOU SAID YOU'D PROTECT ME IN THE TUNNELS! EVERYBODY ALWAYS LEAVES ME!"

Mitchy clutched her stomach with a grimace. "I'm so sorry, sugar." She turned around in agony. "Amber is it?"

Amber stepped forward nervously. "Yes, that's me."

"I need you to do something for me."

"Ok, what do you want me to do?"

Mitchy scratched at her arm and her ill-fitting trousers. "I need you to kill me."

"WHAT!?"

"You can control fire, can't you? I need you to burn me."

"I CAN'T! I WON'T!"

Mitchy dropped to her knees. "Please? You have to kill me, I can feel the change happening."

"But I haven't killed anybody in my life?"

Aphrodite walked up behind her with a smooth, soft padding of bare feet. "You just tried to fire bomb me to death darling, you weren't holding back there."

Amber shifted her feet, looking to the ground. "I was, I was always holding back, we were never meant to kill you Aphrodite, Apollo said you were always off limits, Norton unfortunately wasn't, it was just meant to scare you and keep you busy."

"Oh no!" Mitchy whispered, slightly frightened. "Get away from me, please go, I think it's…"

She stopped in mid-sentence, it was becoming harder for her to speak and she grunted slowly. "Amber… please?…kill me."

Amber stepped back and shook her head, her face showing a mask of confusion, all the bravado she showed earlier was long gone, she began to cry as well.

"I can't…I can't do this, this wasn't supposed to happen!"

Mitchy's face twisted with pain. Aphrodite looked hard at Mitchy. "We haven't much time"

"God! It hurts!" Mitchy cried.

She quickly ran forward to her and to everyone's surprise tenderly held Mitchy's head.

"Happy birthday, Mitchy." She kissed her forehead.

"You y-y you k-knew?"

Aphrodite nodded and whispered in her ear.

"Thank you for saving my sister's life."

Mitchy smiled her warmest and then any trace of human was gone, she had enough energy left to summon up a scream of pure agony. She pushed Aphrodite away violently and coughed up blood.

"WHAT DID YOU SAY TO HER?" Gemma demanded.

"Doesn't matter now," Aphrodite replied solemnly.

More blood sprayed from Mitchy's mouth as she began to cough up her stomach, her eyes bulged from their sockets and then turned black. Slim Pickings began to retch as Mitchy's body began to convulse.

"Whatever we're going to do, we have to do it now!" Odysseus called out.

Gemma's heart was thumping so much faster now and her face was warm from her own tears.

"AMBER, YOU HAVE TO DO SOMETHING NOW!" Gemma shouted.

"BUT WHAT CAN I DO?!"

Odysseus bolted forward in his heels, eyes wide. "You gotta do what Mitchy asked you kid, it's the only way."

Amber's voice came clearly in defiance and calm. "I'm not going to kill her."

Mitchy's body turned and twisted like a snake, then she dropped on all fours, black bile spewed from her mouth and she hacked up more, grunting solidly she moved faster than her bulk should allow and went for Gemma.

"NOOO!" Gemma screamed and stumbled backwards, Odysseus made a grab for Mitchy and strained to hold her back, Gemma doubled over on her knees to catch her breath.

"DO IT NOW, LADY!" he shouted whilst struggling with Mitchy's right arm. Echo made a dive for her left arm and held it tight, not even her glow had an effect on the newly infected Mitchy. Mitchy hissed and wriggled as Gemma's face showed the true horror of what her friend had become.

"AMBER! I SAID DO IT NOW!" Odysseus face snarled.

Amber felt more scared than she'd ever felt in her life and ambled forward towards the captive Mitchy who pulled hard at her friend's restraints, her now black teeth gnashed hard at her, Mitchy's fists hammered on the ground trying to get free, black eyes wide with rage and fury.

"HURRY!" Odysseus's voice shocked Amber closer.

"Oh God! oh God! I'm so sorry! I'm so sorry Mitchy, please forgive me."

As Amber's eyes glowed orange with her flame power about ready, Mitchy's head shook vigorously trying to break free, Amber kneeled down nervously in front of her.

"Mitchy, stay still for me please?"

Mitchy's neck twisted awkwardly still trying to lunge.

"Please? She won't stay still."

With her arms folded and tears still streaming, Gemma walked closer to Mitchy and stood behind the frightened Amber, she wiped her eyes and nodded.

"MITCHY!" she shouted once and hard at her friend and former human.

The voice from Gemma gave a spark of what little humanity which was left in Mitchy, her dark eyes flared up the briefest of recognition and looked up at the two girls.

"Do it," Gemma sadly told Amber.

Amber's went stiff and stopped shaking.

"Look into my eyes, Mitchy...this will sting a little."

A powerful concentrated flame burst shot out from Amber's eyes and struck Mitchy right between hers, the flame burned her head and exited the other side with parts of charred brain matter. Mitchy was dead before she made the short journey to the ground.

Amber's shriek of sorrow split everyone's ears and Gemma's tears returned as she sobbed uncontrollably and dropped to the ground also.

13. BROKEN STONES

The sounds of the protesters at the foot of the Messiah's Complex were gone, some had probably fled for their lives whilst others had definitely been infected by the virus. The infected bumped into overturned cars, the occupants were either dead or had made a hasty retreat. Olympia's streets were smeared with blood, the infected lingered around waiting for their next meal like opportunist hyenas. It was well into the night and still car horns were honking away and burglar alarms blared out constantly. Sirens wailed throughout, a mixture of all the emergency services were out and various vehicles collided with escaping civilians.

Big Man's eyes flicked open, as he awoke from his unconscious state. He was back in his Messiah's Complex, laying broken and battered in his master chamber. Looking around the room, a voice made him turn in his blood stained sheets. "You should keep your eyes shut, Father, there is nothing to see here, your beloved city of Olympia is shattered beyond repair." It was the voice of Apollo, back in his 'Green Man' garb and no longer a toddler. "Forgive me if I startled you."

Big Man grimaced and held his cracked ribs. "Why didn't you just kill me?"

Apollo seemed genuinely hurt by that request. "Where would be the fun in that? If I wanted you dead, believe me you'd be six-feet deep by now."

"What are you going to do with me?"

"You've been part of a game, you and the city have been involved in my new game for the whole day now and I just wanted your feedback."

"What do you mean?" Big Man grew impatient.

"This whole day was a test for my new show, I'm the new games master in this city now, well this dead city, you had your chance years ago and messed up with that silly programme 'Game Show'. I always wondered why you called your game show 'Game Show' – pretty ridiculous if you ask me."

"Is that my punishment then? Being bored to death buy a clown in a cheap suit?"

Apollo wheezed a laugh. "You will never change, but's let's hope you'll listen, the reason why I have terrorised my own city of Olympia today was not purely for revenge on you, it was for money, plain and simple. Apollo picked up a remote control and turned on a massive flat screen television hooked onto the wall. "You have a working television set in your home? I thought television was banned in this city?"

"Perks of being a bastard I suppose," Big Man replied, trying hard to brace the pain around his body.

"The 'Dead Run' is what I've called my new game show, get it? Quite apt I thought, anyway, with crime and unemployment rates hitting an all time high in cities in the inner rim I went to various governments with a proposal, and most of them accepted. I take some of my infected people and set them in the centre of a city whilst the good and the rich seal themselves in their homes with specialised security systems, supplied by me of course and the infected will multiply and rid the cities of the homeless, the poor, the criminals and all the scum that reside there and afterwards my clean up crew will go and destroy the infected making a better city, making a utopia if you like?"

The pain hit Big Man again but he had to get his point across. "Just because you're unemployed or homeless doesn't make you a bad person, you're killing innocents."

"I know that and you know that, but it's not about what's right and wrong, it's about power, you of all people should know that."

"But at least the people in my game *wanted* to be in it, they weren't forced."

"Really? What about the school children?"

"That was a mistake, I know that now."

"That may be so, but that was the plan and it's already started."

"So this whole day was never really about getting revenge on me and obtaining the 'entry keys' to my complex?"

Apollo shook his head. "Merely entertainment for the watching cities, like I said Olympia was a test for the others, I have cameras all around this city, more so than before, like I mentioned before if I wanted you dead, you would be. The same as if I wanted you out of the complex, the key thing and the bounty on your head was just a rouse to get you out, the whole 'revenge' thing with Amber and Tara was just a bonus, just bought in millions of new viewers around some of the world, you should be proud of the idea, I have infected the whole city of Olympia for entertainment, for television, the dead run the city and it's all for ratings.

"You can't keep me here, the girls are coming to get me."

"Really Father? How will they get in?"

Apollo began to pace up and down the room.

"Norton, your head of security had a key and he's dead, Melissa, your PA had a key and she's dead, that young girl who was the head of housekeeping, what was her name again?"

Big Man thought long and hard. "Enya I think, she was new, she got given the job this morning."

"That's it Enya, with the flying sister Echo I think? Well she got killed which wasn't down to me let me add, she had a key, Gemma lost her key, so no one is coming for you and even if they do, Gemma is going to kill you for what you did to her father, so you can't win."

"How will you get rid of the infected all over the city?"

Apollo chuckled. "I apologise for spitting in your face earlier, but I did say I had another surprise for you." He pressed a button on his familiar wrist control. "Are we ready, Ares?" He waited. "We are? Ok coolio, meet my cleaners."

Apollo pressed the controls on the TV remote, cameras flashed feedback from another building which wasn't the main Messiah's Complex, it was a laboratory somewhere else, an underground complex filled with countless television monitors and armed guards still wearing the ponchos, various technicians sat at their workstations tapping away on their keyboards.

Ariel, the team leader stood next to Ares, her concern for the project deepened. She began to scratch her arms slowly, they were itching and the surge of pain in her arms grew worse. A loud female voice could be heard shouting in the background, the voices sounded annoyed and frustrated and eager to make an appearance. Ares walked into view back in a white lab coat and out of his battle gear, he gave a thumbs up to the camera, and

Apollo returned the gesture. The lab technicians tapped their keyboards in a rushed manner and looked excitedly at the readouts on their screens.

Apollo, The Green Man, spoke again into his wrist control.

"Are you still afraid?"

The female voices in the laboratory replied, "WE ARE ALTERED, WE ARE UNAFRAID. WE HAVE BEGUN A NEW JOURNEY. WE ARE FIT TO JOIN YOUR ARMY OF RECKONING. WE ARE TOGETHER AS ONE. WHERE THERE WAS ONCE FEAR IS NOW POWER. WHERE THERE IS WAR WE WILL BE. FOR WE ARE KIMBERLEY WATSON, AND WE ARE AFRAID OF NOTHING!"

Big Man looked at the screen to see hundreds of faces of the same lovely girl enter the lab all dressed in white leather jackets and mini skirts with white skyscraper heels. Their eyes were black and riddled with a haunting emptiness. "That girl looks familiar, they all look familiar, what the hell is this?"

Apollo turned slightly and watched Big Man closely.

"When you put those kids from that school into that game show of yours years ago, we all took blood samples from everybody involved under your own orders, which you've obviously forgotten about…well we started a cloning process years ago with one of the girls known as Kimberley Watson. She was the one who died in the great escape from Gommerstall prison, their features have finally taken shape and there's some existence of slight retaining of memory, which we're trying to remove."

Big Man tried to snarl a warning to Apollo, but could only muster a dry moan. "Cloning? You've cloned people?"

"Just one initially, but the carrier started developing abnormalities with the memory stuff, so we got rid of her, but this new batch has no memories of their original past and have kept their power from the serum.

"What are you going to do with them?"

Apollo looked away from the TV, disappointed. "Weren't you listening to a word I said? Those girls, those clones are my clean up crew, they will go from house to house, pillar to post and destroy all the infected in the city with their bombs and then we'll move on to the next city for entertainment and money and do the whole thing all over again, televised of course. Do you know how many cities at war with their neighbours want us to go in and wipe them out? It's a win-win situation for us."

"But if you wipe out all the infected, who will you use to start the new infection in the next city?"

Apollo nodded and started to leave.

"Glad you're paying attention, Father, when your daughters come for you and they will come…they will be captured and infected with my virus and begin the next phase."

"Next phase?! They're your sisters and you want to kill them?"

"We have had our family reunion, Father, kill them? Actually no, you're right, I won't kill my sisters, but I will clone them though, it's all about business now, so after the girls come and are cloned or infected whatever comes first, after my clones destroy your beloved city of Olympia and leave it in ruins and after you have nothing left in this world, oh pathetic father of mine, then I will allow you to die."

As Apollo began to leave, his father struggled to call to him.

"One thing, that 'stranger' who told you everything about your past, I mean *everything,* who was it?"

His son stood amazingly still in thought, and then walked back to Big Man. "I'm surprised Ares could keep this act up for so long, but I'll tell you as you'll be dead soon, it was Jago, he's back."

Apollo left the room with a smile, keeping the television on. Zeus 'Big Man' Wylde had enough strength to watch the Kimberley clones stride purposely out of their laboratory. The clatter of high heels on metal floor was loud but not loud enough to keep him from slipping back to sleep.

Gemma stared at the dead body of Mitchy on the ground, even with her fried brains scattered next to her she thought that her friend would simply stand up and dust herself off like she had done previously through out the entire day, but this wasn't going to happen now and her tears had dried to her face, the scene was complete confusion.

"Ok we have to move now."

"Move where?" Echo asked.

"Nothing has changed, we still have to get to the Messiah's Complex to reach my…" She corrected herself quickly. "To reach Big Man."

"That's right, nothing has changed, we can't get into the complex as none of us have a key to get in."

"But you can fly us there, right?"

Echo nodded. "Yes, but we can't get in without a key!"

Slim Pickings tapped Amber on the shoulder. "Dude, here they come."

The whole group turned to see a few of the infected, burnt but still making their way towards them. Gemma shouted angrily, "DON'T THESE BASTARDS EVER GIVE UP?!"

"Don't worry, I got it."

Echo's wings began to flutter and the effect made the infected stand still in a daze.

"Yeah I bet you have," Gemma mumbled.

Echo's wings stopped flapping and she turned to her best friend. "What do you mean, Gemma?"

Gemma's eyes bulged with a mixture of fury and confusion. "Well, because you're the girl with the wings, the girl who can control the infected, the girl who with the indestructible skin, why should you stay here anyway and help us?"

Echo grew more uncomfortable.

"Why are you saying these things? We're friends, remember?"

Gemma stopped her rant and looked back in anger.

"Friends? If we were friends you wouldn't have let me sneak out to your place for a sleepover years ago, if I had stayed in my house I could have saved my dad and not let it burn down to the ground."

"WHAT ARE YOU TALKING ABOUT?" Echo said with deep shock.

"I'm talking about you taking the piss with me when we were kids and messing up my life now."

They made eye contact with anger. "Messing with your life?" Echo's wings buzzed with ferocity and her voice increased. "YOU'RE BLAMING ME FOR THAT?!

"Yep, I've had a pretty bad day don't you know."

"YOU'VE HAD A BAD DAY? I LOST MY SISTER YOU STUPID BITCH!"

Gemma turned away seemingly unbothered, Echo stormed over to her and grabbed her arm. "HEY, I'M TALKING TO YOU."

Gemma shoved her away. "GET OFF ME!"

"YOU TWO STOP IT!" Amber shouted. "We have to decide what we're going to do."

"We? We?" Gemma's face turned into a question. "Remind me who you are again? Only moments ago you wanted to kill us and now you want to be all 'best friends' with us? It was *us* who were trapped for hours on end below the city, *us* who had to hide from those street zombie things and it was *us* who had to run for our lives from a massive dragon." Gemma rolled her big brown eyes. "You killed Mitchy too."

"You saw how she was Gemma, she was infected."

"SHE WAS MY FRIEND!" Gemma yelled.

"Whilst you were just bitching about how your old man got tricked by mine, my fake one anyway, serves him right if you ask me."

Amber's right hand began to burn with an angry flame.

"Dude, just ignore her, she's not worth it, I thought she was though," Slim Pickings sighed.

"I'd listen to your stoner douche bag brother if I were you…honey."

Odysseus stepped in now, looking over his shoulder at the infected, still dumbstruck with Echo's glow.

"Don't use 'honey' that was Mitchy's word and she's a good person."

"SHE'S DEAD YOU PRICK!" Gemma's green hair streaks caught in her mouth as she whipped her head round.

"I don't know what's gotten into you girl, this isn't like you?"

"How do you know me, Odysseus? Can you honestly say you do? I thought I knew you until you disappeared and came back an ugly drag queen."

Aphrodite caught Gemma's angry glare.

"As for you? Stay away from me you skank whore."

Aphrodite put her hands up in mock surrender, preferring to stay silent, Echo chewed her lip in thought and then spoke.

"To hell with this, I'm leaving!" Her glorious wings purred back into motion. "Look I'm sorry about what happened to Mitchy, really I am, but I'm not going to stand here and listen to you bad mouth everyone because you're upset?"

Gemma's eyes strained at her as Echo's glow grew more blinding in anger in the dark.

"FINE! JUST LEAVE THEN, WE DON'T NEED YOU!"

"GEMMA!" Odysseus scolded.

"NO, I MEAN IT! LET HER GO!"

"Ok," Echo whispered.

She hovered over to Odysseus and gave him a big hug. "Thank you for saving our lives."

"You don't gotta do this, babe."

She stroked his grizzled face tenderly and her glow soothed him slightly. "Yes I do, look after her for me… please?"

Odysseus nodded. Echo turned to Aphrodite. "You can keep the jacket by the way."

Aphrodite nodded and spoke softer than usual. "I'm sorry about your sister, Echo."

"Thank you," Echo replied.

Then the smile left Aphrodite's face when she remembered the burn holes in the jacket.

"Ridiculous."

Amber's gaze rose to Echo's. "Where are you going?"

"Anywhere, away from here."

Amber closed her eyes and opened one in faint hope. "I know you hardly know me or my brother, but could you possibly take us with you? There's nothing here for us now, we just need to get away."

Gemma butted in.

"Thought you wanted to get back at Big Man? That was a quick revenge don't you think?"

"I think your issues with Big Man are worse than ours, we thought we had problems until we met you." She turned back to Echo. "Can you take us?"

Echo saw Gemma jam her middle finger up in the air at her in a final show of defiance.

"Yeah, let's go."

Slim Pickings held on to his sister as they allowed themselves to be carried away by the fluttering wings of Echo. Amber managed a quick wave before being lost in the dark, the remaining infected watched her fly away and turned to follow her glitter trail, the others were safe until the glimmer thing from Echo disappeared from the night sky.

"Right, that's that, I'm off now."

"What are you talking about, Gemma?" Odysseus asked with a disappointed voice.

"I'm going back into the Labyrinth underground to find Connor."

"Are you an idiot? Wait? Let me rephrase that... you're an idiot," Aphrodite muttered. "You do know Connor is dead, darling."

Gemma turned to walk away.

"But he had my entry key on him, so when I find his body, I'll get the key to go back home to the Messiah's Complex and kill Big Man and when I'm finished with him, I'm going to track down that bastard dragon and kill it after what it did to my poor spider."

Odysseus felt a churning sensation in his stomach. "You don't mean that, do you kid?"

He met her eyes, shocked at the look of pure hate on her face.

"Watch me...dead dad first and then dead dragon."

She turned and walked a few paces away to the nearest manhole cover, a sight she'd seen all too often today and with a sigh and an almighty heave she lifted the cover open and waved to Aphrodite. "See you later, slut."

The tunnels had been her home for most of the day so without a sound and effortless precision, she lowered her little body into the hole and disappeared from view, the innocent, shy, nervous little sister Aphrodite was meant to take swimming earlier today was gone and only a hate monger remained. Gemma's head resurfaced quickly and called to Aphrodite.

"You know what? I only wanted to go swimming today, in a normal pool and not an infected one, and you couldn't even get that right, what's that word you always say? Oh wait never mind I remember...ridiculous."

She disappeared from sight for the last time.

"And then there were two," Odysseus sighed.

Aphrodite let out a long and tired breath. "I really don't have time for this."

"I know."

"Any ideas?"

"I'm all out now."

She smiled, a rare comfortable all across her face. "If anybody had told me yesterday, by this time tonight I would have encountered horrible plague-like ruffians, be chased by a dragon and find out I have sister and another brother who can change into toddler, I'd have thought they'd be quite deluded or drunk, oh plus my only friend left in the city is a drag queen who's fooling nobody that he can fit into a size twelve skirt."

Odysseus forced a smile and shook his head. "This city is pretty much dead now."

"I'm inclined to agree with you."

"You leaving?"

"Yep."

He cleared his throat. "What about Gemma, you just planning on leaving her?"

"Yes, but you're going to follow her and make sure no harm comes to her."

He raised an eyebrow. "Oh really? So what are you going to do then?"

"I'm going to Gommerstall, to find the only people who beat my dad, my headmaster Elias Glaucas and his loser nerd buddies, if they can't beat Apollo and Ares then we are in trouble."

Odysseus had a smile, which turned into a small frown.

"You forget they have a dragon guarding them? You can't get past that."

"Then I'll fight fire with fire and bring back my own dragon, a bigger one, and believe me, if she's still alive, then we're all in for some more fireworks from my sister."

"She's a dragon?" Odysseus asked, eyes raised again.

"She's more than a dragon, she's a Paintshark, and we all know only idiots fuck with sharks."

"Excuse me?"

"It gets more complex darling, I wouldn't worry your tiny little mind about it."

"What about my wife?"

"I think saving the city comes a bit higher on your 'things to do list' than date night with your missus, just go after Gemma and look after her, I'll sort the rest out."

Odysseus swallowed uncomfortably.

"How will you find me, I mean...us?

"You still have your phone, right?"

Odysseus slapped his forehead. "Yeah, shit I forgot."

"Well if that doesn't work just head to the Messiah's Complex anyway and if you can get in, then do so, just keep Gemma on a leash until I get there."

"On a leash, that's funny coming from you."

Aphrodite started a witty retort, but stopped and moaned her frustration. "Too tired."

"Well, if you want me to look after Gemma, I'm going to need help."

Aphrodite looked at her battered nails and her mouth curled up in disgust. "Who? Everyone's either dead or has left us."

Odysseus thought back to his encounter at the bus stop that morning. "I think I can get someone, he's a bit slow on the uptake but built like a brick shithouse, he's more than enough muscle if he's still there, and alive."

She stretched her legs and pulled Echo's jacket again tighter on her, completely ignoring his previous comment.

"How far is the city of Gommerstall by the way?"

Her eyes darted around and pleaded for direction. "Hundreds of miles."

He pointed behind him. "That way, look it's pitch black, you're semi-naked, you must be starving and the city is overrun with the infected, why are you doing this?"

She gave him a long, thoughtful look and started walking away.

"Are you sure you're doing the right thing, Aphrodite?, I mean I know he's your dad, but he lied for years to you about that Paintshark girl, lied to Gemma about her true father and also turned you into a werewolf if I'm correct?"

Aphrodite recoiled at the madness she heard coming from his lips and answered with a stamp of efficiency.

"I know what he did, but he's still my father and I have to help him, people can change you know?"

She continued walking away from the theme park, just a leather jacket for company, the night wind stirred and blew sweet wrappers all around her.

"Aphrodite," Odysseus called out.

"I know he's your father, but I think you're wasting your time."

She turned around, her chest heaving hard from annoyance. "We'll see about that, my father *can* change."

Odysseus smiled at the sincerity of her voice and called again. "Aphrodite..."

"What now, Odysseus?"

"You ever heard about the story of the Frog and the Scorpion?"

EPILOGUE

The dragon was breathing easily again and slowly lifted its head as its glimmering crest fin was the only thing visible on its bruised and battle-scarred black body. Its incredible vision was returning slowly after being blinded by Echo's light, it had being relying on its sense of smell to get back home. The creature reached its destination and squatted down at the foot of the massive hole in the ground. The moonlight showed the terrible scars from the evening battle at the theme park, its left eye was beginning to shut and its jaw was slightly crooked as well as some shattered teeth.

Brushing away some debris used to conceal its opening with its giant padded claws, it paused for a moment, hearing movement nearby; it was visibly annoyed and let out a slow, guttural snarl as a warning. When sensing the coast was clear the dragon entered the hole and used its snake-like neck to weave itself round and pull its huge bulk further down the winding tunnel network.

Reaching the end of the tunnel, it was met with another set of eyes, although not as big as the dragon they were brighter and had more life in them. The eyes blinked slowly and the dragon bobbed its head, agitated, and roared at the smaller eyes. The smaller eyes were of a baby dragon, an injured hungry baby dragon. The baby tried to crawl to the large one, its mother, Hannah Wylde. Its right leg was bent at a strange angle and it was tired and hungry, too weak to roar itself it whimpered like an upset dog for food.

Its mother didn't bring anything back for its young, even with a city overrun with the infected, the mother did not bring any food, she knew something was wrong with those people, she knew the fresh meat was tainted somehow and she would not give that infected food to her offspring.

Hannah moaned her disappointment to her young and curled up next to the injured dragon, she began tenderly licking at it's wounded leg as it went back to sleep.

She wheezed softly with hunger knowing that she had to find food tomorrow or her baby would die, the older dragon had been severely wounded by the giant spider's webbing earlier and venom and also the long battle with Echo.

It could have fed at the theme park, but there were so many of the infected intertwined with humans that it was difficult to distinguish between them, hence why her flame wiped everybody out. The young dragon's leg was getting worse and she did not know how to fix it, only loving licks from her giant tongue would have to do for now.

Further down the nightclub tunnels, deeper under-ground where the dragon had fought the giant spider, Buckby, was a number of damp and massive caves. It was where the spider had seemingly protected its mistress Gemma from the dragon's unforgiving flames.

Keeping the teenage girl away from the fire wasn't the only thing on the spider's mind. Several ball-shaped egg sacs lay hidden in Buckby's webbing affixed to the cave wall in a silken pouch, each sac containing hundreds of eggs, Buckby wasn't a male spider, but a female and her eggs decorated the cave walls.

Soon they would hatch, the hunger would overtake them and then they must feed and grow. The food source from the caves would soon disappear and they would head to the surface to hunt, but the only inhabitants left in Olympia were the infected, but for the offspring of Buckby the spider, that would have to do.

Mr Tidy was still stood in the same spot since earlier in the morning with his phone in his hand, shivering slightly in the rapidly increasing wind; he looked down to his little dog who was also shaking.

"I can't get any replies from food delivery places in Olympia boy, might have to try out town services."

The bus stop was littered with the dead bodies of the infected, all with broken necks which Mr Tidy had despatched quickly and without question. He was more concerned with his stomach than most of the humans in Olympia turning into savage killing machines, patches of urine also were apparent near his spot. He rang another number and waited patiently for a reply, then a woman answered.

"Hello, this is Kelsey City Food Deliveries, how can I help?"

Mr Tidy punched the air in delight. "Hello yes, do you deliver?"

"Yes sir, it's in our title."

"Ok, can I get a ham and cheese sandwich but hold the cheese please?"

"So what your saying is sir, you'd like a ham sandwich then?"

Mr Tidy's face turned into a confused frown. "I'm not sure, I'll suppose that'll have to do then." He hung up his phone forgetting to reveal his location. Mr Tidy looked at his watch and gave a normal smile to his dog. "He's not going to come is he?" The little dog barked and rolled over playfully in the dirt. "Ok, we'll give it ten more minutes and that's it."

The End